BELLS

by

JO VERITY

HONNO MODERN FICTION

Published by Honno
'Ailsa Craig', Heol y Cawl, Dinas Powys
South Glamorgan, Wales, CF6 4AH

The author would like to stress that
this is a work of fiction and no resemblance
to any actual individual or institution
is intended or implied.

ISBN 978 1870206 87 7

Published with the financial support of the Welsh Books Council

Cover illustration by Rebecca Gibbon

Printed in Wales by Gomer

For Jim

Acknowledgements

I would like to thank: Honno and the Welsh Books Council for their continuing confidence and support; Caroline Oakley, my editor, for her guidance, expertise, good humour and enthusiasm; the members of Cardiff Writers' Circle for their encouragement and invaluable criticism; and everyone whose brains I have picked in the course of writing *Bells*.

1

IN THAT NO MAN'S LAND that lies between wedding reception and evening 'do', Jack Waterfield surveyed the hotel car park. The window of the fourth-floor room made an excellent vantage point as, clad only in creased-from-the-packet boxers, he watched his nearest and dearest, barely recognisable in ill-considered finery, criss-crossing the melting tarmac. Distant yet connected, remote yet concerned, he experienced a hint of the bewilderment that God – if such an old gentleman existed – unquestionably derived from scrutinising his flawed creation.

Jack pulled the waistband of the underpants away from his hot flesh, stretching the stiff elastic, encouraging the dead air to circulate around his crotch. Putting a hand inside the pants he cupped his genitals, the soft flesh clammy in his palm, then, bending his knees slightly, he allowed everything to settle more comfortably. He sighed.

Turning away from the window, he stared at his sleeping wife. Fay had chosen the bed nearest the door. The brochure claimed that 'All our twin rooms are furnished with queen-sized beds – the ultimate luxury' and as she lay there, the extra width of the bed made Fay look more like a robust child than a dumpy fifty-three-year-old. He studied 'his' bed. Crisp white sheets, a snazzy reading lamp and a clock radio – all to himself. Luxury indeed.

After the meal and speeches they had escaped to their room. He had stripped off the stifling layers of morning dress but she had refused to remove anything, not even her shoes. 'I'll never get them back on again.'

'At least take your hat off, love.' He'd made the same suggestion several hours earlier when she'd been complaining of one of her 'heads'. The hat's wide brim, forcing her to hold her head at an unnatural angle, was, without doubt, the cause of the trouble.

'I can't,' she'd snapped. 'My hair's a mess.'

He'd known better than to mention that the hours and small fortune she'd spent at the hairdresser's had, therefore, been completely wasted. Now the hat, envy of any large, nesting bird, lay on his bed.

Even in sleep, Fay looked discontented. Lips pursed and eyebrows drawn together in a slight frown, an ugly little crease running up between them, she might have been in pain. Her features were tensed but exhaustion and alcohol had slackened her neck muscles and the flesh around her lower jaw sagged. Gravity was triumphing over determination.

The gauzy dress and matching coat she wore were chiffon. He knew that because he'd heard the ensemble described at every dinner party and in a hundred telephone conversations over the past six months. The predominant colour of the outfit was strident turquoise, a colour Fay often chose. He'd asked her, a long time ago, why she never wore red – his favourite.

'My hair.' She'd spoken slowly, as if talking to a child. 'Redheads shouldn't wear red. Or purple. Or pink.'

'But Caitlin looks wonderful in red.' He'd pointed to their daughter as she skipped across the lawn, chased by her brothers. Fay hadn't bothered to reply.

Although she'd finally removed the hat, his wife's

sweat-damp hair had retained its shape and now resembled a sandcastle tipped out of a seaside bucket. Were it not for her monthly visits to 'Le Salon' her hair would be grey and then she could wear any colour under the sun.

Fay lay on her back, perfectly still, arms at her sides, fists clenched. Her legs, too, were straight and stiff, ankles puffy and ill-defined, feet splayed, flesh bulging between the straps of her gold sandals. The body showed no sign of life. Had she died whilst he was watching the woman park the yellow 'Beetle' or the golfers on the driving range beyond the car park?

And what did he feel, seeing her laid out on that hotel bed? *Be honest, boyo.* He watched her, waiting for terror or remorse to rear up and grab his throat. He waited. Nothing came. Nothing at all. Neither desolation nor delight. Neither loss nor release. This woman who had shared his life for thirty years might be dead, and he didn't care either way. He didn't care enough to take five paces across the room and search for a breath or a pulse. Or to call her name gently, then louder and louder until he was sure, one way or the other.

The awareness that he felt nothing for her had the same effect as a mugging. His legs buckled and he crumpled, leaning back and sliding down the cool wall. Sobbing quietly, shoulders shaking, he rested his forehead on his raised knees. He licked his lips, tears mixing with snot and tasting of childhood miseries as they trickled down his neat beard and dripped into his chest hair. Needing to get away from the source of his collapse, he crawled across the floor to the bathroom, grazing the white skin of his insteps on the heavy-duty cord carpet. Once inside, he pulled himself up on the chrome rail, locked the door then sat on the lavatory seat, face buried in a towel, until the weeping subsided to an intermittent judder.

He breathed deeply in an effort to slow his frantic heartbeat, then, when he was calmer, he pushed his underpants off and stepped into the shower cubicle. Shoving the lever around to 'maximum', he released the blistering water to scour his body. It seared his scalp through the thinning grey hair, pounding his slight shoulders and coursing down his torso. Where it touched the tenderest areas – inner thigh and grazed feet – the skin turned lobster pink. When he could bear the heat no longer, he thrust the lever across to the other side and ice cold water powered down onto scalded flesh. He stifled a shriek. All the while he scrubbed himself with Fay's loofah-glove, cleansing himself of unforgivable thoughts.

As he crept back into the room, Fay's feet twitched, and the low sun flashed off her sandals.

'Jaaaaack?' A yawn lengthened the vowel, distorting his name, 'Did I sleep?' She pushed herself up to half-sitting, plumping her hair with her fingers. 'You couldn't make me a cup of tea, could you?'

'Of course, love.' He unplugged the kettle and took it into the bathroom.

'And for goodness sake put some clothes on.'

If she had commanded him to stab himself in his cold, cold heart he would have rushed to find a dagger.

The disco had driven most of the guests out of the function-room, onto the terrace or into the shrubbery beyond. Occasionally Jack heard giggles or caught glimpses of pale clothing – *or flesh?* – and wished that he, too, were having fun. At least he was out of the hired suit and feeling like himself for the first time that day. And what a long day it had been. The alarm had gone off at five-thirty and, from that moment, Fay had kept him to a tight schedule.

All day he had done his duty; done whatever was asked

of him without questioning or arguing. This was the first moment he'd had to himself – his first opportunity to reflect on his son's wedding day. Where had the initial plans for an intimate family celebration gone adrift? At some point, the whole affair had been rail-roaded and the unstoppable wedding juggernaut had run away with them.

'I don't know what you're getting so het up about, Jack,' Fay had said. 'Nia's parents are footing the bill.'

'I'm not het up, love. And, to be fair, we *are* paying for the evening 'do'. It's just that I didn't think Dylan *had* 200 friends.'

'You don't begrudge your son a proper send-off, do you?'

So here he was, watching 'The Day' take its predictable course, indistinguishable from scores of weddings that he'd attended over the years. Amongst the frightful outfits, bizarre gifts and banal speeches, Dylan and Nia had made promises that were impossible to keep. Side by side, listening to those arcane words, Fay had squeezed his hand taking him back thirty years, to an instant when everything had been possible.

Fay had spent the first hour of the evening party complaining that she couldn't persuade the guests to 'mix and mingle'. He'd tagged around with her on her failing mission, but, in the end, she gave up and he tried to placate her. 'Have a drink, love. Look, everyone's having a great time. You've been the perfect hostess and now it's your turn to relax.'

'It's all right for you, Jack, but someone has to stay sober,' she snapped. 'I'd better check the buffet arrangements. They're bound to get it wrong if I don't keep after them.'

'I'll just circulate, shall I?' He watched her hurry off towards the kitchens.

After a day of following instructions to the letter, he

was unsure what to do now and he drifted, pausing here and there for a quick 'Enjoying yourselves?' or 'How's it going?' No one offered him a seat or included him in their conversation. And something rather weird was going on. It wasn't that he was being cold-shouldered, they simply weren't seeing him. Or hearing him, either, come to that. After an unsuccessful attempt to join a crowd of Dylan's workmates, he tested his 'invisible man' theory by walking straight towards four young women, who were making their way from the car park. Although he smiled at them, they didn't acknowledge him and, without deviating from their route, two passed to his right, two to his left.

'Wow. Did you clock the Best Man's butt?' a leggy girl in a clinging dress asked her friends. Hands extended in front of her, palms forward, she squeezed imaginary buttocks with her long fingers. He didn't catch the reply, lost in their laughter, as they moved away from him.

In all the years that they had been lovers, Fay had more or less avoided mentioning his body. There had been lots of remarks about his 'lovely eyes' and 'nice smile' of course, but nothing that she wouldn't say about a brother or a friend; nothing to arouse him and make him feel like a raging animal. In the beginning, when he'd explored her body, he'd sometimes used the ancient, crude words when referring to her intimate places and his actions in and around them, the coarseness of the language increasing his pleasure. Fay seemed to enjoy what was going on but said nothing, as if she had taken a vow of silence. Those young women, striding up the path, would have no such qualms.

The path from the terrace sloped down to the overspill car park at the rear of the hotel complex. As he meandered on, the music was reduced to a bass beat and the tunes became un-nameable. Soft yellow lights, set in bollards, lined the paths through the manicured grounds, their half-glow attracting flutters of moths. The disco was scheduled to continue until midnight and it was out of the question for him to leave before the end. Room four-oh-eight, with satellite TV and his very own bed, beckoned, but that would be the first place Fay would look for him. Out here, wandering in the grounds, wasn't a bad option. Technically he was still circulating and available, should anyone wish to find him. He wandered on, filling in time, only feeling a tiny bit guilty.

Not far off a car started, revved and pulled away. He and Fay had been chauffeured to the church and on to the reception, but his car must be somewhere down here in this car park. Caitlin had used it to bring his parents and had returned the keys to him when they were checking in. He tapped his trouser pocket and heard the familiar *clink*.

After the shadows of the shrubbery, the car park was harsh and threatening. The large compound, surrounded by a high wire fence and illuminated by security lights, made him think of a prisoner of war camp. He had never *been* in a prisoner of war camp but John Mills, caught in the glare of searchlights, flashed onto the silver screen of boyhood memory. He wandered up and down the ranks of vehicles, the distinguishing colours of paintwork modified by the mercury lights. Where on earth was his car? He pressed the bulge on his key fob, looking and listening for a flash and bleep. There it was, three to the right.

He slumped into the driver's seat. The drinks that he had consumed through this endless day must have put him way over the limit but, starting the car, he edged out of the row. He drove slowly around the car park until he found a space under an oak tree, where the leaves obscured the relentless light.

He switched on the radio and abandoned himself to the second half of 'The Moral Maze'. The panel were discussing the case for and against euthanasia. He pushed away the remembrance of Fay, corpse-like on the bed, and within five minutes the reasonable voice of Radio Four, and the smell of still-new car, lulled him to sleep.

2

FAY WAS LOOKING FORWARD TO THE JOURNEY. Train travel was such a civilised mode of transport. Expensive, though, and if she and Jack were both making a journey, they went by car. According to the departures board, the Nottingham train was due in twenty minutes.

Although it was August, a cold wind swept down the platform, peppering her face with grit, and she retreated to the café in the station concourse for her third coffee of the morning. There were a few tables, outside the main area, set aside for smokers. Of course she wasn't a proper smoker like these desperate people around her. The only time she smoked was when she *needed* a cigarette. She *wanted* about twenty a day but *needed* nearer ten. In any case, she could kick the habit any time she put her mind to it. But after her early start, and with the prospect of several hours on the train, she *needed* a cigarette.

The coffee was dangerously hot and the cardboard cup deformed as she lifted it. The apple Danish, included in the promotion, was sticky and far too sweet and when she tried to wipe her fingers, the paper serviette shredded and small pieces stuck them. She recalled her father's freshly-shaved face, dabs of toilet paper on his cheek and neck where he'd nicked himself. They'd bought him an electric razor for his seventieth birthday but it had still been in the box four years later when she'd helped her mother clear his things.

The station announcer 'regretted to inform passengers that the train from Cardiff to Nottingham is running approximately twenty-five minutes late' and expressed a hope that 'it will not cause passengers too much inconvenience'. All around her people were making calls and she rooted through her handbag for her mobile. *No point.* Jack was on his way to mid-Wales with the Wicker Men and it made better sense to ring Laura when she was sure of her arrival time.

Jack had dropped her at the station over an hour ago. If she were driving, she would be on the M5 by now. She raised the coffee to her lips again and a droplet coursed down the outside of the cup, splashing on to the lapel of her pale Burberry. 'Shit.'

The train pulled in. It was a two-carriage Sprinter, already full with passengers who had joined at Swansea or Port Talbot, but she had no misgivings about evicting the girl who was occupying her reserved seat. Muttering obscenities, the girl hauled herself up and dawdled down the carriage. Fay stood her ground, more than a match for any insolent teenager. She dealt with dozens of them every day in the classroom.

By the time the train groaned out of the station, she felt as if she'd travelled half way round the world. The man in the adjacent seat left the train at Newport and she colonised the vacant space with her raincoat. To strengthen her claim on the territory she piled her newspaper, book and handbag on the table in front of her, then turned to the *Guardian* crossword.

They trundled on, losing more time. The man opposite, lapel heavy with enamelled badges, several of which had something to do with the Boy Scout Movement, informed her that once a train was late, it was very likely to get later. 'It's missed its slot, you see.' He knew far too much about rolling-stock for her liking and she made an effort to avoid eye contact in case he felt the urge to do a good deed.

Sometimes fellow travellers had fascinating tales to tell. Returning from a conference in Manchester a few years ago, she'd chatted with a woman whose husband had attacked her at the breakfast table that very morning. The battered wife unwound a paisley scarf to reveal violet bruising where he had tried to throttle her. The social workers had found her a place in a refuge in Taunton, and she'd left her home in such haste that she'd had no time even to pack an overnight bag. The children were still with her husband. When Fay had expressed surprise, she'd boasted, 'He wouldn't lay a finger on them. He loves them to bits. He's a wonderful father.'

Fay was off to spend the weekend with friends from her grammar school days. They kept in touch through phone calls, emails and occasional letters enclosed with birthday or Christmas cards. Naturally Fay had wanted to give Laura and Isabel the full details of Dylan's wedding and they'd all agreed that it was a good reason to get together. The last time had been a couple years ago, at Isabel's house in Chelsea. On that occasion they'd been summoned to inspect her new conservatory.

The train buff had been right. They were losing more time. 'Look on the bright side,' he announced, 'If we're more than an hour late, we can claim a refund. It's all there in the Passengers' Charter.' She half expected him to produce the document from his carrier bag.

They pulled in to the station fifty-four minutes late. 'Sod's Law,' Fay said to him gathering up her belongings and sidling out of her seat. Her back twinged as she straightened up and her stomach felt unsettled. The hot chocolate she'd bought from the trolley, to take away the taste of the tuna sandwiches, had been a bad idea. A sweet silt coated her tongue and she longed to clean her teeth.

Ignoring Laura's instruction to catch a number twenty-nine bus from the station – 'It'll drop you at the local shops and then it's less than a ten-minute walk,' – Fay took a taxi, happy to part with seven pounds and save the hassle. Laura had never had much money and, not wanting to embarrass her friend with what might be considered an unnecessary show of wealth, she asked the driver to stop on the main road so that she could arrive, on foot, from the direction of the bus stop.

Although this was her first visit to Laura's present home, she was confident that she would identify it immediately. She dragged her wheeled suitcase along the uneven pavement, studying the little red brick houses. The terraced properties were modest but well cared for, their tiny front gardens jolly with sunflowers and nasturtiums; their windows sparkling. About half way down the row, a tousle of passion flowers shrouded a purple door. No net curtains obscured the bay window. A tabby cat watched her from the garden wall. *That's got to be the one.* She checked the number on the wooden gate. It was, indeed, number forty-four.

Laura opened the door, releasing a smell of coffee and baking fruit cake. They hugged and laughed, whilst the cat wrapped itself around their legs, its tail upright and quivering.

'Isabel phoned a few minutes ago. Surprise, surprise, she's running late. I thought she was going to cry off. You know what she's like. Never mind all that. Come in and dump your things. It's wonderful to see you.'

They went down the narrow hall to the kitchen and, as Laura put the proffered flowers in an earthenware jug, Fay had her first chance to look at her old friend. Laura's hair, tied loosely at the nape of her neck, was streaked with grey; she had soft jowls at her chin-line and her face looked thinner but her hands and her legs and her voice had barely altered since that first day at school. 'You *so* made the right decision never to dye your hair,' said Fay. 'Heaven knows what colour mine would be if I let it grow out.'

'Sheer laziness,' said Laura. 'Painters spend enough time agonising about colour. I just don't have the energy to agonise over my hair too. Or my face, come to that.'

'You've never needed makeup. You're skin is such a lovely tone. I look like the living dead if I don't slap a bit of something on.'

Laura had been the creative one. While the rest of the form giggled about boyfriends and periods, she was working in the art room. While Fay and Isabel had been in the cloakroom, back-combing each other's hair and scratching initials on the lavatory doors, Laura was off somewhere painting or carving something. Clothes weren't important to her, either. At home she lived in paint-spattered shirts and jeans so, by default, she appeared to have the confidence to be different. This was unusual in a girls' grammar school during the sixties and her reputation for being 'a weirdo' lent their threesome certain kudos. Fay had never fathomed what Laura got out of it until, years later, Laura explained that being with them gave her an insight into contemporary youth culture, essential to inform her work. 'I liked you, too,' she'd added, when she saw Fay's jaw drop.

She showed Laura the wedding photographs and the snaps she'd taken when she and Jack had spent a few days in Paris. 'It would have been good to get away straight after the wedding, to avoid the anti-climax, but I had another week before school broke up. There was so much else to think about that we hadn't organised anything. It was Jack's idea to go to Paris. I'm not entirely sure why. We spent our honeymoon there so perhaps it was nostalgia. Weddings always dredge up strange emotions, don't they?'

'And *did* Paris reawaken love's young dream?' Laura bowed an air violin.

Fay shook her head. 'God, no. Paris in late July is unbearably hot. And we were both exhausted. Every time we lay down, we fell asleep. I think we were both glad to get home.'

'Death stirs up strange emotions, too.' Laura handed Fay a mug of coffee. 'I mean apart from the obvious ones.'

Fay reached out and touched her friend's hand. 'I was desperately sorry about your dad.'

'Thanks. You wrote me such a brilliant letter. I love the idea that other people, besides me, remember what fun he was.'

'I know how close you two were and I really envy you that. I don't have a clue what my father was like, under that three-piece suit. I'm not sure he cared much for me.' She patted her hand. 'Anyway, how are you coping?'

Laura shrugged. 'Oh, it's easier than it was in the beginning. But now that the grief and anger are subsiding, other things are surfacing.'

Fay raised her eyebrows. 'D'you want to talk about it?'

'Maybe later. Let me have another look at those photos.'

They drank coffee and ate warm fruit cake, waiting for Isabel to arrive.

Jack's day wasn't going well. After dropping Fay at the station, he'd gone home to collect his kit. He needed to be in Llandrindod Wells by eleven-thirty for the Trans-Wales Morris Dancing Championships and, from past experience, he knew that anywhere in Wales was further away than it should be. Normally his 'side' – the Wicker Men – packed into two or three cars to travel to a venue but, on this occasion, Jack had found himself without a lift. He'd set off once, then been forced to turn back when he realised that he was without his buckled shoes. Fay couldn't bear the smell of shoe-polish in the house and he'd taken them down to the shed to clean them and left them there. Anything else he could manage without, but his shoes were essential.

He headed north for the second time. It wasn't often that he found himself making a journey on his own. Had Fay been with him, she would have a packet of soft-mints or a bar of chocolate at the ready, and no sooner did the thought of Fruit-and-Nut cross his mind, than he craved something to suck. He switched on the radio and prodded his way through the pre-set channels, looking for some distraction. The selection of music was unappealing and a gloomy item on the hole in the ozone layer depressed him. He switched off and resorted to tuneless whistling.

The road climbed up, past valley towns synonymous with coalmining, choirs and tragedies. After half an hour, the scarred landscape and the marching ranks of terraced houses gave way to round-topped mountains, sheep grazing on their lower slopes and streams gathering into tiny waterfalls. He opened the car windows, allowing the rarefied air to blow away the city staleness.

It was perfect dancing weather – dry and fresh. Soon he would be slipping on pleated shirt and white breeches, woolly socks and shiny black shoes, and strapping on the bright little bells. He would abandon himself – dentistry left little room for abandon – to the rhythms and hypnotic music, setting Jack Waterfield free. He would connect with the world through his senses, by-passing his brain – the cause of so many problems. Great stuff. Why would anyone pay money to lie on a psychiatrist's couch, when they could dance their way out of discontentment – at least for a few hours?

The needle on the petrol gauge was edging into the red sector and he pulled into a garage, on the outskirts of a small village. He filled the tank and bought a selection of snacks and a fruit drink to leave in the car for later. Before setting off on the last leg of his trip, he checked his mobile for messages. There was nothing from Fay, which he took as a sign that all was well. There was, however, a rambling message from Stan Colley, bagman for the Wicker Men. The upshot was that three of the team who were driving up together had been 'involved in a minor prang' before they'd even left Cardiff. *Prang for God's sake?* Nothing serious, but they were in Casualty, waiting for X-rays, and they would have to pull out of the competition. The message had been left an hour or so earlier.

Jack phoned a couple of the others and established that he was the last one to hear the news. The rest had turned around and were already back at home, whilst he was somewhere in mid-Wales. He sat in the car, eating a Mars Bar and wondering what to do. Fay was in Nottingham for the weekend so there was no need to rush back. Out of the blue, he had this glorious day to himself. Added to that he was in a place where he wouldn't normally be. It was the most exciting thing that had happened to him for ages and an opportunity not to be wasted.

His initial impulse was to pinpoint his location on the

map and make a plan for the rest of the day. Maybe he should let someone know where he was and what he was up to. But who? And what was the point? *Bugger it.* He tossed the road atlas onto the back seat. Good grief, how lost could anyone be in such a small country?

By the time Isabel turned up, Fay and Laura had almost finished the bottle of Chardonnay that Fay had packed in her overnight bag. It was tepid but effective and they were flushed and giggly. Isabel, keen to catch up, produced a bottle of vodka and they spent an hour or so settling into each other's company.

Little had changed in Fay's situation since they last met. She was teaching in the same school; Jack was still working in his own practice; her older son was married and her daughter looked like becoming an old maid. And her younger son? Kingsley was still on the other side of the world.

'Don't be ridiculous, Fay,' said Laura, 'Caitlin won't be an "old maid". She may choose not to marry but what's so terrible about that? Look at the mess Sadie's making of her marriage.' Laura had two children by different fathers. Sadie, the younger one, had married when she was barely twenty and the relationship had been on and off several times. 'It's on at the moment, thanks to Joe's refusal to give up on her,' Laura crossed her fingers, 'But I don't hold my breath.'

'What about Cassidy?' asked Isabel. 'How old is he now?'

'Getting on for thirty-four. Scary, isn't it?'

'He's a lot better looking than he used to be,' said Fay, holding up a photograph of a young man with a ponytail. 'Or is my eyesight deteriorating? Where does the blonde hair come from? David was dark, wasn't he?'

'That was in Australia. The sun had bleached it. Cass worked out there for a couple of years. He wears it short now.'

'What's he doing? Didn't you mention carpentry, or something?' asked Isabel. She took the photograph and whistled. 'I bet he's broken a few hearts.'

Isabel had been the glamorous, giddy member of the trio but Fay wasn't sure she deserved her nickname Dizzy Izzy. After a string of handsome boyfriends, she had ended up marrying a rather plain barrister, Geoffrey Lauderdale, and living in a huge house in Chelsea. She'd driven up to Nottingham – although Isabel insisted on saying 'down' – in a very flash car. The jacket hanging on the back of the kitchen chair had an Armani label. It seemed to Fay that Isabel had been very shrewd indeed.

'How on earth d'you keep your figure, Izzy?' asked Laura. 'You've had four children and you can't be more than a ten. I don't want to know what size I am. I just put a big shirt over everything and hope for the best.'

Fay glanced across at Isabel's flat front and pulled in her own stomach.

'I watch what I eat, and I go to the gym or swim most days,' said Isabel, who had the time and the money for such things.

The conversation progressed from diets to health to old age to death and, inevitably, they ran through the lengthening list of contemporaries that had suffered dreadful illnesses and untimely deaths.

'Would you want Geoffrey to marry again if you died?' asked Fay. 'I wouldn't like Jack to be lonely, but I can't quite picture him with another woman. Who'd want an ageing dentist, anyway?'

'Geoffrey can do what the hell he likes when I've gone,' said Isabel. 'We hardly see each other now, so he might not even notice I wasn't there.'

'Let's talk about something else,' said Laura, picking up the empty glasses and taking them to the sink. Fay shot a glance at Isabel and grimaced. Laura's beloved husband, David, had died a long while ago and she had never remarried. Laura had always been a private person and it hadn't seemed right to press her on the question of Sadie's father. She had once told them that he wasn't around for long, adding, 'But I had a choice, didn't I, and chose to go through with it.'

Jack tucked in to his teacake. It was not yet five o'clock but the mellowness of the afternoon had evaporated and he'd fancied something warm to eat. He was the only customer in the place. He'd spent the afternoon roaming through mid-Wales, stopping to browse in bookshops or sort through the bargain boxes outside junk shops. As a result, he now owned a first edition of a Cecil Sharp biography, a garden fork and a vase in the shape of Nelson's Column – a little gift for Fay.

The waitress wandered around with a J-cloth, sweeping crumbs from the table onto the vinyl flooring.

'Anything else?' she asked, glancing at the clock above the counter.

'No thanks,' said Jack, 'But perhaps you could tell me where I am.'

Since making the decision to let destiny direct him, Jack had done everything he could to avoid establishing his location. Obviously the settlements along his route had all sported signs but fortunately he'd never heard of any of them. He'd had a smashing day and the time had come for him to be heading home.

'The Corner Café.' She pronounced it 'caffee'.

'That's in…?' he prompted.

'Bridge Street.'

'Which is in…?'

'Llangwm,' she said, giving him, what his mother would have called, an 'old fashioned look' and scurrying back to the kitchen before he could push her further. He tucked payment for his snack under his plate and left.

Llangwm was more than a village, yet didn't seem big enough to be called a town. It straddled a meandering river, and the criss-crossing streets, meeting at odd angles, made for a quaintness more often found in England than in rural Wales. He passed a row of shops and a pub on his way back to the moss-covered car park, where his car was still the only one in sight. He turned the key in the ignition. Nothing. He tried again. More nothing. It had been running perfectly, without a hint of trouble, which made diagnosis of the problem impossible. Anyway, he was useless with cars. His time was better spent earning the money to pay someone who knew what they were doing – a perfectly sound decision. Where he'd made the mistake was to let his AA membership lapse.

He locked the car and traipsed back to the café. By this time 'Closed' dangled on the door and there were no signs of life. The street was deserted. Whistling to convey nonchalance, he began walking, hoping that he'd come across a garage or someone who could direct him to one.

At the far end of the street, standing out amongst the row of stone-built houses, he spotted an Italianate villa, bedecked with hanging baskets. The Welcome Stranger Guesthouse in jaunty yellow lettering on a dark green board, hung over the central entrance. After no more than a second's hesitation, he climbed the three steps up from the pavement and pounded on the door.

A young woman opened it and smiled at him. She was, he thought, a few years older than Caitlin, mid-thirties perhaps, and not as tall. Her long, blue-black hair was gathered in a ponytail. She wore a tee-shirt and ankle-length cotton skirt, printed with a hectic pattern of butterflies.

'I hope you do.' He grinned back at her and pointed up at the sign. 'Welcome strangers, I mean.'

'That's the general idea. The stranger the better,' she laughed, ushering Jack past the reception desk and into the untidy sitting room, where a fire, cheery but not too hot, crackled in the grate and a ginger cat snoozed on the rug.

They introduced themselves, 'Jack Waterfield.'

'Non. Non Evans.'

He explained his predicament – a non-functioning car; no AA membership; no phone number for a garage; no sign of life in the village; no idea where he was; no plan of campaign. No mention, either, of a wife and grown-up children. But, sitting by the fire, cat purring at his feet, none of it was a problem. He was immediately and sublimely at peace, as if he'd arrived home after a long and difficult journey; as if he had found the person to whom he could relate his brightest hopes and darkest fears.

He felt even more at home after he'd eaten a supper of lamb stew followed by creamy rice pudding. Non had insisted that, as the other guests were out, he should have a meal with her, in the kitchen and, while they were eating, she made a suggestion. The car couldn't be fixed before the morning, when Non would contact her cousin, Gareth: 'He's a dab hand with motors.' It was futile trying to get back to Cardiff by public transport because the daily bus had passed through Llangwm at noon. Anyway, he would only have to come back for the car and face a similar problem in reverse. Jack agreed that the sensible thing would be to spend the night at The Welcome Stranger and Non went off to prepare a room for him.

There were two other guests in residence. Melvin and

Bonnie Meredith were over from Boston, hot on the trail of their forefathers. They arrived back at nine o'clock after a fruitful day touring the churchyards in the area. Non opened a bottle of wine and suggested a game of Scrabble by the fire. There was dissent over the spelling of a word, here and there, but they agreed to adopt the indigenous dictionary, on the understanding that this ruling would apply when they played a return match in the United States. By the time they'd had a night-cap of hot chocolate laced with rum, they were the best of butties and buddies.

It was only as Jack was slipping into bed that he wondered whether he ought to phone someone and tell them where he was. He checked his mobile but there were no messages and it was well past midnight. There seemed little point in causing a fuss.

3

Fay and Isabel agreed that Laura's fish pie and apple crumble were better than anything they might get in a restaurant.

During the meal Fay noticed how little Isabel ate, and how much she drank. From what she said, her life sounded equally unbalanced. She talked about Geoffrey as though he were a professional acquaintance and her children no more than a logistical problem. Fay had not met Piers, Max, Johnny and Esme often enough to know them as individuals. In her head they were 'Izzy's four', and their mother's disjointed ramblings about 'gap years' and placements with 'friends of ours in Chile' served only to weld them inseparably into Piersmaxjohnnyandesme, a four-headed, over-indulged monster.

Fay noticed how intently Laura listened as if committing every word to memory. Occasionally she asked a question or made a comment that pinpointed the essence of the discussion, elevating it to something more meaningful than gossip. She had always been attentive and, had she been a writer not a painter, Fay might have worried that these intimate conversations would appear in a novel or TV drama.

Isabel stopped talking and relinquished her place in the confessional. It was Fay's turn and she knew that, having been through the superficial stuff earlier, they were expecting some in-depth revelations. But Fay was accustomed to promoting the Waterfield family myth of harmony and success. 'I'm really, really getting a lot out of being HoD.'

'What's HoD?' Isabel interrupted.

'Head of Department.' *Didn't everyone know that?* She continued with the sanitised patter. Jack was well respected within his profession, still loving his work and was very trim for his age. Caitlin was lecturing at the Dental school in Cardiff. She owned her own flat and had a silver sports car. Dylan had just married a charming young woman from a very good family. And Kingsley…? Oh, Kingsley was fine – learning lots of life-skills on the other side of the world. There. All done.

'Does Jack still do that whatd'youcallit? With bells?' Isabel giggled.

'Yes, he does.' Fay had hoped to avoid the Morris dancing. People sometimes forgot his name but nobody forgot her husband's hobby. If he played chess or collected stamps or went fishing it wouldn't get a mention. She, too, found the whole dancing thing ludicrous but she kept up the PR. 'It's a very strenuous activity you know. Excellent for the cardiovascular system. Better than aerobics. And it goes way, way back. Before cricket was…invented. *Invented?* If you've ever read Hardy,' she paused for her words to penetrate Isabel's alcohol-dulled consciousness, 'If you really *know* your Hardy, you'll remember that it's pivotal in several of the novels.' She avoided Laura's gaze, dreading that she would demand chapter and verse.

'I think back all those years, to that last day, when we stood on the bridge and skimmed those sodding school hats across the river. Everything seemed possible. God, I'd have drowned myself there and then if I thought I'd end up like this.' Isabel made a pistol with her fingers, holding it to her temple, as if drowning were not enough.

'Well I'm perfectly content with how things have worked out.' Fay smiled brightly. 'Perhaps I'm not quite so demanding.'

Isabel ploughed on. 'Come off it, Fay. I can't believe that Jumping Jack, successful and healthy though he may be, has been the only man in your life. Spill the beans. Dish the dirt. No dalliances in the stockroom or extra-mural activities? We all know what goes on in the staff room. And in the dentist's chair, come to that. Has Jack been a good boy? Actually, my dentist is dishy. He can give me a filling any time he likes. What's yours like Laura?'

'She's certainly very efficient.' Laura, the slightest of smiles crossing her face, collected the plates. 'And I'd change only one thing about my life. I should have told that bloody editor that David wasn't available.'

Fay leaned across and put her arm around Laura's shoulder, and remembered David Ford. David had been working as a junior photographer on one of the major dailies. A big story had broken. A man was holding a group of teenagers hostage, at a youth club, and all the other staff photographers were occupied so David had been asked to cover it. He'd jumped at the chance. As activity around the youth club stepped up, and police marksmen were called in, the man had become agitated and started firing towards the crowd. At the inquest it was revealed that one of the bullets had ricocheted off the wall of an adjacent building and penetrated David's skull, even though he had been well out of the line of fire.

Try as they might, they couldn't regain their high spirits and soon after they had cleared the table and done the washing up, Laura wished them goodnight. 'You can stay up and natter if you like but I need my bed. Help yourself to anything you need.'

Isabel wandered into the sitting room with two glasses and the remnants of a bottle of wine. Fay followed. It was cooler in here and she pulled her jacket around her as she flopped onto the shabby Chesterfield and yawned. 'I really should go to bed, too. I was up at six. I've eaten and drunk far too much, though, and I shan't sleep.'

Isabel proffered the bottle and when she declined tipped its contents into her own glass. 'I never sleep.' She drank the wine, gulping it down until the glass was empty. 'I've always suffered from insomnia. The only thing that does the trick is a good fuck. And those are few and far between these days.'

Fay was used to Isabel's outrageous statements and whilst her friend prattled on, she looked around the room. The walls were painted in shades of dusky pink, but little of it showed between the patchwork of Laura's paintings and David's photographs. One wall was completely fitted out with bookshelves, the contents dancing in higgledy-piggledy rows. Painters, poets, cooks, travellers, story-tellers and historians, cheek by jowl. Her own shelves were classified along the lines of the school library, and she wondered how anyone in this house could ever find what they were looking for.

Isabel had fallen silent and was lolling to one side. Her cheek, pressing against the high arm of the sofa, was folded and wrinkled like the worn leather. Leaning closer, Fay inspected her friend's hair and could see a few gratifying millimetres of grey, almost white, at the roots. And the skin above her upper lip was furred with soft, bleached hair. The face of her mother's sister, Violet, sprang up before her. Auntie Violet had been glamorous, too, and as a child she'd loved watching her aunt applying blood-red lipstick, then clamping her lips to a Rizla paper to blot off the excess. When she got older the lipstick flooded into the tiny wrinkles around her lips – a scarlet centipede walking across her face.

A noise from the kitchen made Fay jump. Someone was coming in through the back door. She froze, wishing that she had closed the door to the sitting room and could hide from this midnight prowler. Holding her breath, she prayed that Isabel wouldn't wake and start babbling.

It sounded as though the intruder was running the tap and clattering in the cupboards. Now he was whistling. She reached into her bag for her phone, switching it on, ready to call nine-nine-nine.

Something tinkled on to the kitchen tiles. 'Bugger.'

With the phone clasped in her hand, she tip-toed across the hall and leant around the half-open kitchen door. Silhouetted against the white light from the open fridge, was a young man, crouching. He must have felt her presence because she certainly made no noise and he swivelled round to face her, still on his haunches.

'Oh, God. Sorry. Did I wake you? Mum'll murder me.'

'Cassidy?'

'I'm *so* sorry. I wasn't supposed to come home but I missed the last bus to Beeston. I was planning to stay with a mate.'

'You nearly spent the night in a police cell.' She held up her phone. 'I'm Fay, by the way.'

'I know. You haven't changed a bit.'

They shook hands, calculating that it was six or seven years since they'd last met. 'I remember it very clearly,' he said, 'Mum and I dropped in on our way somewhere and I managed to kick a cup of tea all over your white carpet. You were terribly nice about it.'

'Was I? That doesn't sound a bit like me.'

They laughed.

'Well this calls for a drink, don't you think? I know Mum's got some brandy stashed in one of these cupboards. I'd hate to think she's going to waste it on cooking.'

Out of the blue, Fay felt the party mood return and didn't protest when Cassidy poured two generous brandies from the dusty bottle. He raised his glass. 'To reconnecting.'

Fay wasn't fond of brandy but, not wanting to appear a spoil-sport, tossed it back, straight away feeling her cheeks flush and her heart race.

Now that he was standing up, she had to tilt her head right back to look at his face. 'Gosh. I thought my sons were tall but you're...' She stopped. 'How rude of me. I shouldn't make personal remarks.'

'No sweat. And it's a fact. I *am* ridiculously tall. Six-five. The only place I can get lost in a crowd is Sweden. They all seem to be tall over there. But I don't think Dad had any Scandinavian genes.'

'Maybe not, but he was a lovely man. D'you remember him at all?'

'Not really. I used to think I did, but now I realise I was remembering all the things people told me about him. Their memories of him, not my own.' He paused. 'I do remember something of my own, actually.' She waited, wondering why he seemed so uncertain. 'It must be mine because it's something horrid.'

'You don't have to tell me if it's a private thing.' She wanted to keep the conversation light.

'I want to. I don't often meet anyone that knew him. But you won't tell Mum will you? It would be pointless to upset her.'

She promised, dreading what he was going to say.

'He died when I was five, so it must have happened a little while before that. We were in the garden and he

34

had the hose-pipe fixed to the tap outside the kitchen door. We were living in South London then. Did you ever come to that house? Anyway, he was watering the garden, or whatever, and I remember looking down at the hose, lying across the lawn like a big black snake, and I stood on it. God knows why. To see what would happen I suppose. The pressure blew the pipe off the tap which didn't really do any damage but Dad went mad. He smacked me across the legs with it and locked me in the shed. I don't know how long I was in there but it was stifling hot. The smell of creosoted wood still makes me feel ill.' He pushed his hair back with his hand and shook his head. 'Can that be the only memory I have of the man that everyone tells me was so wonderful? He thrashed me and locked me in a shed. Sometimes I think I dreamed it. I wish I had.' He poured two more brandies and this time he, too, tossed his back.

She wished her cheeks weren't burning and that she could think of something comforting to say.

'Shall I tell you another secret?' He paused then obviously seeing concern cloud her face continued, 'Don't worry. This is something nice. I used to love it when you came. Mum, bless her, was a bit laid back but when you came we had such a great time. We did *proper* things.'

'Proper things?'

'We went on outings. To museums. Out for meals. You took me to the zoo for the first time. Things that proper families did.' He paused again, looking directly at her. 'I know this sounds disloyal but I distinctly remember wishing that *you* were my mum.'

Overcome by something she didn't quite understand, she grabbed him in a lingering hug, her head barely grazing his chin. How bony he was beneath his sweater, so different from her well-built son.

'Fay?' Isabel's voice croaked from the sitting room.

35

'Where is everyone? What's the time?'

Fay felt unreasonably miffed at the interruption. 'Just getting a glass of water.' Cassidy raised his eyebrows and she put her finger to her lips then went to the sink, making lots of noise as she filled a tumbler with water. He followed her and standing very close whispered, 'Sorry about all that. I shouldn't have offloaded. You won't tell Mum, will you?' She shook her head.

'Fay? Ooops.' There was a crash from the sitting room which might have been books falling off the shelf or a chair toppling over. 'Shit.'

'Coming.'

Like a sleepy child, he offered her his cheek and she kissed it gently. 'See you tomorrow?' she whispered, then went to persuade Isabel that it was time for bed.

4

IT TOOK JACK A FEW WAKING MOMENTS to pinpoint his location. The window wasn't in the right place – unless he'd moved into the spare room during the night, something he often did these days, prompted by Fay's 'Snoring, Jack,' and prod in the kidneys. They agreed that it was a sensible solution – they both needed to get a decent night's sleep, ready for the working day ahead. But the spare room didn't have crisp white sheets or smell of lavender. The bed creaked as he rolled on to his front, enjoying the long-forgotten sensation of cotton against his naked flesh, before rolling over again to locate a cooler spot. It had been like this when he was a child, hot and feverish with measles, mumps or something that children weren't allowed to have anymore. He would lie in the middle of his tubular metal bed, getting hotter and hotter until he could stand it no longer, then wriggle out of the dip in the mattress to a cool patch right at the edge, anchoring himself with a skinny arm thrust between the mattress and the tucked-under bedding.

The sash window was open a few inches and he dozed for a while, enjoying the fresh morning air, until the distant babble of running water drove him out of bed in search of the bathroom. The rooms at The Welcome Stranger Guesthouse did not have *en suite* facilities. Non made sure that he was aware of that before suggesting that he stay the night. 'Lots of people have got a real thing about it,' she said, 'So I always mention it straight away. There are four rooms and we've got two bathrooms so it's not like a camp site.'

Fay would never stay anywhere if she had to share a bathroom and he felt daring as, kitted out in the towelling robe from the back of the bedroom door, he sauntered across the landing. He pulled it firmly around him when he saw Non coming up the stairs, carrying a mug of tea. 'Sleep well?' she inquired as if he were one of her family. She held the mug out to him. 'I thought you might be ready for this.'

Today her hair was roughly plaited, the ends tied with red knitting-wool and she wore a short-sleeved white blouse and pair of well-washed jeans. Her face was without makeup and her feet were bare. All visible skin had the even tan that only comes from working out of doors.

'Yes. Thanks.' He wanted to tell her that it was the most restoring night's sleep that he'd had for years and that it would be the easiest thing in the world to stay here for the rest of his life, playing Scrabble and sharing a bathroom with lovely people like Melvin and Bonnie.

But he didn't get the chance to say a word before she was off again. 'What d'you fancy for breakfast? Oh, Gareth's on his way over to pick up the keys then he'll go and take a look at your car. Full Welsh? D'you want to borrow some slippers?'

He loved the way her conversation darted all over the place, her voice soft as honey dribbling off the spoon.

After showering, he put on his clothes from the previous day. This was forbidden at home. Fay whipped things off him and into the washing machine before they had time to meld to the shape of his body or take on his smell, then they turned up again in the wardrobe with sharp creases down the arms or legs. Fair enough, he needed to look freshly laundered when he was at work or attending a meeting of the Dental Practitioners Committee, but she did the same thing with his gardening togs and his dancing clothes.

Before going down to breakfast, he checked his phone for messages and called in to see whether there was anything vital on the landline. It was a facility that he'd viewed as technology gone mad but, this particular Sunday morning, it put his mind at ease, knowing that there had been no crisis at home and no one was trying to get hold of him.

The smell of bacon wafted up the stairs and Jack traced it to the kitchen where Melvin and Bonnie were already tucking in to a cooked breakfast. 'Hi there. Help yourself, Jack.' Bonnie waved towards the Aga where a baking tray held all the makings of a 'full Welsh' breakfast.

At home, even at weekends, he and Fay stuck to muesli and wholemeal toast but he poured a mug of tea from the large brown pot and only hesitated for a second before loading his plate with a bit of everything, choosing the seat which gave him a clear view of Non, carrying a basket down to the enclosure at the end of the garden.

'What are your plans for the day?' he asked Melvin.

'We try not to make plans, don't we?' Melvin looked at Bonnie for confirmation.

'Not strictly true, honey. But now we've completed our research we can afford to go with the flow. We don't need to be back home for another couple of months so...' she smiled and shrugged.

What must it feel like – not to be constrained by a relentless schedule? The longest break from work that he'd ever had was two and a half weeks when they'd dragged the children around Scotland. Fay had complained that she was expected to soldier on alone, year after year, through the long summer holidays and had insisted that he put in more effort with 'his' children. By some twisted logic she considered his going to work as a kind of treat, some sort of dig at her, and that she was the one who had the rotten deal. The other school holidays were the same but with a smaller discontentment rating. The Scottish trip had been planned down to the last ice cream stop and visitor centre. Often they had driven past intriguing hand-painted signs on the roadside, suggesting that they might veer off down a winding lane to see a 'tartan maze' or a 'rodent sanctuary', but it would have thrown them off schedule and they might never have got back on track.

'How about you, Jack? How's your day looking?'

Before he could answer, Non had come through the back door. 'Sorry to abandon you but I'm sure you don't want me hovering around being servile. I'm not very good at that.' She put her basket down on the draining board and lifted out a dozen or so eggs, splodged with chicken dung and downy feathers. She wiped them with a damp cloth and placed them gently in the egg cartons, stacked on top of the fridge. 'It's a gorgeous day. I don't think we should sit around here wasting it d'you? I know a place where I can guarantee that we'll see red kites.'

She smiled, revealing her perfect white teeth, and there was nothing in the world that he wanted to see more than red kites, even though he had no idea what they were. Of course he knew they were *birds*. Weren't they? Birds of prey?

'Wow.' He recognised that this wasn't an appropriate response and floundered on. 'That'll be a first for me… great…'

'We'll go in my car. Gareth should have yours fixed by the time we get back. Does that sound okay?'

It sounded breathtakingly, gloriously, magnificently

wonderful to Jack.

Unfortunately Bonnie and Melvin were committed ornithologists and the foursome set out in search of the elusive birds.

They drove for ten minutes, leaving the main road and climbing up towards the bluff, taking narrower and narrower lanes, Non driving confidently on, as if she knew that nothing would appear around the next corner.

They left the car on the side of the road and joined a footpath, leading out onto the springy turf of the hillside. The prevailing wind, no more than a gentle breeze today, had distorted the scruffy hawthorns that dotted the landscape and they leaned at crazy angles. These enduring trees and the scrawny sheep that grazed the rough pasture, gave the scene a markedly biblical look. Melvin and Bonnie, although both on the large side, scampered up the steep slope as if it were their natural habitat and Jack, slight and muscular though he was, had his work cut out to keep up. He was carrying the small rucksack which Non had handed him. 'Just a snack. A proper outing has to include a picnic, don't you think?'

'Abso...' he panted '...lutely.'

They reached the remains of a wall, now just a scattering of stones tumbling down the hillside, and found a spot to perch whilst they passed around the bottle of water and shared the biscuits from the bag. 'I like to think that maybe one of my forefathers tended sheep on this very mountainside a coupla' hundred years ago. We found several Merediths in the churchyard yesterday.' Melvin spread his arms wide encompassing the vista. 'My great-great-great granddaddy may have stood on this very spot and looked down into this very valley. Doesn't it make you feel humble?'

41

They walked on holding the contour, circling the belly of the hill, until Non, who was several yards ahead, extended an arm to signal a halt. 'Look. Up and to your left. Towards the outcrop.'

Jack looked up and saw two birds, silhouetted against the cloudless sky, circling and rising. 'Wow.' It was the appropriate word, exactly.

When they got back, Jack's car was parked in front of The Welcome Stranger and Gareth had left the keys, along with a note, on the kitchen table. 'Loose lead. You owe me a pint next time you're up this way.'

'But I must pay him,' he protested, 'It should be double time for Sunday.'

'You could buy him two pints,' Non suggested, 'next time you come.'

He stared at her. *Next time you come?* 'Okay. It's a deal. But be sure to give him my thanks, won't you? Now I'd better make a move.'

He went upstairs to his room. Of course there was nothing to pack, but he wanted to file the details of it in his memory. The smell of lavender; the bathrobe on the back of the door; the patchwork bedspread; the hen coop at the end of the neat vegetable garden; and, beyond, the hills where the kites had soared. He took the unused handkerchief from his jacket pocket and placed it squarely in the centre of the drawer of the bedside table.

They all came out to see him off, wishing him a safe journey, as if he were setting off to circumnavigate the globe. Melvin pushed a card into his hand. 'It's been a pleasure, Jack. Call by if you're ever States-side. We'll have a return game. American spellings, naturally…'

The car started first time and, before he pulled away, Non opened the door and placed a grubby egg carton and a posy of roses on the seat next to him. 'A memento of your country weekend,' she said, slamming the door and waving him off.

He watched her in the rear-view mirror until The Welcome Stranger Guesthouse disappeared around a bend in the road. As he passed the last house on the outskirts of Llangwm he remembered that he had no idea where he was and he stopped in a lay-by, consulting the map he had tossed behind the seat a mere twenty-four hours ago.

It was only when he got home, and was reversing the car into the drive, that he remembered he hadn't paid for his overnight accommodation.

5

FAY SLEPT FITFULLY. It hadn't been terribly late when she coaxed the semi-comatose Isabel up the stairs but, when she eventually put her bedside light out, the evening's conversations had stirred up the sludge of her memory and particles of the past swirled around all night. She found that she was also re-running her encounter with Cassidy and finding it very...*very what?* Whatever it was, she liked it and wanted to keep the recollection bright and sharp.

Early-morning singing drifted up the stairs. It sounded as though Laura was on top form. How wise she'd been to go to bed when she did. Fay could picture her below in the kitchen, chatting to Cassidy, running fingers through his tousled hair or kissing the back of his neck. She could kiss Dylan's neck any time she liked, or Kingsley's come to that, were he not on the other side of the world. Mothers were allowed to do that kind of thing but it was taboo behaviour for surrogate aunts, once nephews had passed their seventh birthday.

A crumpled morning face stared back from the mirror on the wardrobe door. Puffy eyelids and a crease from the pillowcase across her pale cheek combined to make it look as though she hadn't slept for days. Cheek slapping produced angry asymmetrical patches, reminiscent of a badly painted doll.

A knock at the door made her jump. 'Brought you a cup of tea.' Laura tip-toed in and deposited a steaming mug on the bedside table. 'There's plenty of hot water if you fancy a bath.'

'Lovely.' From habit, Fay grabbed the mug off the unprotected wood and slid her book beneath it. 'You'll have a job rousing Izzy, though. She was a little the worse for wear by the time I got her into bed.'

But Laura was shaking her head. 'Well, she seems bright as a button this morning. She's never needed much sleep, has she? She and Cassidy went out for a stroll about an hour ago. They're going to pick up the papers. I thought we'd have a lazy start, then maybe have a pub lunch somewhere, if that suits you.

'Oh, I hope Cass didn't disturb you when he came in last night. He was supposed to stay with a friend.'

Fay lay in the bath, wondering why she hadn't said anything to Laura about bumping into Cassidy. The thought of Isabel swanning around the streets of Nottingham with him, laughing, chatting – flirting even – was irritating, but their absence gave her a chance to wash and dry her hair and take time over her makeup. A half an hour later she re-visited the mirror and was satisfied with what she saw.

'That's a lovely blouse. Green suits you, Fay.' Laura looked up from the black bag that she was filling with the debris from the swing-bin. Something glutinous from last night's meal slurped onto the quarry tiles and she scooped it up with her hand, pushing it down in the bag.

'Help yourself to breakfast. Cornflakes. Toast.' Laura waved in the direction of a couple of cereal boxes and a loaf of bread on the untidy worktop, then hauled the rubbish out of the back door. A dustbin lid clanged. Fay could count, on the fingers of one hand, the times that she had put the rubbish in the dustbin. She was perfectly capable of doing so if she wanted to, or if she had to, but rubbish was one of Jack's jobs.

The rattle of a key in the front door was accompanied by laughing voices. She couldn't catch what they were saying, but they sounded extremely friendly and she made sure she was sitting at the kitchen table, deeply involved in yesterday's crossword puzzle, when they came in.

'Morning, lazy bones.' Isabel could be extremely annoying.

For a Sunday morning in the provinces, Isabel had selected a simple, yet stunning ensemble. Jeans, beautifully cut, neither too indigo nor too washed out; a white linen shirt; navy leather mules which had obviously been hand-made in Italy. Her hair, drawn roughly back, tumbled towards her shoulders and her make-up – surely she had to be wearing *something* on her face – was minimal. Close behind her came Cassidy, laden with newspapers, a smile still lifting the corners of his mouth.

Fay felt frumpish in her tailored shirt and black slacks. She wished that her hair wasn't so short; that she hadn't plastered on all that foundation in an attempt to cover her freckles; that she were six-inches taller. More than anything, she wished she could come up with a cutting reply but Cassidy's smile had melted her brain.

'You haven't met Cass yet.' Laura corrected herself, 'Not for a while, I mean.'

Cassidy held out his hand and she, still seated, took it. 'Hi there.' His handshake, as she remembered from the night before, was firm, and the skin on the palm of his hand, dry and rough. The hint of a wink twitched his left eyelid, drawing her into a silent conspiracy.

They sat together, a companionable foursome, flicking through the mound of papers. Fay noticed that Cassidy turned straight to the sports pages, absorbing the details

47

of the test-match and the first football matches of the season. Earlier in the week she had ranted to Jack, at some length, about the way the football season ran from August to May. 'And if it's a World Cup year or the European Championship, there's no break from it at all.'

Knowing nothing about cricket, she plumped for football. 'Which team do you support, Cassidy? We seem to be an Arsenal household, for some reason.'

'Don't tell me it's Notts Forest. They put up a poor show last year.' Isabel lowered the Sunday Times to join in. 'They've got to get a better striker. And they could do with a goalkeeper who doesn't bottle it on the free kicks.'

'You are absolutely right. And I'm extremely impressed.' Cassidy and Isabel engaged in animated football talk whilst Laura went to make another pot of coffee and Fay fumed.

The plan was to have lunch in the local pub then Isabel would drive Fay to the station to catch the three-twenty back to Cardiff. 'It's on my way to the motorway so it's no bother.'

Cassidy put the cases in the boot of Isabel's car. 'Are you coming for lunch?' Fay asked.

'I'd love to but I've got a few things to sort out.'

She felt relieved and disappointed. With no Cassidy there, she would be able to enjoy her meal without competing with Isabel for his attention. 'Don't forget. If you ever come to Wales…'

'Funny you should say that. I have to go down to Carmarthen in a couple of weeks. Delivering a table to a customer.'

They agreed, there and then, that he would schedule his delivery for the Saturday afternoon, and join them for lunch *en route*. 'It would be great to see Jack again. And Caitlin, if she's around.'

They set off for the pub, Fay elated to have scored a points victory over Isabel.

Jack placed the carton of eggs and the roses into a plastic carrier bag, tied the top with a double knot and shoved it beneath the other household rubbish in the dustbin. It was a shame but what alternative did he have? Then he changed out of the clothes he'd been wearing all weekend and washed them, along with his unworn dancing shirt and socks. Fay would know something was amiss if he turned up at the station in the same outfit that he'd worn yesterday. He was pegging out when she rang from the train.

'Have a good weekend, love?' As he held the phone to his ear he had a distinct feeling that she could hear his thoughts, so he kept the conversation short and to the point. 'See you in half an hour.'

The station forecourt was snarled with cars depositing and collecting travellers. Many of those heading into the ticket hall were youngsters, tottering under the weight of enormous rucksacks. The automatic doors opened and closed, swallowing or spewing out the overloaded travellers, taking him back to when Caitlin and Dylan were at college, making reluctant and infrequent visits home. They used to arrive on a Friday evening, too late for a family meal but in time to meet friends at the pub. Next morning they slept until midday, dumped a pile of washing next to the machine, watched television then went out for a pizza. On Sunday they got up, knowing that Fay would have washed and ironed everything and prepared a slap-up lunch. A dash for the train and they were gone again.

Not Kingsley, though. Kingsley just went.

Log-jammed and unable to leave the car, he peered through the windscreen, wondering whether he would recognise his wife when she emerged, because he had changed in the past twenty-four hours and it was possible that she had, too. But she hadn't. He watched her, the familiar, determined Fay, stomping towards him, dragging her case around the sweep of the pavement. With each stride, the Llangwm magic seeped away.

'Good visit?' He gave her a peck on the cheek.

'Lovely. They all sent their love.'

He didn't imagine for one minute that they had. 'How were they?'

'Laura's soldiering on. And Isabel's as mad as ever. And guess who else was there? Cassidy.'

Fay wittered as they crawled out of the city centre, Jack grunting at what he hoped were appropriate intervals, a strategy he'd perfected in order to escape from prosaic small talk and gain thinking time. He was contemplating changing the car, especially since it had let him down yesterday. Gareth had been sure it was a loose lead but perhaps he should pop it into the garage for them to give it a complete overhaul. There was an option to try something a bit sportier now that there were just two of them. He could always use Fay's car when he needed to take his parents anywhere or if he had to take rubbish to the tip. That roll of carpet and the old push-mower at the back of the garage needed to be disposed of. He would take them next weekend, if the depot was open.

'So is that okay with you?' Fay paused. 'Jack?'

'Yes, that's fine, love.' He had no idea what she was talking about and prayed she would say a bit more and give him a few clues.

'Did I tell you that he's a carpenter now? Well, more of a cabinetmaker by the sound of it. I expect he's inherited Laura's practical skills. David was rather on the arty side, if I remember.'

Cassidy. Something to do with Cassidy Ford.

50

'It would only be for a bite of lunch. He doesn't want us to go to any trouble.'

'That'll be nice.' Over the years he had become adept at this dangerous game.

It wasn't until they were sitting down to supper that Fay asked, 'How did it go?' She always referred to his hobby as 'it', as though she couldn't bear to use the words 'Morris' or 'dancing'.

'It?'

'Yesterday.'

'Yesterday?'

'Stop it, Jack.'

He stopped it. 'Oh, you mean the competition. Fine. We didn't get anywhere but it was a good outing.' All of which was totally accurate. The Wicker Men hadn't *got* anywhere – they'd stayed at home. And he'd had a delightful outing to Llangwm. How easy it was to dissemble. Then, without really knowing where the idea came from, he found himself saying, 'Did I mention that I've been invited to speak at the conference in a couple of weeks?' He experienced a slight pang of guilt as a shadow of confusion crossed her face. 'You haven't forgotten the conference? I told you all about it just before the wedding.'

'Of course not.'

He'd counted on her refusal to admit that she could forget anything and he pushed his advantage. 'Yes. One of the keynote speakers has dropped out at the last minute – dropped dead actually.' He was enjoying himself now. 'So, as I'm reasonably local, the secretary asked me if I could step in.'

'Wonderful.' She paused. 'But what will you speak about?'

'I thought I might talk about that study I did on dental

caries rates in Valley communities.' Now came the moment where it could all fall apart. 'You're more than welcome to come along, love.' He held his breath.

'Where is it?'

'Llandrindod.'

'When?'

'Weekend after next.' *Please, God, just this one small favour.*

She appeared to be making some complicated mental reckoning, squinting and pursing her lips. She shook her head. 'What a shame. Can you believe it, that's the very weekend that I've invited Cassidy to call? I suppose I *could* put him off ...'

Jack crossed his fingers and held his breath.

'... but it would be rather rude.'

'Never mind, love. A weekend with a load of dentists isn't much of a treat. Maybe we could get away, just the two of us, sometime soon.'

'Well, as long as you don't mind going on your own.'

They cleared away the supper things and, whilst Fay was upstairs making a phone call, he pencilled 'Dental Conference. Llandrindod' on the calendar that hung in the kitchen. As an afterthought he scrawled 'Conference. 16/17 Aug.' on a scrap of paper and pinned it on the corkboard near the phone, half concealed by the sheet detailing Bank Holiday refuse collections. It looked as though it been there for weeks.

He pottered through the evening, marvelling at God's beneficence.

6

'You're looking horribly bright for a Monday morning.' Sheila Pearce glanced up from the crossword and shoved a pencil into the strange little twist of hair on the back of her head. 'And you're twenty minutes early.'

'Is that any way to speak to your boss?' Jack opened the cupboard in the corner of the waiting room and removed a pale-blue smock.

'You've put up with it for twenty-odd years, Jack, so I've had to assume that you like abuse. Come here.' She helped him fasten the tunic, pulling it down at the back, brushing out imaginary creases with the flat of her hand. 'There. Ready for the fray.'

Sheila was the older sister that Jack never had. He did, in truth, have an older sister – Marion – but, remote and fastidious, Marion had always been completely useless at those critical moments when he'd needed affection, advice or a kick up the pants. She had been there in the flesh but emotionally distanced; on the sidelines, watching everything that was going on without participating in the game. She would have made an excellent nun or driving examiner.

So when Sheila, statuesque and full of fun, had turned up in response to the advert for a receptionist he'd placed in the *Western Mail*, it had been a revelation to meet a woman

53

who could laugh and hug people, often without any reason. When he and his partner in the new practice had conferred, Dafydd Morgan, who freely admitted that he'd become a dentist for the money and consequent *pulling power* – a pun which didn't improve with repetition – wasn't totally persuaded. 'Couldn't we go for someone a bit more…I don't know…sexy I suppose?'

They came to an arrangement. Jack would choose the receptionist and Dafydd, the two dental nurses.

Jack basked in the cheery warmth that Sheila brought to the practice. And the patients adored her. Often he would be left hanging about in the surgery whilst they stayed in the waiting room, chatting to her about children or holidays. This time wasn't wasted. After five minutes with Sheila, even the most apprehensive patient would sit confidently in the chair. Dafydd Morgan moved on to higher things – he became a consultant and the rumour was that he'd slept his way to the top – and the vacuous blondes were long gone, but Jack and Sheila, assisted by a series of competent dental nurses, made a great team and the practice flourished.

'How was your weekend?' she asked. 'Weren't you dancing?'

Jack didn't like lying to her so went for a non-answer. 'It was the Mid-Wales Championship.'

'Any good?'

He shook his head and turned to the matrix of names in the appointment book on the cluttered desk.

Jack found August unsettling. Something about Fay being at home made him jittery. When the children were young, needing to be looked after during those long school holidays, it was a necessity but, as they grew up and no longer required supervision, it unnerved him. What did she do all day while he was working so hard? It was a well-documented phenomenon that holidays precipitated dental problems. The stress and anxiety involved in planning and preparing for vacations led to tooth grinding, which, in turn, caused teeth to crumble and fillings to fall out. Several times he'd treated patients who were on their way to the airport, clutching a passport as he tilted the chair back. Parents took the opportunity to while away aimless summer days by dragging their offspring in for check-ups and orthodontic treatment, as though it were an outing, like going to the cinema.

Throughout the morning, his thoughts wandered away from erupting wisdom teeth and receding gums. He pictured Non, polishing the huge brass doorknocker at The Welcome Stranger Guesthouse or taking feed down to the hen coop. Had she come across his handkerchief yet? Had she thought of him at all as she stripped his bed? Was she sniffing the white sheets to see if the smell of him still clung to them? If roles had been reversed, that was something he certainly would have done. He pondered the events of the weekend as he treated his patients, the memories becoming a soothing mantra, sending him into a reverie.

'How's Fay? Haven't seen her for ages.' A family acquaintance was in the chair, and Jack tore himself away from Llangwm to make the compulsory small-talk, but it disrupted his train of thought and he was unable to recapture his mood. Instead he pictured Fay, snooping around the house, rifling through his pockets and checking the car for clues. Unfortunately there *was* the possibility that she might find something incriminating. What if a dog had torn the rubbish bag before the bin men came? Fay would surely demand an explanation for the full carton of eggs and bunch of roses lying on the drive. Then there was the note from Gareth about the car. He remembered scrunching it up but what had he done with it then? Had he shoved it in a trouser pocket without thinking?

In a spare moment, he phoned Fay. 'D'you fancy meeting for lunch? Try the new Italian? It's warm enough to sit outside. Come in on the train. You could do a bit of shopping and we could drive home together.' Even to himself, the suggestion sounded uncharacteristically well thought out but she agreed without comment. He was reassured by her tone. So far he was in the clear and, if he could lure her away from the house for the afternoon, there was no chance that she would be rifling through his belongings. The outlay on a shopping spree could be written off against peace of mind and, once he was home, he would make a thorough check.

Fay was on top form, vivacious and bubbling with good humour. It had slipped Jack's mind that she was quite a nice-looking woman, in a gingery, freckly way and, as they ordered their meal, he wondered if he had been misinterpreting his recent feelings.

The trip to Paris, after the wedding, had been by way of an experiment, to see whether time spent alone with Fay, in that quintessentially romantic city, might be all it took to reconnect with his wife. The experiment failed but his medical training had taught him that it was foolish to rely on one set of results.

He couldn't help equating the situation with that of a stalled car. Perhaps all it needed was an emotional spark to jump-start things and he ran through several extreme scenarios, hoping to reignite his feelings for her. How would he feel if she were having an affair? What if she was held hostage by a mad axe-man? What if she were to die? He already knew that this particular 'what if' left him feeling nothing. The more excessive the imaginary calamity, the less it touched him but the motoring metaphors took hold and he came to the conclusion that obviously, somewhere along the highways and byways of marriage, they had taken a wrong turn; slipped out of gear; run out of petrol.

Now, sitting opposite her, under the trees, he experienced a stirring of something, somewhere and he wished they were at home. He pictured how it would be in their bedroom, voile curtains billowing in the breeze as they undressed and took a shower together. He imagined the two of them, twisting in the cascade of cool water, lathered and smelling of summer meadows. But by the time they were in the bedroom, drying each other with soft, white towels, Fay had turned into a lithe, dark-haired young woman, butterfly skirt in a crumpled heap on the floor.

As Jack made his way back to work, undulating bosoms and bare midriffs wobbled by. The August sunshine seemed to have blinded the shopping public to its physical inadequacies, depriving them of all modesty. To be fair, there were some nice-looking young women in the crowd, brazenly confident in skimpy dresses or snug tee-shirts. But passing them, and feeling neither stirrings nor regrets, confirmed that he wasn't merely another middle-aged man in crisis. Non's loveliness had nothing to do with glossy lips, hair-free legs or an all-over tan. It came from within – he might go so far as to say, from her soul – spilling out to create an aura of goodness around her.

Smiling and humming 'Handsome John', he zig-zagged through the crowds, barely preventing himself from dancing his way back to the surgery.

Considering that Jack had been given free rein of the house for a couple of days, Fay was surprised at how tidy it was. Of course he'd been away most of Saturday and had probably spent Sunday in the garden or the shed. This would explain why everything was more or less as she'd left it before she went to Nottingham. After he'd gone to work and she'd cleared the breakfast things, there wasn't much to be done. The laundry basket was empty, household admin was up to date and Colleen, her cleaning woman, was due tomorrow, so there was no point in dusting. Jack's phone call, suggesting that they lunch together, was unexpected but welcome. She wondered whether Sheila had put him up to it, although she couldn't for the life of her think why she would.

Watching him, across the table, she thought how old he looked in the bright, revealing sunlight. His hair was thinning at the crown and his neck was beginning to look scrawny. His beard, too, was peppered with grey and sharp vertical creases, which she hadn't noticed until today, ran down his cheeks. He had worn a neat beard all the time she'd known him. In the early days, he used to say it was to convince patients that he was old enough to be trusted with their teeth. One of her college friends had, rather cruelly, observed that he looked like one of the guests at the Last Supper, but that was mainly due to his fondness for wearing sandals. It hadn't taken Fay long to change the footwear but the beard had remained.

'It's almost two,' he said, waving to the waiter for the bill. 'I'd better get back.'

He kissed her cheek and she watched him, tall and loping, disappear into the crush of lunchtime shoppers, before turning in the opposite direction and heading for her favourite department store.

On the train into the city centre, Fay had written a shopping list. Inspired by Isabel's weekend outfits, she'd decided to re-think her own wardrobe. There was no problem with what she wore to work. As a teacher she had to look smart and feel comfortable yet confident, but there was no call for her work clothes to be stylish or of particularly good quality. In her off-duty hours however, she may have been selling herself short. Perhaps the tee-shirts and slacks should make way for something a little 'classier'. She wasn't sure what she was looking for, but, whatever it was would definitely be in Robertsons – and would undoubtedly be expensive.

The revolving doors swung her into the perfumery and cosmetics department. As she passed between the island counters, the concoction of scents – floral, zesty, exotic – caught in her throat and mixed with the after-taste of her garlicky lunch. Predatory sales assistants, all of whom had gone one step too far in their bid to be noticed, patrolled the area. A young man in black shirt and trousers, lemon yellow tie and braces, advanced towards her, holding out a perfume atomiser. His hair, presumably dyed yellow for some promotion, was drawn up in spikes, not unlike the outer casing of a conker. And he appeared to be wearing mascara. She avoided eye-contact and kept walking, but he called after her. 'Mrs Waterfield?'

She sighed and turned back. Encounters like this were one of the hazards of life as a teacher, and one of the reasons that she preferred to shop further away from home. Nick Morris, one of the maths teachers, had horrified the staff room with the statistic that during a twenty-five year career, a secondary school teacher in an average sized comprehensive school might teach ten thousand different pupils. Furthermore, it was likely that every one of those pupils would remember their teachers, either with affection or hatred, for umpteen years after they had left school.

'Mrs Waterfield? It's Neil. Neil Bentley. Remember me?'

Why on earth did this lad think she might remember

him – or recognise him, come to that? It must be years since he left school and here he was, in heavy disguise. She smiled brightly and held out her hand. 'Neil. Hello.' *Neil Bentley?*

'Fancy a squirt?' He grabbed her wrist and sprayed it liberally with 'Jaune'. She raised it to her nose. 'No.' He shook his head. 'You've got to give it a few minutes to mature. Wait for the undertones to surface.'

'You're clearly an expert.' She waved her wrist around, marvelling at the stupidity of an education system that imagined Keats and Milton would benefit any of the youngsters that passed through her hands.

'I often think about King and the band. Those were the days, eh?' He smiled and nodded, like a man four times his age.

Of course. Besides being a pupil at the school, Neil Bentley had been one of Kingsley's friends. But he'd looked completely different then – acne and a lot of metal-work in his mouth; played in that dreadful band that used to practise in the garage. The Scourge or something like that. In the end the neighbours got up a petition.

'What's he up to at the moment? I kinda lost track.'

So had she but she wasn't ready to confess that to anyone. 'He's in Australia. Having a whale of a time.'

He laughed. 'Yeah. I can imagine. And he was a seriously brilliant songwriter.'

The young man's guileless enthusiasm combined with this unexpected reminiscence of her son, caused tears to well up. Neil Bentley's two-day training in scent retailing had evidently not included instruction on dealing with a tearful woman and he peered down at his trendy trainers.

'It's nice.' Fay sniffed the inside of her wrist and reassembled her smile. 'I'll take the small *eau de toilette*. And why don't you call in sometime, Neil? We're still in the same house. We could have a proper chat. Now, I mustn't hold you up any longer.'

She stood on the escalator, looking back over her shoulder at her son's friend, wondering what Kinsgley was doing. She looked at her watch. It was two-thirty which would make it the early hours of tomorrow morning in Sydney. He might be asleep. Or playing ghastly music in a club. He might not even be in Sydney any more. They hadn't heard from him for a while, even though they kept emailing, and, all through Dylan's wedding day, she had clung on to the hope that he would show up.

Jaded, she reached the second floor and meandered from rail to rail, hoping to rekindle her enthusiasm for the task in hand. Hobbs. Bluestocking. East. Great Plains. She wandered from one to another, without any strategy. Maybe she should leave it until Caitlin was with her, although it might be difficult to explain to her daughter what she was looking for. And what *was* she looking for? This discontent had started when she'd seen how elegant Isabel was looking. It had made her feel frumpy and provincial but, of course, Isabel was tall and thin, with more money than she knew what to do with. It was easy to wear a linen shift dress when you had no hips and next to no bust.

The 'Hair Zone' was also located on the second floor. The girl reading a magazine behind the reception desk looked up and caught Fay's eye. Before she had time to agonise, she was shrouded in a lilac coverall, her hair frothy with shampoo. It was only three weeks since the wedding, when she'd spent goodness knows how much on having her hair trimmed and coloured, so when the young man came to talk to her about what she wanted doing, she was unclear.

'I could do you a complete re-style?' he suggested. 'Something softer? More modern? More casual? Maybe lose a bit of this orange?' Every sentence ended with an interrogative upturn.

'Shouldn't I look at pictures or something?'

'Leave it to me?'

For a moment she feared he, too, might be one of her past pupils, now hell-bent on wreaking revenge for some imaginary injustice suffered at her hands. But as he chatted away, explaining that he was a Swansea boy and had only lived in Cardiff for a few months, she relaxed, entrusting her hair to his deft fingers, whilst thoughts of Kingsley drifted around in her head.

'D'you need to brush your hair?' Jack asked when she arrived at the surgery. 'You look a bit wind-swept.'

'I've had it re-styled.' She was relieved that Sheila was in the cloakroom, out of earshot. On the unit there was a hand-mirror, for patients who wanted to inspect their new dentures or orthodontic appliances, and she grabbed it. 'I think it makes me look a lot younger, don't you?' She paused but he didn't say anything. 'Obviously not.' He stared blankly at her and she wondered, not for the first time, if his hearing was going.

Before she could press him further, Sheila popped her head round the door. 'Your hair looks nice, Fay. Makes you look less…more…more glamorous.' She smiled. 'I'm off now. It's my Tai Chi night.'

It took Jack a further fifteen minutes to tidy up and change out of his tunic. Fay watched, irritated by his slowness, as he double-checked that all the equipment was locked away and set the security alarm. As the years went by, he was going to get even slower. And deafer. Could all that prancing about, shaking bells and beating sticks together, have anything to do with it?

7

'SO WHAT'S HE LIKE, MUM?' Caitlin sat with Fay in the garden. Junior lecturers were expected to take annual leave during August, while the students were on long vacation, and Caitlin was not in her usual rush.

'Tall. Thin. No, slim. Light brown hair that looks as if it might go blonde in strong sunshine. Lovely voice. Capable hands. Rather sensuous lips.' Fay avoided her daughter's gaze. 'I don't know really. He only breezed in and breezed out.'

'And when's he coming?'

'Nothing's definite. It was only a general invitation to drop in if he was in this part of the world.' She gave it a couple of seconds. 'Possibly Saturday week.'

Caitlin took a bulging desk diary from the cotton bag that lay on the grass next to her deckchair, turning the pages. 'Oh, what a shame. I'm away that weekend.'

'At the conference? Your father's been asked to speak at some meeting or another that weekend. Llandrindod Wells I think he said.'

'I hadn't heard anything about that one. Maybe it's just for practitioners. No, I'm going down to Devon to visit Mira.'

Fay was relieved when the conversation turned to Caitlin's plans. Whenever she spoke about Cassidy, she tended to give out too much detailed information. She would have to watch out for that.

Over the years, she and Laura had thought how satisfactory it would be if their children teamed up. Laura's daughter, Sadie, had been too unconventional for Dylan and too old for Kingsley but Cassidy and Caitlin were an obvious pairing. Now she wasn't sure whether she even wanted Caitlin to meet him. Since their midnight encounter, she wasn't at all sure what she was feeling, or wanting.

As Caitlin was getting into her car, she said, 'The hair looks great, Mum. Very flattering colour.'

'Well *I* like it but your father keeps suggesting I brush it.'

'He's not a great one for change, though, is he? What did he say about the leg-waxing? Surely he can't want you to brush your legs, too.' Without waiting for answers she sped off towards her waterfront flat.

Fay couldn't decide what she should do. If Jack and Caitlin were both going to be away on, what she had come to think of as, the 'Cassidy Weekend', wouldn't it appear strange if she pressed the invitation? She hadn't spoken to Laura since her return from Nottingham, but had written a postcard to thank her for the hospitality, and she was intending to reiterate her invitation a day or two before Cassidy was due to drive to Wales. Knowing that she would be on her own, he might feel that it was inappropriate to call – although what could be inappropriate about calling on an old friend for a cup of tea? Maybe if she included Dylan and Nia in the invitation it would appear more suitable.

Her re-styling project was progressing. She had made two more shopping expeditions and was getting a better idea of the aesthetic that she was after. She was surprised that Jack hadn't commented on her jaunts to Swansea and Bristol. To be on the safe side, she had camouflaged the former with a visit to the University Library, under the pretence of digging out additional information on Dylan Thomas for her A-level group. She had returned with sheaves of photocopied sheets, along with a very nice slubbed linen trouser-suit and a pair of mules, similar to Isabel's. The Bristol jaunt produced the perfect jeans, a cashmere cardigan and a tiny leather rucksack. Hanging in the darkest recess of her wardrobe, they looked reassuringly classy. She'd tried on each item in the shop, but hadn't yet found the opportunity to see what they looked like when worn together.

Jack was always home by six o'clock on Thursdays. They ate an early, light supper before he went out to dance practice. It annoyed her that this silly hobby of his disrupted their routine. Who on earth wanted supper at six o'clock? In fact most things about the Wicker Men annoyed her. The outfits. The music. The terminology. If Jack been a Morris dancer when they met, she might have allowed herself to be persuaded by Dafydd Morgan. Daffydd had made several attempts to woo her but, sexy though he was, she'd resisted, convinced that he viewed her as no more than a trophy to be snatched from the grasp of his friend. Maybe she'd misjudged him and, had things gone the other way, she might be living in a detached house in Buckinghamshire, wife of an eminent orthodontist.

'I'm off then, love. Sure you'll be okay?'

'I'll survive.'

'Back about ten-ish.' And off he went, whistling something rustic.

When she was sure that he'd gone, she took the new items, price-tags still dangling, from the wardrobe. She slipped off her tee-shirt and cotton skirt and studied herself in the long mirror. Not bad. When she was a child her grandmother and aunts, who were still hung-over from wartime deprivation, praised her for being 'bonny'. And she'd remained 'bonny' all her life. As she grew older she preferred to think of it as feminine and curvaceous and had never – *well* – envied her skinny friends. Hadn't research shown that men were programmed to choose shapely women as part of the evolutionary imperative?

The new clothes weren't quite as stunning as she'd hoped. She still looked mumsy. Recently she'd noticed that her bust was descending towards her waist, a phenomenon most noticeable when she sat in the bath or on the sofa. Being not much more than five foot tall, these landmarks started off a lot closer together than if she'd been a beanpole like, say, Caitlin. She looped her thumbs under her bra straps and pulled upwards, raising her breasts a good three inches. If only she were a few inches taller. Maybe a new bra and a pair of high heels would sort it out.

There was nothing on the television and her library book was proving to be heavy going. She browsed their video collection for something to while away the evening.

Jack had bought 'The Graduate' years ago, when HMV had an offer on. 'Great music. Great dialogue,' he'd explained to teenaged Dylan and Kingsley as they wriggled with embarrassment, watching Mrs Robinson go into action. This evening, cup of coffee and bar of dark chocolate to hand, Fay wriggled with pleasure, calculating the age differentials. Dustin Hoffman was twenty-one. Mrs R, what, late forties? But, when Katherine Ross turned up to distract the young man, she stopped the tape, rewound and went for a long soak in the bath.

Jack pulled out of the drive and drove down the hill, passing the community centre where the Wicker Men met. During

August there were no evening-classes and the building was locked up. The same applied over the Christmas and Easter breaks, but Fay hated it when he chopped and changed his routine so, for years, it had been easier to go out to dance practice, regardless of whether there was one or not.

He had started dancing by mistake. (He was beginning to think that most of the things that he did had been the result of mistakes.) One September, in nineteen-ninety-six, he'd gone along to sign up for an evening class in psychology, thinking that it might come in useful when he treated nervous patients. The class had been oversubscribed and, whilst waiting to get a cup of coffee, he'd been attracted by jingling bells and the twinkling notes of a concertina. Bucolic music had lured him to the hall, where the Morris men were in full swing. That first sighting of swirling hankies and puffing men – antithesis of the stuffiness he associated with the waltz and foxtrot – had intrigued and entranced him. Their leaping and stamping filled the room with wholesome vigour and, when the dancers had given a rousing shout to signal the end of the piece, Jack had shouted with them. Spying the enthusiastic stranger, several of the dancers had given him a run-down on the Wicker Men, explaining that they were recruiting new members. Despite Oscar Wilde's famous caution, he'd signed up on the spot and, for the first two terms, Fay had been under the illusion that he was studying Freud and Jung. It was only when she heard jingling coming from his brief-case that he'd been forced to come clean.

In the beginning, the children were mortified by their father's hobby. They spent weekends on pins in case someone they knew spotted him leaping about in a public place. As they grew older, and realised that dentists had the reputation of being a boring crowd, turncoats that children are, they began to boast about his off-beat hobby. It put him in a different league from golfing or philatelic fathers. In fact, at the wedding, he had overheard Dylan telling an acquaintance that 'Dad's a Morris dancer. And he does a bit of dentistry on the side.'

Fay, on the other hand, never changed her opinion and accused him of trying to humiliate her. 'I think I could almost understand the attraction, if there were hordes of glamorous women involved, but the Wicker Men are just that, aren't they? Men.'

Leaving the community centre behind, Jack headed out of the city. It crossed his mind that he could just about make it to Llangwm and back in the three hours at his disposal, but he wouldn't be able to spend more than ten minutes at The Welcome Stranger. Never mind – he was cooking up a much more ambitious plan.

He left the dual carriageway and took the road that wound up through the grimy little town, perched on the valley side. Past the shuttered shopping parade, dowdy and disfigured by the unimaginative graffiti; past the chapel with the sagging banner that pronounced 'Jesus said – I am the way'. He'd attended chapel as a child, like everyone else. He'd enjoyed the singing, but when he left home, he discovered that there were other places to go for a sing-song, and not once since had he considered going to chapel, apart from 'hatchings, matchings or despatchings', as Sheila put it.

He parked half way up the terrace, pulling hard on the handbrake and angling the wheels into the gutter. In nineteen-sixty-one, even a brick beneath the back tyre hadn't stopped Merve Bowen's Ford Popular rolling down the hill and demolishing itself and the telegraph pole.

His mother must have been watching from behind the net curtains that obscured the parlour window and, before he had time to knock the door, she came out, wiping her hands on her apron. 'We wondered if you'd come, love. I kept back a bowl of trifle. Just in case.'

His mother, smaller than ever, led him down the narrow hall to the kitchen. 'Where's Dad?' he asked.

'Out the back. Watering his tomatoes. It's a bumper year.' His father, who had a small strip of garden as well as an allotment down near the railway line, had always weighed or measured his vegetable crops, keeping a tally in an exercise book that lived on the shelf in the kitchen. Each year he would look back and compare successes or failures. There was nothing to be gained from this, apart from confirmation that, with so many variables – variety, weather, cats and garden pests – some he won and some he lost. 'So we've been having a lot of tomato sandwiches and salad.' His mother made no further comment, simply raising her eyebrows.

He laughed. 'Poor Mum,' and gave her a consoling hug. Then, seated at the Formica-topped table, he ate the trifle that she brought out for him in the familiar blue-and-white ringed bowl. This was proper trifle, made with raspberry jelly, Swiss roll and thick yellow custard, not a pale sugar-free replica or something fashionable with kiwi fruit and hard bits masquerading as trifle. With each spoonful, he tasted the Sunday afternoons of his childhood, when tea was laid in the musty front room and the bread came ready-buttered to the table. It had taken him some time, when he first left home, to master the etiquette, or understand the rationale, of transferring butter from the dish on to his bread via the rim of his plate.

'What did she give you for tea, then?' His mother always checked that the woman who had stolen her son was taking good care of him.

'Salad. With smoked salmon.'

She shook her head and he felt rotten for giving her this

69

ammunition but, if he explained the reason for the light meal, he would have to reveal a lot more. When he next visited, he must be sure to report that 'she'd given him' lamb chops or steak pie.

The back door opened and his father appeared, using the doorstep like a bottle-opener to push off his laceless gardening shoes. 'Hello, John.' He held up the pan from the weighing scales, piled high with tomatoes. 'What d'you reckon? Three, three-and-a-half pounds?'

Harry and Vi Waterfield had christened their younger child John and that's what they always called him. Similarly, Marion was always Marion. The 'Jack' business had started with his crowd from the grammar school and it had stuck, although his parents hadn't liked it. 'It sounds a bit…unreliable…a bit fly-by-night to me,' his mother had said.

The tomatoes weighed in at an ounce under four pounds. 'Mum, put a few in a bag for John to take back with him. Show the city folk what a real tomato tastes like, not that rubbish from the supermarket.' Jack hoped that they only called each other 'Mum' and 'Dad' when he was with them, but he couldn't be sure because he had the feeling that, even now, they were marking time, waiting for Marion and him to come to their senses and settle back where they belonged.

This was the second time he'd visited his parents since the wedding, but the snaps that they'd taken with their little point-and-shoot camera had only come back from Bonus Print that day. 'We got an extra set done. Only two-ninety-nine.' His father wiped the table with the tea-towel and spread the prints out. Despite angled horizons, closed eyes and thumbs across the lens, these gave a better impression of a family wedding than the proofs which the professional photographer had sent. There was Fay, pointing, shouting, organising; Dylan looking handsome and uncomfortable; Nia, beautiful and untouchable. Caitlin figured in several shots, staring beyond the camera, as though looking for a latecomer. She had been – they all had been – but he hadn't shown up. There was one particularly touching photograph of his parents, standing to attention, shoulder to shoulder, nervous but proud. 'Who took this one?' Jack asked his father, holding it up.

'You did. Don't you remember? You kept telling us to relax.'

Jack shook his head. It was odd that, in the thirty-six pictures, he couldn't find one of himself, unless the ear in the shot of the giggling bridesmaids happened to be his. And, thinking about it, he had little recollection of the day, as if some kind of local anaesthetic was numbing that area of his memory. He shivered.

'Take the spare set. We got them for you.' Harry shook his head as Jack reached towards his pocket. 'A little gift, son.'

Jack glanced at his watch. 'I'll love you and leave you then.' He did truly love them, this uninspiring couple, whom it was so much easier, more comfortable, to visit on his own.

'Don't forget these.' His father twisted the neck of the paper bag and offered the tomatoes to him.

'Give her our regards. Perhaps she'll come with you next time.' His mother's face was once again deadpan.

'Or perhaps you could come down to us.'

'We'll see.'

They stood on the front step waving him off, and a feeling of shittiness engulfed him as he abandoned them to whatever their life had become.

He retraced his journey, this time diverting in to the community centre car park. The car was filled with the

71

prickly scent of tomatoes and he was a six-year-old again, watching his father's stumpy fingers nipping out the side-shoots which would, if left, ruin the Moneymakers and the Gardener's Delights.

He got out of the car and, before dropping the damning evidence into the concrete litter bin – something which appeared to be becoming a habit – he took the largest tomato from the bag, squeezing it to test its ripeness. *Perfect.* He bit through the thin skin, into the yielding flesh, noisily sucking out the pips, leaning forward to let any dribbling juice splash on the tarmac. The taste of tomato burst inside his mouth – sweet and sharp, intense and exotic – and he wondered how supermarkets had the nerve to call those hard, flavourless spheres 'tomatoes'. Finally he tucked the wallet of wedding photographs into the bottom of his holdall, covering them with his unworn dancing kit.

Fay was watching the news in their bedroom when he went upstairs. 'How was your evening, love?' he inquired.

'I watched a video.'

'Anything good?'

'*Sense and Sensibility.*' There was a clunk from downstairs. 'What was that?'

'The washing machine. I shoved my togs in, on a quick wash.'

He undressed and went into the bathroom, leaving the door open so he could hear the weather forecast. 'Sounds as if the weather's holding for the weekend. Fancy doing anything?' He was prepared to trade this weekend off against the next.

'I wouldn't mind going to Bath. Or Cheltenham, maybe.'

'You're on. I'll treat you to something nice.' *Mustn't overdo it.*

'I could do with some navy heels and a pair of sunglasses,' her answer came straight back.

If there was one thing he admired about Fay, she knew exactly what she wanted.

8

'But I don't understand why you have to go this evening.' Fay stood, arms crossed, watching Jack pack his suitcase. 'Wouldn't it be better to get up early tomorrow? You'll feel fresher.'

Jack shook his head. 'Registration's at nine a.m. I'd be cutting it a bit tight. 'Specially as I'm speaking. Don't want to risk getting stuck in traffic. Getting flustered.' It all made perfect sense. 'Could you pass me my wash bag, love?' She tossed it onto the bed and he jammed it into the vacant corner of the case.

Jack had spent the week writing his conference presentation. He was pleased with his efforts and had enjoyed digging out the information, then weaving it in with personal anecdotes. Caitlin had cast her eye over it and put him right in a few places. She was up-to-date on current trends and her input was invaluable. He'd read it out loud several times and timed his delivery, making sure that Fay was in earshot. He almost convinced himself that there *was* a dental conference in Llandrindod Wells and that he would be speaking at it.

'That's it then. Mobile. British Dental Journal. Couple of shirts. Pyjamas. And most important,' he patted his briefcase, 'my presentation.'

'What time will you be home?'

'Late Sunday afternoon, I should think. I'll give you a ring when I'm on my way.'

'I may be out.'

'Fine. You don't have to hang around for me. I'll have had lunch so I won't want a big meal.'

'Good.'

She followed him as he took his things out to the car and stowed them in the boot. 'It's cooler now. Nice for driving.' She said nothing. 'Shall I give you a ring to let you know I'm there?'

'You're going to Llandrindod Wells, Jack, not South America. Anyway, I'll probably be asleep.'

'Fair enough.' He bent to kiss her cheek. 'See you Sunday.'

As he started the car he called back. 'Give Cassidy my apologies. Sorry to miss him', but she had disappeared into the house.

He could not have been more excited if *had* been setting off for South America. All week, as well as writing his speech, he'd been envisaging his return to The Welcome Stranger. Longing and subterfuge, in equal measures, create an intoxicating cocktail. He became restless and lost his appetite. Several times he'd burst into song whilst treating patients.

Sheila had remarked, 'If I didn't know you better Jack Waterfield, I'd think you were up to something.' She'd peered at him, giving the distinct impression that she could read his thoughts.

'See, I'm not as boring as you all make out.' He'd attempted the double bluff but she'd looked at him even harder, forcing him to withdraw to the safety of the lavatory.

As a child, when he was moping about, wishing the

days away to Christmas, birthday or their annual holiday in Tenby, his mother had always insisted that 'To travel hopefully is better than to arrive'.

'Enjoy today, John,' she'd say. 'Nothing ever lives up to expectations.'

What was she talking about? Those jewels of celebrations shone out, bright and beautiful, in a prosaic schedule of school, chapel, homework and household chores. Days when uncles sang and drank too much; when there were mounds of presents and double helpings of chocolate cake; when they voyaged to Caldy Island in the leaky boat or, screaming, taunted the freezing waves. How could such days ever fail to keep their promise?

The saying had been with him all week as he plotted his way back to Llangwm. Maybe it should be rephrased, 'To travel hopefully is almost as good as arriving, but not quite.' He could go along with that. And now, as he drove away from the city, towards the round-topped hills, glowing golden in the setting sun, he wanted to catch this sweet moment and ride it, as he'd seen the youngsters ride the surf in Cornwall.

When he'd phoned on Tuesday to reserve his room at The Welcome – as he'd taken to abbreviating it to himself – he'd been surprised to hear a man's voice. Jack explained that he'd stayed there recently and that he would be most obliged if he could have the same room. 'On the back, overlooking the garden. Blue walls. Smells of lavender.'

There had been a long silence, and he wondered whether they had been cut off, but he caught the sound of pages flicking over and eventually he was rewarded with, 'That seems to be in order. Will you be coming on your own, Mr…?'

Could he detect a knowing undertone in the man's question? 'Waterfield. Jack Waterfield. Yes, I'll be alone.'

It was ten o'clock, and dark, by the time he reached Llangwm. The main street, decked with bunting and fairy-lights for some kind of carnival weekend, was thronged with strollers. The tables outside the pub were all taken and overspill drinkers perched on the garden walls of the adjacent houses. He slowed the car and opened the windows, searching the faces and listening to the voices, but there was no sign of Non and he drove on.

The front door of The Welcome Stranger was open but Jack stayed in the car, savouring the moment that he had schemed towards for twelve days. It was as if he were coming home after a long spell as a prisoner of war. Or, better than that, as if he'd completed some rigorous initiation ritual and was about to be accepted by the tribe. He glanced up. A scarecrow, wisps of straw emerging from his battered hat and jacket, was coming down the steps towards him.

The scarecrow leaned down and spoke through the window. 'Mr Waterfield? We spoke on the phone. I'm—'

'Worzel Gummidge?' Jack threw himself into the situation.

'Hah, hah. Well spotted. No, I'm Iolo Evans. Most of the time anyway. Can we get you installed, then I'm afraid I'll have to dash off? I'm needed elsewhere.'

This hadn't been how he'd pictured his arrival and, although it was all very jolly, he felt a bit let down. He'd imagined that Non would be in the living room, reading or doing a jigsaw puzzle and, delighted to see him, she would greet him with a hug and maybe even a welcoming kiss.

Following the trail of straw that Iolo Evans was leaving, he arrived at the bedroom. *His* bedroom. 'Thanks. That's fine.'

'You know where everything is.' A statement, rather than a question. 'Here's a key. Come along and join us if

78

you like. Just pull the door to.' And he disappeared down the stairs.

Jack sat on the bed. His plans for the weekend had never progressed beyond this point, because this was where it should go into free-fall. When he entered The Welcome Stranger Guesthouse he was crossing an invisible frontier and journeying into another land, where the inhabitants and their customs were unique, and he was sure that, if he played by their rules, the outcome would be even better than he'd anticipated.

He unpacked his case and the hairs on his arms stood up when he noted that his hanky was no longer in the drawer. The knowledge that Non had found it, held it, maybe carried it in her pocket, went a little way to ease his disappointment that she wasn't there.

The familiar smell of washing powder clung to his pyjamas, reminding of home, and he checked his mobile. There was one text message: 'gd lck 4 2moro. S.' He smiled. Poor Sheila. Friday night and she'd be alone in her little flat, watching a video. Surely one day someone would come along to give her all the love and support she gave to everyone else.

Fay, on the other hand, had neither phoned nor texted and he didn't know whether to feel resentment or relief. Ten-thirty. Well, she had more or less told him not to ring so he put his mobile on the bedside table.

What had Iolo said? 'Come along and join us.' *Where, though?* Switching off the light he went downstairs and checked the sitting and dining rooms. The house appeared to be deserted so, too keyed up to contemplate an early night, he strolled back towards the pub. As he drew nearer he heard strains of music, punctuated with applause and laughter which was coming from an ugly, flat-roofed building set a little back from the main road. Unable to resist the lure of the music, he went in.

Several low tables and tiny chairs cluttered the deserted foyer. He was in a school of some sort. From the scale of the furniture and the décor – bright red and yellow doors – he guessed it was a primary school. The music and laughter appeared to be coming from beyond the set of double doors, at the end of a corridor straight in front of him. Before he reached them, a woman emerged, chasing a small boy who had taken off like a rocket and was heading directly towards him. 'Loo?' she pleaded, spotting Jack.

He shrugged. 'Sorry.' Too late. The child, freezing at the sound of a strange voice, vomited noisily and productively over Jack's shoes and lower trouser legs. The boy, deathly pale and crying now, began to heave again and his mother, gasping apologies, hustled him out of the front door. Jack stared down at his feet, aware of a warm dampness on his shins. He had never been much good with vomit. Occasionally a patient would gag whilst having treatment, but it seldom came to anything and he always had enough time to stand out of the way.

Loud applause came from beyond the doors, followed by the sound of chairs scraping on a wooden floor, as the audience – this had to be some kind of performance – stood up. If they came out now and found him standing in a puddle of vomit, they would obviously assume that he had been sick and, as the smell wafted up from his splattered turn-ups, he very nearly was. He turned and fled.

Once in the fresh air the nausea subsided but, as the moisture on his navy blue trousers cooled, they stuck to his shins. It was unpleasant but he kept moving, hoping that, in the darkness, none of the passers by would notice the mess or the smell and, in a few minutes, he was back at The Welcome Stranger. Outside the front door, he removed his shoes and socks and, holding them as far away from himself as possible, let himself in and shot upstairs where he locked himself in the bathroom.

As he grew calmer, he wondered why he had panicked. Why hadn't he stood his ground and explained to them? These were people who had spent the evening singing and having fun and there was no question about it, they would have laughed and helped him sort it out. Who knows, he might even have achieved some kind of mythic status? But it was too late for that. He'd blown it and bolted which wasn't a very mythical thing to do.

He filled the bath with water as hot as he could bear, stripped off and climbed in, scrubbing his legs and feet with the lemon-y soap from the shelf. He'd forgotten to collect the towel from his room and did his best to dry himself with the hand towel that was on the rail. Taking a deep breath, he sluiced the gobs of whatever the child had eaten for supper down the sink, then washed his shoes, socks and trousers in the bathwater, again using the soap. He wasn't sure how this might affect the shoe leather but it was a chance he would have to take. Finally, wringing as much water as he could out of his clothes, he wrapped the scrap of towel around his waist and scurried across the landing.

He was in bed by the time he heard voices in the hall, trousers and socks hanging over the bed-end and shoes, tied together by the laces, dangling over the window latch, fumigating in the night air. He felt satisfied that he had coped with a tricky situation remarkably well and accepted that it was the kind of thing that would often happen in his new life.

When he went back home, Fay and Caitlin would want to know how the conference had gone. He would need to convince them that, this weekend, he'd been 'Jack Waterfield – Keynote Speaker' and, if he weren't to slip up, it would be safer to convince himself, too. He lay on his back, rehearsing the speech which was now becoming as familiar to him as the Lord's Prayer. How often had he listened to interviews with actors who said that, to give a realistic performance, it was vital to wear the appropriate shoes? His speech was his shoes.

9

FAY WOKE AN HOUR BEFORE THE ALARM. Without Jack at her side, she had spent a restless night wriggling around the double bed. A fluttery stomach alerted her that this was a special day, although it took a few seconds to remember why, and by that time it was impossible to get back to sleep. Pale dawn sunshine already filled the room but she made herself stay in bed, hoping that horizontality would reduce the usual morning puffiness around her eyes and ensure they were bright and clear.

When they had spoken two days earlier, Cassidy had been planning to make an early start and beat any holiday traffic. 'I should be there by about noon. Promise you won't go to any trouble, Auntie Fay,' he'd said. She'd have to knock this 'Auntie Fay' nonsense on the head. 'Just a sandwich and a coffee.' So, she had five hours to eat breakfast, bathe, wash and organise her hair, tidy the house, do her nails and makeup, set the lunch out and get changed.

She'd made up her mind what she would wear several days ago. The navy linen wrap-round skirt and dusky pink raw silk shirt, gifts from Jack when they visited Bath last weekend, were pressed and hanging on the picture rail. Lunch was in the fridge, cling-filmed and ready to go. She must remember to chill the white wine, although Cass wouldn't be able to have more than a couple of glasses.

At seven-thirty the alarm released her from bed. Whilst the kettle boiled, she phoned Jack. If she spoke to him now it would be another thing she could cross off her list. His phone was switched off and she left a short message. 'Jack? It's me. I expect you're having breakfast. Good luck with the talk. Hope it goes well. I'll see you tomorrow. Love you. 'Byeee.'

And she supposed she did love him. He was gentle and funny, kind and loyal. But so were Labrador dogs and favourite uncles. He reminded her of a Catherine wheel on bonfire night, blue touch-paper smouldering, whizzing round a few times, raising her hopes then stopping, needing another prod to get some action. Fay was a great prodder and chivvier, and she didn't object to that role, as long as he played his part and followed through. But recently Jack's touch-paper had fizzled out altogether and nothing she did could activate him. Look how pathetic he'd been at the wedding, wandering about the place as though he were concussed, leaving her to organise everything, when he knew how distraught she was at Kingsley's failure to show up. The only thing that he ever enthused about was the Wicker Men. Could he not see how ridiculous they were? A sort of cavorting Dad's Army of misfits and oddballs. If he felt compelled to go out and perform weird rituals in fancy dress, he might as well have joined the Masons and done himself a bit of good. Yes, she did love him but he had failed to come up to scratch. Before they were married her father had warned, 'Jack Waterfield may be a dentist, Fay, but don't forget, Taffy was a Welshman.' This made no sense but nevertheless it caught the essence of Jack's failure.

The morning went smoothly. Her attempt at the new hairstyle, only the third time she'd tackled it since her

84

visit to the hairdresser, worked out well. Caitlin had introduced her to wax, the secret to achieving and retaining the windswept effect. Her new bra was doing its job of increasing the space between breasts and waist and the sleep-bloated look had gone from her face.

After pondering the pros and cons, she had invited Dylan and Nia to drop in. Scarcely unpacked after their honeymoon, the newlyweds were completely disorganised and Fay was confident that they would forget to come but she would not need to feel guilty about failing to include them. As noon approached, she had little left to do but plump cushions, wipe work surfaces and make frequent trips to the lavatory.

The bell rang and she went to the door, wishing that the tell-tale noise of the filling cistern wasn't coming from the cloakroom. This needn't have concerned her. The four people standing in the front porch, talking and laughing, were making such a racket that they wouldn't have heard Niagara Falls.

'Hi, Mum,' Dylan hugged her then held her at arms length. 'You look … different.'

'Loo? I'm desperate.' Laura – *what on earth is she doing here?* – pushed past her, pointing upstairs and raising her eyebrows. 'Up?'

Nia sidled in. 'Hi. We're on time for once.' She hovered in the hall, waiting for direction, fragile and Bambi-like.

'Hello, Auntie Fay.' There he was, tall and calm, above the confusion.

'Fay – please. Hello, Cassidy.' *It's all going wrong.*

'Hi.' He brushed her cheek with his lips. 'Dylan hasn't changed a bit. I'd have known him anywhere.'

'Your mother…?'

'We didn't tell you she was coming in case something cropped up at the last minute.'

85

By this time Laura was back in the hall. 'That's better.' She hugged Fay. 'A bit childish, but I thought it would be fun to surprise you.' She assessed Fay's expression. 'But if it's not convenient, or you have other plans, I can easily go on to Carmarthen with Cassidy.'

'It's a wonderful surprise. I don't know why I didn't think of suggesting it myself.'

Fay watched Cassidy as he followed Dylan and Nia into the back garden. She couldn't hear what they were saying but it was evident from the laughter and shoulder punching that they were getting on well. Nia, hugging herself even smaller with her own folded arms, smiled and looked on.

'She's very beautiful, isn't she?' said Laura.

'I suppose so.'

'What does she do? You told me but I've forgotten.'

'Accountant. Works at the same firm as Dylan. She was his boss when he started there. I do like her but she's too quiet. I have no idea what's going on in her head.'

'It's not easy coming in on a mother-son thing, and you're a hard act to follow, Fay. It's bound to take her a while to find her feet. Remember what it was like with Jack's mother when you were first married?'

Fay thought back to her first encounter with Violet Waterfield. Jack had been living in a flat with Dafydd Morgan and a couple of other students, near the city centre. She had a room in one of the halls of residence. It was a Sunday, about six months after they had started seeing each other, and Jack had mentioned that he was going to visit his parents. 'D'you fancy coming with me? We might as well get it over with.'

An only child, Fay had spent a great deal of her childhood in the company of adults. She preferred the predictability of their world and was more comfortable sitting with her mother's friends than joining their children in boisterous play. At an early age she had learned the art of small-talking to strangers, so she'd had no qualms as they set off up the valley that Sunday afternoon in Jack's little car. He hardly spoke and she assumed it was because, being a shy young man, he was feeling his way in their relationship. Nothing prepared her for the Waterfield's ugly little terraced house. She was furious with him for not explaining their circumstances and dismayed that these ill-educated people were his parents; this dreadful place his home. Throughout their courtship, whilst being perfectly civil, they seemed merely to tolerate her, as if waiting for their son to come to his senses and find someone of his own kind. Even now, all these years later, when she had given them three grandchildren, they made her feel as if she were a temporary aberration.

'That's not very encouraging,' said Fay, in reply to Laura's question. 'They've always seen me as some stuck-up English woman, hell-bent on setting their beloved son against them.'

'That seems a bit strong. D'you have much to do with them?'

'Not really. The last time I saw them was at the wedding. They seem so uncomfortable when they come here and, quite frankly, I find it totally depressing when we visit them.'

Dylan came to the open window. 'Can we start lunch, Mum? Cassidy has to get on his way.'

Cassidy joined him. 'Please don't hurry on my account. A coffee will do me fine and then I'll get out of your hair.'

It was Fay's first opportunity to look at him. Apart from his height and deliciously sensuous voice, there was nothing to mark him out from dozens of young men that she passed every day in the city streets. He wore a white tee-shirt with some kind of Aboriginal design on it – a crocodile or a lizard. Clean but faded cut-offs reached below his knees. His tanned limbs sprouted a fuzz of bronzed hair and his cork-soled sandals showed a salt-water tide-line. Just a run-of-the- mill young man.

By the time the five of then were eating lunch, and because of this same ordinary young man, she was suffering breathing difficulties. He sat across the table from her, next to Nia, coaxing more from the girl than Fay had ever heard her say. She wanted to reach under the table and run her hand down his leg, to feel if the hairs were as soft as they looked. From time to time he glanced up, holding her gaze a little longer than was necessary and, once, she was sure he winked at her. She blushed and busied herself, pouring more wine and pressing the remaining food on everyone. Laura, who had been having a gentle disagreement with Dylan about a film they had both seen, looked at her watch. 'D'you think you should be off, Cass?'

'S'pose so. It seems a shame to break up the party.'

'No, we've got to go, too. IKEA calls, doesn't it?' Dylan looked to his new wife for affirmation.

'Lampshades and picture frames,' Nia directed this at Cassidy, as if he were the only person worth talking to.

They left the table and, whilst the others strolled to inspect the pond in the corner of the garden, Fay led Cassidy into the house.

'Can I use the loo before I get on my way?' he asked.

She showed him to the cloakroom and pottered about in the hall, straightening the rank of photographs on the wall and checking if the pot plants needed watering. 'Sorry if lunch was a bit chaotic,' she apologised when he emerged. 'We didn't really have a chance to chat, did we?'

'Well, I'll be back again tomorrow to pick Mum up. It was great to see Dylan again and meet Nia. And lovely to see you, too, Fay.'

Her whole body tingled, anticipating a farewell kiss, but he turned aside to look at the photographs. 'Is this Caitlin?'

'Yes. Last year. She was on holiday in America. Colorado, I think.'

'Mmmm.'

'What does that mean? Mmmm.'

'She has an interesting face. Strong. Masculine.' He looked at Fay. 'I don't go much for girlie girls.'

Fay regretted her choice of pink shirt and curled her fingers to conceal her painted nails.

'Not gone yet?' Laura came in carrying a pile of dirty plates.

Fay and Laura went to see him off and he drove away amidst a flurry of instructions and telephone numbers. Fay watched until the car disappeared around the corner.

The two friends stacked the dishwasher then took their cups of coffee into the garden, moving the sun-loungers into the shade. Fay wished she felt more pleased to see Laura, Dylan and Nia but resentment dampened her enthusiasm. They were like three meddlesome guardian angels, hell-bent on saving her from herself. She'd barely had a chance to speak to Cassidy and, when they *had* been alone, they'd talked about Caitlin.

'This is lovely.' Fay hoped she sounded convincing. 'We've got twenty-four hours to ourselves. Is there anything you'd particularly like to do?'

'I'm easy. After all, I've railroaded your weekend.'

'Don't be silly. We could go and have a look at Cardiff Bay. It's quite fun down there. Lots of cheap and cheerful places to eat.'

'I'm hopeless at the tourist thing.' Laura hesitated.

'There is one thing I wouldn't mind doing, but I'm not sure, after what you said earlier.'

'What's that?'

'I've only met Jack's parents once. At your wedding. Could we go and visit them? But not if you can't bear the idea.'

'Why on earth would you want to do that?'

Laura screwed up her face. 'It's a kind of project I'm working on. I don't want to make a big thing of it but it would be really useful. Perhaps we could incorporate it into a trip out. If you wouldn't mind driving...'

Fay shook her head and laughed. 'Not my idea of an entertaining afternoon but, sure, if it will help with your mysterious project. I'd better give them a ring to check they'll be in. Although, heaven knows, they never go anywhere.'

It served her right for asking. It was one of those questions she always asked visitors, assuming that they would leave it up to her. But Laura had never been like other people. Then, as she was phoning her parents-in-law, she remembered. *Laura's father.* Death evoked the strangest reactions and it was natural for Laura, an artist, to channel her grief and loss into something creative. Her 'project' obviously had something to do with that but she would let her friend tell her about it when she was ready.

10

JACK SNIFFED HIS SHOES. There was the faintest hint of something, but it might be nothing worse than damp leather. His trousers and socks were okay too – a little creased but pleasantly tangy from the lemon soap.

Whilst he was in the shower, there was a knock on the bathroom door and a woman's voice – definitely not Non's – asked 'Full Welsh for you, Mr Waterfield?'

'Yes please,' he shouted above the gushing water, unfazed by the intrusion. 'And tea. Thanks.'

The normal B & B rules didn't apply at The Welcome. 'Etiquette' was the word Fay would use but Jack always felt uneasy that, merely because he'd paid some money, another human being should feel obliged call him 'sir'. 'You Welsh are all the same. Inverted snobs,' Fay had snapped when she spotted him sitting with the off-duty waiters at Dylan's wedding. 'They won't respect you for it.'

By eight-thirty he was downstairs, refreshed by nine hours sleep and ready for his breakfast. The dining room was deserted. 'Somewhere Over the Rainbow', whistled rather badly, caught his ear and he traced it to the kitchen. Iolo, dressed this morning as a Formula One racing driver in red boiler suit plastered with advertising slogans and a baseball cap worn backwards, was whizzing up a large bowl of something with a hand-held mixer. A PVC apron bearing the title 'Bosun's Mate' broadened the sporty spectrum. Jack wished he'd packed something more original than a denim shirt and khaki trousers. He'd have to try harder when he next came.

'Morning. You couldn't pass me the salt, could you?' Iolo jerked his head in the direction of the cupboard. 'I thought we'd have pancakes this morning, for a change.'

Jack didn't know whether to mention that he was already committed to a 'full Welsh', but he let it go.

'Pity you didn't make it to the show. It's on again tonight if you're stuck for something to do.'

'Ahhhh…'

'I know. Amateur dramatics are dire. Much more fun for the cast than the audience. Anyway, see how you feel. In the mean time, you couldn't give me a hand with these, could you?'

They were tossing pancakes when Non appeared at the back door. 'Promising start. Poor follow through,' she laughed as Jack's pancake, descending after an ostentatious flick, slithered off the rim of the pan onto the floor. 'Mum said your breakfast's in the bottom oven.'

'Hi.' He bent to retrieve the pancake, his face burning.

She spotted the mounting pile keeping warm on top of the Aga. 'You'd better be hungry.'

This woman was perfect. Today, with her hair loose and wearing a simple cotton shift, the colour of fading bluebells, she looked like a woodland sprite, tanned and mischievous. Such natural grace. Such strong, white teeth.

'Having fun?' An older version of Non – same shaped face, same stature, maybe a little broader in the hip, iron grey hair and shining eyes – appeared in the doorway.

'Yes, we are, aren't we?' Iolo looked to Jack for

confirmation.

'Ummm…'

'That's not fair, Dad,' Non laughed. 'Jack needs a decent breakfast before he gets embroiled in a family argument.'

Iolo put down his pan and wiped his floury hands on a tea-towel, before taking the woman into his arms and planting a noisy kiss on her lips. 'Argument. I never argue with my soul mate.'

Instead of pushing him away, she drew him to her and kissed him back, whilst Non rescued a burning pancake. 'Where are the other guests, Dad?'

'The Bevans are having a lie-in and Freya's gone off to photograph the preparations for the parade.'

Mrs Evans stopped kissing her husband and advanced towards Jack, and for one second he dared to hope that she was going to kiss him too. 'I'm Zena. We met through the bathroom door.'

Jack beamed. What an excellent start to a Saturday.

'I shan't need another thing all day.' Jack placed his empty pancake plate on top of his equally empty breakfast plate, and took them to the sink.

'That's the point of B & B, isn't it? You're paying for it, so you might as well stoke up for the day.' Non poured him a third cup of tea.

'Did you think I'd done a runner? I was almost home when I realised I hadn't paid my bill.'

She looked up. 'I wasn't concerned. When you didn't send the money, I knew you intended coming back.' There was no guile in her remark. 'And I couldn't forward your hanky because you didn't leave an address.'

On his previous stay, he had revealed little about himself. He'd mentioned that he had to get back to Cardiff, once the car was fixed, but no-one had asked him anything about his job or his family. The Merediths' tales of country churchyards, the hard-fought Scrabble match and red kites had eliminated any need for that 'what do you do for a living?' stuff.

'I've a confession to make about that,' she said and he waited for her to tell him that she'd worn it in the left cup of her bra, next to her heart. 'I cut my hand on the vegetable knife and I grabbed it off the washing pile to bind the wound.' She held out her hand, displaying a red scar at the base of her thumb. 'I'll buy you another one, of course.'

He shook his head and took her hand, running his forefinger across the scabby scar. 'Does it hurt? Perhaps it needed a stitch.' She showed no embarrassment or annoyance that he was holding her hand. But something about her child-like scrutiny of the injury made him realise that she'd hardly registered his touch.

The long-case clock in the hall struck the half-hour and she withdrew her hand. 'I must get on. Festival Saturday's one of our busiest days.'

'Are you involved with the celebrations?' Iolo had already told him a bit about the village carnival and craft fayre.

'No. I'll have to miss all that. I'll be on duty.'

'Duty?'

'Didn't I tell you? We've got a little garden centre. Mostly herbs. About a mile in that direction.' She pointed away from the village centre.

'But you work here.'

'I help out, now and again, when Mum and Dad busy. Last time you came I was filling in because they were away.'

'But you *live* here.'

'No. Sorry. Wrong again. My partner and I live in the

94

cottage next to the garden centre.'

He should have known this delightful woman would have a fascinating job and a 'partner'. For two weeks he'd been picturing her here, at The Welcome Stranger Guesthouse, cooking breakfasts and changing sheets but, in fact, she'd been pricking out seedlings and potting things on – when she wasn't making love to a handsome horticulturist.

'You must come and let me sell you some plants, if you've got time. What are your plans for the day?'

'I'm flexible. I expect I'll watch the parade. Try my luck on the hoopla stall. That sort of thing.'

'I may see you later. Did Dad tell you about the party? They always throw a party here after the last night of the show. He should have warned you. It gets a bit wild but we can fix you up somewhere else if you need a quiet night. There's always room at our place.'

Jack went to his room to collect his jacket, and sat for a while. He could see how, to the outside world, he might appear an old lecher but it really wasn't like that. He'd never expected to become Non's lover – *well* – but he would give anything to spend time with her. In her company, he knew he could do anything and be taken seriously. She could help rescue the Jack Waterfield who had wandered off the path and was now floundering, up to his knees in the mire. The fact that she had a partner needn't change that one bit.

Llangwm was more complex than he had appreciated. For a start, many of the buildings were multi-functional. One displayed a small sign, 'Honey & Beeswax Polish – Local', directing customers around to a stall in an immaculate back garden. Another sold hand-knitted garments, in bold colours, from a front room. Fay would have condemned the clothes as being hippy-ish and very badly finished. The grand stuccoed house on the corner had a comprehensive selection of second hand books, devoted to cricket, displayed on bookshelves arranged along its garden wall. He was flicking through 'Pavilions of Splendour – a guide to corrugated iron cricket pavilions' when Iolo tapped him on the shoulder.

'Got a minute, Jack? We could use an extra pair of hands with the float.' He spotted the title of the book. 'You don't play do you?'

With the prospect of something interesting on the go, Jack's mood lifted and he followed Iolo, at a brisk trot, to the school playground. Dotted around the tarmac were a dozen or so vehicles and trailers, each with a team of people decorating them. The scene buzzed with conversation, laughter and children's voices, all to the accompaniment of the Beach Boys over the public address system.

'I used to play a bit. Bowler,' Jack answered when he finally caught Iolo up. 'Which one's ours?'

'Over there.' Iolo pointed to a trailer. 'LADS.'

'Pardon?' Several women were looping yellow fabric along the side of the trailer but there wasn't a lad in sight.

'El-Aye-Dee-Ess. Llangwm Amateur Dramatics Society. We've got the Oz costumes until Monday so we might as well get our money's worth.'

'What's the problem?'

'Typical LADS scenario. Bags of enthusiasm but sketchy on the details. We need a rainbow by two o'clock. Any ideas?'

All over the car park, local organisations were putting the finishing touches to their efforts. The Young Farmers had done something spectacular with big bales and the WI members were, for some reason, dressed as bumble bees.

'Brilliant.' Iolo, back in his scarecrow outfit, handed Jack a mug of tea and a cheese sandwich, 'Bloody brilliant.'

Jack beamed. 'It just came to me. As soon as you said 'rainbow' I had this kind of flashback.' It was one-thirty and they stood looking on as Gareth backed the tractor up to the LADS float. The Wicked Witch of the West – Zena – was sorting out a band of Munchkins, whilst an energetic woman pegged brightly-coloured jumpers on a clothes-line rigged up to span the trailer. 'I promised that we'd give her a credit.' He pointed to the piece of card gaffer-taped to door of the tractor. 'Rainbow courtesy of Harriet's Handknits.'

He watched Cowardly Lion, Tin Man and the rest clamber up onto the rickety benches and gave them the thumbs up as the vehicles manoeuvred to form a convoy. It crossed his mind that perhaps Non might find time to come to see the parade, but he didn't care either way because he was having such a wonderful time. After his busy morning, in the course of which he had made at least a dozen new acquaintances and also promised to bowl a few overs in the evening match, he was content to wander round to the pub and watch his rainbow pass down the main street.

And that's where, pint in hand, he bumped into Stan Colley and his wife. Stan still had his wrist bandaged after the car accident and he was sitting on the wall of the pub, whilst Millicent helped him out of his jacket. 'Jack. Good Lord. Jack Waterfield.'

'Stan. Millicent.' Jack first instinct was to melt into the gathering crowd. This might have solved his immediate dilemma, but it would certainly make for a few tricky questions when the Wicker Men convened again at the start of September, so he raised his pint in salutation and gathered his thoughts.

'What on earth are you doing in this neck of the woods,

Jack?'

'I might ask you the same thing, Stan.' Superb delaying tactics.

'Millie and I always come up for the Festival, don't we, love? Been doing it for years. Is your good lady with you?' Stan peered around the crowd. It was unlikely that he would have recognised her if she had been, because Fay had met Jack's dancing friends on very few occasions during his dancing years.

'She's popped back to the car. And then I think she was going to have a look at the stalls.' Anything to avoid explaining why he was here alone. Now all he had to do was shake them off and make sure he kept out of their way. 'When are you off back?' he asked hopefully.

'We usually make a day of it. Get a meal in the pub. Maybe go to the show in the school hall.'

Millicent, who up until now had done nothing but smile and nod, squeaked and pointed to the parade appearing around the corner. Jack shuffled across behind the privet hedge as the floats moved slowly, oh so slowly, past. Scouts and Guides. Attwoods the Seed Merchants – 'Seeds that grow faster than weeds'. The Local Chamber of Trade. Then, there they were, with Gareth at the wheel of the scrubbed and sparkling tractor, and Jack's jumper and cardigan rainbow swaying to the strains of 'We're off to see the Wizard'.

He sagged lower behind the hedge but the elevation of the trailer enabled all his new friends to see him quite clearly. The singing stopped and they waved, shouting, 'Great rainbow, Jack', 'Coming to the party tonight?', 'Gareth's got some whites you can borrow for the match.' Everyone on the LADS float had a message for him and, because they were in thespian mode, they enunciated beautifully and projected well.

Millicent pointed at the float. 'Got family connections here?'

'Watch out. Wasp.' Jack swiped at the air around Millicent's perm, feeling not the slightest twinge of guilt as her attention switched from the float to her imaginary assailant.

'And you'll never guess who we bumped into the café. Richie Turner and his wife. Small world, eh?' Stan beamed.

'Sure is. Good grief. Is that the time?' Jack, making great show of checking his watch, gulped his beer. 'Well, lovely to see you both.' And he was off down the hill, heading for the sanctuary of The Welcome Stranger.

The house was quiet and cool. Jack went up to his room and opened the windows as wide as they would go. It was only three o'clock but, after his double breakfast and busy morning, he felt exhausted and it was all he could do to slip off his shoes and climb on to the bed. There, in the lavender-scented calm, he drifted in and out of sleepy shallows, like a cork on the tide-line. He wondered what Fay was doing. How was she spending the weekend without him? Of course Laura's son was going to call, wasn't he? But Caitlin was away and the newlyweds were still so immersed in themselves that they wouldn't think that their mother might appreciate some company.

He sat up and stared out of the window at the round-topped hills and saw a straggle of people, wearing coloured shirts and white sun hats, toiling up the worn path. And there, at the highest point, the silhouette of ant-humans broke the smooth arc of the summit. Those tiny blobs, those insignificant dots moving in the vast landscape, were as important to someone – wife, father, lover and even, to be sentimental, God – as Caitlin, Dylan and Kingsley were to him. Yet if one of them, say that one on the very top,

99

fell off the edge, he could turn over and go back to sleep without even missing a heartbeat.

He swung round to sit on the edge of the bed and fished his mobile phone out of his jacket pocket. He listened to the message that Fay had left early that morning, wishing him well for the conference. She sounded cheery and full of beans, and suddenly a wave of love or guilt or panic swept over him. He listened to her message twice more before deleting it.

It took him no time at all to pack his case. Ripping a sheet of paper from his notepad he wrote:

Dear Iolo, Zena and Non,
> *Called away suddenly. Sorry I can't play in the match or see the show or come to the party. Thanks for everything. See you soon.*
> *Jack x*

As an afterthought he added two more kisses, one for each of them, and left the note on top of the chest of drawers, along with a cheque to cover this and his previous visit. Finally he placed the customary clean hanky in the drawer and drove back to Cardiff.

11

FAY EXPLAINED TO JACK'S MOTHER that she was taking an old school friend for a sight-seeing tour and, as they would be more or less passing the door, it would be a good opportunity to drop off the wedding photographs which Jack had ordered for them. Vi's responses were monosyllabic and brusque, making it impossible to gauge her reaction to the proposed visit, but that was no different from usual.

'It'll do them good to see a fresh face,' Fay said. 'They sit in that little house, reinforcing their prejudices, soaking up all that prurient rubbish from the tabloids.'

'Aren't you being a bit harsh?' asked Laura.

'Yes. I am. They're not unintelligent people but it's as if they're just whiling away time until they die. As if they've outlived their usefulness and they've got no right to be alive. And I'm terrified that Jack will go the same way.'

Laura shook her head and smiled. 'No chance with you in charge.'

'I'm not joking, Laura. He never had much get-up-and-go but he's doing less and less. He's perfectly happy to fall asleep in front of the television every night. He never reads anything apart from his work stuff.'

'He still dances though, doesn't he?'

Fay grimaced. 'Don't start me on that.'

'Well, I think it's rather romantic. Brave. Singular.'

'You've obviously never seen the Wicker Men in action.'

They turned up the steep street and Fay parked outside the house, yanking the handbrake hard. Many of the front doors stood wide open and children, some no older than three or four, were out on the pavement playing in the afternoon sunshine.

Laura had a camera on a strap around her neck and, as soon as she got out of the car, she started to take photographs. 'It's wonderful. Timeless, apart from the cars and the trainers.'

'"Wonderful" is pushing it a bit, don't you think? Deprivation is more the word I would use.'

'Maybe. But these children are lucky to be able to play out in the street. They must feel very secure. Where I live, parents don't let the kids out of their sight.'

'Could that be because they care what happens to them?'

Vi answered the door and, after the introductions and mutterings of 'there was no need' to Laura's gift of luxury chocolate biscuits, she ushered them into the tiny sitting room. It was packed with furniture, leaving little room for human occupants. There might have been a view of the street had not a swathe of net curtains obscured it, along with most of the daylight. An ugly clock ticked on the sideboard and ranks of relatives, past and present, stared out from the photograph frames clustered around it. 'We had the new TV from John and Marion. Last Christmas.' She turned to Fay, 'You haven't been up to see it, have you?'

Fay ignored the snipe. 'Shall I make some tea?'

'You won't know where to find anything. I'll do it. You stay where you are.'

Left to themselves, Fay whispered, 'See what I mean? She does it all the time, making out that I never come here. But can you blame me?'

Laura squeezed past the sofa to look at the photographs and was studying a picture of two children, sitting neatly on a garden wall, smiles fixed, when Vi returned with the tea tray. 'That's Marion on the right, John on the left. We were visiting my sister in Swansea. You can just see her in the background.'

Fay looked on, amazed at the ease with which the two women chatted. Laura put up a valiant show of being interested in the rambling details of the Waterfield and Price families, saying little but, with quiet prompts now and again, encouraging Jack's mother to talk. Anecdotes emerged, some of them quite fascinating, which Fay had never heard before.

Fay, a little miffed at their casual intimacy, watched them, noticing that her mother-in-law was wearing the navy blue dress and matching shoes that she'd bought for the wedding. It affected her – touched, surprised, irritated her – that Vi had made such an effort for, what was after all, an informal visit.

Laura, maybe feeling Fay's scrutiny, looked up. 'Haven't you brought some wedding photographs for Mr and Mrs Waterfield?'

Fay produced the fancy cardboard wallet. 'Where is… Dad?' She never called Harry Waterfield 'Dad' because he wasn't her father but, without the children or Jack around, she couldn't use 'Grandad' or '*your* Dad,' the devices she generally employed.

'He's in the garden, talking to his vegetables.' Vi shook her head in mock despair.

'D'you think he'd mind if I went and picked his brains?' Laura asked. 'There's something horribly wrong with my tomatoes.'

'Carry on, lovely. A word of warning. If you get him started he might never stop. It's through the kitchen.'

Lovely. Laura had certainly made a hit.

Now that Fay was alone with Vi, the usual awkwardness returned. They looked through the wedding pictures, Fay describing each one as they went along. 'Dylan and Nia. Dylan, Nia and both sets of parents. Dylan, Nia, best man and bridesmaids.'

'We were there, you know,' Vi chipped.

'Sorry. Of course you were. I wasn't thinking.' Why was it always like this?

'What did you think of those snaps we gave John last week?'

They hadn't seen Jack's parents since the wedding. The old woman must be confused. 'Snaps?'

'Yes. The extra set we got for John. And you. And Harry gave him some tomatoes, too. It must have been, let me see, last week. His regular Thursday visit.'

Was Vi losing it or was Jack up to something? Fay, unwilling to let her mother-in-law see her confusion, played for time, 'They were great. Some really nice shots. And the tomatoes were delicious.' She waited, hoping to pick up a few clues, but none were forthcoming and, whilst Vi wittered on – something to do with a cardigan she'd ordered from her catalogue – Fay tried to work it out. Her mother-in-law's horizons might be narrow, her life prosaic, but she wouldn't have made a mistake about a visit from her precious John, or miss an opportunity to point out an unacknowledged gift.

They went through to the immaculate back garden, with its black soil and tidy rows of lettuce and beetroot. Laura and Harry were in the greenhouse, surrounded by shoulder-high tomato plants. Out of earshot, it was nevertheless apparent that they were already friends. Fay stood with Vi, unable to think of anything to talk about, wondering how Jack could possibly have visited his parents on a Morris practice evening. And, if he had, why he'd not mentioned it to her.

Before they left, Laura took several photographs of Harry in his greenhouse; Vi, in front of the row of runner beans; and one of them, side-by-side, on the front doorstep.

'You were a big hit,' Fay accused as they drove away. Laura's success held an implicit criticism of her own inability to connect with her parents-in-law.

'Probably because it makes no odds to me. Like when we were teenagers. Don't you remember how *reasonable* other people's parents seemed? But you couldn't bear your own?'

'There's one flaw in your argument, Laura. Vi and Harry *aren't* my parents.'

'Okay. But you've got a high stake in the relationship.'

'The way I look at it, just because I'm attached to Jack, it doesn't mean that I have to like his family. They all disliked me from day one.' Fay shot a glance towards the passenger seat. 'What was that all about, anyway?'

'About?'

'Why did you want to visit them? Something to do with the photos you took?'

'Kind of.'

Fay left it for a moment then prompted, 'Anything to do with your Dad?'

'Sort of, I suppose.'

'As I said, whenever you need to talk about it…'

It was clear that Laura didn't want to talk about her father or discuss her mystifying project. Her friend had always been one to keep her own counsel, and Fay doubted whether anyone knew more about Laura than she allowed them to know.

They drove on, discussing the cruel events which had, over the centuries, shaped the humble valley towns.

Before Jack got out of the car, he knew that there was no one at home. Despite the heat, the windows were shut and Fay's car wasn't on the drive. He was disappointed. Having given his speech he'd manage to sneak away from the conference and come home to keep her company – at least that was his story – but without her here to greet him and be grateful, his early return lost its impetus.

He checked his phone, but there was no explanatory message, then went into the house to see if there were any clues as to where she might be. From the utensils and glasses dotted around, it seemed that some sort of a party had taken place, but he was sure she hadn't mentioned anything like that to him. Hang on. Wasn't what's-his-name calling? Maybe he'd brought a crowd of his mates.

He changed out of his conference suit. In Machiavellian mode the previous week, he had gone into W H Smith and purchased a pack of clip-on badges, printed his own name and qualifications on a piece of paper and slipped it into the see-through sleeve. So that his effort had not gone to waste, he jabbed this in to the cork-board, next to his appointment card for the opticians.

Wandering around the garden, he dragged himself back to being Jack Waterfield, suburbanite, but he hankered after Llangwm. Iolo and the gang would be in the school playground after the parade, sharing jokes and reminiscences as they undecorated the trailer and returned the rainbow to Harriet's shop. The kitchen of The Welcome Stranger would be pungent with the smell of sausage rolls and apple pie, as Zena prepared food for the after-show party. Non and her partner would be watering neat rows of marjoram and thyme, then counting the day's takings, before falling into lavender-scented sheets in their little cottage.

After a miserable hour failing to settle to anything, he made himself a cup of tea and a bowl of cornflakes. He took his tea upstairs and, as he headed for the bathroom, noticed that there was a shabby holdall on the bed in the spare room. Feeling almost an intruder in his own home, he knocked quietly on the door and, when there was no reply, tiptoed in. A jacket, constructed from patches of different coloured velvets, hung over the back of the chair, a pair of well-worn Birkenstock sandals stood on the floor beneath it and 'A Short Walk in the Hindu Kush' lay on the bedside table.

It was almost eight o'clock when Jack, sleeping in front of the television, was woken by car doors slamming and female laughter. He remained in the chair.

'Jack?'

'Yes, love.'

'What on earth are you doing here?' Fay pushed the living room door open and he saw that there was someone standing behind her.

'I managed to escape.' Jack looked past Fay at a woman whom he knew that he knew.

'Hello, Jack.' She came out of the shadows and stood, hand extended.

'Laura?' She grinned confirmation. 'Laura.' Ignoring the hand, he hugged her.

'Aren't you supposed to be at some high-powered conference?'

'I did my bit this morning so there was no real need for me to stay. More to the point, how come—'

'Cass dropped me off. He's collecting me tomorrow afternoon.'

They followed Fay into the kitchen where she was filling a bowl with a large quantity of tomatoes. 'I hope you've had your supper.' Fay pushed an empty carrier bag into the dispenser on the back of the larder door 'We've eaten already, haven't we Laura?'

'Yes. Where was it, Fay? Somewhere unpronounceable, but the food was delicious.'

Fay said nothing as she clattered the crockery which Jack had carelessly left on the worktop. Something about her was different. Not just the new hairstyle – he was getting used to that. She was wearing the outfit she'd bought on their trip to Bath. That was it. But the blouse seemed too tight and the skirt too long, making it look as though she'd borrowed the clothes from a tall, skinny librarian. She continued to ignore him with antagonistic disdain, making it clear that he was in the dog-house for something or another.

Laura had changed in the seven or eight years since Jack had last seen her. She was plumper. Her hair, flesh and eyes were less colourful – probably because she didn't bother with makeup and hair dying. Laura had never been like other women he'd come across, that is until he'd stayed at The Welcome Stranger Guesthouse.

They sat in the scented evening garden and, wanting to gain membership of the secret society that the two women appeared to have formed in his absence, he went flat out to amuse them with tales of the dental conference. Fay remained icy and detached but Laura giggled at the *faux pas* made by the chairman when he announced the guest speaker, and was entranced by the titles of the lectures – 'The Best Dentures are made on a Friday afternoon' was one she found particularly amusing. How easy it was to invent details of the phantom meeting. He simply cobbled together bits and pieces from a lifetime of dental conferences, stopping only when Fay butted in: 'I'm amazed you came back early if it was so hilarious.'

'I'm glad you did though,' said Laura. 'It would have been a shame to have missed you.' She patted his knee.

'We called on your parents when we went out for our drive,' Fay snapped.

'Oh.' Now Jack had the explanation for Fay's coolness. 'How were they?'

'Much as they were last Thursday week when *you* visited, I should imagine.' She glared at him and stood up, brushing the creases out of her skirt. 'I'm exhausted. I think I'll have a bath and an early night, if that's okay with you, Laura. See you in the morning.'

She stomped across the lawn to the house and he felt a rush of sympathy for her, and extremely sorry for himself, as he anticipated the difficult night ahead.

The light went on in their bathroom. 'Go and talk to her Jack, before she gets too entrenched. You know how stubborn she is.' Laura spoke softly.

'Is that what she wants me to do?' How much pleasanter it would be to stay here talking to Laura.

'Yes. I think she does. The trouble with being strong, like Fay, is that no one allows you to be anything less. When did you last see her cry or not quite know what to do?' She was right. He'd never thought of it like that. 'Go on, Jack. I'll sort myself out.'

As he crossed the lawn, memories of post-natal Fay, pushing him away, and grieving Laura, longing for human contact, lurked in the purple shadows.

In thirty years of marriage, Jack had never walked into their bathroom without knocking. When there was no response to his gentle tap he tried the door. Locked. He knocked a little harder. 'Fay. You okay?'

'Of course I am.'

'Sorry. As long as you're okay.' From the bedroom window he peered down into the garden but, as far as he could make out, Laura wasn't there. No longer convinced that Fay would appreciate his attention, but also knowing that the next hour could be critical to whatever was festering between them, he stayed where he was.

First he sat in the bedroom chair until, the unyielding wickerwork digging into his flesh, he shifted to the bed. From beyond the locked door came the occasional swish of water, but there was nothing to indicate his wife's state of mind.

Eleven o'clock. The celebrations at The Welcome Stranger would be in full swing. There would be loud, wild music, dancing in the streets and snogging on the front steps. He should be there himself, dancing with Non and getting drunk with Iolo and Gareth. *Bloody Stan Colley.* And now Fay had found out about his visit – maybe visits – to his parents. What rotten luck that Fay and Laura had called in on them.

Laura. It was reassuring to see her again. Jack had never felt bad about what had happened between them, all those years ago. It certainly did not fall into the 'being unfaithful' category. A more accurate classification might be 'bereavement counselling' or 'faith healing', although he was pretty sure counsellors or healers didn't offer love-making in their treatment plans.

He and Fay had gone to David's funeral but, assuming that a happy couple would be the last people a young widow would want to see, they had thought it kinder to keep out of Laura's way, for a while anyway. Then one evening, a few months later, she had phoned, begging them to visit her. 'Everyone's avoiding me. I feel unclean.

If it goes on like this, I'll not only have lost David but all my friends, too.'

They had driven to London the next day.

Fay had been continually exhausted after Caitlin's birth, showing no interest at all in lovemaking and, although he was besotted with his daughter, he'd begun to wonder whether celibacy might be the price of fatherhood. That Saturday evening, tired from the journey and the demands of Caitlin and Cassidy, Fay had gone to bed, leaving him with Laura, for whom sleep, even with pills, was proving impossible. They had been sitting side-by-side on the sofa, watching television, when she had asked in a very matter-of-fact tone 'Can you hold me Jack? Tight. I'm disintegrating.'

He drew her to him, realising how much he was missing the warmth and softness of a female body. He pushed his nose into her dark hair, smelling lemons and a hint of perspiration. He sighed and settled lower into the sofa, 'It's wonderful to touch someone.' The problems that Fay and he were having came tumbling out, amidst apologies for burdening her, when she had so much to bear.

'No. Thank you for not treating me like a pathetic invalid.'

Hugs had turned to caressing and kissing then they had, without discussion, gone up to Laura's room and made gentle, tender love as an offering, each to the other. When it was done, they agreed that physical satisfaction could, indeed, be a healing force and the act of making love had helped them both feel whole once more. But it would never happen again. On subsequent meetings over the years, neither of them mentioned what had taken place. There was no need.

Jack had placed their lovemaking in a sealed box which he'd eased into a shadowy corner of his mind, where it could harm no one. But, lying on the bed, relaxed and receptive, the lid slipped off the box and the memories of that weekend spilled out, mingling comfortably with those of his superb day in Llangwm. It was all very pleasant and he was content to be in the company of such agreeable people. It was enormously encouraging to recall that once, twenty-odd years ago, he'd had the guts to do what his heart told him was right.

The bathroom door opened and a shaft of light cut through the darkness of the bedroom. Fay, wrapped in a bath-sheet, crossed to the bed and took her night-dress from beneath the pillow. 'I'll sleep in Caitlin's room.'

12

Fay watched the rain bouncing up off the decking and splashing the patio doors. With Bank Holiday approaching, a change in the weather was inevitable. She closed her eyes and eased her head back, unsure if the headache which had been lingering for days was due to atmospheric pressure or to the row fermenting between her and Jack.

Jack had offered no satisfactory explanation for his visit to his parents. She was only too happy for him to go on his own, but it made her look ridiculous when it emerged that she knew nothing about it. All she asked was to be told what was going on. By the time Cassidy had turned up to collect Laura, last Sunday afternoon, she had been furious with the both of them, too. From Cassidy's manner – half mocking, half flirting – she felt sure that he was aware of the effect he was having on her. Laura, simply by being her easy-going self, made Fay seem hoity-toity; unbalanced; school-ma'am-ish, even. Why on earth had she wanted to take photographs of Jack's parents? It seemed like everyone in the world was hell-bent on visiting Vi and Harry.

And yet another week had gone by without word from Kingsley.

The phone rang. It was Jack, from work. 'Hello, love. I've just had a message. From Stan.' He hesitated. 'No practice this evening—'

'So I expect you're popping up to see your parents.'

'No. Unless *you* want to go of course.'

Fay snorted.

'No? Only I wanted to let you know that there's no rush for supper.' He paused. 'We could go out for something if you like.'

'I'm defrosting some fish.'

'Lovely. Sounds great. See you about the usual time then.'

The roses which she had picked at the weekend were dropping their petals and she lifted the vase to take them in to the kitchen. Looking up, she caught sight of herself in the gilt-framed mirror which hung above the sideboard. She appeared to be carrying a huge bridal bouquet, her white shirt and pale trousers reinforcing the effect. She allowed herself a few moments to reflect on the failed dreams of her wedding day.

Probably like most brides, she'd assumed that her marriage would be 'different'. She knew that Jack's unpromising image concealed, amongst other virtues, a sharp intellect, a dry humour and a real sense of justice. She'd imagined that only she was capable of peeling away the outer layer of dullness to reveal his true sparkle. But the task had been virtually impossible – like getting corned beef out of a tin once the twisty strip of metal has snapped. If the metal hadn't broken, they would be living in Surrey or Buckinghamshire now and Jack would be a senior consultant, or even a professor, at a teaching hospital, with several text-books to his name. Dafydd Morgan had managed it so it couldn't be that difficult.

She sighed and was watching another shower of petals tumble onto the carpet when the doorbell rang. 'Just a minute,' she shouted and took the vase through to the kitchen before returning to open the door.

'Hello, Mrs Waterfield.' Someone, a man judging by build and voice, in a dark green nylon waterproof – although it obviously wasn't – stood in the porch. The fabric clinging around his face and shoulders gave the impression that he was wrapped in cooked spinach. 'It's Neil.'

'Neil?'

'Neil Bentley.' He shifted from one foot to the other, surges of water bubbling from his sodden trainers. 'I was passing so I thought…'

'Good gracious. Neil. Come in.' She tried to ignore the puddles forming on the hall carpet. 'Come through.'

He followed the trail of rose petals into the kitchen, then stood, legs slightly apart, arms a few inches away from his torso, like a child coming out of the sea, waiting for a grown up to sort things out. She unzipped the cagoule and peeled it off. The white tee-shirt and denim jeans beneath were wet through. He began to shiver.

'You'll have to get out of those things, Neil.' She thought for a moment. 'And you need to warm up. Have a hot shower and I'll dig out something for you to put on. The bathroom's at the top of the stairs. Jack's bathrobe's hanging on the door.'

She half expected him to answer 'Yes, Miss,' but he did as she instructed without question or discussion. The latch on the bathroom door clicked across and she heard the shower running. Picking up the wet cagoule, she draped it on a hanger, putting it to drip in the utility room, then went up to their bedroom. She went through Jack's wardrobe, searching for something for the boy to wear. What sort of thing could she offer him? Sweatshirt and socks were straightforward but Jack was thinner than Neil, and taller, so trousers posed more of a problem. It was possible that Jack wouldn't care to have a stranger borrowing his clothes and equally possible that the young man might object to looking like a middle-aged dentist.

The answer lay in the room next to theirs. Kingsley's room. It was five years since her younger son had used it but it would always be 'Kingsley's Room'. She hadn't preserved it in every detail, as mothers sometimes did when a child died, but neither had she done anything to make it look or feel different. The furniture was the same. Double bed. Desk. That plastic chair he'd insisted on hauling out of a skip. The books on the shelves. And his clothes, still in the fitted cupboards. When a charity bag came through the door, she often got as far as cramming it with his tee-shirts, jeans and jackets, telling herself that it made sense for someone to benefit from his absence, but the bag never made it to the doorstep.

She heard the latch go on the bathroom door and smelled the herbal tang of shower gel. 'I'm in here, Neil.'

Neil hovered in the doorway, Jack's bathrobe wrapped tightly around him.

'Thanks, Mrs Waterfield. I think I was going a bit hypothermic.' He looked around the room. 'This was King's room.' It was a statement, not a question. 'We used to spend hours up here. Writing lyrics. Talking about girls. Making plans. I loved it in this house.'

'Plans?' She remembered how irritated she used to get when Kingsley brought home streams of gormless friends. How they would shut themselves in the bedroom for hours, making a lot of noise and ignoring her offers of coffee or suggestions that they would be better off out in the fresh air. It had never crossed her mind that they might be making plans.

'Yeah. Plans for the band. We were going to be more successful than Oasis. And we weren't going to let success ruin our friendship. The usual stuff.'

She noticed his large, pale feet, tufts of wiry hair sprouting from the flesh of his big toes. His thin hairy legs. The last time she'd seen him he was looking like something from a fashion magazine, with spiked hair and trendy black clothes. 'Look. Why don't you have a dig through Kingsley's things? Find something to put on.' She waved in the direction of the wardrobe. 'Just until we can dry your stuff out.'

'I don't want to be a nuisance.'

'You're not a nuisance. And then come down and I'll make us a cup of tea.'

She closed the door and went into the bathroom. His clothes lay on the floor where he had stepped out of them. Tee-shirt. Jeans. Underpants – the tiny posing-pouchy things that Dylan favoured. Trainer socks. She took them downstairs.

The kitchen suddenly seemed too silent and sterile. No crockery on the draining board, no clutter on the table, no piles of papers or library books. Exactly how she liked it in fact but maybe, to an outsider's eyes, it looked lifeless, as if the people who lived here had tidied up before going away for a long holiday, leaving only two pieces of fish defrosting under cling-film.

She took a few mugs and plates from the cupboard and dotted them about on the work surface then pulled yesterday's newspaper out of the recycling box under the sink and tossed it on to the table. The digital radio, Jack's recent present to himself, stood on the window sill and she put it on, pressing the button marked '1'. The pounding bass beat echoed round the kitchen, frantic and disturbing. She tried '2' and recognised the voice of Elton John. She had no idea what twenty-somethings were listening to these days but was sure it wasn't Elton John and she switched it off.

'Anything I can do?' He stood in the doorway, and she caught her breath when she saw that he had chosen Kingsley's navy-blue sweatshirt, John Lennon's picture on the front and 'Imagine' in swirly lettering across the back. She'd bought it for him in Liverpool when she attended a conference on 'Shakespeare for the ethnic minorities'. When she'd told him she was going, he'd been appalled at the arrogance of the British education system. But he'd still accepted the sweatshirt. He must have been about sixteen then and they were already having those dreadful arguments which went on for days, poisoning the very air in the house.

'I hope it was all right, turning up like this.'

'Don't be silly. I told you to call, didn't I? Tea or coffee? Or hot chocolate?' Young men couldn't resist something chocolatey.

He grinned and licked his lips, 'Chocolate sounds good.'

She heated the milk and opened a packet of shortbread biscuits while he wandered around the kitchen, inspecting the photographs and postcards pinned neatly on the noticeboard.

'Who's this?'

She knew that he was looking at a photograph of the wedding which one of Dylan's friends had sent them. 'That was at Dylan's wedding. A few weeks ago. Did you know him? He was probably at college about the time you used to come here.'

'No. But I do remember King's sister – Katy was it? She used to terrify us.'

'Caitlin. Yes, she can be quite sharp.'

'I used to love coming here.'

He dunked the chunky biscuit in his steaming mug and

noisily sucked the liquid from it. 'I packed in the perfume job last week.'

Avoiding mentioning the dunking, she nodded. 'I have to admit, you did look a bit...it was an odd get-up.' She pointed to his hair, drying to a mousey brown. 'And that's a definite improvement.'

'I dyed it back to what it should be.' He took another biscuit. 'After I saw you in the shop, I started thinking about King and the rest of them. They would've thought I was really pathetic, poncing around in yellow braces...' He stopped. 'Sorry, Mrs Waterfield.'

'Fay, please. And I'm not your teacher any more, Neil.' She waited a moment, watching him stir the drinking chocolate. 'Have you had a lot of jobs?'

'When I left school I joined the army. It was okay. I got through basic training and did a couple of years but we were on exercise once, up in Yorkshire, and I passed out. Woke up in hospital. They did all the tests. Didn't find anything but that was that. I was out.'

'That's dreadful. Did you appeal?'

'No. No point. It's all there in the small print. If they think you might be a liability or a danger to the rest of the lads, they can turf you out.'

Fay had always been affronted by the idea of guns and fighting but nevertheless, if Neil was foolish enough to put on combat gear and risk his life for some ridiculous cause, he shouldn't be banned from doing so on the basis of one fainting fit. 'What did your parents think?'

He shrugged. 'They moved to Spain just after I signed up so they weren't really involved.' He stated this without a hint of self-pity or anger. 'I don't see much of them.'

'You're on your own?'

He laughed. 'I *am* twenty-three.'

'Brothers and sisters? Girlfriend?'

'An older sister. Married. Couple of kids. Lives in Neath. No girlfriend.'

'Where do *you* live, Neil?'

He didn't seem to mind the interrogation. 'Off City Road. I've got a room in a student house. It's okay. Handy for town.'

Student houses, sinks crammed with greasy plates and bathrooms festooned with grubby washing were places to grow out of. A living proof that you couldn't laze about being a student all your life – it's far too depressing. Visiting Caitlin and Dylan, when they were at college, caused her so much anxiety that she and Jack took to meeting them in a park or a restaurant.

'What's it like?'

'Okay.'

'But you *are* looking for a job?' The unspoken criticism was out before she could stop herself. 'Sorry. It's nothing to do with me.'

'No. I need a kick up the arse. I keep meaning to sort out a CV. Not that there's much to put on it.'

The newspaper that she'd tossed on the table happened to have fallen open at the 'Jobs' page, and they worked their way through the adverts. He pointed out one for a warehouseman and another recruiting call-centre staff but Fay was dismissive. 'I'm sure we can do better than that. Can you drive?'

'Yeah. But I haven't got a car. Can't afford one.'

'How about money? Can you claim anything?'

'Not entitled. But I'm okay for a couple of weeks.' The kitchen clock caught his eye. 'Four o'clock. I'd better be going. Thanks for the chocolate.'

Fay took his clothes out of the tumble dryer and tested them against her cheek. 'Still a bit damp. I'll put them in a carrier. Bring those back,' she nodded at her son's clothes, 'and we'll have a go at your CV.'

She wrote their phone number on a piece of paper and folded his clothes. The rain had stopped and, as he walked away from the house, watery sunshine was reflecting off the wet paviers.

13

THE BEGINNING OF THE WEEK WAS DIFFICULT FOR JACK. Fay continued to sleep in Caitlin's old room, insisting that it was too hot to share a bed. To be honest, this suited him. The curtailed trip to Llangwm and Laura's visit, with the memories it dredged up, unsettled him. There was something steadying about the solitary night-hours, when he could let his mind wander without fear of Fay's heat-seeking interrogation.

He knew things would have to change. Covert Thursday evening visits to his parents were definitely off and Fay would be likely, for the foreseeable future, to keep tabs on him, whatever day of the week it was. But soon they would be into September and Fay's return to work, along with the resumption of his *bona fide* dance practices. Unfortunately, if Fay *were* in detective mode, escaping to see Non, would become much trickier.

And it wasn't only Non who beckoned, but Iolo and Zena, too. Over the preceding days, affection for the whole Evans family had overwhelmed him. Iolo – zany and spontaneous; Zena – earthy and nurturing; and Non – the embodiment of wholesome womanhood. It was as if he'd been lost on a beach and the rising tide, creeping across the warm sand, had lifted him and carried him home to his long-lost people. Jack Evans – what a great name.

The most pressing task was to plant the seeds of weekend absences to come. The dental conference had been easy to concoct but he must put his mind to other plausible reasons for spending a night or two away from home, and this would be a great deal simpler if he had an accomplice. Sheila was the obvious candidate and there were several moments when he came close to confiding in her. It would be a great release to tell someone about The Welcome Stranger, and, at the same time, allow him to relive every golden moment. Furthermore, he was pretty certain that, were he to go for the full, soul-bearing confession, Sheila would understand, maybe applaud, his reasons for making love to Laura all those years ago. After all, it had only happened once and had hurt no one. The idea of getting it all off his chest became unbearably appealing, and he made up his mind to tell her everything, but each time he plucked up the nerve, the phone rang or a patient turned up.

It rained for most of the day, the first rain for three weeks and, when he went out for a lunchtime sandwich, he shivered in the chilly air. What excuse could Fay possibly dream up for spending tonight in Caitlin's room? Would they ever sleep in the same bed again? Or the same room? He'd noticed that old people invariably slept apart, but he'd never been curious enough to wonder how and why they'd arrived at this arrangement. Were they disentangling themselves from each other in preparation for the inevitable parting? He was only fifty-something – if he and Fay *were* disentangling it had nothing to do with intimations of mortality.

He arrived home to an absence of cooking smells and Fay nowhere to be seen. The kitchen was in bit of a mess, too, by Fay's standards. Newspapers on the table and dirty mugs on the worktop. Should he be alarmed?

A door banged upstairs. 'Fay?' he shouted from the hall.

'Up here.'

She wasn't in their bedroom or the bathroom and he called again. 'Where are you?'

'In here.'

He tried the door to Kingsley's room but it resisted.

'Hang on. Let me move these.' There was a slithering noise and the door opened to reveal his wife surrounded by black and green bin liners, an assortment of carrier bags and several suitcases. She was holding a pair of frayed jeans. 'What's the time?'

'Seven. Just gone.' He held his wrist out to confirm that he was telling the truth. 'You okay, love?'

'Fine. Why shouldn't I be?'

'No reason. Just …' He pushed the door wider. The bed was piled high with Kingsley's clothes and the posters had gone from the walls. There were several stacked boxes of books and CD's and a half-deflated inflatable gorilla sagged in the corner.

'I'm having a sort-out.' She glared at him, chin thrust forward. 'It's ridiculous keeping this room as a shrine. You only have shrines to saints. Anyway, everything's full of moth-holes.' To prove her point she pushed her finger through a hole in a black tee-shirt.

He could tell, from her flushed cheeks and shining eyes, that she'd been crying and the sight of her, surrounded by years of dashed hopes, touched him. He moved towards her, not quite knowing what he was going to do but she fended him off with an outstretched hand. 'Don't. You'll get covered in dust. I'll leave the rest until tomorrow.' She pointed to two bulging bags, their tops firmly tied. 'If you want to be useful, you can take those down.'

He carried the bags downstairs to the utility room,

then tidied the kitchen and, by the time Fay appeared, the newspapers were back in the recycling bin and the mugs washed and hanging on the mug tree.

'Busy day, love?' He needed a steer, a clue, as to why, on this particular Thursday afternoon in August, she had given up on their son. For five years her refusal to admit that Kingsley wasn't coming back had sanctioned in *him* the tiniest glimmer of hope, but today she had snuffed that out.

'I had a visitor this afternoon.' She paused and he scampered through the roll-call of candidates who might possibly have triggered her drastic action. The police with dreadful news? His parents, telling tales? Stan Colley, blowing his cover? Laura, salving her conscience? Non—

'Neil Bentley. D'you remember him? He was one of Kingsley's crowd from school. Played in that dreadful band. I met him a few weeks ago, selling perfume in Robertson's.'

'Ooohhh.' He relaxed, shaking his head. 'Robertson's are selling perfume, door-to-door now, are they?'

She laughed. It was unusual to hear her laugh these days. 'No, silly. He's given that up. He was passing the house.'

'He can't have been. We live in a cul-de-sac.'

'Jack. Don't be so pedantic,' she scolded. 'He was soaking wet, so I asked him in to dry off.'

He sat back and kept quiet, assuming that, at some point, the story of Neil Bentley's visit would join up with the clearing of Kingsley's room.

'He's a nice lad. His parents have moved to Spain and he's more or less on his own. He's out of work at the moment and doesn't seem to have a clue how to go about finding a job. I said I'd keep my eye open for something suitable. Give him a hand with his CV. Help him with application forms.'

Fay wasn't one to take pity on waifs and strays. Teachers, he'd discovered, like policemen, were hardhearted. They'd seen it all before, in classrooms and corridors, pathetic youngsters trying to worm their way out of punishment, blaming everyone but themselves for their misfortunes. So why had this one, this Neil Bentley, breached the defences?

She smiled again. 'He said that he loved coming to this house. He even remembered Caitlin. Said they were terrified of her.' She picked up the plate of fish and removed the clingfilm. 'Nice lad. Polite. Grateful. He just needs a push in the right direction.'

There it was, at last. A harmless, compliant young man had turned up on the doorstep and surrendered himself.

'Are you sure that he's on the level? You can't be too careful. There are reports in the paper every day about con men, talking their way in to places.' It had been a while since he'd had anything to lecture Fay about and he was ashamed to admit that he was enjoying it.

After supper, Jack went upstairs. Now that most of the contents of Kingsley's room had been displaced into bags and boxes, it looked smaller and shabbier. He sneaked in here occasionally, when things were getting to him. He'd learned to be extra vigilant on dangerous days – Christmas, birthdays, bonfire night – but sometimes, if he saw a long-haired lad juggling or heard aimless guitar chords issuing from an open window, he was caught off guard and found consolation in the room where his son had juggled and strummed.

Kingsley had been *his* son. Fay, with her customary efficiency, had produced 'one of each'. Resolved to stop at that, their third child had irritated her from his very conception. She felt nauseous throughout the nine months of the unplanned pregnancy. Her waters broke in Sainsburys, much to her embarrassment, and a long labour, culminating in an emergency Caesarean section, had been the final straw. But as the cards stacked up against the baby, Jack grew to love him more and more. Having fulfilled a teenage promise to herself and named her first children after Dylan Thomas and his wife, she'd lost interest by the time this colicky scrap of life arrived to upset the balance of the family.

'I'm too tired to think,' she'd moaned. 'You decide.'

Jack had reflected on it for two weeks before announcing that their second son would be called Kingsley. Not after Charles Kingsley or Kingsley Amis, as many of Fay's more literary friends assumed, but Edward Kingsley, the eminent dentist, who, at the turn of the last century, had perfected a revolutionary procedure for root canal work.

Jack opened the wardrobe. A selection of items hung there, neatly spaced, as if left merely to demonstrate how a wardrobe worked. A couple of shirts; trousers draped over a hanger; a black jacket. The drawers, similarly, held tokens of a young man's presence. Two folded tee-shirts; a sweater; several pairs of balled socks. These clothes could have belonged to any eighteen-year-old but the thing was, Kingsley was twenty-three now and might no longer be that gangling, slouching boy who had slammed out of the house with a rucksack, a guitar and a passport. He lifted a tee-shirt from the drawer and buried his nose in it, hoping to catch the faintest whiff of his son, but all he could smell was wood glue.

After the ten o'clock news, Fay went to bed and he stayed downstairs to check their email. The 'in box' contained three new messages. The first from Stan, with the Wicker Men's autumn fixtures. The second from a businessman in

Nigeria, offering him a share of a huge amount of cash if he would open a bank account in their joint names. And an email from Caitlin, accepting their invitation to a barbecue on Bank Holiday Monday.

Fay took the initiative when it came to planning holidays and family events but, even so, she usually tried to give the impression that he was involved. Today, however, she had obviously dropped all such pretence and was carrying on as if he didn't exist. Clearing Kingsley out. Inviting odd-bods in. Arranging a barbecue.

He locked up and went upstairs. Caitlin's door was shut but he hesitated outside and called softly, ''Night, love.' There was no reply.

This wasn't surprising as Fay was in their room, already in bed, sitting up with a book propped on raised knees. Unsure how to interpret this, he undressed whilst she watched him over the top of her reading glasses. He felt oddly self-conscious, turning his back to her until he had put on his pyjamas. When he had finished in the bathroom, he was uncertain if he should hold his ground or retreat to Caitlin's room. Was this the start of a nightly scramble for territory? First upstairs gets the choice of beds?

'It's much cooler tonight,' she said and patted the space next to her, folding in the dust jacket of her book to mark the place.

They lay side-by-side in the darkness, not quite touching, and he listened to Fay's snufflings as she fell into a twitchy sleep. There were things that he should talk to her about, but he needed to be sure where their conversations might lead. In a short space of time, since the wedding day in fact, his life had become one of subterfuge and fantasy. Hankerings and plots. Sooner or later it must be sorted or he was going to drop some dreadful clanger and blow it. In his head he rehearsed various openings but found it difficult, more difficult than a game of chess, to follow through all of Fay's possible responses.

His opening:
I've decided to go and live with the Evans family in Llangwm.

Her possible replies:
1) Don't be ridiculous.
2) I want you to be happy, darling. When are you thinking of going?
3) Good riddance. I hope they can stomach Morris dancing.

His responses:
1) I'm not being ridiculous / I am being ridiculous.
2) I knew you'd understand. I'm going soon / probably never / I'll have to go and have a chat with Iolo. See whether they need an extra pair of hands at The Welcome Stranger.
3) Aren't you going to put up a fight? / Have you ever really cared about me? / You're the only person who has a problem with my dancing.

Next game:
I slept with Laura twenty-odd years ago because we were both unhappy.

Fay:
1) Don't be ridiculous.
2) That was a really altruistic act and I love you for it.
3) You complete bastard. Any ploy to get inside someone's knickers.

<u>His come-backs:</u>
1) Not all women see me as a figure of fun. / I was only joking.

2) It seemed the natural thing to do. / It meant nothing to either of us. / She was warm and giving and we both enjoyed it. She was uninhibited and bold and we did wonderful things…

3) Well you wouldn't let me anywhere near you for months. / You seemed pretty friendly with that history teacher. What was his name? Brian?

<u>Best of three:</u>
'I can't forgive you for driving Kingsley away, Fay. You have to win every single battle, don't you? We all have to do what you want. Always.'

'You're a loser Jack. This family would go to pieces if I left it up to you to. Anyway, if I remember correctly you didn't say a word. You just stood there and let him go.'

'Yes, I did. I was pathetic. And there's not been a single day when I haven't regretted it and wished that I'd run down the street after him. Maybe even have gone with him.'

He pictured the empty room across the landing, the bin bags of clothes awaiting dispersal to the charity shop or landfill site. Fay stirred and turned towards him and he rolled away from her.

14

THERE WOULD BE NINE OF THEM ALTOGETHER – Caitlin, Dylan and Nia, Jack's parents, Neil Bentley, Sheila, Jack and herself. It was supposed to be an informal get together, but she'd been writing lists for several days and they now hung in neat strips on the fridge door, held in place by Shakespeare, Byron, Dickens and someone whom she assumed was T S Eliot. She disliked the studenty air fridge magnets gave to the kitchen, but it kept the lists in full view and demonstrated to Sheila Pearce that her last year's Christmas present was indispensable. Fay had even had the foresight to push the freshly-opened gift box right to the bottom of the bin, where it wouldn't be spotted.

They were going to be lucky with the weather. After several stormy days and drenching downpours, yesterday had been warm and dry and now the sky was cloudless. From the kitchen window she watched Jack setting extra chairs out on the decking. He'd spent yesterday afternoon cleaning grease and rust off the barbecue and Dylan was bringing their state-of-the-art model – one of the wedding presents.

She phoned him but after several rings the answer machine cut in. 'Dylan? It's Mum. You'll need to be here in good time with the barbecue… We have to light it at least half-hour before we start cooking…and don't forget you're picking Sheila up... but you'd better drop it off first. You're not still in bed, by any chance?'

Jack came in and they sat at the kitchen table, drinking coffee and running over the schedule. 'I don't quite understand why you invited this lad. Neil, is it?'

'For the same reason you invited Sheila,' she countered.

'Come on, love. Sheila is virtually part of the family. Won't this Neil feel a bit awkward?'

'I can't see why. He knows me. And Caitlin. And you, despite your insistence that you've never met him.'

'Well, it *was* about ten years ago...'

'Six. Six years. And anyway, you wouldn't like to think of him spending Bank Holiday on his own, would you?' She stood up, signalling the end of the conversation, and began wrapping cutlery in paper napkins, placing them alongside the plates on one of the many trays lined up on the worktops.

Why *had* she invited Neil? He would, as Jack pointed out, be the odd one out but he was a very nice young man. No, not 'nice' exactly. Grateful, that was it. And malleable.

Family gatherings had become games or, more accurately, battles in the long, low-key war which had broken out almost without them noticing. The most recent major offensive had been the wedding, followed by a skirmish when she uncovered Jack's sneaky visits to his parents. She marshalled her troops for the coming offensive. Dylan was definitely on her side, along with Nia, who appeared to be grafted to her new husband both mentally and physically. Caitlin always played it cool, keeping a foot in each camp, removing herself if things came to a head. But Sheila was Jack's, as were his parents, obviously.

Neil had phoned a couple of times since Thursday, thanking her for her hospitality and asking advice about an advertisement that he'd seen for trainee managers at Tesco. And when she'd asked if he'd like to come to the barbecue, he'd jumped at the invitation. 'That's so kind, Mrs Waterfield. Fay. It'll be great to meet Mr Waterfield again. And Caitlin, of course. Can I bring anything?' Nice lad that he was, she'd have to make it quite clear that Caitlin was out of bounds.

'Jack.' She tapped on the kitchen window to attract his attention. He was standing in the shed, reading a newspaper. She opened the window and shouted, 'Jack. It's getting on for twelve o'clock.'

'D'you think I should light the barbecue before I go?'

She sighed. 'We went over that yesterday. You'll be gone at least an hour, won't you? Longer if your parents dither around. Didn't we decide that Dylan should light both barbecues and then he can pop and collect Sheila? I think we should aim to start cooking at one-thirty. Eat about two.'

'Okay. Everything's organised outside. I might as well be on my way.'

It was a relief to hear the car pulling out of the drive. She had an hour to put the finishing touches to the salads and whip the cream for the trifle.

Jack swung into the street where his parents lived and jammed on the brakes. Two small boys, no more than four or five years old, held a rope across the road. He wound down the window to speak to a third, who was pointing a twig, roughly shaped like a gun, at his head.

'Yoomunnyooyoolife, mistuh.'

'It's really not a good idea to play on the road, lads. If I'd been going any faster…'

'Yoomunnyooyoolife,' The boy rested the thorny twig on the bonnet of the car and stared straight at Jack. His oversized tee-shirt, proclaiming 'I'm With This Bitch', coupled with his near-shaven head and insolent gaze gave him the appearence of a malevolent dwarf.

Jack, needing to divert the boy from his criminal intent, began quoting one of the few poems he could dredge up from his school days—

'The wind was a torrent of darkness de-dum-de-dum-
de-dum,
The moon was a ghostly galleon dum-de-dum-de-dum,
Dum-de-dum-de-dum-de, dum-de-dum-de-dum
And the highwayman came riding – riding – riding –
The highwayman came riding, up to the old inn-door.'

The mini-thug stared at him and drew the stick lightly across the paintwork. Jack plunged into his pocket and drew out a handful of change. 'Here, lads. Get yourself an ice cream.' The boy examined the coins and, apparently satisfied, withdrew his weapon and signalled to the rope-holders to lower their barrier.

Outside the house, he pulled hard on the handbrake and wondered what life held in store for the boys. Presumably the parents weren't aware that their sons were demanding money with menaces. Or maybe they were. Either way he wasn't optimistic about their future. But being brought up by educated parents was no guarantee of success. Look at the mess they'd made of rearing Kingsley.

'Ready?' he asked when his father came to the door.

'Tell him to come in a minute.' His mother's voice came from the kitchen.

'You'd better come in.'

His heart lurched at the sight of his father dressed in grey

136

flannel trousers, blazer and highly polished black shoes, more appropriate for the chapel choir than a barbecue.

'It's only an informal get-together, Dad. Just family. No need to dress up.'

His mother, too, was in her Sunday best – flowery dress and white cardigan – and she'd done something to her hair that had turned it into a white scouring pad. She sat at the table. In front of her was a large paper bag which he knew held tomatoes, a bunch of washed beetroot and a box of thin chocolate mints. A lump of love and pity rose in his throat but, nevertheless, he wished that they weren't coming. 'Ready for the off, Mum?'

She stayed where she was. 'Before we go anywhere, there's something I have to say…'

'Leave it, Vi.' Harry put a hand on his wife's shoulder.

'No. I want to clear the air. John would prefer me to speak my mind.'

Jack, sick with apprehension, smiled and nodded, 'Come on then Mum. Spit it out.'

She wiped the tiny hanky which she was clutching across her mouth. 'It's very nice of you to ask us to this "do", but we'd rather not come if Fay doesn't want us.'

'Don't be daft—'

'No. Let me finish. We don't want to make things awkward for you, but you have to see it from our side, too. I know we're not well-educated and we can't keep up with all your clever friends—'

'Mum—'

'Just hear me out, please. We have our pride, too, and if Fay is going to ignore us, like she did at the wedding, p'raps it would be better if we didn't come.' She turned to her husband for his support. 'I've got a bit of pork in the fridge so we won't go without.'

Jack wanted to take the cast-iron frying pan from on

top of the gas stove and beat Fay over the head with it. He wanted to gather his parents in his arms and tell them how sorry he was for all his wife's snubs and cold-shouldering; all her tutting and eye-rolling. But he'd been there when it had gone on, hadn't he? He'd stood by and allowed it to happen. To be truthful, there were times when he, too, had wanted to hide them away in a dark corner, where he couldn't hear their accent and their ignorance.

He pulled out a chair and sat next to his mother, massaging his forehead as he summoned up the right words. 'I know Fay can be difficult. Impatient. And I know that, if we're being honest, you don't like her much. A lot of it's my fault. I should have tried much harder in the beginning. Maybe if we'd all spent more time together…' He looked up to see if he was making headway. His mother was fiddling with her sleeve. 'Please come, Mum. For me. And the kids.' It was below the belt but he knew that mention of Caitlin and Dylan would sway her.

His father had turned away and was standing at the sink, staring into the garden. He recognised this strategy. He used it himself when people started speaking their minds.

His mother pushed the hanky into the folded-back cuff of her cardigan. 'If you really want us to come, we'll come, won't we Dad?' Without waiting for an answer, she stood up, gathering the things off the table into a Co-op carrier bag. His father locked and bolted the back door and they made their way to the car.

Alone in the house, Fay soon completed the outstanding tasks on her list. As she worked, she considered what Isabel might wear to a barbecue but soon abandoned that train of thought. If Isabel wanted to feed people in a garden, the last thing she would do was incinerate sausages and beef burgers. She would hire a marquee and bring in caterers. Probably give her guests 'themed' food. Moroccan or Swedish. Black or green. And her outfit would be appropriate to that theme.

Searching through her pre-Nottingham wardrobe, she chose cropped denim trousers and a pale blue tee-shirt. Barbecues were greasy affairs and the whole lot could go in the machine on a forty-degree wash.

The doorbell rang. Jack had his keys and Dylan would come round to the back. Fay glanced at her reflection in the hall mirror and flicked her hair before opening the door. It was Neil Bentley. He was holding a bunch of, what Caitlin scathingly referred to as, 'garage flowers' and six cans of lager.

'I'm not too early am I Mrs Water— Fay?'

'Neil. No. Not at all. You're bang on time. Are those for me? Lovely.' She took the flowers, in their dusty wrapping, and held them to her nose. 'Mmmm.' It was almost possible to imagine a scent.

He followed her into the silent kitchen and peered out of the window at the empty garden. 'I *am* too early, aren't I?' He looked miserable and confused. 'Shall I go away and come back later?'

'No, it's fine. Dylan should be here soon and you can help him get the barbecues going.' She gave him a tea towel and pointed towards the tray of already sparkling glasses. 'Could you wipe those for me?' It was a long while since anyone had done what she instructed, without arguing. Handing him a polythene bag filled with the trimmings from the salad, she tested his willingness a little further. 'Be a dear and pop these bits in the dustbin for me.' He smiled, set down his cloth and glass and trotted out to the bin.

When he returned, she noticed how diligently he wiped his feet on the doormat before stepping inside. 'Any news on the job applications?' she asked.

'Well, I haven't heard anything on either of them. But I see that as a positive sign, don't you?'

Polite, compliant, tidy and optimistic. Neil Bentley would be an asset to any organisation. 'And life in general?'

'There is one problem that I wasn't anticipating. The landlord wants us out of the house. He's selling it.'

'Can he do that?'

'Yeah. We're on a month's notice. At least I've got time to look round and sort some accommodation out before all the students get back.'

Jack turned the last few sausages and checked to see what his parents were doing. The sun was fierce and they had dragged their chairs into the corner of the garden, under the ash tree. Caitlin was with them so he could relax for a minute. He was still feeling sick in the pit of his stomach as a result of his mother's outburst of honesty. Fay's failure to get on with them had gone on for so many years that he'd accepted it, supposing they would muddle on somehow. Now he had to find a way of persuading her not to treat them like distasteful peasants, without reporting the exchange he'd had with his mother.

Where was Fay, anyway? Dylan, Nia and Sheila were in the kitchen, looking at yet more pictures of the wedding. She must be somewhere with that Neil lad.

'Another sausage anyone? Burger? Drink?' There were no takers so Jack removed his butcher's apron and announced 'Comfort break. Won't be long.'

Caitlin laughed 'We can probably cope until you get back, can't we Gran?'

Vi nodded and patted her granddaughter's hand.

'Has it changed much since you used to come here?' Fay and Neil stood in Kingsley's room.

Neil went across to the window and looked down into the garden. 'Well the view's the same but with three or four of us and all King's stuff—'

'Rubbish, you mean.'

'Whatever, the room used to look smaller. And darker.' He sat on the bed, bouncing a few times and smiling. 'They were great days.'

'They all are, when we're young.' She had no idea why she said this because she certainly didn't believe it. Hers had been a miserable adolescence, dominated by old-fashioned, overanxious parents and she'd never had the courage to rebel. When she was parenting teenagers, she'd intended to leave them to make their own decisions but it wasn't always possible to bite her tongue as they rushed headlong towards the next mistake. Wasn't a mother supposed to protect her offspring? It seemed to have worked with Caitlin and Dylan. Perhaps two out of three was a reasonable result.

Neil was talking about something, '… and there were always arguments going on. Correction, not arguments, discussions. You all *discussed* things. I loved that. In our house, whatever my Dad said, went.'

Did we discuss things? 'You make us sound like a debating society. What sort of things Neil?' He looked confused and she shook her head. 'Don't worry. I can't expect you to remember conversations that took place six or seven years ago.'

'I do, actually. There was one about whether it would be better if families swapped children and brought up someone else's.' He paused, 'And another to do with why we shouldn't eat food off our knives.'

She reached across and picked a thread of white cotton

off the back of Neil's shirt, picturing Kingsley, defiantly shovelling mashed potato into his mouth with his knife. 'I'd better get back and sort out dessert. You can come and give me a hand.'

As they came down the stairs, Jack was emerging from the sitting room. 'There you are.' He held a small leather-bound volume aloft. 'Found it. Come on.'

Fay looked at Neil and shrugged but followed Jack, who Pied Piper-like had rounded up Sheila, Nia and Dylan on his way through the kitchen. Once out in the garden he took up a position in the centre of the lawn. 'I want you all to listen to this.' He waved the book in the air again. 'It's absolutely fantastic.'

It took him five minutes to read *The Highwayman* from start to finish. When he snapped the book shut there was a smattering of applause, reinforced by Dylan's wolf-whistles. Caitlin gave her father a hug and suggested that he might like a strong black coffee. Sheila was giggling with delight. Vi and Harry remained impassive.

Fay took Neil's arm and pulled him onto the recitation spot. 'While we're all here it seems a good time to make an announcement.' It was Jack's turn now to look bemused. 'You all remember Neil, I'm sure. He was Kingsley's best friend—'

'Well, I wasn't exactly his—' Neil, looking apprehensive

'And he's going to be living here with us for a while, until he gets himself sorted out with a job and new digs. Aren't you Neil?'

Neil looked as though he had been doused with icy water. 'Blimey.' Then his confusion changed to delighted amazement. 'Yeah. Thanks. Blimey. Thanks.'

15

'I STILL THINK WE SHOULD HAVE DISCUSSED IT.' Jack bit into his slice of toast and marmalade. 'It's a big step – taking in lodgers. There are implications.'

'We aren't "taking in lodgers". It's more like having a friend to stay for a couple of weeks.' Fay got up from the table and took her breakfast plate to the sink.

'Well, not really.' It had gone too far to rescind Fay's invitation but he needed to register his misgivings so that, if the whole thing went wrong, he couldn't be blamed. 'It could be months before he finds a job. And having a stranger about the place is going to have a huge impact on our lives.'

She turned towards him and raised her eyebrows. 'Huge impact? We'll put a television in his room. We've got two bathrooms. Obviously he'll have to use the kitchen but, apart from that, I don't imagine we'll see much of him at all.'

'You won't be able to wander around in your nightie.'

'Is that a good enough reason to deny someone a roof over their head, when we have several spare bedrooms? I'd like to think that someone, on the other side of the world, might be doing the same for Kingsley.'

Jack had to hand it to her – she was good.

*

The holiday weekend had thrown up the customary dental emergencies. As well as dealing with the routine appointments, Jack replaced a crown – yanked off by reckless chomping of seaside rock – smoothed the jagged edge of an incisor, chipped by a ricocheting frisbee and made a temporary repair to a disintegrating molar – probably caused by tooth grinding.

Whilst he drilled and polished, he thought back over yesterday. Immediately after Fay made her startling announcement, the barbecue party had foundered. For once, his parents obsession with needing to be 'safe home' by six o'clock was a godsend, giving him the excuse to escape before it became obvious that Neil's imminent residency had been as much of a shock to him as everyone else. By the time he had deposited Vi and Harry back in their kitchen, then crawled back to Cardiff with the rest of the holiday traffic, only Caitlin was left. As she helped clear things away, she had kissed his cheek and whispered, 'It might be exactly what Mum needs.' What on earth could she mean?

The morning sped by and it wasn't until lunchtime that Sheila and he had a moment to chat. 'Thanks for yesterday, Jack. It's always good to catch up with Dylan and Caitlin. I don't see so much of them these days.' She offered him a segment of orange.

He was reluctant to talk about Neil Bentley, a topic which Sheila was bound to bring up, and was trawling around for a means of diverting the conversation when she clapped her hands to her mouth. 'Oh, I nearly forgot, someone called in to see you. It was rather odd actually. He didn't seem at all sure that you were the *right* Jack Waterfield. But he gave a reasonably accurate description so I thought he must be *bona fide*. Said he'd come back at five-thirty.'

Jack raised his eyebrows. 'Did he leave a name?'

Sheila lifted the notepad pad from the desk and wriggled her spectacles on to her nose. 'Evans. Iolo Evans. Rather a nice name, Iolo.'

A piece of orange caught in Jack's throat. 'Back in a minute,' he choked, rushing to the cloakroom and locking himself in.

He kept swallowing but the fibrous fruit refused to go down, lodging somewhere around his Adam's apple, burning and stinging. His eyes streamed and he began to fear that he was in danger of inhaling it into his lungs and he leaned against the cool tiled wall, taking shallow breaths, swallowing continuously until the obstruction cleared his oesophagus.

Sheila called gently from beyond the door, 'You okay?'

'Yes, thanks. I'll give it a couple of minutes.'

Had he used an alias and made out that he was a bus driver, from Aberystwyth, when he visited Llangwm, he could have kept his two worlds apart. To be honest, it didn't come as much of a surprise to him that he had been found out. With a name like Waterfield and a carelessly abandoned British Journal of Dentistry, it wouldn't take MI5 to track him down.

At six o'clock that evening, sitting in the bar of the Park Hotel with Iolo, the topic of Fay, his children and his life in Cardiff didn't arise. Iolo was in such an alarming state that he wasn't interested in hearing about anyone else. His bank manager had summoned him to Cardiff, to discuss the loan that he'd taken out when they'd bought the guesthouse. The Welcome Stranger had needed a lot of attention. It was a listed building and the restoration work had to be done properly. The business plan he'd presented, to back up his case, had underestimated the time it would take to recoup the outlay and now he was behind with his repayments.

'It looks like we'll have to sell up.' Iolo drew the palms of his hands down his face. 'Sorry to bother you with all this, Jack. Thank God I saw your name on the brass plate. It's comforting to see a friendly face after those cold-blooded bastards at the bank. I can't tell anyone at home. It'd be all round the place in minutes.'

'You mustn't,' Jack shook his head. 'You mustn't sell. What about re-mortgaging?' He was sketchy about finance but he knew it was the sort of thing people did to raise capital.

'No one wants to back a loser. I don't know why we thought we could make a go of it. Stupid. Christ. How am I going to tell Zena? She doesn't have a clue that we're in trouble.'

This astonished Jack. As he and Fay fell out of step with each other, he'd been thinking a great deal about Iolo and Zena. He'd taken for granted that they shared everything, from the last chocolate in the box to candlelit baths. In particular, during his long solitary night-musings, he imagined that, when the Evans's made love, they reached mutual climax and the proof of this perfect conjunction was their faultless daughter.

'I can't go home.' Iolo lifted the glass and gulped down the dregs of beer. 'Can't put it off much longer, though. She'll have the police out.' His gloomy face was flushed and shiny with perspiration. Dressed, as he was, in a crumpled navy blue suit, top button of his shirt undone and his tie askew, he was no longer the jaunty scarecrow nor the Formula One pancake flipper, whom Jack so envied.

'Did you drive down?' Jack tried to sound off-hand, but before Iolo could reply his phone rang.

146

It was Fay. 'Where are you? It's gone seven. I thought you'd be home by now.'

'Aaahhh. Sorry love. Last minute emergency. Young lad with an abscess. Didn't have the heart to turn him away.'

'But where *are* you? You're not in a pub are you?'

'Course not. I'm—'

'Well don't be long. I'm putting the potatoes on.'

Jack hadn't appreciated how drunk Iolo was when he'd come back to the surgery after work. He could well have been drinking all the afternoon and now here he was, fishing in his pocket for his car keys.

'You can't drive, man.'

Jack filtered the options. The simplest, but the least possible, was to offer him a bed for the night. There would be no problem in concocting a story about bumping into an old colleague from somewhere or another but Iolo was too far-gone for playacting.

There was no way he could drive him home. Fay was already cross with him for ruining her supper schedule and would instantly sniff out a lame excuse for another two or three hours' absence.

Sheila could put him up. If only he'd confided in her last week and brought her up to speed on his Llangwm adventures. But maybe it was asking too much to expect her to spend the night with a drunken stranger.

He toyed with the idea of contacting Zena, but how would she get down to Cardiff? And anyway he didn't want to get involved in the row they would surely have over the business with the bank.

Iolo was slumped on his chair, head back and eyes closed, moaning slightly.

'Come on, mate.' Jack took the car keys from his limp hand, patted him on the cheek and, standing in front of him, grabbed the shoulders of his jacket, lifting him up off the seat. 'Let's get you in a taxi. You can come back for the car tomorrow.' He slipped the car keys into one of Iolo's trouser pockets and buttoned the flap.

The cooler air outside the bar revived Iolo to some extent and Jack steered him around the corner, to the taxi rank. He coaxed him into the back of a car and negotiated a price with the driver to deliver the already sleeping passenger to Llangwm.

As Jack drove home, he felt drunk with excitement. An element of recklessness had entered his life, too, and although he would pass a breathalyser test, he wasn't sure that he was in a fit state to drive. Visits to Llangwm would be risky and challenging but he felt confident that he was up to it. Was this the buzz that youngsters got from a shot in the arm, or a snort up the nose, of the latest 'designer drug'? Then there was the recent satisfying reminder that he had once, albeit philanthropically, made love to another woman. See – it was perfectly possible to bend the rules without bringing the world crashing down around his ears. His morale was high. No one made films or wrote books about moderately successful, middle-aged dentists but, now that he was emerging as a more colourful character, whom would he cast in the role of Jack Waterfield? Nigel Havers? Women seemed to go for him. No, too English. Too good-looking. Someone a bit grittier; more of a working-class hero. James Nesbitt would be the man for the job.

He pictured Iolo, fast asleep as the taxi sped north. He should be back at The Welcome Stranger in an hour or so and would have some tough questions to answer, but it was high time that Zena knew what was going on. He wished he could be there to help and comfort them, but he had his own corner to fight.

Fay was tipping vegetables into the serving dishes as he came into the kitchen. 'Sorry about that, love.' He kissed her warm cheek. 'Something smells good.'

'Coq au vin. I thought we'd better have something civilised after all that rubbish we ate at the barbecue yesterday. Could you open the wine?'

He rinsed his hands under the cold tap and took the wine from the fridge. He would have liked time to relax and change out of his work clothes but the meal was ready, so he slipped off his jacket and rolled up his sleeves. 'Busy day?'

'I sorted out the room for Neil.'

'When's he moving in?' There was no point in holding out any longer.

'He has to be out of his flat by the end of the month. That's next Sunday. But I told him he can start bringing his things over whenever it's convenient.' She sat facing him, her hand reaching for his. 'It'll be fine, Jack. I promise.' Her voice was gentler than it had been for months.

'Yes. It'll be fine.' He raised his glass. 'Here's to our new lodger. Who knows, he may even be a dab hand at mowing lawns or washing cars.'

After supper, Caitlin rang and, whilst she chatted to Fay, Jack stacked the dishwasher and tidied the kitchen. He should phone to check whether Iolo had arrived safely but, having paid the driver forty pounds to take his friend home, there was little he could do about it either way. He was curious to know what Iolo would tell Zena and Non about their meeting – that was if he could recollect anything at all about it. It was touch and go if Iolo would remember where he had parked his car.

Fay returned after ten minutes. 'Caitlin's got the rest of the week off. She's going to Derby tomorrow to visit

Sarah Forrester. Remember Sarah? The one with greasy hair and no sense of direction.'

The description fitted the majority of Caitlin's friends from student days, male and female. Jack had spent hours calling them by the wrong name and drawing simple maps to navigate them round the country. 'Vaguely.'

'She suggested I cadge a lift with her and spend a couple of days with Laura. It would be company for her on the drive and she'll be more or less passing Laura's door.' Getting no immediate reaction she continued. 'I know she was only here ten days ago…'

Oh, dear. Fay and Laura and endless hours of chatter. For an instant, a cloud crossed his clear blue sky, vanishing as quickly as it had appeared. In nearly thirty years, Laura hadn't divulged their secret, why would she do so now? And, joy of joys, Fay's absence would provide an unplanned opportunity. 'Of course, love. You must go. Take the chance while you can.'

'You'll be here if Neil wants to drop anything off, won't you?'

Bugger. The roller coaster had reached the summit and was plummeting down again. 'Actually, if you don't mind, I'd rather you were around when he moves in. He'd probably find it a bit…awkward…here on his own with me. At least in the beginning. You know how useless men are at making small-talk.'

She crossed the kitchen and put her arms around him, resting her head on his chest. 'That's very thoughtful. You're right. I'll give him a ring and suggest he leave it until Saturday. I'll be back by then and we'll be able to make him feel properly at home.'

He kissed the top of her head, content that she would have a pleasant few days with her best friend and that he could, for an evening if not longer, get back to Llangwm.

16

'Of course you must come,' Laura replied. 'Gosh. Three times in one month. What have we done to deserve it?'

We. Could Laura have picked up on her feelings for Cassidy? Fay didn't go into it, not wanting anything to interfere with her unexpected opportunity to see him again.

She wasn't best pleased therefore when, an hour later Laura, rang back. 'You'll never guess what. Ten minutes after I spoke to you, Isabel phoned for a chat. When I told her you were coming, she suggested she pop up, or down, or whatever she calls it, tomorrow. Just for the day. She's got to get back for some big charity "do". That's okay with you, isn't it?'

'Lovely.' Fay hadn't appreciated that Laura and Isabel were quite so pally. 'If Caitlin picks me up about twelve, we should be with you by, what, four-ish?'

The clothes she laid out on the bed were from her 'new wardrobe'. The silk shirts – she wouldn't take the pink one – and linen trousers were a nightmare to fold without creasing. It was a good job that Jack wasn't hovering, asking why she needed so much for a two-night stay, and pointing out that Laura had turned up with just a toilet bag and a change of underwear. She felt a pang of guilt about

151

abandoning him at such short notice, especially as he'd been so cheerful when he'd left for work. 'Don't worry about me, love. I may pop up and see Mum and Dad. Have a bite to eat with them. I promised Dad I'd give him a hand with something.'

They'd been travelling for over an hour before Caitlin got around to Neil Bentley.

'What's that all about, Mum?'

Fay had anticipated a grilling on the subject and had been trying to formulate a realistic explanation. This had proved to be quite difficult because she wasn't sure, herself, why she'd offered to take him in. Seeing him in the kitchen in the Lennon tee-shirt, looking vulnerable and needy, had a lot to do with it. Then, once she'd addressed the problem of Kingsley's room, the notion of sorting out a young man's problems, albeit not her son's, became progressively more appealing. Lots of people felt driven to acts of charity without being asked to explain their motives. That's what it was, an act of charity.

'Good gracious, I don't know what all the fuss is about. It'll only be for a few weeks. We've got masses of space and it's not as if he's a stranger.' Put like that, it sounded perfectly reasonable.

'Kingsley would be pleased. And surprised.' Caitlin smiled. 'I think it's a great idea.'

It was true, Kingsley *would* be pleased, although she hadn't considered him when she'd issued the invitation. It was just the sort of thing he might have done, but Kingsley would probably have taken it that bit too far and filled the house with deserving cases.

'And remind me about Auntie Laura. I don't want to put my foot in it. It seems a shame that she never married again. She must have had lots of offers.'

'If she did she's never talked about them. But then she wouldn't. We lost touch for a while. I'm sure it's because she didn't want us to meet Sadie's father.'

Caitlin grimaced, 'Why d'you think that?'

'Oh, I don't know. Isabel reckons he must have been a drug addict or something arty and disreputable. He can't have been that nice, to have walked out on her when she'd just given birth to his baby.'

There was no sign of Cassidy's car in the street outside Laura's house and Fay smiled to hide her disappointment. By the time Caitlin was locking her car, Laura was on the pavement to greet them and she took Caitlin's hands in hers, patting it. 'This is lovely. We were so sorry to miss you when we came to Cardiff.'

Caitlin accepted the invitation to stay for a cup of tea and they followed Laura in to the house. 'I'll ring Sarah and let her know where I am. It shouldn't take long from here.' She went in to the back garden to make her call.

Laura hugged Fay, who was attempting to massage the creases out of her trousers.

'Are you sure you're not sick of the sight of me?' Fay asked.

'Don't be ridiculous. I'm really glad you came.' She cupped her face in her palms. 'To be honest I think it's only these past few weeks that I'm coming to accept that Dad's really gone so it's good to have old friends around.' They hugged again.

There were voices in the garden and Fay peered through the kitchen window. Cassidy, stripped to the waist, was carrying lengths of timber in through the back gate, which opened on to a lane running behind the terraced properties. He and Caitlin were laughing about something. She had steeled herself for this, recalling Cassidy's interest in the family pictures in the hall. He'd said he didn't care for '*girly* girls', but Caitlin would soon be on her way to Derby.

'…it's not far and I think you'd find it interesting. We might go there tomorrow, if I can get this wretched thing sorted out.' Laura pointed to the boiler on the wall near the sink. 'It's been on the blink since Monday. All my appliances have a built in gadget that makes them self-destruct at Bank Holidays.' Fay hadn't noticed until then that the kitchen was particularly chaotic. Piles of dirty crockery covered the worktops and there was a heap of tools and a torch on the table. 'We twiddled a few things but …' She shook her head. 'The plumber promised he'd get here by four. Never mind. We can manage, can't we? Let's have some tea.'

Caitlin and Cassidy showed no signs of returning to the kitchen, so Laura put the teapot and mugs on a tray and they went outside to join them. Fay lowered herself into the deckchair, trying not to picture what this would do to her linen trousers.

'We've been catching up,' said Caitlin.

'Refreshing memories,' Cassidy added. 'Cait's got amazing powers of recall.'

'The sight of you kicking tea over Mum's white carpet isn't easily forgotten. Nor the inquest after you went. If *we'd* done it we'd have been grounded for weeks.'

'It wasn't "my carpet",' Fay jumped in. 'I wish you wouldn't make me out to be such an ogre, Caitlin.' Her protestation sounded childish and she hurried to temper her remark. 'You can barely see the stain now.'

The garden was small, but Laura had utilised the space thoughtfully to create a jewel of a garden, bursting with colour and scent, and they lounged in deckchairs, enjoying the late afternoon sun. 'Is that where you work?' Fay asked, pointing to a small shed in the corner, where Cassidy had stacked the timber.

'I do the odd repair here, but I rent a workshop out on the bypass. That's where I spend most of my time.'

Caitlin asked for directions to Derby. 'I've got a large scale map in the house,' he said putting his arm around Caitlin's shoulder and shepherding her back inside.

'You look disapproving.' Laura closed her eyes and lent her head back against the striped canvas.

'Not at all,' Fay laughed. 'I forgot to ask about Sadie. How are things?'

'Quite good, actually. The last time we were together – it was after Dad's funeral, in fact – she and Joe were talking about having a baby.' She paused. 'You won't have experienced this yet, Fay, but the death of your second parent has a galvanising effect. It shifts you up a rung on the ladder. You're that much nearer the top and it makes you think, "I'd better get on with things; get things sorted." I think Sadie feels she's moved up a rung, too.'

Laura looked beautiful, in a dishevelled way, the stray wisps of grey hair forming corkscrew curls around her tanned face and, for the first time, Fay envied her ability to ignore creases in her clothes and wrinkles on her face.

'Does Sadie have her father's temperament?'

Fay held her breath wondering if, at last, Laura would divulge her secret, but all she got was: 'Maybe.'

Caitlin came to say goodbye. 'I'll call you tomorrow about going back, once I know what Sarah's got lined up.'

Cassidy appeared behind her, wearing a tee-shirt now. 'I'm trying to persuade Cait that she'd have much more fun here with us.' He came alongside her and put his arm, in brotherly fashion, across her shoulder and she flushed slightly. 'Ditch your dreary friend and get back here as fast as you can.'

'She'd be better off in Derby if her friend has a functioning boiler,' Laura pointed out. 'You do what you want to do, Caitlin. You know you're very welcome.'

'I must admit, I'd be intrigued to meet Isabel again. She made quite an impression on me last time we saw her.'

'Did she kick *her* tea on the carpet?' Cassidy slipped his arm down to her waist.

'No. She downed a whole bottle of white wine without getting the slightest bit drunk. I was well impressed.'

'Shouldn't you be on your way?' Fay prompted. 'You won't have any time at all with Sarah at this rate.'

They trooped out to see her off and Cass whispered something in her ear then kissed her on the cheek. 'She's almost as beautiful as her mother,' he said as the car pulled away and his fingers brushed Fay's arm, sending a tingle fizzling down her spine.

For once, Jack kept strictly to appointment times, determined to be away from the surgery by five-thirty, and in Llangwm by seven at the latest.

'On some sort of productivity drive, are we?' Sheila joked as he took a short lunch break.

'Need to be out of here on the dot,' he half-explained.

'Oh, by the way, was that Iolo chap okay last night? I thought he looked a bit…well, drunk I suppose, when he came back.' Not for the first time he wondered whether Sheila was clairvoyant.

'Ha,' Jack laughed. 'Iolo drunk? Good heavens no. He's not well, poor man.' Realising that laughter at the expense of an ailing friend was inappropriate, he drew his face into a frown. 'His medication makes him a bit woozy.'

Sheila let it go. 'When's that lad moving in?'

'At the weekend.'

'If you don't mind my saying, it's very un-Fay-like.'

Was this the moment? 'Can I talk to you about something important, Sheila?'

Sheila stood, calm and receptive. 'Of course.'

But if he were going to tell her everything, he would need more than a few minutes and he could hear the first patient of the afternoon plodding up the stairs. 'It'll keep 'til tomorrow.'

That morning he'd sneaked a change of clothes out of the house and into the car, not wanting to arrive at The Welcome Stranger looking, or smelling, like a dentist. He wished he'd had time to shower, too, but every minute was precious and he tried not to sweat as the rush-hour traffic crawled out of the city. He had no idea how the evening would pan out but, from his two previous visits, he knew that plans were superfluous where the Evans family was concerned.

Passing the slip road which would have taken him to his parent's house, he could picture them now, his father pottering in the garden, whilst his mother washed the dishes after tea, chewing over the events of the barbecue for the umpteenth time. 'She should show a little more charity towards her family,' his mother had grumbled as he'd driven them back. 'Blood's thicker than water. Who is this Neil boy, anyway?'

'Poor sod,' his father would mutter, under his breath.

Jack made good time, the traffic easing as homeward bound commuters slipped off to the estates of modest houses, clinging to the sides of the broad valley. It was before seven when, singing to himself, he dropped down the hill and coasted round the final bend into Llangwm.

A 'No Vacancies' sign hung from the board outside

The Welcome Stranger but the front door was wide open. He paused in the hall, trying to identify the muted voices coming from the kitchen. 'Hello,' he called. 'Hello.' The voices stopped and the house, usually bustling with people and filled with laughter and singing, fell silent.

He waited and, after what seemed far too long, Iolo, wearing a striped apron over khaki shorts, appeared from the direction of the kitchen. 'Jack.' He gave a relieved smile, grabbed Jack's hand and pumped it, 'Jack.'

'Iolo.' Jack pumped back. 'Thought I'd better check you're okay. Did you retrieve your car?'

'Yes. Took a while to track it down, though. Cost me a packet in car park fees. Still…' Hanging on to Jack's hand, he slapped him on the shoulder. 'Can't thank you enough for last night. How much do I owe you for the taxi?'

Jack shook his head. 'Forget it. You've told Zena about…things, I assume.'

'Mmmm. Made a bit of a dog's breakfast of it I'm afraid. Here, what am I thinking about? Let's get the kettle on.'

Non was sitting at the kitchen table, the area in front of her a sea of papers, cheque book stubs and brown envelopes. She looked strained but her face brightened when she saw Jack. 'It's our guardian angel,' she said and, seeing her lovely face again, that's exactly what he wanted to be. 'Dad told you about our difficulties.' She waved her hand over the table. 'We've spent all day going through this lot. Trying to work out where it went so wrong.'

When Iolo went into the garden, to empty the tea-leaves from the familiar brown teapot, Non whispered urgently, 'Mum's gone to her sister's. Sshhh. He's coming back.'

Their faces gave them away. 'She told you that Zena's gone?' Iolo swished hot water around the pot. 'Taken it into her head I'm a devious, drunken shit. Seems to think that I've been keeping other things from her, too. Couldn't persuade her that I was only trying to save her the worry, until I get things sorted.'

Non laid a hand on her father's arm. 'We've agreed it's a bit beyond sorting, Dad.'

His shoulders sagged. 'Bastard bankers,' he muttered. 'Keen enough to lend you the money but don't want to know when you hit a sticky patch.'

Jack wanted to comfort Iolo and he envied women, who, at times like this, could hug the sufferer and make soothing noises. This option denied him, he resorted to hard facts. 'This is rather indelicate, and you can tell me to mind my own business, but how much money are we talking?'

'We've past the "indelicate" stage. Twenty thousand pounds.' Iolo shook his head. 'There's no doubt we can make enough to live on but we can't seem to get on top of the initial loan.'

Non nodded confirmation. Past her, through the window, the setting sun was casting an orange glow across the hills; a huge bunch of asters, shaggy and jewel-coloured, stood in a lustre jug on the dresser; hens crooned in the enclosure at the end of the garden.

The solution came to him in a flash, as though someone had raised the curtain to reveal an entrancing stage set. 'Well, I've been giving it a lot of thought.'

Non frowned, 'How long have you known about it then?'

Iolo was quick to dispel any idea that he had confided in a stranger before telling his family. 'Yesterday. When I was down in Cardiff.'

Jack elaborated. 'I mean I've been thinking about it all day. I couldn't say anything until I knew what sort of money's involved.' He linked his hands behind his head and lent back in the chair. 'Twenty thousand's nothing in the scheme of things.' His heart raced in anticipation of what he was about to propose. 'Look. I've got some money sitting in the building society, earning very little. Why don't I invest it in The Welcome Stranger?' Jack held his breath.

The cat, curled in the shabby chair in the corner, yawned and stretched a paw; the tap dripped into the sink; Jack's proposition settled. Then a grin split Iolo's face and he clapped his hands 'Hallelujah. We're saved.'

But Non silenced him. 'Hang on, Dad. If we can't repay the bank loan, how on earth is Jack going to get his money back?'

Jack did, in fact, have a great deal more than twenty thousand pounds or, more accurately, he and Fay did. It was money that Fay's father, an astute investor all his life, had left them when he'd died a couple of years earlier. As they were comfortably off and could expect generous work pensions, and Caitlin and Dylan were both in good jobs, they'd stashed it away in the building society, where it was accumulating at a healthy rate. Considering how on the ball she was in every other area, it was odd that Fay left fiscal matters to him. In the beginning he'd wondered whether she wasn't confident with numbers, then he'd come to the conclusion that she found it all rather tedious – the sort of thing a dentist should deal with. But, at that moment, he was grateful for it and for the fact that the money was accessible on either signature.

His mind raced in all directions. 'I'm sure we can work something out. For starters, I'd only want to match the interest I'm getting at the moment, which is bound to be a lot less than the bank's charging. You can pay it off, as and when. And,' the plan was firming up, 'if you decide you want to pack it in, you can pay me back when you sell up. At least it buys you time to make alternative plans. How does that sound?'

Iolo flapped his apron, as though his thighs needed cooling. 'Wonderful. Fan-bloody-tastic. If we can just have more time, I know we can put this place on the map. And,' he banged the table with the flat of his hand, 'you can come up whenever you like. Treat the place like home.'

This possibility had crossed Jack's mind.

But Non wasn't looking convinced. 'It's terribly generous, Jack, but we couldn't accept. For a start, you don't know anything about us. We could be con men for all you know.'

She looked so earnest and innocent that he couldn't help smiling. 'I don't think so. Con men don't generally get people's cars fixed for free then send them home with half a dozen eggs.'

While Iolo pottered around the kitchen, whistling and rustling up wedges of fruit cake, Non collected the papers together and tapped the pile. 'I wish you'd take a look at this lot before you make a decision, Jack.' She checked that her father was out of earshot. 'Dad's not the most shrewd businessman and,' she searched for the right words, 'I couldn't bear the thought that he might fail a second time. It might be kinder to draw a line under it now.'

Her beautiful face was full of concern for her father. There was no sign of the irritation or impatience that she might be excused for having with an incompetent, ageing parent. Her consideration for Iolo raised her even higher in Jack's esteem and he wondered if she might not, in fact, be a kind of secular saint, radiating a top-to-toe halo of goodness. It would certainly explain the glow he felt when he was near her. 'How long do we have?'

'The bank's given him a couple of weeks.'

'I hope you don't think I'm overstepping the mark, but shouldn't your mother be involved in the decision?'

161

Non closed her eyes, raising her hands to her face and pulling the flesh taught across her cheek bones. 'It's not that straightforward. They've had a bit of a rocky ride over the years. They came here to make a fresh start. Mum has a huge emotional stake in the place. The silly thing is, Dad was so desperate not to mess up again, he was scared to tell her when things started coming adrift. Then, when she discovered that he's been keeping her in the dark, she said she couldn't trust him any more.'

He wondered how loveable, generous Iolo had 'messed up' the first time. Women? Drink? Gambling? It surely couldn't have been *that* bad or the bank wouldn't have lent him any money in the first place.

They drank their tea and Iolo babbled on, expounding schemes that he had cooked up to improve the profitability of The Welcome Stranger, and Jack wondered whether the man was on anti-depressant medication. His naive enthusiasm, so appealing and contagious on carnival day, seemed inappropriate in the current crisis.

When Iolo went out to shut up the hens for the night, Non insisted that Jack read through the letters from the bank. 'You must be wondering why I don't sell up the nursery to raise the money.'

'It hadn't crossed my mind,' he gave the honest answer.

'In fact it's not mine to sell. It belongs to my partner. We run the place together but she actually owns it.'

She. Non's 'partner' was a woman.

17

After their meal, Laura suggested that they go for a stroll. 'It's a beautiful evening and there's a pub with a beer garden, down by the river.' She went outside and shouted towards the shed, 'Cass? We're going to The Plough. D'you want to come?'

Cassidy hadn't eaten supper with them, explaining that he'd had a late lunch, with friends. 'Sounds good. I've still got a bit to do here, so you carry on. I'll catch you up.'

Fay hurried upstairs to collect her bag and check her hair. It seemed days since she left Cardiff. Her scalp felt itchy and she longed for a shower. The plumber had phoned while they were eating, promising that he would be along first thing in the morning. Laura had offered to boil a kettle so that she could wash her hair, 'Or we could go down to the leisure centre, have a quick swim and make use of the facilities.' The frightening thing was that she'd meant it.

Fay splashed her face with cold water and, noting that Laura was still in her old tee-shirt, decided not to change. Her clothes were creased beyond trendiness but, uncertain what the next day might bring, it seemed safer to keep a clean set in reserve.

The walk to the pub took over half an hour. Victorian terraces gave way to wider streets of semi-detached houses, driveways blocked with cars and caravans. There was nothing to distinguish this part of Nottingham, a city which she'd always associated with Lawrence, coal miners and the privations of the industrial revolution, from the suburbs of any other English town.

'I meant to ask if you wanted to phone Jack,' Laura said.

'He's going to see his parents this evening, I think, so he won't be home.'

'How are they?'

'We saw them on Monday. They came to us for a barbecue.' It sounded so natural; so everyday.

'But how are they?' Laura persisted.

'The same as ever,' Fay laughed. 'Critical. Miserable. Inflexible. Thoroughly heavy going. They never change.' She expected Laura to leap to their defence but the conversation was curtailed when a girl, aged three or four, running full tilt along the pavement ahead of her mother, tripped and fell and the three women spent several minutes calming her down.

'How d'you feel about grandparenthood?' Laura asked as they continued on their way. 'Kingsley's got a child, hasn't he?'

Why did Laura ask such direct questions? Most people hedged around, making it easy for her to respond with vague generalisations.

'Possibly.' It sounded ridiculous. 'I know that the girl, the woman, whatever, whom he's with, has a son but I don't know if the child is his. You'd think he'd have the decency to set the record straight.'

'Perhaps he's not sure himself,' Laura ventured.

It was an odd thing to say and Fay wondered where this was leading. 'That's all well and good, but I think Jack and I deserve to know if we *are* grandparents. I see it as a basic human right.'

Laura nodded. 'I know what you mean. When we're young, all that genealogy stuff seems irrelevant. We feel it's dragging us back, slowing us down. All we want is to get on with things. But I do feel that there comes a moment – maybe some deep-seated imperative clicks in – when we *do* need to set the record straight.'

They walked on in silence.

Fay had trained herself to block thoughts of Kingsley. When he left, and it became clear that he wasn't merely making a gesture, concern for his safety drove her mad and she'd had to take the term off work. The police had been disinterested once they learned that he was eighteen – even though he'd gone only three days after his birthday – reeling off statistics on the numbers of young people who left home and were perfectly fine. Then, when the note arrived saying that he would be in touch again if he had anything to tell them, the police were proved right and there was nothing she could do. Occasionally they received cards and emails. Once he'd written a three-page letter, reassuring them that he was fine, whilst avoiding telling them anything about his situation. Then postcards had turned up from India and Thailand but more recently they were from Australia. He mentioned 'Anya and the baby' but, despite explicit requests for information, all she knew was that he was still alive.

'Maybe the woman isn't sure herself,' Laura continued.

'Strangely enough, I don't find it at all comforting to think my son has taken up with a tart who isn't even sure who's fathered her child.'

'It's not always straightforward, Fay. People said I was a tart when I had Sadie,' Laura replied softly.

'But that was different. At least you knew—'

'No, I didn't,' Laura interrupted. 'Are you sure you want to associate with me?'

*

By the time they reached the pub, Fay's feet were sore where the stitching on the handmade shoes had rubbed. She went to the Ladies and sat in the locked cubicle, cooling her feet on the tiled floor and wishing that she were at home, with a water heating system that worked. It was likely that Jack had gone to visit Vi and Harry but she rang home, on the off chance that she might catch him. When there was no reply, she left a brief message, letting him know that she'd arrived safely.

Although it was midweek, the pub was crowded. They carried their lemonade-shandies to a rickety table in the corner of the beer garden, watching the dark river eddying and racing just beyond. It was picturesque but, as the light faded, it altered and became sinister and Fay turned her chair to face away from it, keeping an eye on the door.

By nine o'clock it was dark. Strings of coloured fairy lights illuminated the garden and all that remained of the swirling water was a scatter of dancing reflections and the sound of it, lapping against the stone wall beneath the terrace. But there was no sign of Cassidy.

'I expect he got a better offer.' Laura appeared to be explaining to herself more than Fay.

'Wouldn't he phone?'

'I'm terrible about carrying my phone. He's given up nagging me about it.'

'You can use mine.' Fay volunteered her mobile.

'Oh, it's hardly worth it now. We'd better be starting back.'

Fay had slipped her shoes off under the table and her feet had swollen. She rammed them hard into the toes and pulled the back of the shoes up, feeling the sharp pain of the blister that had bubbled up on her right heel.

'Have you got a plaster?' she asked when they had gone

a little way, and Laura had magic-ed one, rather fluffy but perfectly serviceable, from a compartment in her shabby purse.

They walked back through the dark suburb. At home she hardly ever – never in fact – walked anywhere in the dark. Why would she? To be honest, now that the streets were deserted, she would be nervous to walk here alone. The city held the dubious reputation of being 'murder capital of the UK', but she assumed that Laura wouldn't bring her here unless it was pretty safe. It *was* fascinating to observe, in the few seconds that it took to pass each house, the snapshot of the lives which animated the rows of semis. Lights illuminated sitting rooms and hallways. She was surprised how many people had left the curtains open and how few of them had net curtains. Her mother had been obsessive about excluding prying eyes and had communicated her fear to Fay. 'Un-curtained windows – God's gift to peeping Toms,' she'd explained.

In one sitting room, illuminated by a bare light-bulb, a young couple were stripping wallpaper. She wore shorts and a bikini top. He was sipping from a can.

A few doors along, the room glowed cosily from side lamps and a woman stood at an ironing board, in front of the television, clothes dangling from hangers hooked on the picture rail.

Little semi-detached lives.

Laura must have read her thoughts. 'Crazy, isn't it? All of us, living out our dreams in tiny boxes. Don't you love walking in the dark? There's something sensuous, dangerous, about it. And such exotic smells.' She sniffed the air noisily. 'It's like wine. I'm getting honeysuckle. Mmmm. What else? Carbon monoxide. A hint of curry.'

The streetscape changed and they came into some sort of housing estate, dominated by ugly concrete blocks of flats. The inefficient street lights revealed the litter that had accumulated, caught by the straggly clumps of municipal planting between the graffitied buildings and the road. A cyclist drew up alongside them. It was Cassidy, breathing heavily. 'There you are. I've been riding around like a maniac, trying to track you down. Can't you persuade Mum to carry her mobile, Fay?'

They walked three abreast, Cassidy on the kerb with the wheels of his bike in the gutter, Laura in the middle. Fay had to trot to keep up with her long-legged companions and she felt the interloper, almost the gooseberry, as mother and son conversed in a kind of affectionate shorthand. Had she not known better, from tone of voice and body language, she would have guessed they were partners. Cassidy had been the man in Laura's life, the constant man, since David died and there was a rapport between them that she'd never had with either of her sons.

During his previous visits to Llangwm, Jack had been playing a minor role in a zany romantic comedy, where anything might happen. But he'd foolishly believed the 'anything' would always be on the positive side. This evening, glumness hung about the place. The current guests were a colourless bunch, keeping themselves to themselves as they came back from wherever they'd spent the evening, barely stopping to say goodnight before they crept up to their rooms.

'We're full, I'm afraid, Jack' Non apologised, 'But I could easily put the camp-bed in Dad's room.'

'No worries. And "full" is what we want to hear,' he said. It had been his intention to stay overnight. He'd calculated that, if he made an early start in the morning, he could get home, shower, change and be in work for his first appointment at eight-thirty, but this evening he felt peculiarly out of place.

There wasn't much traffic about and, as he drove back to Cardiff, he pondered his evening with Non and Iolo. He was sure that he would be able to lend Iolo the money, as he'd offered, and soon replenish their savings account from his salary. In any case, the whole sum would be repaid within the next ten years or so, whenever Iolo and Zena decided to retire. Fay need never know.

The financial side of things was straightforward compared to Non's disclosure concerning the ownership of the nursery. The English language was getting much too confusing. There was a time when the word 'partner' was used purely in a business context. Or ballroom dancing. Or, at a push, in cowboy films. But when Non had mentioned that her partner owned the business, already having told him that she *lived* with her partner, he hadn't know what to think. He had no problem with anyone's sexual orientation, as long as it wasn't the woman he loved.

When he got home, there was a message from Fay to let him know that she was safe at Laura's, her voice sounding strangely echo-y, as if she were talking to him from the bottom of a well. Neil Bentley had rung, too. 'Hello Mr…Jack. I know Mrs…Fay is away until Saturday, but it would be great if I could drop off a couple of boxes tomorrow evening.' He'd left a contact number in case it wasn't convenient. The whole thing wasn't convenient, if Jack were honest.

There were films and stories that started like this, weren't there? Harmless young man ingratiates himself with gullible couple. Moves in. Starts to take over. Manipulates them. Seduces the woman. Murders the man. Takes over his identity. 'The Servant', Dirk Bogarde. He couldn't quite see how Neil Bentley was going to work at the practice without Sheila, or the patients, spotting that something was amiss, but it was perfectly possible that he might try it on with Fay.

Jack knew that, since their marriage, Fay hadn't slept with anyone else. They'd never discussed it, but he *knew*. If she had, she would have told him because, if there was one thing he could say about his wife, she was blisteringly honest. When they had first got together, he'd envied her that trait. He, from childhood, had done everything in his power to avoid confrontation. Occasionally this was to escape punishment but, more often, it was to spare his parents' feelings or to make life run smoothly. Fay took things head on. This may well have benefited her career but most of the family's problems resulted form her inability to keep her opinions to herself. It was doubtful that she would ever change, so perhaps it was time he did.

It was past his usual bedtime but he didn't feel in the least tired. Here he was, on his own, able to spend the night hours entirely as he wished. He might not even go to bed. Iolo certainly wouldn't lie tossing and turning just because it was 'bedtime'. His thoughts were butterflies in his head, flitting and fluttering from one topic to the next. Money. Non. Neil Bentley. Laura. Kingsley. Always Kingsley. He poured himself a large whiskey, although he didn't really want it, and meandered around the dark house, the street lamp providing enough light to guide him. The first sip of alcohol burned his throat and within seconds he felt flushed and light-headed, not surprising as he'd barely eaten anything all day.

When they were children, he and Marion hadn't played together often, but one of the games they both enjoyed started with Blind Man's Buff and developed into just Blind Man. As soon as they tired of chasing each other, they carried on alone, a scarf wrapped tightly around their eyes, imagining what it would be like to lose their sight. Now, in the hall, he closed his eyes and discovered that he could go straight to the door handle of each room then walk across it without bumping into the furniture. It depressed him to acknowledge how familiar the confines of the house had become.

Negotiating the stairs without even stubbing a toe, he arrived in Kingsley's room but, once there, he couldn't bear to open his eyes. In his darkness he saw untidy piles of clothes littering the floor; posters for obscure bands; the Strat look-alike, cradled safely on its stand; used coffee mugs. And later, angry slogans graffiti-ing the walls. How could Fay invite a stranger to displace those memories?

He wasn't sure how long he lay on his son's bed before he crawled under the crisp, new duvet and spiralled into restless sleep.

18

Jack woke early. His shirt was throttling him and his feet were burning. For a second, he thought he had fallen asleep on the sofa but, no, he was in Kingsley's bed, still fully clothed.

After a shower, he was ready for the cooked breakfast which he'd promised himself. He enjoyed cooking, especially in a frying pan where he could see exactly what was going on and nothing could catch him unawares. Fried eggs were particularly gratifying and he tilted the pan this way and that, coaxing the bacon fat to trickle across the humped yolks, rendering the glutinous layer crisp and white. Iolo would be doing much the same thing for his guests about now, and, with his help, would continue doing so for many years to come.

Jack considered his forthcoming charitable act to be on a par with those of the Victorian reformers – Cadbury and Barnardo and the like. The Welcome Stranger Guesthouse was just as worthy of preservation as Brighton Pavilion or Blackpool Tower. It was too much to expect creative people like Iolo and Zena to offer the delights that they did *and* balance their books.

The phone rang. It was Fay. In a whisper she filled him in on the malfunctioning boiler and her blistered feet. 'We're boiling saucepans of water to wash in. It's worse than camping. Laura doesn't seem to care. It's all very well being laid back, but there comes a point where it's bloody irritating.'

'Poor love,' he commiserated, 'I'm sure you'll rise to the occasion. Look, I've got to dash. See you tomorrow.'

Breakfast was delicious and he decided to have the same thing for his evening meal. This meant that there was no point in washing the frying pan, or the saucepan in which he'd heated the baked beans, and he left them on the hob, ready to go.

During the morning he dealt with a steady stream of patients, none of whom presented him with anything tricky. At lunchtime he went to the building society where the teller reminded him, rather sanctimoniously he thought, that he would forgo interest by way of penalty for failing to give sixty days notice of withdrawal. Apart from that, the transaction was straightforward and he folded the cheque into his wallet and headed back to the surgery.

His next problem was how to get the cheque to Iolo. He was reluctant to trust it to the post but daren't risk another jaunt to Llangwm so soon. Fay expected him to be at home that evening, and Neil Bentley had left that message about boxes, whatever that meant. Spotting an empty phone booth and keen to be out of Sheila's earshot, he pushed a handful of coins in the slot. 'Iolo? It's Jack. Look, any chance that you could pop down to Cardiff this afternoon? I've got the cheque here so the sooner you get it to your bank, the sooner you can get them off your back.'

Iolo, after effusive thanks, said he would contact the bank and make an appointment. He would call at the surgery, to pick up the money, on the way. Jack was apprehensive about this but, with a full complement of patients, he would be unable to get away and he couldn't come up with a better solution. He hesitated before asking, 'Any news from Zena?'

Iolo said he'd heard nothing but didn't sound despondent. 'She'll calm down when she hears that it's all sorted out. Thanks again, Jack.'

Jack arrived home to find Neil Bentley sitting on the doorstep, alongside four large cardboard boxes. He jumped up. 'I came in a taxi,' he said, as if required to explain his transport arrangements.

Jack unlocked the door. 'You might as well take them straight up to Kingsley's... to your room. Can I give you a hand?' He was glad when Neil refused. There was no going back on Fay's invitation but he wanted to distance himself from it and, if possible, avoid entering that bedroom, so packed with the past, whilst this intruder was occupying it.

An aura of the morning's grilled bacon lingered in the kitchen but it no longer made his mouth water. He stood in front of the cooker, inspecting the dirty pans, debating whether he could face another fry-up. Usually, when Fay went away, she left a comprehensive list of what he should eat and where he would find it. He wasn't sure why she did this – he had a feeling that it wasn't totally for his convenience. It would be just like her to have a stockpile of survival rations somewhere which she was determined he shouldn't plunder. He checked the work-surfaces and pin-up board but found no such instructions. He'd change then decide later what to cook.

Neil was taking the last box upstairs. They met in the hall and Jack realised that it was going to be like this from now on. There would be another person in the house, moving about, making noises, cooking in their kitchen, smelling different. Listening to *him* making noises and smells. 'How's it going?'

'Not too bad.'

'Much more stuff?' He gestured towards the box which, he noted, had originally contained tinned peaches. 'Things?' It sounded like a criticism and he hurried to add, 'It's a decent sized room. Plenty of space.'

The boy shook his head. 'Not much more. Just a rucksack of clothes. And my guitar, of course.'

He should have known that the lad would play guitar.

He went into their bedroom, shut the door and listened. No sound at all came from the adjacent room and he wondered how Neil was feeling. Whether he was on the other side of the wall, wondering what it was going to be like, living with his ex-English teacher and her husband. The total silence seemed unnatural now that there was someone else in the house and, to counteract this, he put the bedside radio on, whistling as he stripped off to take his second shower of the day. His mother would have commented on this extravagance, and she was probably right. Only recently he'd read that bathing too frequently washed all the beneficial oils from the skin and caused the sweat glands to work harder. If a human being went without washing for six weeks, 'things' didn't get any worse and the body reached some kind of stasis. He'd mentioned it to Fay but she hadn't bothered to comment.

There was still no sign of Neil when he went back down to the kitchen. Had he slipped away without saying anything? He went into the hall, and called up the stairs, 'Anything you need, Neil?'

Neil came onto the landing and gave the thumbs-up. The gesture looked passé and awkward. 'I'm fine thanks. Been putting a few things away. Oh, and thanks for the telly.'

Jack doubted whether he would be able to pick out Neil

Bentley in an identity parade. Medium height. Medium build. Mid-brown hair. His own children were rather distinctive looking. Caitlin – tall, redhaired. Dylan – tall, black hair, patrician nose. Kingsley – tall, thin, dark-brown hair in a ponytail, earring. At least that's how he'd looked the day he left.

'No problems.'

Out of the blue, a feeling of compassion towards this nondescript young man swept over him. He didn't have a lot going for him, did he? *No problems?* No job, no home, no family – a list of major problems in Jack's book. Could this be the thing that had touched Fay and induced her to take him in? Or might it be because he was a direct, if sketchy, link with Kingsley? No. It was more likely that, having never come to terms with her failure to mould her younger son, she needed to notch up some successes and she'd identified Neil Bentley as a lad ripe and ready to be 'set straight'. *Poor sod.*

'Neil… I was just about to have a beer. Fancy one?'

They stood in the kitchen, sipping from the cold bottles. Jack wished he'd been more attentive when Fay had talked to him. All he could remember was that, up until recently, the boy had been selling perfume in a department store – not a promising starting point for a conversation.

'Heard from King lately?' Neil, probably also searching for a way to connect, asked the obvious question.

Fay would have deflected the inquiry, in an effort to save face, but she wasn't there and Jack could give an honest reply. 'No. We mail him regularly but we haven't heard for weeks. To be honest, we have no idea where he is. Or what he's doing. It's, ummm…' he paused, 'It's worrying.' He took a swig from the bottle.

'Yeah. I had the same thing, in reverse though, when my parents buggered off,' he gave a sheepish grin, 'Sorry.

When my parents went to Spain.' He pondered for a moment, tapping the lip of the bottle against his chin. 'Maybe I can find out for you. We keep in touch. Nothing regular. Nothing heavy. '

It had never crossed Jack's mind that his son might have been in contact with his old friends but, considering the younger generation's love affair with the internet, it was so obvious. 'When did you hear from him last, then?' He tried not to sound too desperate, too anxious.

Neil thought for a while. 'Well, it was definitely after I bumped in to Mrs Waterfield in Robertson's, so, what, three weeks ago? I mailed him that evening and he replied a few days later.'

'Any idea where he is? Did he mention a child? Did he mention us?'

Neil thought again. 'No. He just said something like "Did my mother tell you to take your hands out of your pockets?" The rest of it was about a big festival he'd been to. Sounds as if he's having a great time.' He took another sip of beer, 'I should let him know that I've moved in. I'll go to the library and mail him, tomorrow.'

'Why not use my machine?' Jack felt as if he were casting a line across a tranquil pool and, sensing a bite, started to reel it gently in. 'Save you traipsing to the library. It's in the study.' He pointed to towards the hall. 'I was going to say, whilst you're here, feel free.'

Neil smiled. 'Thanks. That'd be great. Fay's promised to help me knock out a CV. My English isn't so hot.' The young man rocked on the balls of his feet.

'You can use it now if you like.'

Neil shook his head. 'Oh, I mustn't hold you up. You'll be wanting to get on with your meal.' He tipped his head back, drinking the rest of the beer, then placed the empty bottle on the draining board.

'Have you eaten? We could get a delivery. Chinese? Curry? Pizza?' Jack lifted the dirty pans from the stove. 'Tell you what, I'll wash these up whilst you have a session on the machine. You might as well mail Kingsley right away.' Did that sound weird? 'And anyone else, of course.'

'The Star of Bengal does a good biryani, if that suits you.' Neil suggested.

They found the number in *Yellow Pages* and placed their order. Then Jack settled Neil in the study and switched on the machine. 'Anything you need?' He wanted to stand at the lad's shoulder and tell him what to say, what questions to ask, but he forced himself in to the garden and completed the round of evening tasks. He watered the hanging baskets and tubs before wandering into the shed.

The garden shed had become the butt of many family jokes. Once, when they'd all been ready to set off on holiday, Jack had popped in there to sharpen his penknife and they found him, dead to the world, in the old armchair which he'd rescued from the skip. It was here that he retreated to avoid unwelcome visitors and Jehovah's Witnesses. Sometimes, after Fay had finished mocking his use of *verbal* cliché, she would line his shed up in her sights, too, groaning, 'A man and his shed. You are *so* predictable, Jack.'

He checked the tool rack to make sure everything was dangling from the correct hook, swept the floor, crossed yesterday off the calendar and freed a butterfly that was beating its wings against the window. How long did it take to send an email? 'How long is a piece of string, John bach?' His grandfather's response to unanswerable questions echoed in his memory. This had bemused and frustrated him until his grandmother taught him to reply, 'Twice as long as half of it.'

He managed to occupy fifteen minutes before returning to the house. Neil was in the kitchen drying the things from the draining board. 'Thought I'd make myself useful. Oh, I left the machine on in case you need it.'

The meal arrived, and Jack waved aside Neil's offer to go halves. 'No. My suggestion, my treat.'

They ate in the kitchen, and during the course of a curry, several more beers and a large bowl of toffee fudge ice cream, they got to know each other better. Jack could see that the lad was nervous and he tried to make it easier for him by asking him questions about himself, but this soon began to sound like a job interview and he stopped, whistling to cover the silence as he stacked the dishwasher.

'What's that?' Neil asked.

'Pardon?'

'That tune you're whistling.'

Jack had no idea what he'd been whistling. Whistling had become a sort of automatic thing he did when he was embarrassed or uncomfortable. Fay wittered. He whistled.

'How did it go?' Neil, who had seemed pretty reserved until now, came into his own. With almost total accuracy he regurgitated 'The Rigs o' Marlow', one of the tunes that the Wicker Men regularly used. 'Something like that?'

Jack explained what the tune was, which necessarily led on to an explanation of why he knew it. Neil took the news that his landlord was a Morris dancer without any of the usual smirks and quips about bells and hankies that Jack had come to expect. He appeared to be genuinely interested and asked lots of sensible questions, focussing mainly on the music side of it. 'Any chance of catching one of your gigs?' he asked.

Jack stared at him. There was no hint of mockery or

condescension on his face. 'No problem. We practise every Thursday evening in term time, at the community centre.'

'Thursday it is, then.' Neil glanced at the clock, 'Better be on my way. Thanks for the meal. See you tomorrow.'

When Neil had gone, Jack took the debris from the meal out to the bin. It was a warm evening and he sat on the garden seat, head back and eyes closed, listening to the night noises. Miles above a plane droned; someone laughed a few gardens away; milk bottles chinked and a front door slammed. He thought back a couple of weeks to Laura's visit, when the three of them had sat here together. Then, alone and slightly drunk, he risked another peep at the past, watching himself and Laura making love, imagining how they might look today, grey-haired, less athletic but a lot more experienced. A police siren, out on the dual carriageway, tore through his reverie and he jumped up, like a schoolboy caught doing something unsavoury.

He lay rigid in bed, arms at his sides and he wondered if he was having some kind of breakdown. Every weekend there were articles in the supplements about 'the male menopause', but he'd never bothered to read them. He debated going down to the study and Googling the phrase, but he wasn't very successful whenever he tried to find information on the internet. Maybe the additives in the curry were causing some kind of personality change. Could E numbers trigger off lewd fantasies? Another thing to Google. He tried to calm himself, to get his thoughts under control, by thinking about Llangwm and the wonderful hours he'd spent with Non. There. He was at it again. He couldn't blame his feelings for Non on E-numbers.

Laura. Non. Oh. And there was Fay.

19

'DON'T THINK I'M TRYING TO SAVE THE PLANET or anything like that,' Isabel assured them as she paid the taxi driver for the journey from the train station. 'My car's off the road and Geoffrey refused to lend me his, miserable prick.' She delved into her turquoise leather bag and produced a bottle of vodka, holding it aloft like a sporting trophy. 'I intend to anaesthetise myself for the return journey.'

Before Isabel's arrival, Fay had done the best she could with a few litres of water heated in the kettle. She'd washed her hair and attempted what her grandmother used to call an 'all over wash'. The plumber had turned up while they were eating breakfast but he'd disappeared again in search of a spare part for the twenty-year-old boiler. 'If he can't fix it, I'll ask my neighbour if we can shower next door.' Laura's promise sounded more like a threat.

Isabel was wearing a chocolate-brown linen shift with matching jacket, her hair in a single plait, loose but neat, down her back. Her sandals exactly matched her bag and she looked even thinner than she had a few weeks ago. 'God, I must look a sight. We've had the decorators in and I can't get at half my clothes.'

Laura, today in a different washed-out tee-shirt and baggy cotton trousers, laughed. 'Yeah, yeah. A real sight.'

Fay didn't want to pursue any conversation where

they might end up talking about how smart and young Isabel looked. 'What a shame you've got to go back this evening.'

They discussed what they might do to make the most of their day together. Without a car between them, Laura suggested a few places they could reach by bus.

Isabel shuddered. 'Two train rides in one day – that's my dose of public transport for the year. I'm happy to stay in your sweet little house and get quietly wrecked. Or,' she pointed through the window to the garden, where Cassidy was pumping up the tyre on his bicycle, 'can't we persuade your gorgeous son to drive us somewhere?'

'I'm happy to stay here, too.' Fay didn't care for Isabel's proprietorial tone. 'And someone has to be on hand for the plumber. Don't they?' She looked to Laura for confirmation. Much as she loved the idea of driving around the countryside with Cassidy, her daydream didn't include Isabel, whom she knew would end up sitting next to him. People with long legs always got to sit in the front.

The rest of the morning drifted away in indecision. Laura suggested a trip to a local park, where the annual sculpture exhibition was on display. Isabel favoured a shopping expedition, if they really had to go somewhere. They sat in the garden, Isabel returning to the house at frequent intervals to replenish her glass. During her third or fourth absence Laura remarked 'Something must be wrong for her to get up at the crack of dawn and fag all the way here on the train. And she's half way through that bottle already.'

They stopped talking as Isabel emerged from the back door, drink in hand. 'Talking about me?'

'Yes,' Laura confessed. 'We think something's wrong. Is it?'

Isabel slumped back into her deckchair and shut her

eyes. She took a long gulp from her glass and waited until she had their complete attention. 'Geoffrey wants a divorce. He's found someone else.'

Fay contained her laughter. Last time they'd been together, the implication had been that she and Geoffrey had both had a string of lovers, so why should this particular liaison be causing such a problem?

'Don't you have a what-d'you-call-it,' Laura echoed her thoughts, 'an open marriage?'

Isabel, ignoring this question, stared past her friends, as though the next-but-one garden held the solution. 'She's plain and dowdy. Rather plump. She's called Margaret. D'you know what he said to me?' Neither Fay nor Laura dared hazard a guess. 'He said he wants to grow old with someone "homely and comfortable". He makes her sound like an old cardigan. In fact that's what I'm going to call her from now on. The Old Cardigan.'

They sat in silence, Fay staring into her own lap, picturing a silver-haired Geoffrey and a dumpy little woman, in armchairs on either side of a crackling blaze. A dog slept at their feet and they were, indeed, comfortable.

'What aspect of this are you finding so upsetting?' Laura asked, in a matter-of-fact tone.

'Oh, God, I don't give a stuff who Geoffrey sleeps with, if that's what you mean. It's just that for twenty-odd years I've played the role of Stepford fucking wife at all those fucking law functions. I've produced a perfect set of offspring to continue the Lauderdale dynasty. That was the deal and I more than kept my side of it. How dare the bastard dump me for…' Isabel flapped her hands around, as if trying to grab the right words.

'An old cardigan?' Fay helped her out.

Laura stood up. 'I'll make some coffee.'

Fay emptied the whole bottle of bath foam from her travel toiletries into the steaming water. She was ashamed to have coped so badly during the boiler crisis but, now that Isabel was safely on her way back to London, she felt entitled to reward herself with a long soak. The entire afternoon had been focused on Isabel and her inability to face the future without Geoffrey's money or status. 'And what will people think,' she'd moaned, 'when they see him with her? What will they think about *me*?'

Laura had tried to put it in perspective but Isabel was determined to make a drama out of it. 'I know he's got to support me in the manner, etcetera, etcetera, but I won't get compensation for all the sniggering and finger-pointing, will I? They'll think I'm fucking frigid or something.'

At last she'd gone and Fay could look forward to an evening with Laura and – her heart raced – Cassidy. Laura was chopping things in the kitchen and there was an encouraging smell of roasting chicken, rising up the stairs. The fragrant water and relief after the strain of the day with Isabel released her to a place between sleep and wakefulness. Somewhere a phone rang and she could hear the rise and fall of voices in conversation.

From nowhere, a recollection of Jack popped into her mind. There he was, a young husband and father, carrying Dylan on his shoulders and holding Caitlin by the hand, wandering along a shingle beach. His hair was a little too long, just how she used to like it, and his shapely legs were strong and tanned. Where was it? Cornwall? West Wales? Everything was so straightforward, then, and everything seemed possible. It had started to go wrong when Kingsley was born. The birth was traumatising and he'd been such a fretful baby.

Laura tapped the door. 'You asleep? Caitlin rang. She's going to come for supper. She can sleep in with you. That's okay isn't it?'

Fay sat up and pushed her damp hair away from her face. 'What about Sarah?'

'She didn't say, but I have a feeling that Cass had something to do with it. Anyway, she won't be here for an hour or so. No rush.'

Fay's plans for an intimate evening swirled down the plughole with the bath water. She lingered upstairs, knowing that, once Caitlin arrived, she would become plain 'Mum' and not the vivacious sophisticate that she'd intended to be. Much as she loved Caitlin, she would have been happier not to see her until tomorrow.

The kitchen was hot and messy, every surface strewn with packets, jars and cooking utensils. Laura, flushed and perspiring, still wore the clothes she'd had on all day, without even an apron to save her from the fallout, and there was a white line across her tee-shirt, where she'd leant against a floury worktop. 'It's lovely to be cooking for four people.' She stopped slicing beans and looked up. 'Gosh. Very swish.'

'Can I do anything?' Fay, dressed as she was in navy linen skirt and white shirt, hoped her offer would be refused.

Laura nodded towards the dining room. 'I've dumped all the stuff on the table, if you want to set it. There's white wine in the fridge. Help yourself.'

Fay did her best to smooth the creases from the un-ironed cloth as she moved around the table. Not for the first time, she noted the shabbiness of the furniture and, spotting the cobwebs undulating between the curtain pole and the ceiling, wondered whether Laura's eyesight was deteriorating. She found a paper napkin and was giving the cutlery and wine glasses a vigorous rub, when she realised that Cassidy was standing in the hall, watching her.

'My Grandmother used to say "you eat a peck of dirt before you die". I thought she meant *a speck*, but I think it's more likely to be a peck in this house. As in bushels and pecks?'

'You're much too young to know about bushels and pecks.' Fay blushed and fumbled the glass, catching it clumsily before it fell to the floor. 'Your mother tells me that Caitlin is coming for supper. I'm a little confused.'

Cassidy grinned. 'I persuaded her to dump Sarah. I promised that she'd have much more fun here.'

'Well, as long as she wasn't rude.'

'She told her that you needed to go back to Cardiff this evening. Some sort of family emergency.'

Fay tried to laugh but was shocked, not so much by the cavalier way he and Caitlin had treated Sarah, but how unashamedly he admitted that they'd dragged her into the deception. She felt as if she'd been included in something underhand but, at the same time, exciting. 'It's very hot in here. Could we have a window open?'

Cassidy chose to open the window behind her and, in squeezing past, his arm brushed across her breast. 'Sorry.' He gave a knowing smile as he pushed the sash window up. 'Better?'

When Caitlin arrived, she had the decency to be a little shamefaced about the way she had treated Sarah but they were soon diverted by Laura's announcement that supper was ready. Fay, catching sight of her fiery cheeks in the tiny kitchen mirror as she helped carry the meal to the table, resolved not to drink any more. She and Laura hadn't anywhere near kept pace with Isabel during the emotional afternoon but, even so, she knew she'd had enough alcohol for one day. She would need to have her wits about her this evening.

Laura's dining table was circular. Fay was first to sit down. With only four of them, Cassidy would be sitting next to or opposite her. She was happy with either. He pulled back the chair next to hers for Caitlin and this old-fashioned courtesy seemed somehow intimate, as though he were laying claim to her daughter. He took the seat opposite and, not for the first time, Fay wondered whether this adorable young man was as wholesome as he looked. Perhaps her own less than pure intentions were corrupting her analysis of what she was seeing.

'So, I missed Isabel.' Caitlin sounded genuinely disappointed.

'Yes. She left at about five, to catch a train.' Fay put her knife and fork down and turned to Laura. 'D'you think we should check that she's home?'

Laura glanced at her watch. 'She's due in about now. I'll ring her as soon as we've finished eating. Mind you, I can't think she'll be in any fit state to go to a dinner. Not with Geoffrey, anyway.'

'What's going on?' Caitlin asked and they gave her a resumé of Isabel's circumstances. 'Why would Geoffrey swap her for an old frump? I assumed every man wanted a glamorous wife like Isabel.'

Cassidy let out a spluttering laugh, 'Sorry.' He shook his head. 'Poor Isabel. She tries so hard but someone ought to take her aside and explain where she's going wrong.'

The three women stopped eating. Laura looked amused, Caitlin, intrigued and Fay – she hoped – disinterested. Cassidy carried on eating.

Caitlin was the first to crack, stamping her foot under the table. 'You can't stop there, Cass. What d'you mean "where she's going wrong"?'

'Women have their secrets which, I hasten to add, make them all the more fascinating, so I'm going to keep mine and hope it has the same effect.' He gave Caitlin what Fay could only describe as a 'flirty' look.

'Take no notice,' Laura interjected, 'He's feeling threatened. It's his pathetic attempt to rattle us.' She tapped the back of Cassidy's hand in mock chastisement. 'Behave. Or Cait will wish she's stayed in Derby.'

Laura went to phone Isabel whilst Fay carried the plates and serving dishes into the kitchen. She was aware that Cassidy was, once again, watching her, and she did her best to pull her stomach in, move elegantly and keep a serene half-smile on her face.

Caitlin pointed to a framed photograph standing, with several others, on the cluttered mantelpiece. It showed a girl of about thirteen or fourteen, astride a bicycle that was far too big for her. 'Is that Sadie?'

Cassidy reached up for the picture and wiped the dusty glass with a napkin. 'Yes. That is indeed my dear sister. She'd just swapped her roller skates and Mum's watch for that bike. Didn't think to ask permission but once Sadie's made up her mind…'

'She reminds me of someone.' Caitlin peered hard at the triumphant face. She turned the photograph around for Fay to see. 'Who does she remind me of, Mum?'

Fay, not willing to admit that everything was out of focus when she wasn't wearing her glasses, pretended to study the picture. 'Must be one of your friends.'

'What's she doing these days?' Caitlin asked. Fay waited for Cassidy's answer. She always felt uncomfortable questioning Laura about Sadie, in case there was something dreadful to report.

'They're living in London. Finsbury Park. Sadie's temping and Joe's got a job on a magazine, doing something digital. I saw them last week. They seem to be going through a good patch.' He raised his eyebrows and shook his head. 'The man must be a saint.'

Laura returned after a few minutes. 'Yes. Izzy's home safely. She sounded remarkably bright and breezy considering how miserable she was all day. I think someone was there with her.'

'I'm sure Isabel never has a problem rustling up company.' It was only after the words were out of her mouth that Fay realised how bitchy she sounded.

'Any pudding, Mum?' Cassidy asked. 'It's just that Cait and I are thinking of popping into town. See what's going on.'

'Typical. We prepare a lovely meal,' Laura generously included Fay although she'd contributed nothing, 'And all you want to do is stuff it down and dump us like a couple of Cinderellas.' She dropped her shoulders, as if spurned.

'Yep. That's about it. But we love you both to pieces, don't we Cait?'

Caitlin wasn't used to engaging in this kind of banter with her mother and looked uneasy. 'Is that okay with you two? You're welcome to come with us, aren't they Cass?'

'Of course they are,' he replied, deadpan.

'Don't be ridiculous. There's apple pie and cream in the kitchen. Help yourselves. Fay and I are going to have a relaxing evening here, carry on our chat and go to bed at a reasonable time. I rather fancy doing the crossword, don't you?' Laura waited for Fay's nod. 'You're on the zed-bed in your Mum's room, Caitlin.'

They ate their pie without ceremony and Laura opened the paper at the crossword as the youngsters left to catch the bus into the city centre.

Fay lay in bed, unable to sleep and wondering whether it was even worth trying if Caitlin was going to come in and wake her again. Caitlin – the child who never gave her cause for concern; who behaved impeccably; who was reliable and responsible. But could she have got it wrong? What Fay had interpreted as reserved and well-behaved might be devious and secretive. And she had no idea how she behaved when she was out with her friends. Completely wild and uninhibited, maybe. It was possible that she went to dubious dives, – did they have dives these days? – bared midriff, hair dishevelled and spiky.

Her misgivings dissolved when she remembered that Caitlin was a *dentist* and dentists were a prosaic bunch. Banality seemed a prerequisite for the job. Dafydd Morgan was the only exception she could think of. She pictured him, on that steamy July evening after graduation, in the kitchen of the flat he shared with Jack, singing a selection from Carmen whilst he cooked sausage and chips. He was stark naked and clearly trying to impress her with his skills and assets. Writing him off as an exhibitionist; a buffoon; she'd made her choice. Would she have made the same decision if she'd known that Dafydd would end up as a senior consultant and Jack a Morris dancer?

20

EACH TIME FAY WOKE, SHE CHECKED THE CAMP BED. It was years since she'd suffered this sleep-depriving anxiety and she had no idea whether she should be worrying. Caitlin and Cassidy had gone into the city on the bus, so they couldn't have been involved in a car accident. Unless, of course, they'd accepted a lift from one of Cassidy's friends, who might be over the limit. It didn't help that the city had such an appalling reputation. What if they'd been mugged and were fighting for their lives in A&E? She pummelled the pillow and turned over. Why was she getting into a state? Caitlin was having the time of her life somewhere – probably in Cassidy's bedroom.

At five-thirty the camp-bed was still empty. She crept along the landing to the bathroom. Laura's door was open a couple of inches and she heard the bed creak as her friend turned over in her untroubled sleep.

The adjacent door – Cassidy's door – was shut tight. She paused outside, her ear to the door – but if they *were* together in there, they were well past the noisy stage.

The bright light in the bathroom shocked her into full wakefulness and she peered at herself in the de-silvering mirror above the sink. Beneath her usual crop of freckles which had been accentuated by a day in the sunshine, her face was pale; her squinting eyes particularly insignificant.

Her night, and her face, had been made wretched by two peoples' selfishness. Resentment started to build. 'Sod it.' She pulled the flush, leaving the bathroom door wide open to ensure that the swishing and hissing filled the house.

She climbed back into bed and tried to read but her book didn't engage her. Her imagination gathered momentum, weaving the more compulsive story of Caitlin's night with Cassidy and she was horrified to feel faint stirrings of lust. She got up again and checked her watch. It was six o'clock and when she pulled the curtain back she saw that the night-sky was marbled with the beginnings of dawn. A milk float hummed then stopped and she heard chinking milk-bottles, somewhere beyond the terrace of houses which backed on to Laura's garden. Most of the houses were still in darkness but, here and there, lights shone in kitchens and bedrooms.

She dressed in yesterday's creased clothes, ran a comb through her hair and went downstairs. Whilst the kettle boiled, she unbolted the back door and went into the garden. The world smelled freshly laundered, as it had at the start of every summer's day when she was a little girl. Deciding not to bother with breakfast, she took an apple from the fruit bowl on the kitchen table, grabbed her handbag and went out of the front door.

She chose a different route from the one they had taken to the pub, surprised at how many people were already on the move. Where were they going at this hour on a Saturday? Hospitals changed shifts at strange times; and maybe factories clocked on at seven or seven-thirty. If there were factories in central Nottingham, would they be working on Saturday? She'd ask Laura when she got back.

Fay increased her pace, keeping up with this army of people, every one of whom was heading purposefully somewhere. She came to a dual-carriageway. Two lanes of traffic sped in both directions, making it impossible to cross the road, and she used the dank concrete underpass, graffitied and litter-strewn but which, in the clear morning light, felt completely safe.

The route she took appeared to be leading her towards the city centre. Jack would have been able to tell from position of the sun, or some inbuilt compass, whether he was walking south or west or whatever. She tried to visualise the road-map which they'd used to navigate to Laura's house, but this morning she'd zig-zagged through the streets and couldn't work out where she was.

Houses gave way to shops. Useful shops. Dry cleaner, florist, post office – none of them open yet. The newsagent, however, was doing a brisk trade and she went in. Several paper-boys were collecting their morning deliveries, stashing piles of papers into fluorescent yellow satchels. Gruff-voiced and gangly, they were clones of the lads who would be confronting her next week with uninspired excuses for late homework or lost textbooks. They pushed and shoved, in the way that boys do when they can't think of any other way to show affection towards each other. She envied them, living completely in the here-and-now, at the centre of their own lives, as they spilled, laughing and untroubled, out of the shop.

She bought the *Independent* and some cigarettes. 'Is there anywhere here I could get a coffee?' she asked the Asian shopkeeper.

In lilting cadences, not dissimilar to the Welsh, he directed her to a café in the next street. 'The place looks a little scruffy but it's very clean and they do a delicious sausage sandwich. Tell them Raj sent you.' He made the suggestion of a stiff bow.

It was the sort of down-at-heel place she would

normally walk past but, once inside, the smell of fresh coffee and grilling bacon was irresistible. She ordered a large black coffee and was about to pay when she added, 'And a sausage sandwich, please. Raj tells me they're the best in town.'

The woman on the other side of the Formica counter was about Fay's age. Plump and solid, with dry, home-bleached hair, she smiled. 'You a friend of Raj's, then?'

Did she look like a friend of an Asian newsagent? Maybe she did, in her creased clothes and without a trace of makeup. Before she had chance to respond, the woman continued, 'He's like a dog with two tails since the results came out.'

Results? Was the poor man ill? She must have looked confused because the woman elaborated, 'You heard that his daughter got four As in her exams? Off to be a doctor.'

Fay sat in the corner near the window, half reading her paper, looking up as customers came and went, all taking breakfast out in lidded cups and paper bags. There was something glamorous, European, risqué, about *not* eating breakfast in one's own kitchen. But there were no cafés in the suburb where they lived, and she would have to drive for several miles if she wanted to get a sausage sandwich in a paper bag.

In a quiet moment, the woman came across, refilled her coffee mug and chatted about a film she'd watched on television the previous evening. Fay felt like an explorer, making landfall on a new continent and she regretted that she would never become Raj's friend or meet his industrious daughter. She wished that she could tell someone about her expedition. It was eight o'clock. Jack should be awake now, even if he wasn't up and dressed, and she scrolled through the list on her mobile until she reached their home number. It was engaged. Who on earth could he be talking to this early on a Saturday? Disappointed, she dropped the phone back into her handbag.

The terraced streets had little to distinguish one from the next and she took a few wrong turns before finding her way back. Caitlin's car was still parked opposite. This shouldn't have surprised her but it did because, although she'd only been away from the house for a couple of hours, it seemed to her that she'd taken a week's holiday in a different country. She glanced up at the front bedroom, where Laura slept. The curtains were still closed and she had no keys. She tapped gently and, when no one came to the door, she perched on the wall, lighting a cigarette and trying to fathom out why she'd been so entranced by her early-morning sortie.

'Not *another* dirty stop-out.'

Fay turned to see Caitlin and Cassidy, looking bright and fresh, strolling towards the house from the opposite end of the street. She stubbed out her cigarette and fixed a cheery smile on her face, hoping it would compensate for the lack of make-up. 'I went for a wander and I forgot to take keys.' She stared Caitlin in the eye. 'I didn't want to wake anyone.' She paused, 'But *you* obviously weren't there to wake.'

Cassidy produced a set of keys from his pocket and opened the front door, standing back for her to enter. 'Didn't Mum pass on the message? She said you'd already gone to bed, but I thought she might have let you know. We didn't want you to worry, did we Cait? She's hopeless.'

Caitlin, rather eagerly Fay thought, joined in. 'We stayed with Cass's friends. They've got a fantastic place. Huge. Part of a converted bus depot. We had a sofa each, didn't we?' She looked to Cassidy for confirmation.

'Yes, unfortunately.'

Laura appeared at the top of the stairs, still in her nightdress. 'They've explained where they were? I didn't think it was kind to wake you. And you knew Cait was in good hands.'

Jack was tipping milk onto his cornflakes when the phone rang. He was surprised that Fay was up and about so early. But it wasn't Fay.

'Morning, Jack. Thanks for last night.' It was Neil. 'Is it okay to bring the rest of my stuff over this morning? I've got to be out of this place by midday.

'Of course. Fay's due back this afternoon so I'll be confined to barracks, making sure it's all ship-shape.' He had no idea why he was adopting the persona of hen-pecked husband or speaking in military clichés. In fact he'd better make an effort to be assertive, right from the start, if he were intending to earn Neil's respect. 'Oh, and Neil, anything back from Kingsley?'

Neil explained that he hadn't had time to check his email during the twelve hours since he last saw Jack.

'Never mind. You can do it here,' Jack replied. 'See you soon.'

One thing Jack had to do was ensure that there was nothing – not one single thing – to indicate his transaction at the building society. He put the red passbook back in the bureau, exactly where it had come from. He checked that there were no give-away scraps of paper in the waste-paper baskets. He went through their email to ensure that the patronizing teller hadn't been super-efficient and done something stupid, like confirm the withdrawal of such a large sum. He hadn't.

In his 'Inbox' there was a reminder from Stan that rehearsals for the Wicker Men would start again the following Thursday. Stan was attending computer classes for the 'silver surfer' and he'd become besotted with the technology. However, the temptation to press 'send' was so great that he often forgot to include everything in his first message. A second mail, sent seven minutes later, added a fixture to the schedule which he'd circulated the previous week:

> *An extra date for your diaries, lads. Llangwm*
> *Harvest Celebrations. Saturday 27th September.*
> *Short notice but hope you can all make it.*
> *Stan.*

Elation and panic centred themselves in Jack's lower intestine and he headed for the cloakroom where he sat on the lavatory, marshalling his thoughts. Since his visit to Llangwm a couple of days ago, he'd been trying to come up with a plausible excuse for another weekend away. It was too soon for a second dental conference and, unlike Fay, he didn't have friends whom he might conceivably visit on his own. It was wonderful, therefore, to be supplied with a *bona fide* reason to return to Llangwm.

When Iolo had turned up at the surgery the other day, his two lives, because that's how he'd started think of them, collided. Iolo's second visit was ostensibly to collect some tickets for the Opera. Not wonderful, but Jack needed a credible excuse for handing him a brown envelope containing the cheque. Fortunately, only Sheila had witnessed these encounters and he was confident that his explanations for the events had convinced her. But if the Wicker Men, a thoroughly garrulous crowd, were let loose in Llangwm, anything could happen. He had three weeks to fathom out a way to avoid disaster.

Alarm quenched his euphoria.

Jack was in the shed, cleaning his shoes, when Neil found him.

'Are those your dancing shoes? Cool.'

Jack glanced up. No one had ever called his shoes 'cool' before but the lad seemed genuinely taken with them. 'Yes. I like to give them a complete overhaul at the start of the season.'

Neil looked puzzled. 'I would have thought this would be the *end* of the season. Isn't Morris dancing a *summer* thing?'

'I suppose it is, strictly speaking. But we get booked for events all year round. Mind you, I often think we're there to pad out the programme. You know, along with the bouncy castle and face-painting.' Put like that, his hobby sounded like a waste of time and, to dispel that impression, he grabbed his bells and shook them violently.

Neil asked lots of surprisingly sensible questions about the Wicker Men. When he reached, 'Have you got them on video?' Jack began to feel uneasy.

'Neil. A word of advice. How can I put it?' He needed to warn Neil without painting Fay as some kind of prison warder. 'My wife's never been too keen on the dancing thing. She'd never stop me going or anything like that, but we tend not to talk about it much.' He paused uncertain how to proceed.

'No worries,' Neil winked, 'I don't want to blot my copybook on day one, do I?'

Jack hadn't set out to form an alliance with the lad and he hoped that, when Neil saw Fay and him together, he would realise what a devoted couple they were. This might involve some play-acting on his part but he was becoming pretty skilful at that.

Whilst Neil took the last consignment of his possessions upstairs, Jack put the kettle on and broke out a packet of chocolate Hob-Nobs. He wasn't sure how Fay saw things going when it came to, say, catering and washing. Surely she didn't intend Neil to eat with them, so they would have to agree some sort of cooking rota if they weren't to get in each others' way. Would she invite Neil to use their washing machine? It seemed harsh to expect him to traipse to the laundrette. Did laundrettes still exist?

He thought back to student days and the constant bickering about dirty lavatories and festering pedal-bins. Once, he'd been forced to confront Dafydd, when it became clear that he was helping himself to Jack's groceries. It might have turned nasty but Dafydd had roared with laughter, assuring Jack that he was more than welcome to pinch anything of his that he fancied. 'Except my women, of course.'

'Thanks for coming.' Laura hugged Fay and handed her a carrier bag. 'Lunch. Service station food is so dreadful. And so expensive.'

'Thank *you*. It's been a lovely end to the holidays.' Fay had only half her mind on what she was saying as she watched Caitlin and Cassidy making their farewells in the garden.

Laura must have misinterpreted the distracted expression on Fay's face as having something to do with their friend. 'I'll ring Isabel sometime over the weekend. I'm sure a lot of her bull-shitting is covering up her insecurity. We must give her our support.'

Fay stopped gazing into the garden and concentrated on what Laura was saying. 'Oh, come on. Where was she when *you* were the one needing support?'

Laura shrugged and gave a little smile. 'We're all different, Fay.'

They trooped out to the car. When Cassidy stooped to kiss Fay's cheek, he squeezed her arm, as if to confirm some special understanding between them. She was irritated at the ease with which he reduced her to a breathless schoolgirl, but was uncertain whether this was calculated behaviour or just his natural manner.

On the way home, they stopped at a service station on the M42. It was the last Saturday of the school holidays and the car park was packed. They sat on a grassy embankment, as far as they could from the rumbling traffic, eating the tasty lunch that Laura had provided.

'Did you have a good visit, Mum?' Until now they had limited their conversation to the passing countryside and what was on the radio.

'Lovely.' She paused. 'Well, not entirely lovely. Isabel was particularly wearing. Laura's brilliant at letting it go over her head but I can't seem to do that.' She pulled the pith from a segment of orange. 'What about you? I hope you haven't fallen out with Sarah.' Her words sounded like a reprimand.

'Not fallen out exactly. We don't have much in common any more. She banged on about some chap she's just split up with. And some weird diet she's on. I think she was quite relieved when I said I had to leave early.'

The air was tainted with petrol fumes from the filling station. Cars and lorries came and went.

'You and Cassidy seem to get on well.'

'Mmmm. We do.' A smile flitted across Caitlin's face as she tucked in to a piece of Laura's fruitcake.

21

CAITLIN DROPPED FAY OFF AT THE GATE, declining the invitation to come in. Fay thought this might be to avoid an inquest on her re-scheduled weekend. It was only as she unlocked the front door and spotted the unfamiliar jacket hanging on the newel post – she'd have to put a stop to that – that she remembered Neil was moving in today. She listened but the house was silent. 'Jack?' He must be around. Both cars were on the drive.

The kitchen was immaculate. No cups or plates left draining in the rack, the newspaper neatly folded in the magazine holder, the tea-towels over the rail. 'Jack?' She looked out of the window and saw them, Jack and Neil, chatting on the decking, coffee mugs on the table in front of them, for all the world as if they were life-long pals.

She went out to join them, and, on spotting her, Neil jumped to his feet. She trained all her students to do this when she entered the classroom and was flattered that the habit had stuck. 'Hello, Mrs… Fay.' He blushed, as though he had overstepped the mark by using her first name.

Jack remained seated. 'Good journey, love? You look a bit frazzled. I'll get you a coffee.' He glanced behind her. 'No Caitlin?'

'She had to get back for something.' With an outsider there, it wasn't the right time to tell him about their daughter's uncharacteristic behaviour the previous night.

Ignoring whatever Jack was muttering about extra dance fixtures, she drank her coffee, the rich, brown smell transporting her back to breakfast time. What was so remarkable about having breakfast in that shabby café? Why had she found it so delightful? 'I'd rather like to go out for breakfast tomorrow,' she interrupted. Jack stared at her, evidently not catching what she'd said. She tried again. 'Breakfast. What about finding a nice little place to get breakfast tomorrow?'

'No need, love. There's plenty of bread. And I picked up some milk this morning.'

Neil raised his hand. This pupil-teacher thing might become tiresome. 'There's a great caff near my old flat. Formica tables. Fantastic bacon baps.'

She extended her upturned hand towards him, acknowledging his contribution. 'Thank you, Neil. I was beginning to think I was speaking Urdu.' Seeing Jack's confusion, she relented and put on a cheery smile. 'Shall the three of us go, then? Let's celebrate the last day of the school holiday.' She stood up. 'Could you bring my bag upstairs, please, Jack?'

Jack hovered, watching her unpack. It unnerved her, as if there could be something amongst her dirty washing that she'd rather he didn't see. No doubt a psychiatrist would explain that she was, indeed, trying to hide something. But Jack was exceptionally unobservant. He'd barely commented on her recent 'new look', or her eagerness to re-establish her friendship with Laura. If he came home one day with a trendy haircut, and started wearing expensive shirts and handmade shoes, she would definitely know that he was up to something.

'Neil appears to be settling in,' she said.

'Yes. Nice lad. Seems pretty straightforward.' He squared up the pile of books on his bedside table. 'I'm not quite sure what the ground rules are, though.'

'Ground rules?'

'House rules, that's more the phrase I'm after. For example, will he be eating with us? What about his washing? Will he be allowed to bring friends back? That sort of thing.'

Fay hadn't considered any of these things but wasn't going to admit it. 'Of course he won't eat with us. Unless we invite him to. He'll have to use the kitchen after we've finished. Washing? I don't see any reason why he can't use our machine, as long as he treats it carefully and buys his own washing powder. Friends? No. I don't think so. Not with the pale carpets.' She had an aptitude for making quick, if not always correct, decisions and couldn't bear Jack's inclination to vacillate. 'What's he doing now?'

Jack peered out of the bedroom window. 'He's not in the garden. Must be in his room.'

His room. It would take a while for her to get used to that.

She filled Jack in on Geoffrey's decision to leave Isabel for a more homely woman. 'Very odd. But no doubt Geoffrey will make sure that Izzy's well provided for. She had hysterics at the prospect of people thinking she couldn't hang on to her man.'

'Sounds like a Charles and Camilla job to me.'

She'd forgotten how funny Jack could be; how, when they first knew each other, his quiet, anarchic humour had made him different from the rest. It had been such fun to sit in the pub, eking out one drink, listening to his stories about weird patients or his take on their fellow students.

She told him about Caitlin's premature return to Nottingham and her night on the tiles with Cassidy, trying to keep it light and humorous, not wanting to give a intimation of her own feelings.

'Caitlin's got her head screwed on. Can't imagine she'd be daft enough to get carried away by good looks,' he assured her. 'And how's Laura?'

'Oh, you know Laura. Loveable. Messy. Vague. Wise. Too bloody tolerant of everything and everyone.'

'It's a good job we're not all the same.'

'And, guess what? She told me she doesn't know who Sadie's father was. But I'm not sure I can believe that.'

'Well, as I said, it's a good job—'

'Perhaps she was just ahead of her time. These days, lots of young women prefer to go it alone. They look for a man who fits their criteria, use him as a sperm donor and send him on his way.'

'You're not suggesting that Caitlin—'

'Good heavens, no.' *Could* Caitlin be sizing Cassidy up as a possible father?

Music, not loud but quite distinct, filtered through the closed bedroom door. Neil was making himself at home. After they had run through the 'house rules' with him, she must put her mind to finding him a job and launch him back into the world, before he made himself too comfortable.

That afternoon, before Fay got back, Jack had encouraged Neil to check his email and was unable to contain his excitement when Neil called out, 'Yep. There's one from King.'

The message, sent that morning from an unfamiliar email address, was short but tantalising.

Neil, Mate.
   Not totally surprised to hear from you, considering the situation. On the move again.

I can recommend this nomadic life. I ALMOST came home when we won the Grand Slam. Next time, maybe.

Kingsley.

Tell M&D not to fret. Love to C&D.

Neil gave his trademark thumbs up. 'He's fine.'

'But that's not the email address *we* have for him.' Jack tapped the screen.

'I expect he's got a couple. Most people do. It's a way of filtering stuff.' Neil signed out and got up from the desk. 'I'd better go and unpack a few things.'

Jack tidied the kitchen, trying to recall every precious word of Kingsley's mail. How literally should he interpret the phrase 'nomadic life'? Was his son on 'walkabout'? To be truthful, there was nothing to indicate that he was still in Australia. He could be in Cornwall with a group of New Age Travellers for all they knew. But, if that were the case, even a bitter, angry Kingsley could not be so cruel as to stay away.

Jack put the crockery and cutlery away and scrubbed the worktops, obliterating every smear of grease, every splash of tea, until the kitchen looked like an operating theatre. 'Tell Mum and Dad not to fret.' *Fret.* Did the boy have no idea that his absence dominated their lives, like a smoking bomb crater?

He and Neil were having a coffee, in the garden, when Fay arrived home. Her presence seemed to fluster Neil. Not surprising, really. Jack imagined he would have felt the same if, when he was twenty-three, he'd gone to lodge with Mrs. Watkins – his dishy ex-geography teacher. While Fay was saying something about going out for breakfast and not listening to a word he was saying, he took the opportunity to tell her about the additional dance fixture.

When he decamped to Llangwm for a couple of days, three weeks hence, he would, quite truthfully, be able to say that he'd warned her. And Neil could act as witness for the defence.

After Fay had unpacked, they sat in the living room, Jack trying to identify the muffled music, no more than a bass beat, coming from upstairs. Dylan had lived at home until six months ago but he hadn't been terribly interested in music. He'd had a player in his room, but that was probably more because it was expected of him than to feed a hunger, whereas Kingsley would wilt if he were cut off from his source of musical supply for more than an hour or two.

'Have I missed anything? Is there any news?' Fay asked.

There *was* news. Neil's email correspondence with Kingsley was big news. And the disclosure that their son was on the move again was news. Jack looked up from the paper and cocked his head to one side, as though delving into his memory. 'Don't think so. No.' He wasn't ready to share it with her yet, in case she waded in and did something to frighten Kingsley off.

'Your parents are okay?'

'As far as I know.'

'But you went there on Thursday, didn't you?'

'Yes. Yes. They were fine on *Thursday*.' As Jack, on his way to Llangwm, had driven past the turn to their house, he had made a mental note to check that they *were* okay but it had slipped his mind. He must be more careful in future.

As soon as he could, under the pretext of running through his diary for the coming week, he slipped into the study and dialled their number, letting the phone ring longer than they could possibly take to reach it from anywhere in their tiny house. Five o'clock on a Saturday. They should be at home. He had a sudden but intense hunch that something was wrong. If he'd thought about it this morning, he would have had time to pay them a quick visit but now, aware of the fragility of his alibi, it preyed on his mind and, while Fay wittered on, he ran through it, coming to the conclusion that, if anything were amiss, he would have heard about it by now.

'So, shall we call Neil down?' Fay asked. 'The sooner we let him know how we see this going, the better.'

'Poor kid. We don't want him to feel that he's here under sufferance.'

Fay shook her head. 'I wish you'd make your mind up. You were the one who raised the "house rules" issue.'

Jack went in search of their lodger but the music had stopped and there was no response to his knock on the bedroom door. There was, however, a note, in small, neat writing, propped up against the vase of flowers on the kitchen table.

Just off out. Will try not to wake you when I come back. Thanks for everything. N.

Jack tried his parents several times during the evening. Eventually, at about ten o'clock, his mother answered. When he asked where they'd been, she explained that they'd been at home. 'Dad wouldn't let me answer. He's not feeling too bright but he didn't want you to know, so as you wouldn't worry. I knew it was you ringing all the time, though. I did that one-four-seven-one thing you told me about.'

'What's the matter with him, Mum?' It wasn't the moment to criticise their half-baked reasoning. 'What are the symptoms?'

She explained that Harry hadn't been 'too bright' for a couple of days. 'Nothing drastic, just a bit more breathless than usual. A bit dizzy, like, and off his food.'

'What does the doctor say?' He knew the answer before he asked.

'We didn't want to bother him. You know your dad doesn't like to make a fuss.'

'That'll look great on his tombstone, won't it? "Harry Waterfield – the man who didn't like to make a fuss".' There was silence and he was ashamed of his cruel jibe. 'I'll pop up now. No arguments. I'll be with you in half an hour.'

'I'll have the kettle on,' was all she said.

Fay offered to go with him, but she was the last person his mother would want around if they were in trouble, and he persuaded her that it would be more useful if she stayed at home, 'We might need you here to…coordinate things.' They both knew that this was nonsense but it was the let-out she needed.

He packed his pyjamas, a change of clothes for the next day and the remains of the Christmas brandy. 'One of us might need it,' he explained when Fay raised her eyebrows.

'Don't you think you should phone Marion? You know how funny she can be if she thinks she's being left out.'

'I'll wait until I get the lie of the land. There's no point in worrying her unnecessarily…' he trailed off and gave a sheepish grin. 'I'm as bad as they are.'

Fay kissed him gently and, he thought, lovingly. 'Let me know how he is.'

As he started the car, he imagined how it might appear to a nosey neighbour. Eleven o'clock, overnight bag in hand, he kisses his wife and drives away. Shortly after a young man arrives and lets himself in. That should keep them guessing.

It was the time when restaurants and pubs shut and there was a fair volume of traffic heading out of Cardiff. Jack drove more slowly than usual, reluctant to reach his destination, spinning out the precious moments before he got tangled up in whatever was unfolding in the little terraced house.

22

JACK FOLLOWED HIS MOTHER THROUGH TO THE BACK ROOM, where Harry was lying across the sofa, propped up on a pillow, wedged against the arm. From what Jack could see, his only concession to his 'not too bright'-ness was to have exchanged his trousers for pyjama bottoms. How small his father seemed, compressed on to the two-seater sofa; how invalid-like. This was partly due to his grey face and sunken cheeks but the impression was emphasised by the ever-present coffee table, dragged to within arm's reach, littered with the comforts of the sick room – the bottle of lemonade, the box of tissues, the bag of mint imperials and another of boiled sweets and the plastic bucket discreetly placed on the floor, between its splayed legs.

'Fuss about nothing,' he greeted his son.

'Probably.' Jack touched the back of his hand to his father's forehead, not because he had a clue what it might indicate, but because his mother would find it reassuring. 'Perhaps it would be a good idea to get you checked out. Put Mum's mind at rest.' He turned to her for confirmation and she nodded gratefully.

'I'll take it easy... tomorrow, then pop... down the surgery on... Monday.' Harry gasped his way through the promise. His chest had always been his weak point but tonight it sounded worse than Jack had ever heard it.

'Show John your ankles, Dad.'

His father made a feeble attempt to reach his right ankle but gave up and fell back against the pillow. Jack pulled up the pyjama leg and rolled down the nylon sock. Harry's leg ran straight down from the calf through to the foot without narrowing. The top of his foot was puffed up and there were indentations in the flesh where the elasticated sock had cut in. The other leg was the same.

'You'd be more comfortable in bed, Dad. Let's see if we can get you upstairs.'

But, even with both of them to lean on, Harry could barely shuffle to the door and his breathing sounded more distressed, his chest whistling and gurgling as he gasped for air. Jack recognised how disastrous it would be to get stuck half way up the stairs and they guided him back to the sofa.

'I'm going to phone the doctor.' Jack ignored his father's protestations. Out in the hall, Vi indicated the printed sheet on the telephone table *'What to do in case of a medical emergency out of surgery hours'*. He scanned through the instructions which appeared to forbid anyone to be ill after six pm or at weekends. No wonder his father would rather die than call the doctor. He went through the designated procedure, answering the same questions several times as his call was bounced from one disinterested voice to the next. Eventually he did what Fay would have made him do right from the start, and played the I'm-a-dentist-so-I-know-a-bit-about-it card. 'I've examined my father thoroughly and he needs to see a doctor. Now.'

Doctor Mansel, whom neither Vi nor Harry had seen before and whom Jack doubted was as old as Dylan, arrived about an hour later. 'I'd like to get you checked over, Mr Waterfield. Just to be on the safe side.' He was unconvincingly casual, but Harry played along with it and Jack sensed that his father was grateful to have the decision taken out of his hands. Even in these unhappy circumstances, Vi shone with pride at her son's authority, bustling about making cups of tea, while the doctor located a hospital bed for Harry.

Jack thought back a few hours, to when he and Fay had been cocooned in the safety of the sitting room. Even now, people all over the city – all over the world – were ignorant of what was waiting to come crashing in on their lives. Flood, fire, death, destruction. And it was inevitable that, whatever the hospital tests showed, the Waterfield family's cosy existence was about to lurch out of kilter, maybe for a short while or maybe forever.

'I'm going to make a couple of calls.' Jack went into the hall, glad to escape for a moment. First he rang Fay and updated her on what was happening. 'I shouldn't think I'll be home until we've got him settled somewhere,' he paused, 'And I'll probably have to bring Mum with me. I'll keep you posted.'

Next he phoned his sister. It wasn't a number that he knew by heart and he leafed through his parents' leather-bound address book. 'John and Fay Waterfield' and 'Marion and Richard Wells'. It shocked him to see that his mother had entered the names and addresses of her children so formally, in her neat, laboured handwriting. It was as if they were acquaintances, no more significant than the plumber or the couple they met last year on the 'turkey-and-tinsel' trip to Weymouth.

He dialled Marion's number. It rang seven or eight times before the answering machine cut in. He put the phone down and glanced at his watch. One o'clock. She and Richard would be in bed, ignoring the call. He rang twice more until his sister, terse and full of sleep, answered and he gave her a brief account of the situation, adding,

'There's no point in coming at the moment but I thought you'd want to know what was going on.'

Marion showed no emotion at his news, but she'd never been demonstrative and he left it at that, promising to ring again when he had more details.

The journey through the empty streets, following the ambulance that Kyle – they were now on first name terms with Doctor Mansel – had insisted on summoning, took about three quarters of an hour. The blacked-out windows in the rear door gave no clue as to what was going on inside, but Jack was encouraged to note that the vehicle was progressing at a steady pace, without wailing siren or whirling blue light. Now and then he shot a glance at his mother in the passenger seat. Her hands gripped the mock-leather holdall in which she'd packed Harry's pyjamas and toiletries and she stared ahead, as though her unremitting gaze could keep her husband safe.

He searched for words of reassurance. 'He's in good hands, Mum. They'll get him sorted out.' What he really wanted to ask was, 'How did it get to this stage?', but it might have had something to do with his failure to visit them on Thursday, and that was the last thing he wanted to hear.

The rest of the night was spent in the twilight zone of the Emergency Admissions Department; in stale-smelling unventilated rooms lit by fluorescent strip lights; in cubicles and side rooms, sitting on plastic chairs, drinking tepid drinks dispensed from a machine. Jack was sure that Limbo must be somewhere in the bowels of a city hospital during the night shift.

They stuck as close as they could to Harry as he was taken for blood tests and X-rays. He looked embarrassed to be on display, half-sitting, half-lying on the battered trolley, waiting for whatever might come next. They made small-talk until they ran out of cheerful clichés and Harry drifted into half-sleep. At about five o'clock, two burly porters took him up to the ward. The nurse supervising the process took the holdall, which Vi had been clutching since they left the house, suggesting, although it was clearly an instruction, 'Why don't you pop home? Have a nap and a bite to eat. We'll have him ready for visitors by two o'clock.' In those few hours his father had gone from being an independent man to an invalid, who needed to be prepared for visitors.

Fay watched the car pull away, relieved that, for once, Jack was the one having to deal with whatever this might turn out to be – crisis or false alarm. Without thinking, she slipped the chain on the front door then took it off again. Neil wasn't back, was he? It was so different when the person who hadn't come home yet was another mother's child. He was a nice enough young man but she wasn't obliged to lie awake all night, dreading that he'd been beaten up, or worse.

She went to bed and tried to read. At about midnight she heard the sound of the front door shutting gently, followed by soft footfalls on the stair. Neil or Jack? The footsteps passed her door. Neil.

She was asleep when Jack phoned. He sounded calm but she knew that his brain must already be wrestling with the implications of Harry's impending hospitalisation. The immediate problem would be what to do with Vi. Marion lived in Swansea and had a prestigious job with one of the big building societies. She was an unfathomable woman, without an iota of tenderness. When Marion's only son had been born, Fay had visited her in the maternity unit, and as the other mothers cooed over new babies and revelled in those few brief days when they were considered special, Marion read a book. There was no chance that she would drop everything to come and support her mother. No. It would fall to Jack. He lived near the hospital, had a spare bedroom and was too soft to refuse.

She went downstairs and made a pot of camomile tea, hoping that it would help her sleep. Tomorrow, or rather *today*, was the last day of the long holiday. She should be feeling relaxed and brimming with energy, ready to tackle the coming academic year, but instead she was feeling cross. Cross that they hadn't had a decent holiday. They'd gone away for a few days after the wedding but Paris was hardly the place to unwind and, for some reason, Jack had been irritatingly over attentive. Cross because she'd allowed herself to become infatuated with Cassidy. And crosser still that he could maintain his hold over her at the same time as making overtures to Caitlin.

Now Harry was doing his level best to disrupt her life. At least her own father had had the decency to drop dead whilst he was still in perfect health. In any case, her mother was an educated woman, accustomed to sorting out her own affairs. Fay doubted whether Vi had ever changed a plug, booked a holiday or spoken to the bank manager. The only time the Waterfields had been apart was when Harry was at work, and then it was as if Vi were holding her breath until he came home again. He'd finished work years ago and if anything happened to him, she would become dependent on Jack. How could anyone be so pathetic yet, at the same time, so controlling?

The camomile tea was failing to make her drowsy, and she flicked through the pages of the local paper. God, the stories were parochial – another cat rescued from a chimney; another barmaid shaving her head for a good cause; another petition against the closure of a branch library. She skimmed through the 'Situations Vacant' pages, on the off-chance that there might be something suitable for Neil. If he were offered a job next week, it was unlikely that he would start straight away and then it would be another month before he had his first pay check. Neil would be with them for a couple of months, if all went well, and goodness knows how long if it didn't.

The lavatory flush hissed. If Neil was still awake, he might as well keep her company. She called him down. 'I thought you might be wondering why the phone was ringing.' From his befuddled expression, it was clear that he hadn't heard a thing but he was evidently eager not to contradict his landlady and Fay continued, 'Jack's father's been rushed to hospital. Something to do with his breathing.'

Neil stifled a yawn. 'Sorry to hear that. He seems a nice old guy.'

It had slipped Fay's mind that Neil had met Jack's parents at the barbecue. And Harry *was* a 'nice old guy'. It was Vi that was the difficulty.

Before meeting them, she'd assumed that Jack's parents were working-class but well-educated. She'd imagined they came from the same Welsh stable as Aneurin Bevan or Elizabeth Andrews and it had disappointed, even shocked her, to discover that Jack's mother was so…so uncultivated. She wasn't proud of her reaction and had always told herself that, had Vi been a hilarious, optimistic, feisty woman, her shortcomings wouldn't have mattered. She could understand why Vi had been standoffish in the beginning – her son, her golden boy, had brought home a girlfriend whom she considered to be hoity-toity and 'posh English' – and it was obvious that Vi thought that Fay, in her attempts to dispel this impression, was playing Lady Bountiful. Maybe there *had* been a grain of truth in that. Then, when the children were born, Vi was constantly watching, assessing how good she was at putting on a nappy or getting wind up; silently criticising her decision to return to work or – Jack was never to blame – her choice of school; judging without offering assistance; bullying by aggressive meekness.

'Anything I can do to help?' Neil asked.

'Not at the moment, thanks.' Then, seeing the concern on his face she added, 'But I'm glad you're here to keep me company. Waiting is harder than having something to do, don't you think?' He nodded but she wasn't sure he understood what she was getting at.

They talked about school. It was a long while since he'd left, but he had an excellent memory, asking about various members of staff, many of whom still worked there. He was fascinated to hear the staffroom gossip, tutting like an old woman at any scandalous incidents, and in return updating her on several of his more unforgettable contemporaries.

'You may have disliked school, Neil, but spare a thought for us poor teachers. The whole ghastly cycle starts again on Monday. Oh, God, that's tomorrow.'

'I loved school, actually.' The simple statement sounded like a reproach. 'I would have stayed on but my Dad wanted me to join up. He said if it was good enough for him…'

Fay, reluctant to probe deeper in case she unearthed something she didn't want to hear, changed the subject. 'Did you go somewhere nice this evening?'

'The Kings Arms.'

'With friends? Or *a* friend?' She smiled, knowingly. It was possible that Neil had found a girlfriend.

'I've got a bar job there. Just to keep me going until I get something better.' He looked embarrassed. 'We never discussed rent. Will weekly be okay?'

Rent. Fay laughed. Neil was a child and children don't

pay rent. 'Good Lord, we don't expect you to pay rent.'

'But I can't impose—'

'And you're not going to.' Now it was established that Neil would be living with them, free of charge, she found it easy to lay down the house rules which she and Jack had formulated, and he seemed more than content to go along with everything. 'Anyway, you'll have a proper job in no time at all, and you'll want to find a place of your own.'

'That's so generous, Fay. I'll be sure to switch off the bedroom light when I go out. And I won't use all the hot water. And I can put the bins out for you. Things like that.' These modest promises painted a painful picture of the months he had spent in dismal flats and dreary bed-sits,

The phone rang. It was Jack, letting her know that Harry had been admitted and that he and his mother would be home in fifteen minutes. 'Off to bed you go, Neil. Someone might as well get some sleep. Looks like we'll have to put our breakfast plans on hold.'

It was getting light when the car pulled up. She took one last look around the kitchen – *her* kitchen – before Vi arrived and a new era began.

23

THE FIRST WEEK OF HARRY'S HOSPITALISATION DRAGGED as the medics, with no perceptible sense of urgency, plodded through the endless raft of tests. Bloods. X-rays. Monitoring input and output. Harry, stoic and uncomplaining, allowed himself to be prodded and pummelled; was grateful for the food set in front of him; did as he was instructed. He may have been no better, but he was certainly no worse.

Jack appreciated how hard the new arrangements were for Fay, but could see no immediate solution. When she came home, tired and edgy after a day at school, it wasn't easy having to share the house with his mother. It was as if Vi were an invalid too, dictating what they should eat – 'Now you know I don't like anything…foreign,' and which television programmes they watched – 'If there's one thing I won't put up with, it's bad language.' She issued regular and graphic bulletins of Harry's bodily functions – usually at mealtimes. 'They're flushing a lot of water out of him. He filled three bags in twenty four hours,' she announced proudly as they ate their chicken casserole.

She was disorganised – wilfully so – and most evenings, after popping in to the hospital, Jack was despatched up the valley, to collect this or that, see to the mail and water the tomatoes. Vi didn't go with him because she said that she found the house, without Harry, 'too upsetting'.

'Mum, couldn't you make a comprehensive list of what you need for, say, the next week? And why don't we give Annie Jenkins the key? She could see to the greenhouse and keep an eye on the place.' It sounded perfectly reasonable to Jack.

'Dad may be home in a couple of days,' she countered, 'and that Annie's a nosey madam. She'll be all over the house, poking and prying.'

Jack pictured the house and wondered what Annie Jenkins might find remotely interesting in the damp larder or the mothball-scented wardrobe.

Fay was more direct. 'After Jack's done a day's work and visited Harry, the last thing he needs is to spend another hour in the car.' But Vi wasn't budging. 'She's playing you for a fool,' Fay exploded when she tracked Jack down, in the shed, after yet another unsuccessful attempt to persuade her mother-in-law to be sensible. 'We all know she's as tough as old boots.'

'I know, love. I know. But she's all at sea. If we can just hang in there until we know what's going on with Dad, we can work something out.'

Caitlin and Dylan fitted visits to the hospital around busy schedules, both expressing regret that they were unable to do more to support their parents. Then reinforcements came from an unexpected source. Jack was locking the car after one of his evening sorties – this time to collect his mother's *spare,* spare pair of spectacles, a pale lemon cardigan and last Saturday's lottery ticket, which she'd forgotten to check – when Neil came out to join him. He'd been living with them for less than twenty-four hours when all this had blown up and the timing couldn't have been worse. Now Fay was back at school, he was stuck with Vi every day until she caught the bus to the hospital for afternoon visiting. Jack felt bad about it but there hadn't been a moment, in the past hectic week, to discuss it.

'Neil. How's it going? I wanted to catch you. It can't be much fun for you here—'

'It is, though.' Neil held up his hands. 'I don't mean it's *fun* exactly. But it's fine. It's what families are all about, isn't it? The ups and the downs. The laughter and the tears.'

It was difficult to follow the boy's reasoning. 'It's very kind of you to be so—'

'It isn't. Not really. To be honest, I've never been part of a proper family – a family who care about each other, look out for each other. I spent most of my time at home keeping my head down.' Neil rambled on, cheerily painting the grim picture of the seventeen years before he left home, only to be rejected by the army. 'I've had some great chats with Vi. I could listen to her all day. She's got the most amazing stories to tell. I'd love it if she was *my* gran.'

Jack thought he could see what the boy was getting at, and wondered if recruiting a grateful stranger, preferably one who had suffered childhood deprivation, might be the solution to the bickering and backbiting that plague most families.

He slapped Neil on the back, 'All I can say is that it's a pleasure having you here.'

'And *I* just wanted to say, if there's anything at all I can do, you only have to ask.'

That's when the idea crystallised. 'I think there is something. You've got a driving licence?'

Neil nodded.

'How would it be if we put you on Fay's car insurance? Just for a month or so. If you could do the occasional bit of running around – giving Mum a lift, picking up a few things from the shops – it would take the pressure off.' Fay might not be thrilled but Jack was confident that he could sell the proposal to her.

Jack salvaged every opportunity – alone in the car; in the shower; before he fell asleep or if he woke early – to relive his Llangwm experience, from that first moment when he rounded the bend and saw the village lying before him, like a fairytale hamlet, to his attempt to bail Iolo out and save the Evans's marriage. He ran through it over and over again, filling in details, real or imaginary, as they came back to him. He longed to get away from the relentless routine of work-hospital-bed and be back in the kitchen of The Welcome Stranger, planning the next party or cooking up a scheme to make Iolo's fortune. Occasionally Fay caught the faraway expression in his eyes and patted his arm or kissed him gently. 'Don't fret, Jack. He'll be okay.' He felt wretched at misleading her but, if he had, it was unintentional. Besides, it was comforting to feel her concern and he took advantage of one such moment to broach the subject of Neil and her car.

'I can see your point,' she conceded.

The following Saturday, when Jack and his mother arrived at the hospital, Marion was already at Harry's bedside. It was the first time she had been to visit and she had compensated for her neglect, heaping the bedside locker with flowers, fruit, magazines and chocolate. 'I've had one of those weeks at work,' she moaned, when she and Jack went down to the cafeteria to give their parents a few moments on their own. 'Anyway, I knew that you and Mum would be popping in every day, so he wouldn't be short of visitors.'

The cafeteria served both staff and patients. Saturday afternoon was a popular time for sick-visiting and the place was teeming. Families and friends, some visibly distressed, some excited, others bored, consoled themselves with chips or pizza or cream cakes. Here, too, doctors and nurses grabbed ten minutes away from the ward and Jack was appalled to note that their diet was no healthier than the visitors'.

'Don't they know what fizzy drinks do to tooth enamel?' he asked, but Marion wasn't listening.

'So. What's actually wrong with him, then? What's the prognosis?'

'I'm not sure.'

'For goodness sake, Jack, haven't you talked to anyone about it?'

'Yes, of course I have.'

'Who? Who have you talked to? Not some houseman, I hope.'

Every TV addict knew that housemen were the alarmingly young ones who had no experience, no authority and made critical errors. The only doctor that Jack *had* managed to speak to was, indeed, a houseman but he wasn't going to own up to this. 'When I say I'm not sure, I mean *they're* not sure. Yet. They'll know for certain in a couple of days. But I'm positive that there's nothing to worry about. It's probably a matter of tinkering with his medication. Getting the balance right.' Jack was surprised how unperturbed he sounded. Put like that, Harry's restoration to health was a foregone conclusion.

Marion appeared to be satisfied with his woolly explanation – after all, it let her off the bedside-vigil hook – and she switched to telling him a long-winded story about cowboy builders who had made a mess of refitting her second bathroom. He sat opposite her, wondering why she plucked her eyebrows down to thin, wavering lines; why she dyed her hair the colour of Ribena; why he had no idea what music she liked or food she hated; why he had no clue what made his sister tick.

'I'll have to be getting back,' she said. He assumed she meant back to the ward, but when she explained that she and Richard were going out for a meal with friends and she needed to get home in time to wash her hair, Jack knew that, regardless of Harry's condition, they wouldn't be seeing much of Marion.

As he was going up in the lift, he felt an urge to talk to his father – to have a conversation about things that mattered, not the small-talk that had punctuated a lifetime of silences. He tried to remember the last time they'd discussed anything in depth. Or, indeed, if they ever had. It horrified him to concede that he knew so little about his sister, but did he know any more about his father? He'd assumed Harry voted Labour, approved of the monarchy and believed in God. But were these the things that mattered? What about fulfilment and – he hardly dared contemplate it – happiness? Perhaps his father had discovered his own Llangwm; met his own Non Evans. But if he had, he'd kept his promise to stick with Vi, 'til death did them part.

'Where's Marion?' his mother asked when he got back to the ward.

'She had to dash off. Said she'll be back to see you next weekend, Dad.' The lie was to protect his father not his sister.

Harry nodded and fiddled with the flex on his headphones. 'You two don't have to hang around here all afternoon on my account. I expect John's got things to do.'

'Nothing that can't wait.' Jack wished he could be honest and say how much he hated these visits to the hospital; how it frightened him to see his father, emasculated and pathetic, in that dreary place. And how fearful he was of what lay ahead for all of them.

'How is he?' Fay was in the garden when they got home. 'Did Marion show up?' They had a few minutes before Vi returned from the bathroom.

'Much the same. Nothing happens in hospitals at the weekend. All those sick people, sitting there, on hold until Monday.' He accepted the glass of wine she handed him. 'Yes. Marion was there. Briefly. I think she sees all this as little more than an inconvenience.'

'It *is* an inconvenience, but that's all the more reason for her to do her share.'

Vi appeared, pulling a cardigan around her shoulders although it was a mild evening.

'Drink, Mum? Sherry? White wine?' Jack asked.

'Oh, no. Just a glass of water for me. It wouldn't be right to drink alcohol, while your father's lying there, so sick.'

Fay snorted, muttering, 'Give me strength,' and leaving Jack, once again, the miserable piggy-in-the-middle.

Fay checked the alarm. 'I never thought I'd look forward to a Monday morning. *The Merchant of Venice* with Year Nine is a far more enticing prospect than a day at home with your mother.' She plumped her pillow. ''Night, 'night.'

Jack switched off the lamp and tried to relax but it was impossible. He envisaged his father, frightened, uncomfortable and alone, sweating on the rubberised mattress. After all those years of struggle, all that effort, was this how it ended? It was unbearably sad. Jack began to cry, at first managing to stifle the soft whimpering but, as the anguish took hold, he could no longer control it.

Fay woke and turned towards him, pulling his head

into the soft, slack flesh between her breasts. 'Poor, Jack. I shouldn't take it out on you. You can't help it if your mother's…the way she is.' She tilted his head back and kissed his eyelids, his nose and then his lips.

Was this spontaneous show of affection because she cared about him or pitied him? Either way, it felt good and he sniffled on longer than he might have done, anxious to keep her arms around him. He'd forgotten how effective physical contact was at banishing melancholy and, in an effort to finish the job, he stretched his leg over her thigh and fondled her back. She kissed him again, this time as a wife, not a mother and he responded, signalling the start of the ritual which they'd been performing, on and off, for thirty years. It's like riding a bike, he thought, as muscle memory took over, and they were just getting up a decent speed when there was a thud on the landing and his mother's quavering voice announced, 'I'll be all right… nothing broken… '

Everything stopped and they rolled apart.

'I knew it. She's a bloody witch,' Fay asserted while Jack struggled back into his pyjama trousers and went to see what had happened.

24

WITH THE START OF THE ACADEMIC YEAR, several new members of staff arrived at the school, amongst them a handsome young biology teacher, whom Fay guessed was about the same age as Cassidy. It occurred to her that her summer infatuation might have something to do with her age. Maybe, from now on, she was doomed to lust after every young man that hove into view. She tested this theory by spending time with the newcomer and didn't know whether to be relieved or disappointed when, despite his husky voice and sexy bottom, she wasn't even slightly attracted to him.

In the staffroom, her behaviour didn't go unnoticed. By the end of the first week this, combined with her 'new look', gave rise to ribald accusations of cradle-snatching and suggestions that she was on the lookout for a toy-boy. All incredibly predictable and juvenile, but what could you expect from schoolteachers?

'Coffee?' Neil asked as she dumped her brief case and bag of exercise books on the kitchen floor.

It was only a week or so since Neil had moved in, but it was as if he'd been there for ever, like the umbrella stand in the hall or the busy-lizzie in the bathroom. 'Lovely. Thanks.'

He filled the kettle. 'Vi's still at the hospital. I said I'd pop and pick her up at six-ish. If that's okay.'

'Can't Jack bring her back?' Fay slipped her shoes off and sighed.

'That's the other thing. He can't get to the hospital this evening. He forgot that he had to go to a ...' he read from a scrap of paper that he'd pinned to the notice board 'Practitioners' Committee meeting. And a dinner afterwards. He rang after lunch. Said not to wait up for him.'

She wished Jack would log his commitments on the Year Planner. It was a simple enough thing to do and essential, considering current logistical complications. And, had she known that he was going out after work, she would have made sure he'd taken a clean shirt to change in to.

Before leaving to collect Vi, Neil asked, 'Okay if I cook later? After you and Vi have eaten?'

Ten days ago, it had been simple to formulate 'house rules' for their lodger but it was ridiculous to eat in two sittings, when there were only three of them. '*I'll* make supper, Neil, and we'll eat together, as soon as you get back with...Vi.'

During the first few days of Harry's hospitalisation, routine had been abandoned. Fay had found herself marking books in the early hours of the morning and ironing at breakfast time. They'd eaten strange meals at even stranger times and snatched sleep when they could. Harry's condition was stable, but Vi was showing no signs of returning home and Fay presumed that the present setup might continue for months. With that came the prospect of autumn days filled with little else but work, hospital visits and invalid talk. To make it worse, Vi's refusal to touch 'foreign food', intimations that a glass of wine with supper heralded the slippery slide into alcoholism and sideswipes at their extravagant use of hot water were ruining the modest satisfaction she derived from a leisurely meal and a soak in the bath.

To give him his due, Jack had been doing his best. He went out of his way to fend off his mother's digs, spent less time than usual in the shed and even missed the first dance practice of the term but, despite his efforts, the dynamics within the house had changed. Having Neil about the place, amiable and undemanding, helped defuse the tension, although there were moments when he seemed almost *too* eager to please, and it bothered her that they were starting to rely on him. She must apply herself to his CV and put out some feelers in the school careers department. How long had it been since Neil and Vi moved in? Nine days? The house already felt like sheltered accommodation for the unemployed and the aged.

She changed out of her school clothes, wishing that the evening ahead was her own. What a treat it would be to linger in the bath with a book, or sit with a glass of wine and the crossword, or watch something challenging on the television.

When her father had died, without warning, five years ago, she and Jack had agreed that there wasn't much point in second-guessing what lay around the corner for their three remaining parents. But now that they were faced with the possibility of Harry's slow decline, Fay wished that they had at least devised a strategy, no matter how sketchy, for dealing with the survivors.

She sat at the dressing table and brushed her hair, leaning forward to inspect the roots. The evening sunlight, bright and revealing, fell on her face, illuminating the fuzz across her upper lip, the enlarged pores on the sides of her nose and the sharp frown-creases between her eyebrows. She pulled her lips back in the parody of an enthusiastic smile hoping that, by exercising her facial muscles, the sagginess along her jaw and the wrinkles around her eyes would disappear, but all it did was reveal her teeth, no longer as white as they used to be, 'Christ, woman, get a grip.' But hearing her own voice, railing against the unstoppable clock, had the opposite effect and she began to cry, adding bloodshot eyes to the depressing list.

The catastrophes that had reduced her to the pathetic woman in the mirror were piling up, casting a sombre shadow: the loss of Kingsley – he might as well be dead; Jack's lack of oomph, on-setting deafness and recent erratic behaviour; Harry's inconsiderate illness and Vi's overbearing presence in their home; the daily grind of a job which gave her little satisfaction but which was wearing her out; and her body, wrinkling and plumping and sprouting, no longer capable of attracting the likes of Cassidy Ford. Faint but ominous alarm bells sounded, as her life veered towards the rocks, or worse still, the Doldrums.

The phone rang and she jumped up, mopping her nose and eyes with a tissue from the box on the dressing table. It was Caitlin, inquiring after Harry.

'I haven't heard today,' Fay reported. 'Neil's bringing Gran back now. Your father's had to go to a dinner.'

'What dinner's that?'

'Oh, I don't know. GP Committee, I think. We never have a moment to talk to each other these days.'

'Poor Mum. Poor Dad. I'll try and get in to see Grandad tomorrow and perhaps Dylan and Nia can do Thursday. You two need to spend some time together. Get away from it for a few hours.'

Fay heard a key in the front door. 'They're back now. I'd better go.'

'Mum?' Caitlin caught her before she put the phone down. 'I nearly forgot. Cassidy's invited me to the private view of a furniture exhibition. On Saturday. In London. He's got some pieces in the show.'

Caitlin was seeking Fay's approval but she was not in the mood to give it. Cassidy's blatant pursuit of her daughter, whilst he was still sending out unashamed messages of encouragement to her, was reprehensible. He had, without a shadow of a doubt, deliberately touched her breast when he'd reached across to open that window. 'Really? I remember you made that little stool when you were in school, but I had no idea you were that interested in furniture.'

Jack enjoyed the rhythm of work. He liked putting on the pale blue smock which transformed him from an ordinary bloke into a dentist. He started most mornings with routine checkups, bright and breezy, the patients in and out in five minutes. The bulk of the day's appointments were for fillings or running repairs and he took a pride in his workmanship and his ability to calm and reassure those of his patients who were nervous. At the end of each morning session he dealt with emergencies – cracked fillings, lost crowns or abscesses, that sort of thing – proud that his skills could relieve the misery of toothache. Today, however, he felt edgy, his stomach fluttery, and several patients mentioned that he looked pale, joking and saying that it made a change for the *dentist* to be the nervous one in the surgery.

The cause of his apprehension was that, in the early hours of the morning and unable to sleep, he'd finally made up his mind to confide in Sheila. It wasn't so much that he was seeking her blessing but rather that he needed her help. Planning future jaunts to Llangwm was tricky enough before his father's hospitalisation but now, without an accomplice, it was going to be impossible. He was sure that Sheila was the woman for the job – she'd always enjoyed putting one over on Fay. Sheila couldn't bear snobbery in any form and his wife did occasionally display, what Sheila referred to as, 'English tendencies'.

By late morning he was feeling sick with anticipation. He looked for the right moment to raise the subject, wandering into the waiting room to check if she were on her own, then back to the surgery until, in the end, Sheila confronted him. 'For goodness sake Jack, what's the matter with you? You've been hovering around like a…' Failing to find a suitable simile, she shook her head.

'Have I? Sorry.' He stood in front of her desk, fiddling with the paper-clips in the desk-tidy. 'What are you doing for lunch today?'

'Same as I do every day. I shall lock the door and eat my round of sandwiches and my apple, then drink two cups of green tea.' Her face gave him neither encouragement to continue nor warning to stop.

'Sounds good. D'you mind if I join you?'

'What? You want to scrounge half my lunch?'

'No, I didn't mean—'

'I know you didn't. Look, why don't I pop out and fetch you something then we can have a chat about…whatever it is?'

When she'd gone, he stared out of the first-floor window. The pedestrian area surged with lunch-time shoppers, scurrying along on a thousand different assignments. In the middle of the throng, and the only stationary being, stood a man wearing, despite the warmth of the September day, a tweed cap and belted raincoat. Strapped to his torso, by some kind of harness, was a sign that reared up above his head demanding 'REPENT'. Jack was too far away to see if the man was speaking but, if he were, his words were failing to halt the shoppers. How pathetic. How embarrassing. Was it worse to be ignored or sniggered at by the unrepentant mob? The man held his ground, chin up and defiant, and suddenly Jack envied him his conviction, his willingness to risk abuse and ridicule.

He turned away from the window, trying to involve himself in the list of afternoon appointments. Two crown prep's and an amalgam replacement. But he couldn't stop himself drifting back to check if the man was still there. *Repent.* It left no room for compromise.

The door banged. 'They'd sold out of ham so I got cheese,' Sheila held out a cellophane-wrapped baguette. 'And now perhaps you'll tell me what's going on.'

They sat, side by side, in the waiting room and he told her the whole story… The aborted dance fixture; the faulty car; the first night at The Welcome Stranger. He told her about Non; playing Scrabble; seeing the red kites. Then the second visit; Iolo and Zena; tossing pancakes; the carnival float. Finally the financial mess Iolo was in and the money he'd lent to bale him out.

'Aaahhh,' Sheila nodded, 'I thought there was more to Mr Iolo Evans than dodgy medication and a couple of opera tickets.'

He waited for her to voice the understanding and approval that he craved and had counted on, but all he heard was the muffled *snick, snick* of the wall-clock as it ticked away the first seconds of the new age, when Llangwm was no longer his secret.

'I haven't done anything wrong,' he asserted when he could bear her silence no longer.

'You may not have done anything *wrong,* Jack, but it doesn't follow that you've done everything *right.*' She snapped the lid back on her sandwich box, signalling the end of the conversation and leaving Jack with an even sicker sensation in the pit of his stomach and an urge to run away.

While the first patient of the afternoon was chatting to Sheila, Jack phoned home, asking Neil to pass a message to Fay about a fictional dinner that evening. 'Tell her I'm ever so sorry. It completely slipped my mind.'

He made a second call to the ward, to check that there had been no change in Harry's condition. 'And can you let him know that I can't make it tonight?'

Finally he instructed Sheila to cancel his last hour of afternoon appointments. 'I'm not feeling well,' he mumbled, avoiding her eyes. 'I'll be leaving early.'

The road climbed up towards the Beacons and a layer of low cloud blotted out the sun. Jack shivered and shut the car window. Since he left the surgery, he'd been thinking about his *tête-à-tête* with Sheila. She'd been barely civil to him all afternoon and when, finally, he'd asked her what she was thinking, she'd snapped, 'To be quite honest, Jack, I'm disappointed. I thought you, of all people, wouldn't succumb to…whatever you want to call it. The male menopause.' She intoned the last three words as if they were an accusation of murder.

Over the past few days, a blanket of wretchedness, leaden and stifling, had settled on him, culminating in his decision to confide in her. But how could he have misjudged her so badly? He'd presumed that she would be delighted that he'd found such amazing new friends and such an idyllic bolt-hole; that she'd be the person he could talk to about Non's shiny black hair and Iolo's latest escapade. Undeniably, the female mind was a conundrum but he'd never thought of Sheila as female, more a third gender, capable of tapping in to both the male and female psyche. Now it looked as though he wouldn't be able to talk to her about anything ever again.

When he reached Llangwm, he pulled in to the car park near the bridge, the very spot where his car had broken down on that first visit, five weeks ago. What should he do now? He could drive straight back to Cardiff and tell Fay that the dinner had been cancelled. A fire in the hotel kitchen should cover that. Or he could hang about all evening until an after-dinner sort of time and get home in time for bed, as Fay would expect. Or perhaps he should go back to Sheila's flat. Try to win her over. Mmmm. No good. Tuesday was her motor maintenance class. Anyway, who was he fooling? He didn't have any options. He was an addict and he was here to get his fix of the life that he deserved to be living.

Soft drizzle, barely heavy enough to fall to the ground, enveloped the village, glossing the slate roofs and tracing the cobwebs that looped the hedgerows. His visits, both real and imaginary, had been made in bright sunlight and he'd never seen the place in the rain. He might have known that Llangwm rain would be perfect rain. He opened the car window and closed his eyes, breathing in the fustiness of wet leaves.

Hearing the swish of cycle tyres on the wet tarmac, he opened his eyes, catching a glimpse of a figure in a yellow waterproof, cycling past. He started the car and edged out into the road, following the cyclist.

He was positive it was Non, going at quite a lick, long butterfly skirt flapping like a slack yacht sail. The bike she was riding was the old-fashioned sort, with a black frame and a basket in front of the handlebars, just like the one his parents had bought Marion as a reward for passing her eleven-plus exams and gaining a place at the girls' grammar school. A Trent Tourist – that was it. Ever even-handed, when he went to the equivalent boys' school, they bought him a bike, too, but they must have been going through a lean time because his was second-hand, advertised on a postcard in the local newsagent's window. In the end, neither he nor Marion took to cycling. They lived in a valley town and if the outward journey was easy, then the return was agony.

He drove as slowly as he could, keeping a cautious distance behind her as she slipped in and out of sight along the twisting road. She was probably heading for home. Sure enough, after a mile or two, she turned left into a lane where a brightly painted board proclaimed 'Coed Melyn Nursery – shrubs, plants, herbs', a 'Closed' sign dangling from hooks beneath it. He passed the end of the lane, driving on until he came to a wide grass verge where he could pull off the narrow road. Before getting out of the car, he checked his phone. There was a text from Sheila, terse and ambiguous. 'Hope you are soon yourself again.' She would never tell tales to Fay but her loaded text message, for once in standard English, indicated that she was taking what she saw as his aberration very seriously.

The murky evening was perfect for concealment as Jack, hunched over, crept from bush to bush. Fifty yards or so from the road, the lane curved off to the right and led into a small parking area and, if he straightened up, on the other side of it he could see greenhouses and a display of large glazed pots. To his left there was a wooden gate. The white plastic letters on it spelled out 'Coed Melyn Cottage' and, beyond it, a brick-paved path led to a plain, squat house. It wasn't the roses-round-the-door cottage that he'd pictured but, now that he'd seen it, the grey stone house with the slate roof and small, deep-set windows was the most perfect house in the world.

He slipped in through the half-open gate, taking care not to touch it for fear of squeaking hinges, and, calculating that it would be safer to get off the path, dodged between dripping laurel bushes, weaving stealthily through the shrubbery. When to scurry and when to stay? How low to crouch and when was it safe to stand up? The skills acquired decades ago, during endless summer games of heroes and villains, came back to him as he worked his way towards the house.

Although it was not yet seven o'clock, the lights were on and he made a final dash for the flower bed which ran beneath one of the lighted windows. He knelt for a few seconds, catching his breath before risking a peep. Yes, there she was. His heart lifted when he saw her, still wearing the yellow waterproof, taking items from a carrier bag and stacking them on the kitchen table. It looked as though there was someone else in the room or within earshot because, although he couldn't hear anything through the closed window, her moving lips paused every now and again and she turned her head as if to catch a reply.

He'd forgotten how faultless those lips were; how gracefully she moved; how lovely she was.

25

JACK LEANED AGAINST THE WALL, knees drawn up to his chin. Here he was, less than three metres from the woman who occupied his waking thoughts, and he didn't have a clue what to do next. He checked the time. Seven-fifteen. To keep up the myth of his attendance at a dinner, he would need to leave Llangwm by ten o'clock at the latest – a little earlier if he wanted time to compose himself when he got back to Cardiff. That would give him a couple of hours with Non. But first he must dream up a convincing excuse for knocking the door. 'I was just passing …' Not really. 'I was wondering how Iolo's getting on.' Why call here then, rather than at The Welcome Stranger? 'I needed someone to talk to and you sprang to mind.' Almost as feeble as 'a wife who doesn't understand'…

The phone in his jacket pocket vibrated against his ribs. It was Fay. Not daring to ignore it yet anxious not to be detected, he crawled hastily away from the house, taking refuge amongst the lower branches of a yew tree.

'Jack?'

'What's the matter? Anything happened to Dad?' He kept his voice down, cupping his hand around his mouth.

'No. He's much the same, from what your mother says.' There was a pause. 'Why are you whispering, Jack?'

'Was I?' He risked a slight increase in volume. 'What's

wrong, love?'

'Nothing really. It's just that…'

He heard her voice catch. 'Come on. Spit it out.'

'Oh, I'm being pathetic. I must be overtired. Go back to your meeting. I shouldn't have bothered you.'

'Don't be daft. That's what I'm here for. We're a team.' *What a load of tosh.*

'I don't know what the matter is…' She paused. 'And Caitlin's worried about us. She thinks we don't spend enough time together. Perhaps she's right.' She was sniffling now. 'Life's so bloody banal at the moment. So directionless. So bleak.'

'I know. I know.' He crouched amongst the sodden branches, muttering soothing clichés whilst peering at the window, hoping he might glimpse Non. What kind of a heartless monster must he be? 'Tell you what, I'll sort out a few things here, show my face to the committee, then skip off as soon as I can. How does that sound?' He made a kissing noise into the phone, switched it off and stashed it in his pocket.

He stayed where he was for a few minutes, reluctant to abort his mission but consoling himself with today's sightings of Non on her bike and in her home – two new images to add to the cache of pictures in his mental scrapbook.

It was only when he arrived back at the car that he noticed the muddy patches on the knees of his trousers, and felt damp seeping through the seat of his underpants. Although it wasn't cold, in an effort to dry out he put the heater on 'max' then he doubled back through the village, past The Welcome Stranger. The lights were on in the big, solid house but the front door was shut and he drove away feeling excluded, like a child who hasn't been allowed to join in a thrilling playground game.

'That's what I'm here for...' 'We're a team...' The phrases he'd so readily trotted out nagged away as he drove home, trying to remember the last time that Fay had called upon him for emotional support. In the terrible period after Kingsley's disappearance, Fay had girded herself in armour that had become thicker and more impenetrable as days became weeks, and weeks extended to months. They certainly hadn't been a team then, just two individuals, drifting apart, each struggling to survive.

He turned the heating down a notch and tried, not for the first time, to fathom out why they had ended up together. He'd first seen Fay – in fact he'd first *heard* her – in the college cafeteria, holding forth about inadequate grants, whipping up a gaggle of lethargic students, instructing them to hoist their banners and join the protest march. She was a different creature from the sallow, sulky girls that pursued him up and down the valley. Confident and urbane. Intelligent. Brave. Shockingly foul mouthed. It had amazed him that so much noise could issue from the diminutive redhead with the startling green eyes and cheeky breasts. Dafydd Morgan was with him at the time and he was used to his best friend, a good-looking, cocky bastard, getting any girl he wanted, and wanting them even more if he sensed another man was interested. Going in to the second year of their course, Dafydd already had seventeen notches on his double bed-head, so it had come as a flattering surprise when Fay gave Dafydd the cold shoulder – 'Arrogant, mouthy little prick,' were her exact words – and chose him as her suitor.

Sex; love; marriage; parenthood. Yes, for the first few years he and Fay had functioned well together, in an 'opposites are complementary' kind of way, and, if anything, he'd been the one needing support through several episodes of self-doubt. To be honest, it was easier having an independent wife than one who looked to him to take the lead, but he accepted that it may have made him lazy when it came to teamwork. Then again, if his life was so bloody satisfactory, why was he risking it all for a stolen glimpse of a young woman?

He hovered a hundred feet above the earth, watching one Jack Waterfield driving through the winding lanes that lead away from Llangwm; taking the main road that climbed over the mountain and down the other side, past the reservoirs, pewter-coloured and grim in the moonlight; joining the dual carriageway that led travellers home to ugly-sounding places and inconsequential lives.

Vi had commandeered the sitting room and was watching a television programme about a pensioner who had won several millions on the lottery. Neil was in the kitchen, clearing up after supper and being far too cheerful. Fay, feeling marginalised but without the energy to defend her territory, hid behind the shed and smoked two cigarettes in quick succession before retreating to the dining room to mark Year Ten essays on 'The Role of the Fool in Shakespeare's Tragedies'.

She had only three more to tackle when car tyres crunched on the gravelled drive. She hurried to the front door, pausing in the hall when she caught sight of a dumpy, middle-aged school-teacher in the mirror. Mrs Fay Waterfield, aged fifty-three, Head of English. She placed her fists on her hips and pushed as hard as she could, as if brute force could pulverise the adipose padding. Then, turning sideways-on, she took a deep breath and stood tall, thrusting out her chest whilst pressing the bulge below the waistband of her skirt with the palm of her hand. For a few seconds she managed to thrust back time.

The security light came on and, through the frosted

glass panel in the front door, she watched Jack coming up the path, feeling an unaccustomed satisfaction that he was home.

'What's this in aid of?' he asked when she clung to him, nestling her forehead into his soft beard. 'Sure there's nothing wrong?'

'No. Nothing specific. Just a shitty day.'

Neil came out of the kitchen, pulling up sharp when he saw them, intimate and entwined. Suddenly and unexpectedly, Fay felt aroused. It was the sensation that she experienced whenever Cassidy looked at her, but it wasn't Neil causing the hot flush, centred in the small of her back and the tingle in her intestines – or lower down. No, it was having someone observe her intimacy with Jack. A sort of Peeping Tom, in reverse.

She exaggerated her movements to ensure that Jack understood what was happening – and what she'd decided was about to happen. He pulled away but she locked her arms around his neck, clamping him tighter to her, pushing herself hard against him, squirming slightly. 'I think we should get an early night,' she said, as though unaware of Neil's presence.

Jack struggled to untangle himself. 'Fay… Neil's…'

Fay turned her head to glance at Neil. 'Oops,' she giggled.

'No worries…' Neil darted past them, taking the stairs two at a time, clearly desperate to reach the safe haven of his room.

Fay, throwing herself into the role of seductress, pulled at the knot of Jack's tie, loosening it while she groped for his belt buckle with her other hand.

'Fay…' Jack, no longer resistant, was breathing more quickly.

She felt powerful and reckless. 'Is that a drill in your

pocket or are you pleased to see me?' Hackneyed, maybe, but nevertheless effective.

'What? What are you talking about? What about Mum? What's she…? Aagghh.' He moaned gently as she pushed her hand inside the back of his boxer shorts, encountering dampness around his buttocks. Things were hotting up.

'Never mind her. Concentrate on me. Because I'm going to fuck you.' The English teacher in her bemoaned the lack of elegant indecent vocabulary. 'I'm going to fuck your brains out.' Merely uttering the crude phrase increased her tingle to a throb.

Yanking his tie, she led him up the stairs and along the landing to their bedroom. He followed without complaint. Neither of them spoke but Jack's occasional tremulous moan must have been audible to Neil, and he would certainly have heard the unambiguous clatter as she locked them in their bedroom.

Now they were alone, Fay could call a halt to her performance – because her seduction of Jack *had* started as out as play acting. But there was a moment, maybe when he'd cried out, when she stopped pretending. She had not felt like this for years and, sensing that it might well be achievable, hungered for an earth-moving climax, something she hadn't experienced since before Kingsley was born. After twenty-three years of near-misses and disappointingly minor successes, she'd accepted that their physical relationship was limited. Their sexual shortcomings had been a taboo subject, even with her closest friends, because it implied failure and she was loath to admit that she'd failed at anything. Besides, this animal behaviour, messy and crude as it was, had always slightly disgusted her and left her with a guilty aftertaste. Until today…

It didn't need a professional therapist to suggest that

the reason she was, in classroom parlance, 'gagging for it', was probably because power, in all it's manifestations, had always stimulated her. It was obvious. She was a born dominatrix, and her only regrets were, firstly, that it had taken her this long to realise it and, second, that she'd never seen any pornographic films to give her a few pointers. Jack *had* once suggested that they watched something called *Spanking Party*, but she'd banished him to the spare room for a week. It helped the current situation considerably, though, to imagine that Cassidy was spying on them, through a one-way mirror.

Jack appeared to be in shock and it was clear that, if she wished things to reach a satisfactory conclusion, she needed to encourage him. She pushed him backwards on to the bed and straddled him, her knees sinking in to the feather duvet, the button on the waistband of her skirt popping under the strain. She squirmed around on his groin area and was gratified to feel him burst into life. At last he was getting into the swing of it and he pushed his cold hands beneath her tee-shirt, unfastening her bra and pulling the whole lot over her head. The air cooled her skin and it was wonderful to be free from the tight elastic around her chest. She leaned forward, moving from side to side, dragging her nipples across his face, smothering him with her full breasts. 'Lick me', she instructed. It was her turn to moan now.

An understanding passed between them – she would tell him exactly what to do and he would comply with her instructions. For the twenty minutes that followed, they did just that. It was messy, noisy, athletic, inventive and totally successful.

Jack was unable to sleep, although there had been instants when he'd assumed that he was already dreaming. At that moment Fay's left leg was looped around his waist, heavy and clammy with sweat. In the room along the corridor, Neil was playing something blues-y with a heavy bass beat. His mother was muttering to herself as she came slowly up the stairs. 'I don't know...can't understand...never used to...' Disgruntled and complaining, she made her way to bed. On her way past, she tapped on the door. 'Fay? I've pulled the plugs out and locked the back door. But I've left the chain off so Jack can get in.' Thank God she'd failed to notice his car in the drive.

What an extraordinary day it had been. At twelve-thirty he'd been draining an abscess and now, ten forty-seven by his clock-radio, he was recovering from violent, glorious sex with a woman whom he'd decided, less than an hour earlier, he no longer cared about. He'd reached this harsh conclusion on the dual carriageway, passing the B&Q Warehouse. The huge sign, crude and orange, loomed up, a warning of what lay ahead if he didn't act soon. DIY. Little runs in the country. Bingo. Failing eyesight. Arthritis. Meals-on-Wheels. Incontinence. And, all the while, Fay would be at his side, nagging and sniping and mocking. Then, bang, it would be all over. Kingsley had been the smart one. He'd grasped what life held in store for those who got on that treadmill and kept walking. Like Kingsley, Jack had made up his mind to get off.

His plan, still embryonic when he'd reached the front door, was to leave Fay, wind up the practice and move to Llangwm. He'd help out at The Welcome Stranger – maybe at the nursery, too, if Non and her partner needed an extra pair of hands – in exchange for room and board. He'd spend his days dressing up and messing about with Iolo. He'd go bird spotting or play cards with Non, and, occasionally touch her arm, happy simply to be in her presence – only a barbarian would demand sexual favours from a saint. His needs were modest and, even after his 'loan' to Iolo, he still had a fair sum salted away. Initially, Fay would make a fuss but she wouldn't really mind. He knew he did little more than irritate her these days. She might be worse off in economic terms, but she could sell the house and find something smaller if she wanted to release some capital. The children would be shocked but they would come round to the idea and probably think all the more of him for it. His parents? They'd never approved of the marriage in the first place so they couldn't object if it came to an end.

That had been his plan, but it lay in tatters now because he'd been unfaithful to Non, Iolo and his own salvation. He'd allowed his wife to 'fuck his brains out' and he'd enjoyed every minute of it.

26

FROM NEIL'S EXPRESSION, Fay could see that even a brick wall and the Rolling Stones hadn't obliterated the noises coming from their bedroom. She didn't care. In fact she would have been disappointed if their efforts had gone unnoticed. As the three of them went through their breakfast routine – Vi was having a lie in, complaining that she 'didn't get a wink of sleep' – she touched the back of Jack's neck, his shoulder, his thigh, to remind him of last night. She'd hoped for a little more evidence of the deliciously guilty secret that they shared but when she'd woken him at six-thirty, by biting his buttock, all he'd mumbled was 'I can't, Fay. Sorry.'

Before they left the house, they arranged to meet at the hospital after work, spend an hour or so with Harry then go out for dinner. 'Somewhere romantic,' Fay whispered, planting a kiss on his mouth and nibbling his lower lip.

'You look like the proverbial cat,' one of her fellow teachers commented as they gulped their mid-morning coffee. 'If I didn't know you better, I'd suspect you were enjoying some extra-mural activity.'

Fay gave what she hoped was an enigmatic smile.

Throughout the morning a plan gnawed away until it became irresistible. Before bedtime she had to get hold of stockings and a suspender belt – maybe a bra to match – and not the sensible sort available from Marks and Spencer. There was a lingerie shop in one of the arcades and at lunchtime, although she was cutting it fine, she dashed into the city centre. Over the years, she must have hurried past La Passionata a hundred times and she'd dismissed it as a place where men shopped. Men who wanted to bully their wives or partners into dressing, or rather un-dressing, like tarts. Overnight – and *what* a night – she had revised her opinion and could now see that there was, indeed, a time and a place for crotch-less knickers and tassels.

The interior of the shop was airless and thick with patchouli. Low lighting reflected off scarlet, purple and black satin – visceral and oppressive. Fay's relief at being the only customer turned to alarm when the assistant, a blowsy brunette not much younger than she was, with crepe-skinned cleavage and fake nails, advanced towards her. 'Cn'I help you, madam?' she asked, her expression scornful and knowing.

Fay's courage ebbed. 'I'm looking for a gift. For a friend. A woman.'

The woman raised her left eyebrow a few millimetres. 'Yes, madam. Would that be for a special occasion?'

'Yes. Yes it is actually. It's her…her fortieth birthday.'

'What did you have in mind? Satin pyjamas are always acceptable.'

There was no way Fay wanted anything acceptable. She gave a playful laugh. 'Actually I was thinking of something a bit saucier…more of a fun present. Like…' she pretended to ponder, 'like suspenders and stockings. Bra and panties. Nothing too…sensible.'

The woman made it as difficult as she could by producing the most utilitarian items in the shop, until Fay was forced to ask for 'Something more…titillating?' She had to invent intimate details about the 'friend' – size, colouring, personality – parting with the best part of a hundred pounds before emerging with a chocolate-brown carrier bag containing crimson satin bra, thong, suspender belt and black fishnet stockings. They were from the 'Moll Flanders' range, and not one of the items was large enough to cover the palm of her hand.

She made it back to school with minutes to spare then, unwilling to leave the carrier bag unattended in the staffroom, she took it to her lesson with her new GCSE group, placing it on the floor under the table.

This early in the term, teacher and pupils were still sizing each other up. Whilst they were testing her discipline and making their minds up whether to be for or against her, she was assessing their capabilities, identifying trouble-makers and potential allies. It was essential to gain their respect and, after thirty years of playing this game, she knew that this was most easily done by making her lessons unconventional. Hold their interest – keep them guessing. Not a bad motto for other areas in her life, too.

Her knee brushed the carrier bag and she remembered last night. 'Right, Form Four, I'm going to set you a little challenge.' She lifted the bag from beneath the desk and held it up, dangling from its silky cord handles. 'What's this?'

A giggle and murmur ran around the room. 'A bag, miss.' Titters and groans.

'Well done, Emma. A bag. But is it an empty bag?'

Step by step, she drew them out until they agreed that the bag contained *something* but, as there was nothing written on the stiff brown paper, they had no idea what was in it. They began shouting out suggestions and she knew they were hooked. She, too, was hooked – by the risk she was taking. What if the handles slipped from

255

her grasp and the contents of the bag slithered on to the desk? Waving explicit objects in front of fourteen year olds was definitely a sacking offence. The very danger of the situation excited her. 'Okay. We've had a teddy bear; books; a skull; trainers; bananas. Lots of good ideas. So, for tonight's homework, I'd like you to write a story about finding this bag,' she pondered for a second, 'in, let's say, a garden shed. Why is it there? To whom does it belong? What does it contain? Weave your story around the bag and its contents and,' she forestalled the several raised hands as teacher suppressed temptress, 'I know, I know. Obviously, in real life, you'd call the police and report a suspect package, but try and get away from real life.'

Fay couldn't wait for school to finish. Most days she stayed on for at least an hour after the final bell, catching up with paperwork, but today she made her getaway whilst pupils were still trickling out of the rusty school gates. This would give her a couple of hours before she was due at the hospital and she needed to shower and change. There were other things to do, too.

The house was quiet when she let herself in but, to make sure she was alone, she called,' Hello? Anyone here?' Vi was sure to be with Harry but Neil could well be in his room. There was no reply. She made a cup of instant coffee and took it upstairs, tapping on Neil's door, making absolutely certain she was alone. She showered and washed her hair, taking longer than usual, swirling the scented foam over her skin and savouring the moment that she'd been anticipating all afternoon.

Each item was wrapped in black tissue paper, sealed with a red heart-shaped sticker. When she tipped them out on to the bed, they looked like blobs of ink, defiling the *broderie anglaise* cover. The receipt fluttered to the floor and she picked it up. These four featherweight packages had cost ninety-eight pounds. *Ninety-eight pounds.* How many goats would that buy for Africa; how many wells would it dig in Bangladesh? She sat on the bed, wrapped in a bath sheet and, breaking her own house-rules, smoked a cigarette. Did she need to choose between making poverty history and a sex-life? Could she bear to return to what she now thought of as the 'pre-Cassidy era', when her erogenous zones were a no-go area and sex was something to put up with? There had to be an ethical solution.

It didn't take her long. If she gave up smoking, she could donate half the money she saved to charity and buy provocative underwear – or whatever it took – with the rest. She sipped cold coffee and savoured her last cigarette.

Every now and again, Jack glanced up from a patient to catch Sheila peering at him, as if he were a culture in a Petri dish and she were waiting for something to develop. He needed to reassure her that things had changed since they last spoke; that by surrendering to his baser instincts, he had been tested and failed; that by making love to his wife he had dishonoured Non, the Evans family and everything they stood for, thus forgoing his entitlement to happiness. Llangwm had been elevated to Shangri-La – an unattainable paradise beyond the distant hills.

The *outcome* of his actions – continuing to live with Fay and be a dentist – ought to please Sheila, but the way he'd arrived at it certainly would not. Indeed, he was stunned at the ease with which he'd allowed Fay to use his body and was well aware that people – Sheila was the person he had in mind – would claim Fay couldn't have done what she did without his full cooperation. Technically true.

But at lunch time, when he'd planned to set the record straight, Sheila and her Tupperware sandwich-box were nowhere to be found. He was still trying to work out what had made her react so violently to yesterday's revelation. He'd hoped that, after she'd had the night to mull it over, she might be more sympathetic to his position – or the position as it was until he entered the hall last night – but her coolness this morning, and her absence now, indicated that he'd misjudged it again.

He could count on the fingers of one hand the times, apart from holidays and illness, that Sheila hadn't been there between one and two o'clock, eating her lunch and standing for everything that was reasonable in an often unreasonable world. Dental nurses came and went – it was seldom worth getting to know their names – but Sheila had been a constant in his working life. She'd been there through every family, medical and professional crisis; through the crippling months after Kingsley left; and she had never made a single joke about bells or hankies. Now, all he had to do was persuade her to ignore yesterday's revelatory conversation – that it had all been a joke. Then she would chuckle, telling him what a daft old thing he was, and they could settle back into their comfortable camaraderie, as if he'd not said a word.

He sat in the silent waiting-room, waiting.

She returned five minutes before afternoon surgery, without revealing where she'd been to eat her lunch. When Jack followed her into the tiny kitchen, she turned on him. 'D'you want to know what I think, Jack?' This was his opportunity to put her straight.

Before he could speak, she raised her hand. 'No, let me have my say. If I heard this tale of woe from any other man, because, call me foolish but I didn't have you down as being like other men, I'd say he was a complete loser, making a pathetic attempt not to grow old. There has to be a name for it because there are enough of you at it. The Peter Pan Syndrome – that's what I'd call it.' She paused.

'Have you ever read *The Picture of Dorian Gray*? Perhaps you should.'

'But Sheila—'

'I'm not interested, boyo. If you need approval for your…sexual peccadilloes', the rise and fall of her strong Welsh voice endowed every syllable with derision, 'you've come to the wrong woman. Heaven knows, Fay and I seldom see eye-to-eye but after thirty years, she deserves the truth. Why don't you confess to her that you've got the hots for a young woman. And her whole family. And a guesthouse, for God's sake.' She shook her head and that was the end of that.

By the time Jack took off his smock at the end of the afternoon, he had no idea what he wanted. All he *did* know was that if he hadn't allowed Fay to seduce him, he'd be at home now, packing his possessions into a hired van and heading for Llangwm. That wasn't wholly accurate. It would take weeks to sort things out at the practice but it served to dramatise the consequences of his folly.

On the other hand, it *had* been bloody fantastic. It was disquieting that such an everyday act – 'Shock! Horror! Husband and Wife Make Love' – had made him feel so… wanton, so…dangerous. Before Fay came along, there had been fumblings and couplings with a few unmemorable girlfriends. And there was Laura, but that didn't count as having sex, did it? He had never experienced anything like last night so, if he *had* blown all entitlement to a new life, going home to Fay might not be too unbearable.

He was the first one to arrive at the hospital and he sat in the cafeteria, pretending to read a discarded newspaper. But he couldn't concentrate. It was ridiculous how excited and, it had to be said, embarrassed he was at the prospect of meeting his own wife. When she appeared, weaving towards him between the tables, he jumped up, like a young man trying to impress a new girlfriend.

He bent and kissed her clumsily, not quite connecting with her lips. 'You look fantastic, love.' In fact, she didn't. She was wearing too much makeup and her hair was stiff with whatever she'd taken to using. Beneath her blouse, her breasts looked a funny shape, sort of lumpy and squashed.

'I aim to please, sir.' She gave a coquettish smile, and he noticed lipstick on her second incisor.

When they got up to the ward, the contents of Harry's locker were heaped on his empty bed. 'Just having a sort-out,' his mother explained, bustling across to the black rubbish bag suspended from the wall near the sink.

'Where's Dad?' Jack collected two plastic chairs from the stack in the corner and they sat down.

'Tests. They took him off about four o'clock.'

'That's over two hours ago, Mum. What were they testing for?'

'I didn't like to pester. They've got enough to do.' Vi went on tidying.

Jack searched for his father's notes but they weren't in the rack at the foot of the bed, and he ventured down the airless corridor to the nurses' station. The grubby walls were plastered with curling A4 sheets, the information they displayed – visiting times, support groups, hospital cross-infection regimen, the chapel opening hours, the complaints procedure – badly set-out and hard to decipher. A whiteboard showed the layout of the ward and the location of every patient, names written in green block-capitals. Some of the names, including 'Harry Waterfield', were smudged and illegible, as if that person were fading away. Jack shivered.

'Mr Walker's sent him down for tests.' The nurse treated

him to her aren't-you-silly-for-asking smile. 'Shouldn't be long. Why don't you get a coffee?'

Jack stood his ground. 'My mother said he's been gone since four. Anyway, what sort of tests?' But he got nowhere.

The three of them sat around the empty bed. Fay didn't say much but he could tell, from her tapping foot and frequent glances at the wall-clock, that she was calculating how long it would be before they could get away. His mother, twittering and restless, looked worn out. She'd been keeping watch for days and he recognised how exhausting hospital visiting was. He felt bad that he'd not been more tolerant of her presence in the house or given her more of his time.

Just before eight o'clock, nurses shoo-ed the visitors down the corridor to the exit and started the medication round, but there was still no sign of Harry. 'Come on, Mum. I'm sure they'll ring if there's a problem. Let's get you home.'

'Don't you worry about me…'

'It's not too late, if you still want to go out,' Jack said once they'd settled Vi in front of the television. He'd passed the hungry stage an hour ago but was prepared to press on with their plan if Fay was keen. 'Or we could order a takeaway.' He wanted to compensate, in some way, for their dreary evening.

'Oh, I don't know. Whatever.' She was snappy and he began to wonder if he'd imagined last night. 'Actually I think I'll have a sandwich and an early night.'

Early night. A coded message?

'And I do mean an early night, Jack.'

'A sandwich sounds just the job.' To tell the truth, he wasn't confident that he'd be up to another night of passion.

Fay undressed in the bathroom. Removing the silk blouse and linen skirt, at first she tried not to look in the mirror, but her reflected self was inescapable, the efficient lighting emphasising every fold and bulge of flesh, every inch of blemished skin. Taking a deep breath, with hands at her sides, she risked an objective appraisal.

The Moll Flanders underwear had chafed and pinched but, for the first hour or so, she'd accepted the discomfort as reminder of last night, and a promise of what was to come. It had been thrilling to walk towards Jack, the scanty bits of fabric prickling her skin – a secret, waiting to be shared. Then they'd been through the missing patient fiasco and her mother-in-law's pitiful, 'Don't you worry about me. You two carry on and have fun. I'll get the bus home.' As the likelihood of another night of lovemaking faded, the underwear had become downright painful.

The suspender belt, slung around her hips, and the thong, barely covering her pubic hair, framed a cushion of podge, etched with the puckered scar, a constant reminder of Kingsley. The skimpy cups of the bra had almost disappeared beneath her breasts and, obviously not designed to support anything heavier than a couple of marshmallows, the mean straps had gouged deep channels over her shoulders. She turned around to reveal two larger cushions, dimpled and overstuffed, sad and ludicrous. She finished undressing, shoving the preposterous underwear to the bottom of the linen basket, then pulled a white cotton nightdress over her head, covering up the marks gouged by taught elastic and rasping synthetic lace.

Although Jack had already switched off the bedside lamp, the street-light illuminated the room enough for her see that he was lying on his back, eyes open. He remained motionless as she slipped in to bed beside him. Last night, his passivity had helped to unleash her excitement but now it simply irritated her.

'What are you thinking about?' she asked, offering him the opportunity to set the ball rolling.

'Oh, nothing much.'

Thirty years and he hadn't got any better at opening up. 'Come on, Jack. Don't you think we should talk about it?'

He wriggled slightly. 'Perhaps it's more serious than we think. If his chest's the only thing they're concerned about, they'd have sorted out his medication and sent him home by now. Hospitals have to meet targets these days and he's a bed-blocker.' He turned to face her. 'I can't stop thinking about him, alone in there, too bloody frightened to make a fuss. Too scared to ask what's happening, or if he's going to die. Mum's the same. Blindly soldiering on, as though acceptance is a virtue… Two martyrs bound for glory.'

She reached out and stroked his face. It hadn't crossed her mind that he could be thinking about anything but last night. She was ashamed that she hadn't given poor Harry as much as a passing thought. Nevertheless, last night was what she wanted to discuss and she left it a few seconds before prompting, 'Anything else on your mind?'

She felt him stiffen, as if he were assembling the right words to say something vital, but the silence extended for too long. 'No. Nothing in particular.' And she'd lost him again.

The day, which had begun with delicious promise, had fizzled out in a plate of cheese and pickle sandwiches. If her life were on the GCSE English syllabus, this would definitely have been classed as a metaphor.

27

JACK PHONED THE HOSPITAL FIRST THING NEXT MORNING. He hoped to find out more about the mysterious tests but was palmed off with the standard 'the patient is comfortable'.

'I'll pop in and see him straight from work,' he told Fay, 'Then I really ought to go to Morris practice. I can't miss another week.'

Before he went to work, he retreated to the shed to give his shoes a rub over with the duster and snatch a few moments to himself because, beyond a doubt, something was happening to him. The first hints of this change had been evident at Dylan's wedding and, since then, he could pinpoint several other manifestations. He'd gone over and over it during the night, coming to the conclusion that he had become an Existentialist, and he'd crept downstairs at four o'clock to check the dictionary, which stated: *Existentialism, n. an anti-intellectualist philosophy of life holding that man is free & responsible, based on the assumption that reality as existence can only be lived but never become the object of thought.* He liked the sound of it, especially the 'man is free' bit. It seemed to address the dichotomy of his life – or existence as he might have to call it from now on. Jean-Paul Sartre. Albert Camus. *Who else?* He'd Google it later.

He shoved his dancing kit into a holdall and, passing

Neil in the hall, asked if he'd be able to collect Vi from the hospital after Fay got home from school. 'And you mentioned you might like to see what we get up to on a Thursday evening so…how about tonight?'

'Great. Yeah. Cheers.'

He gave Neil instructions for finding the community centre. 'Then listen out for bells.' He shook his bag.

Sheila appeared to be dismounting from her high horse. She smiled at him a couple of times during the morning and, at lunchtime, inquired after Harry, looking concerned when he told her about the tests. 'Ooh, bless him. No point in getting all steamed up, though, until you know if they found anything. I'll try and get in to see him at the weekend.'

'Thanks. He'd like that. And Sheila,' he paused, nervous that he might undo the progress he had made, 'about the other day. I didn't mean to involve you in my personal problems. Could you forget that I mentioned anything? I've sorted myself out now.' Her face softened and, although it was unfair to play on her sympathy, he added, 'I can't have been thinking straight. It's all got on top of me lately.'

He dropped into the newsagents and bought his father a gardening magazine and a bar of milk chocolate – gifts such as he might take any work colleague or neighbour who was in hospital. Jack, himself, had been an in-patient only once. When he was thirty-two he'd suffered a nasty ear infection and been kept in hospital for two nights, in order for the medics to blast it with intravenous antibiotics. The constant noise, inedible food, waterproof under-sheet and, worst of all, the other patients had contrived to make it a ghastly experience. But, when Harry gently grumbled or asked when he might be going back home to his own bed and Vi's cooking, he and Fay scolded the old man for his impatience and lack of gratitude for the attention he was receiving.

He had no idea what might make his father's incarceration less monotonous. He tried to imagine how he'd be feeling after ten days confined to bed, or the armchair next to it, with no date set for discharge. He went back into the shop, searching for anything that might distract Harry from his dreary routine and surroundings. On a shelf marked 'Pocket Money Toys', he found the very thing – a pack of gaudy plastic puzzles. Silver balls to coax through a maze; numbered tiles to slide into sequence; coloured squares and triangles to create dozens of different shapes. By the time he reached the ward, he was feeling delighted with his own inventiveness.

Harry half sat, half lay, flopped against a pile of pillows, eyes closed and denture-less mouth slightly open.

'Dad. Dad.' Whispering to avoid startling him, Jack touched the back of his father's hand, the flaky skin purpled and blackened by ten days of invasive needles. 'You awake, Dad?'

Harry's eyes opened and he moistened his lips with his tongue. 'Pour me a drop of pop, John.'

Jack passed him the plastic beaker, 'There you go. Mum been in?'

'Aye. That young chap – Neville is it? – he's given her a lift home.'

'Neil. That's good. He's a kind lad.' Jack paused, uncertain how to raise the subject of the tests, unsure how much his father knew about his condition. 'Any news?'

A reassuring look of irony flitted across Harry's sunken face. 'Yes, boyo. I scored the winning try. Right between the posts.'

Jack laughed, keen to maintain the offhandedness. 'It's

just that they were doing some tests when I came yesterday. What was that all about?'

'Don't ask me. I'm only the patient.'

Now that Harry was looking brighter, Jack produced his gifts. The chocolate joined the confectionery heaped on the locker, and the magazine went on the pile of unread papers, but his father smiled when he saw the puzzles, 'What's this then?'

While Harry nudged silver balls through the maze, Jack flicked through the medical notes which had reappeared at the foot of the bed. It looked at though his father had gone to the urology department the previous day. What did that suggest? Next to the locker, a flickering TV on an articulated arm advertised its 'pay-as-you-view' services. 'Only four pounds a day.' For that the patient got to watch drivel on a screen the size of a paperback book. *Welcome to capitalism, NHS style.* A catheter bag dangled from the bed's metal frame, its contents alarmingly orange and, free of charge, Jack watched liquid dripping out of his father, debating when he could decently escape from the time warp of the ward.

'Go in, you blighter,' Harry muttered, then smiled triumphantly, 'Done it,' holding out the tiny maze for Jack's approval.

'Well done, Dad.' Didn't they say that, in old age, we revert to childhood? 'Look, I'm sorry I've got to rush off but—'

'Off you go. I'll be fine.' Unlike Vi, this was said without an iota of self pity. 'Just fine.'

Jack leaned over and kissed the top of Harry's head, breathing in the antiseptic smell of coal tar soap which never failed to bring back Sunday nights in the chilly bathroom. 'Sheila says she'll pop in at the weekend, if you feel up to having visitors.' He beefed up this slender life-line with a plausible lie, 'And Marion phoned to check how you were. She sends her love.'

But his father was busy shunting plastic tiles around and didn't answer.

Shouts of 'Here he is,' and 'Hello stranger,' greeted Jack, but the Wicker Men kept leaping and stamping in time to fiddle and accordion, filling the room with panting energy. He changed in the corner, slipping on the old tee-shirt and jogging bottoms which he wore for practice sessions. Next the heavy, buckled shoes, shiny and smelling of feet and shoe polish. Finally, the bells, twelve to a leg, four attached to each of three vertical leather strips. He had strapped the harnesses around his shins scores of times, but the *chink chunk,* exotic and atavistic, never failed to thrill, evoking much more than the rustic dance – Christmases; wizards and witches; troikas across the frozen steppe. Trevor and Malcolm struck up 'Trunkles' and he took his place in the file. In no time at all, the monotony of hospital visiting, the Llangwm dilemma and Fay's extraordinary behaviour the night-before-last evaporated, exorcised by the ritual of the Morris.

When he'd first begun Morris dancing, he'd been inhibited and self-conscious, unwilling to let himself go. It was as if John-the-dentist was struggling to restrain Jack-the-dancer. What with that and all the leaping and counting and remembering, an hour with the Wicker Men left him on his benders. Gradually he'd learned to respond directly to the ancient rhythms and no longer needed to route any of the steps or figures through his brain. He could, within half a dozen squeezes of the accordion, become no more than an amalgam of grunts and puffs and curses; salty snot; twirling ribbons and flying hankies; throbbing calves and aching thighs; stamping feet and tapping toes; sweat and farts and a washing-powder-scented shirt; blood, from a bitten tongue. All driven on by the mesmeric bells.

Jack hadn't done much exercise through the summer and he was relieved when, after 'Trip and Go', they took a break. Pulling up the front of his tee-shirt to mop his forehead, he went to the open door where he'd spotted Neil, hovering. 'You found us okay.'

'No problem.'

'Thanks for collecting Mum from the hospital.'

'No worries.'

'Come on over and meet the lads.' Jack grimaced. 'Lads' was overstating it – he was the second youngest. He introduced Neil to the dozen or so panting men, and to Trevor and Malcolm, the musicians. 'Neil, here, was at school with my younger son. Played in his band. He's staying with us for a bit.'

Stan called for order and dealt with the weekly business, coming, finally, to the matter of the autumn fixture-list. 'You all got my email or, for those of you still in the stone-age, my note? As I mentioned, we've been invited to do a couple of half-hour sessions at the Llangwm Festival on the twenty-seventh. Are you all okay for that? Anyone not available?'

Jack gulped from his bottle of mineral water, the tepid liquid doing nothing to refresh him, but the act of swallowing putting off the moment of decision. He'd Googled 'Existentialism' at lunchtime and scanned through a mere handful of the thousands of entries. *Man is totally free and entirely responsible for what he makes of himself. It is this freedom and responsibility that is the source of man's dread.'* Sounded about right. Yes. From today he would throw his hat in the ring with the Existentialists. And what heady company. Jack Kerouac, Samuel Beckett and Dostoevsky were names that jumped out. *On the Road.*

Crime and Punishment. Waiting for Godot. These men had tapped into his life before he'd even had chance to live it. He wasn't sure about the Marquis de Sade, but it was possible the bloke had been misrepresented. Maybe he'd get a black polo-necked sweater at the weekend.

'You'll be there, Jack?'

'Sure.'

'We were a bit ragged tonight but you got the gist of it?' Jack asked as they drove home.

'Yeah. Dead impressive. Kinda rough and ready but full of energy. The music's something else. Cool.'

It was unnerving to hear anything positive about his hobby and Jack wondered if Neil was being polite, but his open face dispelled all doubt about his sincerity. He chatted about the possibility of using the Morris tunes and rhythms in some sort of fusion music. 'I don't mean folk-rock. That's been done before. I mean something totally new.'

Jack wanted to be encouraging but he didn't have much idea what Neil was talking about. 'You'll have to give me a demo when we get in.'

Then, as they turned the corner and came within sight of home, Neil slapped the palms of his hands on his thighs. 'Sorry. I clean forgot to tell you, Kingsley mailed a couple of days ago.'

'Oops,' Jack over-steered and the car tyre caught the kerbstone. 'Was there any news?' He tried to sound casual, as though Neil had forgotten to water a houseplant or turn the page of the calendar.

Neil chewed his lip, 'Let's think.' He counted the points off on his fingers. 'He asked about Harry and Vi, of course. Wanted to know if I had a job yet. Asked if I was still in his room—'

'He referred to it as "his room"?' Jack interrupted. Might this indicate that he was planning to reclaim it one day? 'Did he say where he was? What he was doing. Anything about who he was with?'

'I don't *think* so. I can't really remember, sorry. Why don't I log on when we get in, and you can check it out?'

Since the crisis with Harry, Jack hadn't thought about Kingsley as much as he usually did. Neil's being in touch with him had slipped to the back of his mind and, despite knowing about this for two weeks, he'd not, for reasons which he didn't quite understand himself, got around to telling Fay. He was eager to see what was in this most recent communication, but he was going to have to make sure she was out of the way before he let Neil anywhere near the computer. 'No rush. Tomorrow maybe. I've got a few things to see to, and I don't want to be too late to bed.'

'Course you don't.' Neil gave a knowing wink.

Fay had planned to spend the evening with Neil, getting to grips with his CV and working out a strategy for his job search. Without any applications in the pipeline, he might still be with them at Christmas. She didn't object to having him living with them for a while – on her terms and as her protégé – but he was getting disturbingly chummy with Jack and Vi. Before she had the opportunity to tell him what she had in mind, she heard him go out.

She fixed a smile on her face and went into the living room. Her mother-in-law was reading the *South Wales Echo*, her lips framing the words as she struggled through the nightly quota of lurid headlines. 'How was he this afternoon?' Fay asked. Every day they went through the question and answer ritual. The facile conversation ritual. The 'being nice to each other' ritual. Rituals that saved them from having to make a legitimate connection – social washers to prevent them grinding against each other.

'Not very special.' Vi lowered the paper and looked at the clock, 'Is that the time?'

Yes, you stupid old woman, that's the time. And why don't you just tell me to fuck off, because all you want to do is get your head stuck in the television so you can be shocked by the sex and bad language in the sodding soaps. 'Shall I put the TV on for you?'

'If it's no trouble.'

How on earth could it be any trouble to walk four paces and push in a switch? 'No, it's no trouble.' Why did they keep up this pathetic pretence? 'If it's okay with you, I'm going to make a phone call then do some marking.'

'Carry on, dear. I'll manage.'

Manage what? Manage to breathe in and out. Manage not to urinate on the sofa? Manage to be incredibly boring. 'Well, give me a shout if you need anything.'

It was twenty-six hours since her last cigarette and, hoping to strengthen her resolve to quit, Fay retrieved the underwear from the linen basket where it had lain hidden since last night's failure. She sat on the bed, fingering the dark red satin and wondering whether to try again. Jack should get home from Morris practice at about nine-thirty, grateful that he'd been allowed out for the evening and keen to please her. An image of Jack as he probably was at that very moment – hankies fluttering – loomed up and extinguished the flicker of interest that the underwear had rekindled. She wondered if a drink would help and, sneaking downstairs, she collected her bag of exercise books and a bottle of white wine, and returned to their bedroom. It was infuriating that she was forced to skulk around in her own home and she gulped down a glass of wine and half the next before she felt up to marking Year

Nine's evaluation of *Cargoes*.

By nine o'clock, she'd covered thirty-one exercise books with scathing comments and finished the bottle of Pinot Grigio. Then, steadying herself on the bed-end, she stripped off and struggled into the painful bra and thong, concealing the scarlet scraps beneath her sensible bathrobe. It would be another half hour before Jack came home and she didn't want to go downstairs and risk a conversation with Vi, especially now that her inhibitions had been slackened. She contemplated ringing Caitlin but wasn't sure she was up to talking about her forthcoming trip to London. She tried Dylan's number but there was no reply and she couldn't be bothered to compose a message. Anyway, she had nothing to say.

Weariness and wooziness engulfed her and she slipped under the duvet. The bed was a boat, bobbing on a gentle swell. Where was she bound? Distant Ophir, perhaps. When Jack came home she'd ask him if he'd take her there for a holiday. Where was it anyway? She'd forgotten. India? Raj, the polite little Nottingham newsagent, with his gentle eyes and slender fingers, swam alongside the boat, smiling proudly at the prospect of having a doctor daughter.

'You okay?' Jack woke her. He sat on the side of the bed and, as he pulled off his tee-shirt, she smelled the not unpleasant tang of his sweat.

'I'm fine. Just a bit tired.' She raised herself up on one elbow and the bathrobe fell open to reveal the scanty bra. 'Good practice?'

'Mmmm. Neil turned up. I think he was quite impressed.' He pointed to her chest. 'What's that?'

'Oh, that.' The wine had sapped her energy, mental and physical, but she was incredibly relaxed. 'D'you like it?' From here on it was up to him.

28

FAY SEEMED TO REQUIRE SOMETHING FROM HIM, mumbling and pulling at her dressing gown, but he made soothing noises and stroked her cheek, as if he were calming a fretful child, and she was asleep in no time.

He couldn't decide whether he was more shocked by her bizarre underwear or her drunkenness. She'd always enjoyed a glass of wine with a meal, but was very sniffy about anyone who drank with the intention of getting drunk, which, as the empty bottle next to the bed appeared to indicate, had been what she set out do this evening. As for underwear, her criteria were rigid – it should always be clean, *could* be attractive but it *had* to be functional. It was there to support, pull in, cover up. The red things – they could hardly be termed 'bra and pants' – failed on all counts.

Occasionally, when the kids were young, she used to go to things called 'Tupperware Parties', explaining that it was really an excuse for women to get away from the children for an hour or two. He'd read an article quite recently which said that saucy underwear and sex toys had taken over from plastic food containers, and that 'Anne Saunders Parties' – was that it? – were all the rage. The red things must have come from somewhere like that. Could Fay and her teacher friends have been whiling away long summer afternoons at risqué get-togethers, giggling and swapping lewd stories? She *had* changed her hairstyle and bought some rather odd skirts, but that was very different from tonight's lap-dancing kit.

When he could avoid it no longer, he addressed the most damning evidence – her incredible performance in that very room. He was still sore from, and embarrassed by, what had taken place. If he'd become an Existentialist more or less overnight, was it possible that Fay had turned into a nymphomaniac?

He longed for a brother or a friend to talk to. Wouldn't it be fantastic to lift the phone this minute and tell this person, this man friend, that Fay was having a breakdown of some kind, acting out a fantasy that she was a hooker. That his father was most likely dying and all *he* was worried about was what would happen to his mother. That it was five years since he'd seen his son, *his* son, and it was more than he could bear, sometimes. But, the worst thing by far was that he was bored with his job and bored with himself.

He used to have friends – mates, pals, chums. They tended to be other dads, whom he got to know through school functions. For a while he'd been the treasurer of the PTA and had helped run the under-tens soccer team, but once the kids progressed to secondary school that had all faded away. If he were truthful, those men were acquaintances not friends and, left without the children to focus on, they discussed cars or rugby or DIY projects. No. He wouldn't have entrusted any of them with his problems.

It was easy for women. They went through life gathering friends, hugging and doing that fake kissing thing, giggling and gossiping. It was okay for them to cry and they were allowed to have tantrums. It was obvious why there weren't too many female Existentialists on the list – women could gather together at Anne Saunders parties and spill all their troubles out in a flurry of underwear and chocolate dildoes, for fuck's sake.

'Soddit.' Jack scrunched up his sweaty clothes and threw them in the direction of the bathroom door. The rhythmic snoring coming from under the duvet convinced him that Fay was out for the count, so he pulled his pyjamas and dressing gown on and went in search of Neil.

'Got a minute?' Jack found Neil in the kitchen, making a pot of tea for himself and Vi.

'Sure. I'll just take Vi her tea and digestives.'

'I thought we could have a look at that email from Kingsley.'

When Neil returned from his errand, Jack hovered behind him whilst he accessed his mailbox.

'Here we go. Sent the day before yesterday.' He moved aside for Jack to get a better look at the screen.

Hey, Neil.

> *How goes it? What's the latest on Grandad? Hope my folks aren't giving you too much grief. Are you letting the side down and keeping my room tidy? What news on the job search? Tell you what, get a decent band together and I might be tempted.*

> *See ya. K*

Jack read and re-read the careless message.

'Sounds okay, doesn't he?' Neil smiled encouragingly.

'Yes.' What did Neil understand about the agonies of parenthood? 'What does he mean about a band?'

'He's taking the piss. He wouldn't come all the way from Oz to play in a band, would he?'

Neil wished him goodnight and went upstairs. As the computer was on, Jack checked their email. Alongside the usual offers of downloads and upgrades there was unopened mail from Kingsley. It had been sitting there for several days – probably sent at the same time as the one to Neil. Up until now, such rare communications from their son had sent him rushing off to find Fay because it was unthinkable to access the precious information without her being there to see it. This evening, he scarcely hesitated before double clicking.

Hi, Mum and Dad.
   Thanks for the newsy mails. It's not easy to pick them up where I am at the moment. So old Dylan went through with it and I've got a sister-in-law. You don't say anything about her so I assume you don't like her much. Hope Grandad's going on OK. Can't imagine Mum and Granny under the same roof.
   There doesn't seem much point in sending twice while Neil's there with you.
      Say hi to everyone. K.

Naturally Kingsley had worked out that Neil would be sharing his mail with them, but the implied decision to keep in touch with an acquaintance, rather than his parents, was hard to take. This mail told them nothing about what he was doing or his whereabouts. He was twenty-three now, for heaven's sake, wasn't it time he got over this teenage petulance? Whatever he felt they'd done to him, however they'd hurt him, he'd made them pay. *They fuck you up, your mum and dad* – fair enough, the man was right, but that was how it was and every parent, including him and Fay, was someone's fucked up child.

As well as making him angry, their son's email presented another problem. If Fay saw it, it would come out that he'd kept silent about Neil's contact with Kingsley. He read the mail again, twice, and deleted it.

He was checking that he'd locked the front door, when he realised that his mother was still watching television. During the fortnight she'd been with them, he hadn't spent a lot of time with her. There were the usual excuses – work, hospital visiting, household jobs – but it was primarily because it was impossible to have an honest conversation with her when Fay was present, conscious, as he was, of the antipathy the two women had for each other. It was as if each of them was checking to see where his loyalty lay, in a kind of if-you're-not-for-me-you're-against-me assessment. When he *was* alone with his mother, he avoided talking about the future and its unpleasant certainties – ill-health, decline and death. The past was no better – a minefield, strewn with inaccurate recollections and explosive resentments. And the present had become an obstacle course of barriers to clamber under, over or around.

Penitent for his shortcomings, he went in to the sitting room only to find Vi, wedged in the far corner of the sofa, head dropped forward, dead to the world in front of the weather forecast. He could see that she *wasn't* dead because, now and again, the hand resting in her lap, twitched as though she were a life-sized marionette and the puppeteer was yanking the string. How was it that, when human beings passed a certain age – say sixty-five or seventy – they lost any vestige of individuality and morphed into generic cartoon characters? Time and again, he'd noticed this. He'd look up and greet the next patient coming in to the surgery with a 'Hello, Mrs. Jones,' when it wasn't Mrs Jones at all, but Mrs Williams. They all looked the same. Specs went on, noses drooped, hair whitened and thinned, flesh sagged and wrinkled. And they did themselves no favours when they adopted the uniform of the living dead – beige, cream, brown. Blokes were even more difficult to tell apart.

'I wasn't asleep,' Vi asserted, floundering amongst the soft upholstery.

'Just resting your eyes?'

'Well I was.' She nodded towards the television. 'I don't know why they can't tell us something cheerful. Terrorists. Strikes. And now we're all going to die of bird 'flu.' She pronounced it *fl-yew* – and glue was *gl-yew* and blue was *bl-yew.* Fay had once tried to put her straight, annunciating the words slowly and clearly – *Gloo. Floo. Bloo.* – as if she were speaking to a small child or a deaf person. He'd had to keep a straight face when his mother had responded – *Gl-yew. Fl-yew. Bl-yew.*

This facile comment sounded horribly like something he'd mentioned to Neil on the way back from the community centre. 'Why don't they have one news bulletin a day that tells us all the good news. Cheer us all up.' Oh God, was he morphing prematurely?

'Neil brought you a cuppa? He's a nice lad, isn't he?' *What can she find to whinge about there?*

'A very nice lad. I only wish my grandsons were half as thoughtful as young Neil.'

'That's not quite fair, Mum, Dylan cares a great deal—'

'One's under the thumb of a wife who won't let him out of her sight.' She shot him a loaded glance, 'And the other one … well, I might as well not have another one.' His mother glared at him, daring him to take up the challenge.

Persevere, persevere. 'So, how are *you* bearing up, Mum? You must be feeling exhausted – all that traipsing back and forth. I know it means a lot to Dad, having you there.'

She patted the sofa cushion, indicating that he should sit down. It was ten-thirty and he was tired and really would like to shower before bed but, mindful of how little time he'd given her in the past two weeks – *or the past thirty years?* – he did as she requested.

Next morning, Fay woke at five. The nausea had subsided but her head pounded and, if she swivelled her eyes from side to side, it felt as if she'd been punched in both eye sockets. She ran her hands down her body and confirmed that she was no longer wearing the bra and thong – she thought she remembered Jack easing them off – but she was pretty sure that they hadn't made love. Jack had been very attentive in the night, sitting in the bathroom with her when she thought she was going to be sick and bringing her several glasses of water. 'You're dehydrated, love. This'll help.' Now he was lying alongside her, his back to her, his arm outside the duvet. From the gentle rise and fall of his shoulders, she could tell that he was asleep. She turned over cautiously, not ready yet to wake him and face an inquisition. She would let him sleep until the alarm went off at seven. Their tight breakfast schedule would leave little time for discussion and it was possible that she wouldn't have to answer any questions until the evening.

Friday. The pupils were skittish, planning the weekend's sexual skirmishes and illegal substances. It was much the same in the staff room. Despite a dull headache and sensitive eyes, Fay free-wheeled through the morning, sustained by paracetamol, black coffee and a couple of cigarettes. Her failure to re-ignite Jack's passion, or her own if it came to that, had lessened her motivation to save up for more lingerie and, things being as they were, the calming effect of nicotine was invaluable.

Jack rang during her lunch break, to ask how she was feeling. 'Better, thanks. And Jack. Thanks for being so… thoughtful.' There was silence on the other end of the line. She should say something about her behaviour last night, and she sensed that each was waiting for the other to bring up the subject, but neither broke the silence. In any case, she couldn't contemplate holding an extended, and possibly life-changing, conversation on a phone the size of a bar of soap.

After lunch, she was timetabled to take Form Four and, once they were settled, she asked them for their 'What's in the Bag?' homework. She noticed that two or three had made title pages with colourful illustrations and the consensus was that it had been 'fun homework'. This made her uneasy. She pushed the bundle of papers into her brief case.

After the lesson, as the teenagers jostled and shoved their way out, one of the boys – a nondescript lad called Darren – lingered by her table. 'Miss?'

'*Mrs Waterfield.*' She was expected to remember his name, the least he could do was remember hers.

'Right. Mrs Waterfield. When can we have them back? Our stories?'

'When do I next teach you lot?' She consulted her timetable. 'Wednesday. I'll mark them in time for the Wednesday lesson.' It seemed an odd request. 'Any particular reason, Darren?'

He looked miserable. 'You won't read them out in class, will you?'

'Why?' She had thought it might be a good idea to read the best ones, especially as the class were so enthusiastic about the exercise.

'Mine's rubbish. I just don't want you to read it out,' he was trying to sound casual, but she detected the earnestness in his voice.

She reassured him. 'No. I promise I won't read yours out to the class.' This was a troubled youngster. 'If you like, you can take it back and let me have another story. Have another bash at it.'

He shook his head. 'No. You can read it, Miss.' He heaved his rucksack on to his shoulder and plodded after the rest of the class.

Jack arrived home early, bringing two bunches of dahlias. 'They're beautiful. Thank you.' Fay kissed his cheek.

Vi, ever looking to identify unnecessary extravagance, called it to his attention that Harry grew dahlias – gladioli and chrysanthemums, too – in their garden. 'No need to spend good money on flowers, John. I'm sure your father would want you to help yourself.' But when he produced a small box of Dairy Milk for *her*, she didn't complain.

'You're getting crafty in your old age,' Fay said when they were alone. Having made a fool of herself last night, she wasn't sure where she stood with her husband.

'I aim to please. Not always easy with Mum, mind you.'

'Jack…about last night…'

He held up both hands to stop her 'No need, love. You don't have to explain. Everyone is entitled to do whatever they want to do. No questions asked.'

What a peculiar thing to say. Their married life was founded upon inquests. Nothing went without question or justification. Jack never went out to buy a newspaper without telling her where he was going, and how long he was going to be away. That wasn't quite accurate, though, was it? What about those Thursday evenings, when he'd let her think he was off dancing and had, in fact, been visiting his parents? And now this 'everyone is entitled to do whatever they want to do' remark. She raised her eyebrows, inviting him to expand but he didn't take the hint.

29

ALTHOUGH IT WAS SATURDAY, Fay got up as soon as she woke, irrationally embarrassed to be lying in bed with Jack whilst his mother and an ex-pupil were within earshot. It was like being in a hotel room, conscious that other guests might be listening through adjoining walls. 'Don't forget we're going out this evening,' she whispered to Jack, who was still asleep – or pretending to be. 'You'd better visit your father this afternoon.'

She was setting the breakfast table when Caitlin rang from the station, reminding her mother that she was off to London. 'Oh. It's this weekend, is it? It had slipped my mind. Have a lovely time and… give Cassidy my love.' She had been determined not to mention his name and was disappointed with her own lack of self-control. She made a pot of coffee, wishing that she were standing on Platform One at Cardiff Central, waiting for the Paddington train to whisk her off to a handsome young lover.

After her triumph with Jack on Tuesday night, swiftly followed by her failures on Wednesday and Thursday, Fay wasn't clear how things stood between them – or how she wanted them to be. Her infatuation for Cassidy would never come to anything but she couldn't bear to surrender the sweet fantasy, which had made her summer so exhilarating. She was all too aware that his physical presence was madness-inducing and that she her strongest resolution would falter if he stood in front of her. The sensible thing, therefore, was to steer clear of him – that was the theory, anyway.

She watched Jack as he buttered his wholemeal toast, spreading thick-cut marmalade across its surface, pushing it to within a millimetre of the crust, evenly distributing the slivers of peel. He always sliced the round from top to bottom, never from side-to-side, explaining that he preferred a section of crusty top and soft base on each half round. He'd followed this formula most mornings for the past thirty years, methodical and unimaginative – exactly what you would want from your dentist.

He looked up, 'Any plans for today?'

'Didn't you say, yesterday, that everyone should do whatever they want to do? No questions asked?' She intended her response to be light-hearted and a little provocative but it sounded bitter, as if the words had been fermenting overnight, ready to boil up into an argument.

He glanced up, expressionless. 'Yes, I did.'

She tried to melt the icy wastes separating them. 'Actually, I was thinking I'd—'

'No,' he shook his head, 'No. You're absolutely right. It's none of my business.'

Silence settled around them, opaque and insulating. Although she would stake her life on the way Jack would butter his toast, she would no longer wager anything on the unfathomable process of his mind.

Saturdays and Sundays these days threw up their own difficulties. Fay could barely cope with weekdays, when she only had to spend the evening avoiding Jack's mother, but it was impossible at the weekend. Unable to come to terms with the outlandish notion that Fay paid someone to clean her house, Vi pottered about, flicking surfaces with a yellow duster or fiddling with the vacuum cleaner. Her behaviour annoyed Fay and probably offended Colleen, the cleaner, who would see it as a criticism of her competence.

'You don't have to do that,' Fay told Vi when she found her in the downstairs cloakroom.'

Vi pumped the lavatory brush up and down in the pan. 'I've got to earn my keep. The Devil makes work for idle hands.'

Upstairs, Neil was playing his guitar and his plaintive strumming brought Fay to a standstill, as if she had received a blow to the chest. There was a time when faltering chord sequences, forging pathways through unwritten songs, had filled the house, as much a part of their lives as the ticking clock or the pictures on the walls. It had driven her mad, but it was worse when Kingsley left and the music ceased.

'Neil,' she shouted. 'Neil? I'm not doing anything at the moment so why don't we have a go at your CV? It shouldn't take more than an hour.' The music stopped and she breathed again.

They spent the rest of the morning in the study and by midday had produced a document which maximised Neil's humble qualifications – five reasonable GCSE passes, the Duke of Edinburgh's bronze medal and several awards for swimming and lifesaving. Fay guided him through the section on hobbies and interests and, by the end of it, had learned that his middle name was Vincent – after Gene not Van Gogh – and his birthday fell on the same day as Marion's – proving that astrology was twaddle.

'Thanks. I wasn't getting anywhere.'

'Well, *I'd* certainly give you a job, with this CV.' She patted his hand. 'And you know you can always give my name as a reference.'

'Thanks, Fay.' He gave an appreciative grin and tears, triggered by his grateful acceptance of her help, blurred her vision.

The car pulled up and Jack got out. The last time she'd seen him he'd been going into the shed, but he must have left whilst she was with Neil. He was carrying a Marks and Spencer carrier bag but, by the time he appeared in the kitchen, there was no sign of it. Under the new rules, she felt unable to ask where he'd been or what he'd bought.

After lunch, Jack and Vi went to the hospital and Neil disappeared to do an extra shift at the pub. At last she had the house to herself for a couple of hours and she made a cup of strong coffee, picked up the newspaper and, lured by the milky September sunshine, went into the garden. The drooping purple blossoms of the buddleia bush were alive with butterflies and, as she watched them, thoughts of Caitlin and Cassidy, flirting over a glass of white wine, fluttered in to disturb the tranquil scene.

In an attempt to block the incapacitating thoughts, she did a tour of the garden. Gardening, for its own sake, didn't interest her but she liked the flower beds to look orderly, the grass just-mown, so that if they entertained guests out here the garden acted as a pleasing backdrop. Jack, unlike his father, wasn't a committed gardener and he stuck with the old stand-bys – roses, gladioli and chrysanthemums – but he did his best and everything was looking neat and tidy. She worked her way along the border, tugging at odd wisps of couch-grass and nipping spent heads from the roses, recalling Dylan's wedding as fading petals cascaded to the ground.

Arriving at the garden shed, she glanced through the cobwebbed window and spotted Jack's M&S bag, at the end of the workbench. So *this* was where he'd left it. She tried the handle, half-expecting the door to be locked but it swung open. Despite the open window, the sun had raised the temperature inside the wooden building and the air, smelling of white spirit and wood shavings, was stuffy. A bluebottle buzzed up in the rafters, loud and sinister. She stepped inside, crossing the unmarked border into Jack's private domain, becoming a spy in alien territory, liable for punishment if she were caught. What was he hiding? What didn't he want her to see?

'This is ridiculous.' Taking two decisive strides, she snatched up the carrier and pulled out the contents. It was a black polo-necked sweater – forty inch chest – Jack's size. What a let down. The thing that surprised her was his driving all the way into town for something so commonplace. Not sure whether to be relieved or disappointed in what she'd found, she re-folded the sweater and placed the bag back exactly where it had been. As she'd always known, parcels were invariably more exciting *before* they were opened – with the exception of those in plain brown carriers, of course.

Her discovery reminded her that she had essays to mark. It was several days before she was due to return them but, with her appetite for mystery whetted, she was intrigued to see what the brown bag homework had thrown up. In particular, to find out what had caused Darren so much anxiety. She made a second coffee and collected her briefcase.

On the whole, the class had produced good work. It might be worth repeating the exercise with other groups she taught. The keenest pupil had discovered a magic carpet, leading to six tedious pages of intergalactic tosh; the laziest – or the cleverest – another carrier bag inside which there was another bag inside which there was … There was a predictable body-part count – heads, fingers, ears – and an alarming amount of food, drink and drugs.

She saved Darren's work until last. Darren's bag contained a brown wig, a pink strappy top, a short denim skirt and a pair of white pumps. In the privacy of the fictional garden shed, he'd stripped off his tee-shirt and jeans and put on the clothes explaining, in awkward, clichéd language, his feeling of happiness as he was transformed from a fourteen-year-old boy into a fourteen-year-old girl. 'Everything seemed okay again. Life could get back to how it ought to be.' Poor kid. No wonder he'd not wanted his work read out to the class. What made it extra touching, extra poignant, was that he'd dressed in the clothes of a typical teenage girl. It would have still have been shocking, but more logical, if the bag had been full of sequinned dresses and six-inch stilettos.

Circling spelling mistakes and correcting punctuation, she re-read Darren's essay. The boy was pleading for help. But why had he reached out to *her*? The homework had been an opportunity, but a rather obscure one. He must trust her, although she'd had nothing much to do with him, until a couple of weeks ago. A crush on an older woman? It happened. What if…what if women of a certain age produced a pheromone, or something similar, that attracted vulnerable young men? There'd been that article in the *Observer*, hadn't there? Women were winning fishing competitions because they gave off a scent which attracted the heavier male fish. And, look. Hadn't Neil come scuttling round to the house after one sniff? Then there was Cassidy. He'd hinted that his memories of David hadn't been wonderful. Perhaps he, too, was planning to come and cry on her shoulder.

'This is fun, isn't it?' Fay leaned across the table towards Jack and gave him a knowing grin.

They were seated in the corner of a dingy, pseudo-

Italian restaurant and Jack's eyes were watering from garlic fumes, drifting from the open-plan kitchen. It wasn't 'fun' and he ought to stand by his new manifesto and tell her so, but truth was too important to be wasted on minor issues like Italian restaurants.

'It was sweet of Caitlin to book this for us, don't you think? All week she's been saying that we should spend more time together. Away from…you know…things.'

Did Caitlin really believe that a couple of hours eating pasta and drinking second-rate *Valpollicello* could set the world straight? 'Where's she gone, anyway?' Jack asked, imagining how much more he would enjoy the evening were Caitlin there with them.

'Oh, I'm not sure. London I think.' Fay brushed invisible crumbs off the red table cloth. 'She's meeting Cassidy Ford and they're going to a furniture exhibition. Then he's taking her to see Sadie and Joe. They live in the East End. Did you ever meet Joe?' She seemed to know a lot of the fine detail for someone who wasn't sure.

Fay chattered on. Now and again she paused but, when he said nothing, she started again, as if his silence were encouraging. While she talked to herself, Jack watched the other diners – mostly couples, like themselves – weighing up which were soul-mates, which resigned to their circumstances.

He'd done further internet research before his trip to Marks and Spencer, unearthing a plethora of definitions, many ambiguous and confusing and he'd printed out a couple of the more straightforward ones, to have by him for handy reference. *Existentialism views the individual, the self, the individual's experience, and the uniqueness therein as the basis for understanding the nature of human existence.* He'd definitely had some unique experiences over the past couple of months but they hadn't cast much light on human existence and, as a novice, he decided it was wiser to make sense of his *own* life before tackling the rest of mankind.

The waiter arrived and poured a splash of wine into his glass, standing back whilst Jack tasted it. It was as bad as he'd anticipated, sharp and lifeless, but he couldn't be bothered to make a fuss.

Fay pushed her glass towards him. 'I've been wondering…'

'Oh, yes.'

'I told you, didn't I, that Geoffrey Lauderdale's leaving Isabel because he says he wants to grow old with someone who's "a bit more homely"?' She wiggled her index fingers, forming inverted commas in the air. 'I think there must be more to it than that, mind you but, I was wondering… Which do *you* think's more essential? Glamour or homeliness?'

He looked at Fay's patchy green eye-shadow, blobby mascara and greasy lipstick. He took in her peculiar, gravity-defying hairstyle, stiff to his touch. He caught sight of her freckled hand, gripping the stem of the glass, the ridged nails painted an unlikely iridescent orange. He remembered peeling the vulgar underwear off her the other night. Glamorous? No. Homely? No.

He ran his finger around the collar of his new sweater, pulling the hot, itchy wool away from his neck. How would the 'big boys' – Sartre and the like – deal with the mess he was in? He wished that there had been a few practical examples amongst the screeds of theory. No doubt they wouldn't have allowed themselves to end up in his position – trapped by convention, responsibility and cowardice. On the far side of the restaurant, the middle-aged waitress who had taken their order, shining black hair caught in a simple twist at the nape of her neck, moved

292

gracefully and patiently between the tables and Non edged into his mind, for a moment filling him with resolution and he knew that, if he were to save himself, this was the moment to tell Fay everything and face the consequences. He felt exhilarated yet scared, powerful yet uncertain. A few words would sever the ropes tethering him to his humdrum existence and enable him to become the man he was meant to be. It should be a piece of cake.

'That's not much of a choice,' he said.

She laughed uneasily. The silent seconds ticked by. 'For God's sake, Jack.' Now she sounded panicky, as if she had strayed into quicksand.

Existentialism does not acknowledge the existence of a god or of any other determining principle – human beings are free to do as they choose and face the consequences of their action.

Was it possible to have it both ways? He wanted to retain the love and respect of his family, and he couldn't deny that the romp with Fay the other night had been pretty amazing. At the same time, he longed to be the man who concocted rainbows and solved economic problems; whose admiration for one woman was so all-engulfing that simply being in her presence brought physical satisfaction. It didn't stack up. Perhaps Kierkegaard and his pals were infertile orphaned bachelors, spared the anguish caused by abandoning parents, wives and children.

The waitress arrived with their food and Fay, who seemed no longer to expect an answer to her glamour-or-homeliness question, switched the conversation to school matters, telling him about one of her pupil's homework. It had something to do with girls' clothes and carrier bags, but he already had enough on his mind and it drifted past him.

By the time the taxi turned up to take them home, Fay

had drunk too much and he was wishing he'd drunk a lot more.

30

'How did he seem to you?' It was Monday morning and Jack's first opportunity to speak to Sheila since her visit to the hospital the previous afternoon.

Sheila screwed up her face, 'A bit subdued. He didn't say much but there were quite a lot of us there, all nattering. Vi, Dylan and Nia, some neighbours – Jenkins is it? – then Marion turned up. So I didn't stay long.' She patted his arm. 'Chin up. He's a fighter.'

A fighter? That wasn't how he saw his father. Had he been old enough to fight in the war, Jack was sure Harry would have found a way not to. He would have stayed at home and worked a double shift in the narrowest seam, doing whatever it took to keep the home fires burning. No, his mother was the fighter – guerrilla warfare her speciality. Harry had been more of an avoider – was there no word for someone who, almost pathologically, steered clear of trouble? – slipping out into the garden whenever conflict loomed. Reticent. Restrained. Fair enough, but what happens when an avoider comes face to face with the ultimately unavoidable?

In the middle of the afternoon, his mother phoned the surgery, something which she rarely did. 'Staff Nurse says that they're going to send Dad home. But John, the house'll be damp. And I've got no food in.'

'Take it slowly, Mum. Tell me exactly what they said.'

In the end, unable to make sense of what she was telling him, he phoned the ward and they told him that, yes, the consultant had mentioned the possibility of sending Harry home before too long, but it was very unlikely to be before next week.

'You couldn't go and calm my mother down, could you nurse? Tell her to hang on there and I'll come in as soon as I can.'

She promised to do her best.

How speedily they'd incorporated Harry's hospitalisation into their routines. Having his mother with them wasn't ideal but they were working around it, thanks, in no small part, to Neil who was turning out to be an asset to the household. Visiting was tedious but the hospital was handy and, to be fair, his mother had born the brunt of it. The unexpected news that his father might be sent home soon, panicked him. Which home did they mean anyway? He shuddered. It was unthinkable that Harry should come to them but, if he went *home* home, would his mother be able to cope? She wasn't a young woman – seventy-seven, in fact – but it wasn't her age that concerned him, it was her dependence on Harry to deal with anything which wasn't 'woman's work'. She could churn out beef tea by the gallon, and make sure the bathroom was spotless but could she unblock a drain or sort out a problem at the bank? It would be best if Harry Waterfield stayed where he was, at least until he was fit enough to climb a ladder and clear leaves from the guttering.

Harry was asleep and his mother folding and re-folding towels when he arrived in the ward. She couldn't wait to ask, 'Could you pop me to the supermarket tonight? Then up to the house?'

'Hello, Mum.' He kissed her cheek. 'Don't start fretting

about that. Didn't the nurse explain that he won't be discharged just yet? I know he's been sitting out in the chair, but they'll have to be certain that he can get himself to the toilet – his mother disliked 'lavatory' – and things like that. We don't want them to send him home until he's—'

'Yes, but I need time to air the house and do some baking.'

He let her babble on, spewing out the disjointed and trivial thoughts that cluttered her mind. Not for the first time, he wondered whether, even hoped that, he'd been adopted and that his *real* mother was a member of Mensa.

He turned to the sleeping man, watching a pulse flicker in the soft depression where scrawny neck met frail breastbone. Harry's battered hands rested outside the sheet, on his chest, one covering the other, as though he were ashamed of them and was trying to conceal the damage done when he hacked and shoved and heaved coal, hundreds of feet beneath the Valley floor. Jack spread his owns hands – pale and soft, the nails short and clean – on the blue cotton blanket and compared them with his father's. But, slight though they were, he detected similarities in the way their thumbs bent back and the oddly undersized nails on their little fingers. No question about it, whoever may have borne him, this man was his father.

He stooped to retrieve a wad of cotton wool from beneath the bed and, as he straightened up, he saw that his father's eyelids were a fraction open. Harry was watching him. The crafty bugger was taking avoiding action again. One eyelid closed and opened again, in a nano-signal of collusion.

'So Grandad's coming home?' Caitlin smiled and patted the back of her grandmother's hand. 'That's wonderful.'

'I'm sure I don't know how we'll manage.' Vi whizzed the teaspoon around, generating a whirlpool in her cup.

'You'll be fine, Gran. You've got great neighbours, and Dad can be with you in twenty minutes.'

Jack had managed, between the front door and the sitting room, to brief Caitlin that her grandparents would be returning to their own home when Harry was discharged. 'They'll be better off. Everything's how they like it. They can suit themselves. Grandad's sure to want to get out in his greenhouse—'

'How was London?' Fay was showing remarkably little interest in the approaching departure of one of their house-guests. 'Have a good time?'

Caitlin flushed. 'Great. It was good. Very interesting.'

'Did you learn a lot about furniture? Can you tell a dovetail from a tenon? Teak from mahogany?' Fay's tone was belligerent.

Caitlin ignored her mother's odd questions. 'We saw Sadie and Joe on Saturday night. Had a meal together. We were reminiscing. The last time I saw her, she was sitting on our sofa, refusing to speak.'

'She always was a drama queen,' Fay said. 'Laura's had a dreadful time with her.'

'Well, she seems pretty normal now, apart from the body piercings. And Joe is such a lovely guy.'

Jack was relieved that his mother had fallen asleep in the armchair, head back, upper dentures dropped on to her lower lip, and they could escape a post-mortem on the current fad for self-mutilation.

'D'you remember, Mum, when we were at Laura's a couple of weeks ago and we were looking at that photograph of Sadie? I said she reminded me of someone?' Caitlin paused and Jack thought how beautiful she was, in an unconventional way. Her green eyes were a little too far apart, her nose too long and her teeth too big, but these imperfect features came together in a bold, intelligent face, made all the more striking by unruly hair, the colour of paprika. She shook her head and shrugged. 'It's Kingsley. I don't know why I didn't twig at the time. She sounds like him, too. All evening I felt as if he were in the room with us.'

Jack choked. *Kingsley. Sadie. Sadie. Laura.* His heart-rate tripled. *Sadie. Laura. Laura. Jack.* He felt perspiration springing out of his armpits, streaming down his back. *Do something.* He tipped the contents of his cup into his lap, then watched the small quantity of orangey-brown tea quadruple in volume as it dripped between his thighs, forming a puddle shaped vaguely like a map of Africa, beneath his seat.

Fay exploded. 'What *is* the matter with you, Jack? It's worse than living with a three-year-old. Here. Let me.'

Sadie's reported resemblance to Kingsley was lost in a frenzy of mopping and swearing . Even if his 'bloody clumsiness' meant buying new trousers and replacing the pale carpet; even if he suffered third-degree burns to his inner thighs, it was preferable to an in-depth discussion about Sadie's parentage.

While Fay and Vi argued about the best way to deal with the spreading stain, he slunk off to change his trousers. Sitting on the edge of their bed, he took slow, deep breaths but his thoughts were bouncing from one unanswerable question to the next. How old was Sadie? *Exactly* how old? When had they made that visit to see Laura after David died? *Exactly* when? Fay was the expert on that sort of stuff – birthdays and anniversaries, knowing which year they went on which holiday – but obviously he couldn't ask her outright.

'What on earth are you doing?' Fay appeared in the

study where Jack, having sneaked downstairs, was rooting through the desk drawers.

'Ummm. Looking for our insurance policy. I wanted to check that the carpet was covered for accidental damage.' He was pleased that he'd come up with such a credible reply, doubting whether even old Camus would have had the guts to say, 'Actually I'm looking for my old diaries, on the off chance that I made a note of when I made love to Laura Ford.'

'For goodness sake. You know we don't keep that sort of thing in the desk.' She pointed to the two-drawer filing cabinet in the corner. 'It'll be in there. But can't you leave that until tomorrow? Caitlin's just leaving.'

When they finally got to bed, he was unable to sleep. Fay, too, seemed restless and they talked for a while about the practicalities of Harry's return home. 'It's going to involve you in a lot more running around,' Fay warned. 'There's bound to be out-patient's appointments and things like that.'

'Let's see how it goes,' he muttered. He pictured Non, brushing her thick, black hair before slipping in to bed. Iolo would be preparing sweet cocoa for the guests and Zena – she was surely back from her sister's – would be setting out the breakfast places.

'What d'you make of that peculiar stuff about Sadie?'

It had been too much to hope that Caitlin's revelation would be forgotten. He might be panicking unnecessarily. If it turned out that he were in the clear, he would be happy to discuss the phenomenon but, first, he needed to establish the facts.

He rolled across the bed until he encountered Fay's body, warm and soft against his. 'Hello.' He kissed her, gently at first, then harder.

'Hello, yourself.' She sounded surprised but not

displeased.

The same act of love that was causing him such disquiet, rescued him – for the time being, at least.

Jack slept fitfully and, at six o'clock, sneaked out of bed and crept down to the study. He'd hung on to all his pocket diaries, supplied annually by the British Dental Association, and made them into neat bundles, encircled by stout rubber bands. They were fiddly things, all fancy cover and useless information about airports and average rainfalls, in print that was too small to read. There was barely space to write more than a key word against each date. 'Seminar', 'Docs. 9.45', 'F's b'day'. Very occasionally he referred back to them for a phone number or date of a particular meeting.

Fay was out cold but, nevertheless, he felt vulnerable in the house and, salvaging a discarded carrier bag from the waste paper basket, he gathered the diaries and took them out to the shed. It had been a clear, cold night and droplets of condensation had formed on the rafters, then dripped onto the floor. He shivered and pulled on his old gardening fleece before perching on the arm of the grubby old chair and settling to his task. All night he'd been going over and over it, struggling to pinpoint the date. They'd visited Laura a few months after David died. What year was that? It must have been when Cassidy was about five and Caitlin, what, two? It was summer, anyway, and definitely before Dylan was born.

He found the diaries for 1976 and 1977 and began flicking through the thin pages. The entries weren't easy to decipher but he limited his efforts to weekends in the summer months and within a few minutes he'd found it. 'L. to visit L.' London to visit Laura. Saturday 3rd August 1976. He took the calendar off its hook next to the window and counted forwards nine months. The 3rd May. A child conceived on 3rd August should be born on or around the 3rd May the following year, unless something out of the ordinary had happened.

Fay was late down for breakfast and they had little time for conversation as they prepared for work. 'I can't believe they're talking about sending your father home. He's no better than when he went in.' She gave him a distracted peck on the cheek as he left for the surgery. 'You'd better get hold of someone and find out what's going on.'

Pushing dates and calculations to the back of his mind, he joined the procession of cars heading into the city centre. It was a perfect September morning, the low sun bringing out the colours of the leaves as they took on the yellows and oranges of autumn. Along his route he passed youngsters in groups of two or three, weighed down by oversized school bags, meandering towards the local school. Despite their loads, they looked cheerful and he wondered whether this generation of schoolchildren suffered from the 'back to school' nerves that had afflicted him at the beginning of every year. When he was thirteen or fourteen, his mother had taken him to the doctor, firmly convinced that he had a stomach ulcer, or worse, but the griping pains always subsided a week or so into the new term. What had been the cause of his anxiety in those miserable, adolescent days? Caustic teachers? Communal showers? Acne? Quadratic equations? Or the ultimate nightmare, that he might die a virgin, which, in retrospect, would have solved all his problems.

For once he was content to be crawling along in the morning traffic, cocooned in the car, temporarily disconnected from his difficulties. This sense of remoteness was reinforced by a humming in his ears, as if he were at the far end of a tunnel. Probably lack of sleep. Were he in charge of a heavy goods vehicle, he would be declared a

302

danger to himself and everyone else on the road, so why on earth did he think he was capable of performing delicate procedures inside the human mouth?

He took the next turn off the dual carriageway and parked in a street of terraced houses. He needed to think and it might be easier here, away from everything that was making his life so shitty and, getting out of the car, he started walking, taking random turns to the left or right. The schoolchildren milling along the pavements here were more of a mixed bag than those he'd seen earlier. The girls wore cheap jewellery and make-up. The boys walked three abreast, insolently forcing him off the pavement. Many of them were smoking. Snatches of conversation that he caught were punctuated with obscenities. One lanky girl, in the sketchiest version of school uniform, shrieked at her dawdling friends to 'get a fucking move on'. They joined her and began taunting the boys on the other side of the road. Individually, trapped in the dental chair, they were harmless enough but, in these little mobs and on their own territory, they made him nervous and he hoped he'd locked the car.

He checked his watch. The first patient would be arriving at the surgery in about twenty minutes. He stood in the doorway of a boarded-up shop and phoned Sheila. 'It's me. Look, I'm feeling really ropey this morning. Dizzy. Queasy. Could you cancel my patients? Apologise to those that you can't catch.' As an afterthought, he added, 'I'm going to unplug the phone and go back to bed. I'll ring again this afternoon. Thanks, Sheila.'

On the opposite corner there was a shop selling pies, sandwiches and hot drinks. He bought a coffee and sat on a high stool at the counter near the window. It was years since he'd been ill enough to take time off work, which was astounding considering the number of germs that he inhaled every day. He felt rotten about cancelling his patients, some of whom would make a fruitless journey, and he felt worse about lying to his faithful friend, leaving her to field any complaints.

Defying his own stricture, he stirred a sachet of white sugar into the instant coffee. Tooth decay was way down his list of things to worry about and he needed all the energy he could muster. It was nine-seventeen on a Tuesday morning and, once again, he had disappeared off the radar. But he couldn't spend the rest of the day lurking in sandwich bars. It was high time to address his increasing tally of anxieties.

Existentialism no longer seemed the cure-all for his life. The bit about being free to do what he wanted was still appealing but the rider – that he would have to face the consequences of his actions – was daunting. Anyway, how was that going to work, if the consequence of his action twenty-nine years ago was Sadie Ford? His mission for the day, and the reason that he'd cried off work, was to establish if he was Sadie's father and the obvious place to start was Fay's birthday book.

31

'IT'S ONLY ME.' Jack had hoped to have the house to himself but Vi and Neil were in the kitchen, leaning over a newspaper that lay open on the table. They looked sheepish, as if he'd caught them doing something that they shouldn't. He explained why he was home again so soon. 'I'm feeling lousy. I'm going back to bed.'

His mother fussed, offering hot-water-bottles and, her cure-all, a mug of hot, sweetened milk. Accepting that there was no escaping her attentions, he opted for a cup of tea.

'We've been going through the jobs.' Neil pointed at the newspaper where a few small ads had been ringed in pencil.

'Anything take your fancy?' Jack, who up until now hadn't been involved in Neil's search for employment, tried to sound interested.

'It's more whether I take their fancy. But now I've got a proper CV to send out, I must stand a better chance.'

Vi brought Jack's tea and, peering at his face, made him sit down. 'Yes. You do look peaky. You always get those funny blotches on your forehead when you're going down with something.'

Did he?

Alice. When the kids were young, if they weren't feeling

well, he used to suggest that they were 'Going down with Alice – like Christopher Robin.' They were at the age when they found that kind of thing excruciatingly funny, giggling and repeating and embroidering it – 'Christopher Robin went down with Alice. He'd better take a pill.' 'He'd better have his tonsils out.' 'He'd better jump off the Severn Bridge.' Until they had worn the joke threadbare and were weak from laughing. He'd forgotten all that.

He took the scuffed, leather-bound birthday book and the tattered address book out of the drawer in the hall table and, concealing them beneath his jacket, hurried upstairs. Safe in the bedroom, he changed out of his work clothes then, sitting on the bed, took a deep breath and opened the birthday book to 'May'.

Fay's handwriting had changed little over the years. Maybe now her descenders were more flamboyant, the crosses on her t's more careless, but it was still the unwaveringly legible, rounded hand that sat so well with her personality. He checked carefully through the entries of familiar names, ambivalent about the secret they might hide. Family, friends and people he'd forgotten they ever knew – all logged there. Some of them had died – a neighbour; an old college friend; Fay's cousin who was killed in a car crash on the M3 – but they remained there, on a level footing with the living, although they would never need another birthday card. But no 'Sadie Ford'. He checked through April. Then June. Finally he went through the whole book and, although Laura, David, *poor old David,* and Cassidy were all there, he found no entry for Sadie and felt unduly miffed on her behalf.

As a rule, a man finds out that he's impregnated his wife's best friend before the baby's born, not twenty-eight years later. But what did time have to do with it? After all, a father's for life, not just for Christmas. Laura obviously didn't think the paternity of her daughter was such a big deal or she would have told him at the time, wouldn't she?

What had he felt when her saw her last month? It was unthinkable to admit but, until she mentioned it, it had slipped his mind that they'd ever slept together. A psychiatrist would, no doubt, have a more complicated explanation. She'd visited them on the Saturday of the Llangwm carnival, hadn't she? Was she there when he'd returned early from his 'conference'? No. He was already home when Fay and Laura came in. Fay had taken her to visit his parents...and take photographs of them. 'Her project', she'd called it.

He lay back against the pillows, eyes shut, trying to think, but each thought generated another until his head felt as if it were full of fish, swimming in all directions. 'This is ridiculous.' Grabbing the address book, he found Laura's telephone number.

It rang only twice before she picked up the phone. 'Hello?'

'Laura? It's Jack. Jack Waterfield.'

'Jack? Is everything okay?' It was understandable that she assumed a call from him at ten-fifteen on a Tuesday morning could only mean bad news.

'Yes. Fine, thanks.'

'Your father's okay?'

'Yes. Not too bad. He's coming home this week sometime.' She *would* have more than a passing interest in Harry Waterfield if he were her daughter's grandfather.

'That's good.' She paused and he knew she was waiting for an explanation.

'Did you know that Caitlin went up to London with Cassidy at the weekend? We think it's great that they hit it off so well. And she was thrilled to see Sadie again.'

Another pause. 'What's this about, Jack?' Her voice was warm yet neutral. 'It's lovely to chat, but I'm sure that's not why you rang.'

'No. I wanted to ask you something.' He cleared his throat and ran his tongue along his lower lip. 'When's Sadie's birthday?'

She was silent for quite a few seconds and Jack guessed she was assembling her thoughts. 'Are you asking me if you're her father?' She had always been very direct.

Muffled music came from the radio in the kitchen below; someone was cutting the grass with a push-mower in a nearby garden, the fresh-cut scent wafting in through the open window; his heart thudded. 'Yes, I suppose I am.'

'She was born on the twenty-first of April, but that won't give you, or me, the answer. You see I don't know who her father is. And that's the truth.' Then, in an almost reproachful voice, 'I'm surprised that it's taken you this long to ask.'

It was his turn to collect his thoughts. 'But surely you must—'

'Must I? I don't know if you appreciate what a pitiful state I was in after David died. I didn't realise that it was possible to be so cripplingly unhappy. I was staggering from one day to the next, doing whatever it took to get through, suffocating in grief.' She paused and he knew she was reliving it. 'You were so gentle and considerate that night and I know we gave each other great comfort. But I had other comforters. Several in the space of a few weeks. Please don't ask me who they were. I think I went a bit mad. Then, when I found out I was pregnant, I had some crazy idea that the baby was David, trying to get back to me. See – I must have been mad.' When he didn't say anything she continued, 'Don't you remember how I kept out of your way for quite a while after that visit? Fay was very understanding – she thought it was because I couldn't bear to be with a couple; to see how David and I might have been. When Sadie was born – and clearly wasn't a reincarnation of David – I was as vague as I could be about her birth date and the missing father.

'Sadie and I struggled through those grim years, when she was desperate for a Dad and punishing me for denying her one. It was hard but it was my problem, my choice. Now, at last, she seems happy. Contented. She's got her Joe, bless him, and it would be cruel to ruin their lives with uncompromising things like DNA tests. Where would it get us all, anyway? I think the best thing for me to do is put the phone down and give you time to consider what I've just told you.'

'But the photos. Why take photos of my parents if you don't think they're Sadie's grandparents?'

'Yes. I shouldn't have done that. You heard that my father died recently? That's probably got something to do with it. Maybe I thought I needed to set the record straight – for myself. It was a stupid, sentimental thing to do. It *is* possible that Harry and Vi are her grandparents but, again, that's *my* problem not hers, or yours or theirs. End of story. I hope you feel the same way. Now, can I ask *you* a question?'

'Of course,'

'Have you said anything to Fay about this?'

'No, of course not. You might find this hard to believe but the possibility had never crossed my mind until last night, when Caitlin told us that Sadie reminded her of Kingsley.'

There was a pause as Laura assimilated this information which was clearly new to her. 'Is that what she said? She didn't mention anything when she was here.'

'Didn't you notice similarities, when they were kids?

Weren't you looking for clues? You must have been a bit interested in who fathered your baby.' It sounded harsh but he didn't mean it to.

'Think back. We didn't get together very often, did we? *We* couldn't afford the train fare; *you* used to work most Saturdays. And when we did, one or other of the kids was off somewhere. Or they had some ghastly hairstyle which made them look like nothing on earth. Or they were sulking in a bedroom, refusing to play happy families.'

'You're suggesting that Kingsley and Sadie are two of a kind?'

'I don't know what I'm suggesting.'

He'd wrong-footed her but it was nothing to be triumphant about. 'Sorry. You're right, Laura. I need to think about this.'

They agreed to speak in a few days time.

'Feeling any better? You don't look it.' His mother was backing down the stairs, dusting between the balusters, and looked up as he came out of the bedroom.

'I could do with some air. I might go for a walk.' He wanted to get away from the house and his mother's ministrations.

'Will you be all right on your own?' Neil offered to keep him company. Jack wished he would go and read some dubious magazines in his room, like any other twenty-three year old, and stop being so bloody agreeable.

'Thanks, but I'm okay.' He took the car-keys off the hook and, before they could ask him why he was going for a walk in the car, hurried out.

He felt rotten about letting his patients down but, now that Sheila had cancelled his appointments, there was no point in going to the surgery. He knew he should make more of an effort to find out the medics' prognosis for his father, and what follow-up treatment the consultant planned – although he was convinced the pompous idiot had no idea what was wrong. He would visit the hospital this evening, after his mother had done her shift.

Until then, this mellow September day was all his own.

Having found the courage to confront Laura, he began to believe that this was his day for action, but, as he drove away from the house, he wished that he'd given more consideration to what he was wearing. The shapeless sweatshirt and baggy chinos placed him firmly in the fifty-plus category – accurate but demoralising. He should have gone for something more stylish, more out of the ordinary. He smiled, imagining the fun Iolo had each morning when he opened his wardrobe and decided who to be. Beret and Breton shirt? Fisherman's smock? Combat trousers? With autumn setting in, he was probably in the garden at that moment, sawing logs in readiness for the first cold snap – a lumberjack, in red checked shirt and sturdy boots.

When he reached The Welcome Stranger, the sight of the open door and the hanging baskets, still crammed with lobelia and trailing geraniums, was tantalizing, but he drove straight past. No yellow-coated Siren guided him this time, but he'd relived the journey so often that he was familiar with every twist in the road, every telegraph-pole, every field gate. He rounded the bend and there, opposite the stag-horn oak, was the sign for the nursery and he swung the car down the narrow lane, into the car-park. Before getting out, he flicked down the sun visor and slid back the vinyl panel that concealed a tiny mirror. This 'vanity mirror' was listed as one of the car's features, alongside air conditioning, air-bags and a sophisticated CD player. Would a potential purchaser, prepared to lash out fifteen thousand pounds on a car, really be swayed by a mirror? He had to admit it was useful, though, as he combed his hair and beard using the emergency comb which Fay kept in the glove compartment.

The nursery occupied a plot about half the size of a football field. Two greenhouses stood on the far side and, next to them, an open-sided shed, roofed with transparent corrugated sheeting. Wooden staging, laden with pots and trays of plants, stretched in all directions and, next to the entrance, there was a quaint wooden summer-house, surrounded by buckets of cut flowers – chrysanthemums, Michaelmas daisies, dahlias. A painted sign on the closed door invited 'Ring the bell if you want anything.' Wouldn't that be something? All one's desires fulfilled by pressing a bell. Savouring the moment when he would see Non, Jack meandered between the rows of plants, noting how well-cared for they were, how reasonably priced compared with those at the DIY superstore and admiring the neat handwriting – her handwriting? – on the informative labels.

When he thought he might burst with anticipation, he rang the bell, gazing across the tops of the taller plants, eager to catch the first glimpse of her. He perched, alert, on the low stone wall, like a faithful dog waiting for his master to return. Suddenly an exotic, spicy smell filled the air. What was it? Christmas. He could smell Christmas. Looking down, he saw that he'd stepped on one of the thyme plants that sprouted from between the paving stones. Sodding Christmas. It was out there, lurking maliciously at the end of the year, beyond the minefield of family conflict. His spirits plummeted.

'Hi. Sorry to keep you.' He swivelled round to see a woman, perhaps a few years younger than himself, short and round-faced, her brown, cropped hair threaded with grey. She wore faded overalls and battered walking boots. 'I was having a bite of lunch. How can I help?'

This is my action day. 'Oh, hi. I … I was hoping to catch Non. Non Evans?'

The woman smiled. Her startlingly white teeth were large with a slight gap between the central incisors, giving her face an open, child-like frankness and he found himself unexpectedly drawn to the person who might be his rival. 'She's in the house.' She pointed towards the cottage then, turning, looked him hard in the face. 'Would you be Jack, by any chance?'

'Good Lord.'

'We don't get too many bearded strangers with, how did she put it, "dreamy grey eyes" and,' she pointed at his car, 'Cardiff number plates.' She extended her hand. 'I'm Ruth.'

Dreamy grey eyes, eh? This time there was no need for covert operations. He hurried up the path to the front door and knocked boldly. The sharp sound reverberated on the far side of the door, soon followed by rhythmic footsteps, getting louder until – *Yes! Yes! Yes!* – she stood in front of him, composed and welcoming, as though she'd been expecting him for days. 'Jack.'

'I was passing…' He stopped and shook his head. 'I wasn't passing, at all. I wanted to see you.' There, he'd said it and the world kept turning.

'That's nice.' She led him down the cool, dim hallway and into the kitchen – already familiar to him after his reconnaissance raid a week ago. The remnants of lunch for two were spread on the scrubbed wooden table.

'Don't let me interrupt…' He indicated the food.

'Don't be soft.' Her voice had a more pronounced Welsh lilt than he'd remembered and he was taken aback at the inaccuracy of his recollection. 'Tea?' She gave the word two syllables, the first long and the second barely, but definitely, there. *Teee-uh?*

Whilst she filled the kettle and cleared the dishes from the table, he had an opportunity to study her. Today her hair was in plaits, the parting which ran down the back of her head, delightfully crooked. The luscious, shining braids fell forward as she leaned over the sink, exposing her neck, the colour of the milky coffee his mother used to make. Her arms, sturdy and shapely, were the same scrumptious brown. How mistaken women were if they imagined beauty depended on straight partings or manicured nails.

'Did you call at The Welcome Stranger?'

'The door was open as I passed but, no, I didn't. Are your parents okay?'

'Well, Mum's back. And Dad's on his best behaviour.'

'They've patched up their differences?'

'For the time being. The cash-flow crisis has been sorted, thanks to you. So we'll just have to wait and see what the next thing is.' She grimaced. 'Trouble is, Dad's a big kid. He sees something that he thinks will make life easier, or more fun, and grabs it. I think he's missing the bit of his brain that understands actions always have consequences.'

They were straying into Existentialist country and Jack had a suspicion that Non considered it to be a bad place. 'I don't mean to pry but what sort of thing does he…grab?'

'Oh, the lot. Jobs. Homes. Cars. Pets.' She paused, obviously saving the most serious until last. 'And women.'

He remembered Zeena and Iolo's tender kisses on the pancake-tossing morning. 'But they're obviously so happy. So…in tune.'

She sighed. 'It's more that Mum's in tune – but Dad's tone deaf. Unconditional love, that's what he expects.

Every now and again he pushes her too far. One day she'll walk out and won't come back. But not this time, thank God.' She fixed him with an unwavering gaze. 'Do you have children, Jack?'

The truth, which had been his ally a few moments ago, bared its teeth, ready to chew him down to size.

'Three.' *Or maybe four.* 'A daughter and two sons. But they've all flown the nest.' *My wife's still there, though. And my mother's come home to roost. And then there's Neil, the cuckoo, who's usurping Kingsley's memory.* He imagined Fay's contempt – 'clichéd metaphor'.

Non showed no surprise at his admission of fatherhood. 'You must know all about it then. Unconditional love.'

'I suppose so.' Keen to steer clear of his domestic details and find out more about hers, he said, 'Ruth seems nice.'

'Ruth's wonderful. Ruth's my saviour. She was the one who stopped me topping myself.' The words sounded doubly ugly, coming from her lovely mouth.

He laughed then, seeing that she wasn't making a joke, waited in silence until she was ready to tell him.

'It was a man, of course. The usual story. I trusted him. He messed around. I chucked him out. Pathetic, really.'

'How long ago?'

'Just after we moved to Llangwm, so that's what, three, three-and-a-half years? Ruth saw me through the black days. She gave me a job here and a place to live.' She pre-empted his question, 'Dad was too busy sorting out The Welcome Stranger, and Mum was too busy sorting Dad, to notice that I was sinking.'

'That's terrible.'

'Yes. It was. But it isn't any more.'

And then Jack told her about Fay and what a determined woman she was. About his clever, beautiful daughter. About Dylan, his steady son, and his marriage to the inscrutable

315

Nia. About his father's illness, his mother's dependence and his fears for all their futures.

'It sounds wonderfully normal. You're very lucky.' She thought for a second. 'But what about your other son?'

Finally he told her about Kingsley – the whole story, even down to the ugly steel shutter that his son's leaving had brought down between him and Fay. 'So, not totally wonderful.'

He would have appreciated a little sympathy but it didn't come. 'Oh, I don't know. You're all alive and healthy – apart from your father and he's an old man. You must know he can't live forever. You're well respected. You're not short of money. Isn't the rest of it up to you?'

Non showed him around the nursery, telling him about the plans they had to branch out into garden design and maintenance. 'Not that anyone here's got enough money to pay someone to do their garden. They'd sooner let it go back to the wild.' She shrugged and grinned, 'It's fun to daydream, don't you think?'

Ruth waved from the greenhouse and he could see how fundamental her unobtrusive and unwavering support must have been, and how important this peaceful place had become for Non after the bastard abandoned her.

'I think I'll buy a plant for Fay,' he said, 'What d'you recommend?' He'd dream up an explanation on his way back to Cardiff.

She suggested a rosemary bush. 'Rosemary for remembrance. And if she makes an infusion with the leaves and uses it to rinse her hair, it'll make it shine.' She lifted a plait. 'I always use it.'

A few customers arrived and Jack knew that must let her to get on with her work. 'Look… I may be in Llangwm again at the end of the month – with a Morris group … but it could be difficult – there might not be time…'

She held her hand up. 'No worries. You know you're always welcome.' Then she made, what to him seemed, the most extraordinary statement. 'Everyone needs a place where they can go to catch their breath; to find themselves. There's nothing wrong in that.'

His recollection of the journey back to Cardiff was hazy, but one thing he was certain about, he'd had some kind of revelation – he might go so far as to say an epiphany. He'd come clean and, not only had it made no difference to Non's attitude to him, if he'd understood her correctly, she'd given him permission to use Llamgwm as his bolt-hole.

32

FAY READ DARREN'S STORY SEVERAL MORE TIMES. In it, the shed where he found the carrier bag was in the back garden of a semi on a new housing estate. After he changed into the girls' clothes, he peered through the window of the house, watching a family – mother, father and two boys – eating fish and chips. Then he/she went in through the back door and, after hugging everyone, joined them at the table. It was Pinter-esque in its menacing simplicity.

In her experience, teenagers were just as crude in their creative writing as they were in every other facet of their lives, piling on sensational adjectives, unable to resist predictable plot twists. This made Darren's story all the more unusual. Without revealing her reasons, she consulted several members of staff about him, attempting to flesh out this lad whom, up until last week, she'd barely noticed. 'Quiet.' 'Nondescript.' 'Unremarkable.' 'Darren Who?' was all she got back. She thought about dumping the matter on the Head. His salary was at least double hers, so why not? The trouble was, once she'd reported it, the whole thing – whatever it might be – would be 'taken further' and the details circulated to the world-and-his-wife. It was tantamount to betraying Darren's trust and as bad as reading his story out to the class. She wouldn't do anything yet.

During morning break she phoned Caitlin. Their conversation, the evening before, had been curtailed by Jack's ridiculous antics and she hadn't heard anything like enough about her daughter's weekend in London. 'Can you sneak away at lunch time?' she asked and they agreed to meet in the coffee shop near the school.

They chose a table in the corner, where passing pupils couldn't see them. 'Sorry about the fiasco with the cup of tea last night. Your father seems permanently distracted these days. And I'm convinced he's going deaf.'

Caitlin wrinkled her nose. 'Don't be too hard on him, Mum. He's got a lot on his mind. And I meant to ask, how was the meal on Saturday?'

'It was nice. A nice change.' How could she tell Caitlin that she and Jack had hardly spoken to each other all evening; that she would have had more fun dining with a total stranger; nor that, to counteract her frustration, she'd had too much to drink?

She had always thought it improper for the children to know the ins and outs of her relationship with Jack. Similarly, Caitlin had never sought her mother's opinion on the men in her life. Up until now, that had been fine but Fay's longing to know every detail of the weekend nagged away like a stitch in her side. 'Was the exhibition interesting? Did you see much of London?'

Caitlin gave a factual account of their movements, reeling off Tube stations and bus numbers, and describing items of furniture in the exhibition. In fact she mentioned everything but Cassidy. Did equivocation suggest that Caitlin, too, had fallen under his spell? In an attempt to verify this, she ventured, 'You two get on well, by the sound of it.'

Caitlin rearranged the cutlery on the table. 'He's very

easy to talk to. I feel as if I've known him forever.' She laughed, her cheeks colouring, 'I suppose I have, if it comes to that.' Then, evidently thankful for the opportunity to shift the focus of the conversation, she added, 'Sadie really does look like Kingsley.'

'A similar thing happened to me.' Fay told Caitlin how, a few months earlier, she'd seen someone in British Home Stores who'd looked so like Barbara Devereux, whom she'd worked with in her first teaching post, that she assumed they were related. 'She had tiny teeth and a snub nose, just like Barbara. And the same warbley voice. There could be no confusion with such an unusual name but the woman had never heard of anyone called Devereux. They could have been twins.' Fay, not interested in talking about Sadie, redirected the conversation. 'D'you two have any plans for another get together?'

Caitlin concentrated on her Greek salad. 'As a matter of fact, he may come down to Cardiff in a couple of weeks. I'm going to see if I can get tickets for the opera.'

'That's nice...' Fay kept at it, 'He's very good-looking.'

'Is he? I hadn't noticed.'

'And very charming.'

'Don't be silly, Mum. We enjoy each other's company, that's all. There's nothing in it.' Caitlin's cheeks flushed a deeper pink and her eyes sparkled and Fay thought how alive she looked.

When Fay arrived home, Neil explained that someone was giving Vi a lift from the hospital. 'Jack's not back, though. D'you reckon he's okay?'

Puzzled, she checked her watch. 'But he never gets home before six, Neil.'

'Didn't he tell you?' Neil filled her in on Jack's

indisposition. 'He was feeling better so he went for a walk. But that was before midday.'

Wrong-footed, yet determined to conceal her confusion, she offered an explanation. 'I bet he's called on one of his dancing friends. I'll try his mobile.' She waited until she was alone to make the call but Jack's phone was off and she left a succinct and unambiguous message. 'What the fuck are you playing at?'

An hour passed and there was still no word from him. Vi returned, full of praise for 'the total stranger' – in fact the sister of the man who occupied the bed next to Harry and whom Vi saw every afternoon – who had so kindly delivered her to the door. 'A real good Samaritan.' She looked around. 'How's poor John?'

Lucky bloody John, more like. He'd managed to escape. Moreover, he clearly felt no obligation to explain where he was or to hurry back.

Vi tagged along behind Fay, telling her the same things several times over and switching lights off, even if they were only leaving the room for a few minutes, until Fay, fearing she would batter the woman, retreated to the study, saying that she had tomorrow's lesson to prepare.

She was curled in the armchair, reading the newspaper, when Neil tapped on the door. 'Cup of tea?'

'That would be lovely.'

Neil would make some lucky girl a completely prosaic husband – faithful, supportive, cheerful and paralysingly boring. It was tempting to label Jack 'prosaic' but that would be a lazy, inaccurate description. He was infuriating, obscure, childish and becoming conspicuously unpredictable. Okay, he was never going to vary the way he spread his marmalade, but what on earth had that poetry recitation been about? Or the polo-necked sweater? Or – obviously the point he was making today – the 'I-don't-

322

have-to-explain-what-I'm-doing' nonsense?

'Is it okay if I use the computer? I thought I'd mail Kingsley.'

'Sorry. What did you say?'

'Mail Kingsley. I've got a bit of news that'll interest him. I've tracked Titch Rowson down. D'you remember Titch? Big guy. Used to play, well, still *does* play, keyboards. He's interested in re-forming the band.'

Fay stared at Neil, who was no longer boring. 'What on earth are you talking about?'

'The band—'

'I don't give a flying fuck about your band. You said "Mail Kingsley". Mail Kingsley? Do I gather you're in contact with my son?'

'Yeah. I thought Jack would've told you.'

'Jack knows?'

He nodded, unhappily.

In no time at all she was in possession of the facts concerning the email exchanges but, on seeing Neil's troubled face, she relented a little. 'I *do* feel betrayed, Neil, but, if as you say, you assumed Jack was keeping me informed, then it's excusable. But you must give me your word that you'll tell me as soon as you get the next mail from him. Is that understood?'

'Yeah. Sorry.' He crept out of the room and she heard him go upstairs and shut the bedroom door.

'Hi, love,' Jack greeted her. 'I was telling Mum the latest from the hospital.'

'You've been to the hospital, too, have you? Goodness, Jack, you've been a busy bee. How are you feeling by the way?' A rictus smile reinforced her icy tone.

'Much better, thanks. Yes, I thought, as I was out and about—'

'You thought you might as well make the most of it. Is that right?'

'Well… I…'

Vi chipped in 'Never mind that. What did the doctor say? Can Dad come home tomorrow?'

'Not tomorrow, but unless something untoward happens, he'll be out on Monday. So, a little celebration is in order.' He poured two glasses of sherry – Vi was already sipping orange juice – and handed one to Fay, then smiled, raising his glass. 'Cheers. They want to get him up and about for a few days, make sure he can cope with the stairs and things like that. Get himself to the toilet.'

Fay winced, 'Lavatory.'

Although he was speaking to Vi, his eyes remained focussed on Fay's fixed smile and she let him continue, until there was nothing more he could possibly add to his account of his meeting with Harry's medical team.

'And what about you, Jack? Did you go anywhere interesting this afternoon?' she asked. 'We were *slightly* concerned at your seven hour absence, but you seem to be restored to rude good health.'

'Yes. Well. I'm sorry about that, love. I don't know where the time went. I started driving and, next thing I knew, I was up in the Beacons. Beautiful up there, it was. I had a good walk, towards Pen y Fan, and it seemed to do the trick. Bought a coffee in a lay-by. One of those mobile canteen places. Nice and clean. I've got a little present for you in the car, by the way.'

'How thoughtful. Why don't we go and find it?' She was gratified to see the unease on his face as she led him out of the back door, sherry glass still in hand. 'No, this way.' She directed him towards the shed where, once inside and the door firmly shut, she gulped her sherry, the liquid coursing down her throat and igniting the fury that had been building up.

'How dare you? How *dare* you?' She could make Jack out but his features were indistinct in the semi-darkness, illuminated only by the light from the kitchen window, shining across the garden. She hurled her empty glass and only knew that it had missed him when it struck the far wall, tinkling as the pieces hit the ground, signalling the start of Round One. She slapped him high across his cheek then waited for some reaction. When he didn't move, she tried again, but a lot harder this time, her rings digging into her fingers as she connect with his jaw. She went for his ears next and he responded, raising his hands to protect his face, but still he didn't speak.

'You don't know what I'm talking about, do you? Do you?' She was shrieking now and punching randomly, desperate to hurt him, desperate to inflict pain. '*Do you?*'

He caught one of her flailing arms. 'Stop. Okay. I plead guilty. Just once in my life I thought *no*, I don't want to go to work today. I don't want to look at rotting teeth. I don't want to—'

'Don't try and be clever with me you... you bastard.' She was sobbing, her energy dissipating, and he managed to trap her other arm but she continued to rail. 'You fucking wanker. You loser.' She summoned up another burst of strength and, deprived of the use of her fists, raised her knee, hoping to find his groin but he twisted out of range. 'You fucking bastard. You've got no right. No right. You... you... cunt.' She spat out the ultimate obscenity, sensing Jack flinch, as if he'd been kicked.

'For God's sake, Fay. I have no idea what you're talking about.'

'How could you.'? She was wailing and mumbling, her accusations coming in short, unintelligible bursts. 'Kingsley... emails... Neil thought... why... you cruel

325

bastard...' Exhausted and running out of steam, she panted and leaned heavily against him, weeping into his armpit.

As she gasped out the disjointed phrases, Jack understood. Her tirade had been triggered by his failure to tell her about Kingsley's email correspondence. He clamped her arms down at her sides, terrified that her violent rage would boil up again, giving her enough strength to harm herself or him. After all, the place they stood in was an arsenal – chisels, gouges, hammers, saws – everything within arm's reach, each tool capable of inflicting nastier damage than most conventional weapons.

Rows were nothing new but their spats generally centred on minor misdemeanours – an overlooked gas bill or muddy shoes or a wine bottle tossed in the black bag, rather than the green. Correction. They centred on *his* misdemeanours. He rarely bothered to complain when Fay left his car low on fuel or threw away a newspaper-cutting that he was saving, because she had the knack of turning the grievance back on itself so that he was in the wrong. By tacit agreement, they had never rowed over important issues – Kingsley's leaving; Fay's rejection of his parents; the way she belittled his achievements. Perhaps they feared that doing so might start an avalanche of recrimination which would bury them both, and it looked as if tonight might prove them right.

She was struggling less violently and, realising that he was no longer in physical danger, he attempted an explanation for his secrecy. 'I didn't want you to be upset...' *Sod it.* Why should he apologise?

He drew in a deep breath and spoke calmly and quietly. 'You've got a nerve. You were the one who drove him out.' She didn't answer but he felt her stiffen as if he'd given her a sharp slap across the leg – something his mother often did when, as a child, he started getting 'uppity'. 'You've got a bloody nerve. If *you* hadn't bullied, criticised, nagged and hounded the boy, he'd be up in that room now. But you couldn't bear the idea that one of your children might not conform – might not go to university – and then you wouldn't be able to boast to all your smug-bastard friends. You saw it as a failure and Fay Waterfield never fails at anything, does she? Now you've roped in Neil Bentley, poor bugger, and you're trying to beat him into shape. Mrs Frankenstein, that's what we should call you.'

He pushed her and she seemed to slip, staggering backwards, grabbing the back of the chair, trying to regain her balance but crashing to the floor.

'Aagghh.' It was a cry of pain, not anger.

It was impossible to see what had happened in the blue-black shadows below workbench level, but he could tell it was serious. 'What is it?'

'Just put the bloody light on.'

The fluorescent tube stuttered into life, and its weak, cold glow revealed Fay, sprawled on the floor, blood dripping from her left hand.

With his foot, he scuffed aside the shards of the smashed sherry glass and, grasping her beneath her arms, he hoisted her onto the chair. She avoided looking at him, staring out of the window as he inspected the cut, but the combination of dark blood and poor illumination made it difficult to make an accurate assessment. 'Let's get it under the tap,' he said.

When he tried to put a guiding arm around her, she twitched her shoulders, hurrying ahead of him towards the house. 'No. I can manage.'

Sluicing with cold water revealed a jagged gash, deep and untidy, and Jack sent Neil to the bathroom to fetch a wad of bandage. 'Hold it firmly against the wound,' he instructed, 'until we can get you to Casualty.'

His mother fussed, mumbling about 'lockjaw' and severed tendons and, even as they were getting into the car, he could still hear her droning, 'But how did it happen? They only went to fetch something out of the car.'

He drove to the hospital for the second time that day. The unyielding, barbed silence was the conclusive proof that after five spineless years he'd confronted Fay with the truth – single-handedly, she had driven their son to the other side of the world.

When the triage nurse called her name, Fay dismissed Jack's offer to go with her and left him surrounded by the jetsam of distressed, bewildered humanity that was accumulating in the A&E reception area.

The X-rays revealed that there was a sliver of glass lodged in the fleshy pad at the base of her thumb, and whilst she progressed slowly from one grubby-walled cubicle to the next, waiting to have the glass removed, then to be stitched, bandaged and given a tetanus jab, she had plenty of time to mull over what had taken place. She could never forgive Jack for keeping Kingsley's emails secret – she wouldn't have believed him capable of such calculated cruelty, or, for that matter, of physical violence. She regretted that she hadn't hit him harder.

After almost five hours she emerged from the treatment room, to find Jack where she had left him.

'Does it hurt?' he asked as they made their way to the car park.

'Yes.' It didn't but that was only because of the local anaesthetic – the administration of which *had* bloody hurt – and why should she let him off the hook?

'I'm sorry—'

'Not now. Can we leave it until tomorrow?'

328

'Fay, I'm apologising for pushing you over. Nothing else.'

As they drove off she noticed that it was well past midnight and the adrenalin, or whatever wonder-substance had kept her going, was seeping away, leaving her shivery and queasy. Her head pounded, her back was aching – maybe from the jolt when she fell – and she needed to pee. The street-lights, as they flashed past, illuminated her bandaged hand, turning it into a huge, exotic mushroom, resting in her lap.

Even with the double bed to herself, her hand kept getting in the way and she fidgeted, turning on her back, then her right side, stretching her left arm out or propping it on a pillow. Without any immediate opportunity to refute Jack's allegations – she wasn't even sure where he was – she rehearsed her defence.

Who backed you, Jack Waterfield, when you went through that flaky patch and were close to packing it in and being a – what was it – a greengrocer, for fuck's sake? And Caitlin. She's fine now, but it was touch and go when that idiot dumped her and she fluffed her exams. You realise that she'd be a dental hygienist if I hadn't bullied her into those re-sits. And Dylan certainly wouldn't have got his current job had I not made a few phone-calls. Mrs. Frankenstein, eh?

Her examples did seem rather career-orientated but jobs were important and it would have been downright irresponsible to leave them muddling along – disorganised, directionless and clueless.

By four o'clock, her bandaged hand was no longer a mushroom but a throbbing football, exactly as the nurse had predicted.

33

FAY WOKE AT NINE AND, after phoning school to explain her absence, swallowed two painkillers and sank back into a restless sleep, surfacing now and then to wonder where Jack had spent the night, before reminding herself she didn't give a damn.

She inspected the neat, clean bandage then pressed it cautiously, experiencing a discomfort, similar to a bruise, where she imagined the stitches were. At least it was her left hand. She would be able to write and apply her makeup, but two-handed activities, or anything involving water, were going to be tricky, especially as Jack might not be around to help.

Finally, the craving for coffee drove her downstairs. The house appeared to be deserted – unusual at this time of day. Her mother-in-law stuck to a rigid routine, hardly ever going out before early afternoon when she caught the bus to the hospital. Neil was less predictable but it was generally possible to detect his presence by the aimless whistling that accompanied his every activity. Wherever they both were, it was a relief not to be forced into explanations of the accident.

A note, propped against the stainless steel coffee canister, read –

Dear Fay,

> *I have taken Vi home for the morning. She wants to get things ready for when Harry gets out. Jack said it would be OK to take your car as you aren't going to work today and probably won't be able to drive anyway.*
>
> *Cheers. Neil. Hope the hand is OK.*

Jack said it was 'OK' did he? Three stitches in her hand and he'd decided she was incapable of making her own decisions.

A couple of cushions from the sofa and an unzipped sleeping bag lay on the single bed in Dylan's old room, indicating where Jack had spent the night. She imagined that he'd gone to work but didn't want to risk Sheila Pearce's curiosity by checking. Hell, why should she care where he was?

In other circumstances, a day at home would have been a welcome opportunity to get on with things, but everything she tried to do called for two functioning hands – making the bed, carrying a tray, even pulling her chair up to the table or fastening her bra. She tried to settle with a book but the individual letters refused to form recognisable words as last night's battle raged on in her head. Eventually, when she could bear her own thoughts no longer, she phoned Laura but there was no reply. In desperation she tried Isabel, slightly ashamed to be contacting a person whom she no longer respected and certainly didn't trust.

'Hello,' a woman answered. 'Hello?'

'Have I got the right number? I wanted to speak to Isabel. Isabel Lauderdale.'

There was a pause, then, 'She's not here at the moment but hold on, I'll fetch Geoffrey.' Her tone was pleasant and assured and she sounded nothing at all like an old cardigan.

'May I ask who's speaking?'

Fay had no idea what she would to say to Geoffrey, whom she had only met a few times, and she was on the point of replacing the receiver when a plummy voice inquired, 'Fay? How are you?'

'I'm fine, thanks.' The truth was too complicated. 'Don't let me disturb you, though. I'll try Izzy's mobile.'

'The truth is, Fay, she's not living here any more. I thought she might have told you.'

It felt good to speak to *anyone* after her morning of isolation and that encouraged her to take the next step. 'Geoffrey, we don't really know each other and it's very unlikely that we'll ever meet again, so, can I ask you something?'

'How intriguing, Fay. How could I resist such an opening? Fire away.'

'Why did you throw Isabel out? She always told us that you two had an "open marriage", so I can't see why you didn't just carry on carrying on, as it were.'

'Is that what she told you? God, what a heartless pig I must be.'

Spurred on by the amusement in his tone, Fay warmed to her mission: 'Actually, what she said was that you decided you wanted to grow old with a 'comfortable' woman, whatever that means, and that you weren't fussed about glamour and sexiness. I'm sorry to ask such personal questions but—'

'A word of advice, Fay. Never apologise when you're pursuing truth. It reveals a chink in virtue's armour and gives the guilty hope.' He cleared his throat. '"Glamorous" to me is a pejorative term, evoking falsity and fakery. "Sexiness", another dreadful concept, is not at the top of my list either. Of course there should be… a magnetism… a visceral connection between a man and a woman, but it should never be blatant. More a secret shared.' He cleared his throat and raised his voice a little. 'Loyalty, companionship, mutual endeavour, and humour, of course – are the qualities that should transcend our baser instincts and set us above the primitives, unfashionable and stuffy though it may sound.' He paused and Fay pictured him in the courtroom, decked out in wig and gown, putting the case for the defendant in the dock. 'How am I doing?'

'Very impressive. But I'm surprised. Surprised that you and Isabel ever got together in the first place. Even more surprised that you stuck together for so long.'

'Yes, but remember, Isabel is an interesting woman. In the beginning I was naïve enough, arrogant enough, to think I could modify her less agreeable traits – and I know, on her part, my income and status were enough to outweigh my many shortcomings. When we first got together, we did lots of exciting things – trips, parties, moving house. We were constantly on the move – in fact we spent hardly any time on our own. Then, the four children came along – something I will never regret – and we entered into what seemed like, in retrospect, a twenty-year logistical exercise. I admit I spent too much time at work and Isabel looked elsewhere for…companionship. I sometimes think that, if we'd had less money, we might have been forced to pull together more resolutely, but I don't think that would have appealed to Isabel. It's not a very edifying story. Now it's no longer a viable relationship. Viable – from the Latin, *vita*, meaning life. Isabel found it impossible to come to terms with my need, as I grow older, for loyalty and companionship.'

'I see.' She wasn't sure she did. Despite his elaborate vocabulary and flamboyant delivery, when it boiled down to it Geoffrey's explanation was slightly agony aunt-ish, and it was hard to understand how such a clever man hadn't anticipated the inevitable outcome of marriage to anyone as calculating as Isabel.

'Now it's my turn, if I may.' His resonant voice was imposing. 'How long have you and… Jack, isn't it?…been married?'

'Thirty-two years.' Was she for the defence or the prosecution?

'And during that time, how many other partners have you had?'

'Me? None.' It sounded a pathetic, as if she were some kind of freak, and she added quickly, 'But I've had several offers—'

'Which you haven't accepted. That's *loyalty* in my book. Next. Do you and Jack enjoy each other's company? Share the same tastes?'

'We used to do lots of things together. Concerts. Theatre. Going for walks. Not so much, lately though. We're always too… too…'

'Too busy? I see.'

'And he can be hysterically funny.' She was determined to clock up some points on Geoffrey's desirable traits scale. 'That chippy, subversive, Welsh wit. He used to keep us in stitches.'

'Did you say *used to?* Mmm. Rather a lot of 'used to's' aren't there? Finally, your children. Are they getting on well? Achieving their potential?'

The sleepless night, a throbbing hand and Geoffrey's probing questions had lowered her resistance and she crumbled, pouring out the whole story, from the day Kingsley slammed the door to Jack's searing accusation, the previous evening. He said very little, occasionally easing her back on track if she rambled away from the point and, by the time she'd finished, she understood why men like Geoffrey Lauderdale commanded huge sums of money.

'So, to sum up,' she found it impossible not to adopt his technique 'you're saying that all we need to do is spend more time together? Support each other more? Have a few more laughs?' She paused. 'But Geoffrey, Jack's hobby is *Morris dancing*. It's *so* humiliating.'

'Rubbish, woman,' he exploded. 'I admit I was dubious when you reminded me that your husband is a dentist but Morris dancing…glorious.' He seemed to be serious. 'Look, Fay, I'm going to let you in on something.' He lowered his voice to a near-whisper, 'Cross-stitch.'

'Pardon?' Had she missed something?

'My hobby is cross-stitch. I'm sure Isabel never mentioned *that*, did she? My grandmother taught me and I've been at it since I was seven. Can't get enough of it. I'm just completing a replica of the Bayeux Tapestry. A small section, of course.'

Fay pictured a large man – she had only a hazy recollection of Geoffrey Lauderdale – sitting at a casement window, canvas held in a wooden frame, whilst the mysterious Margaret, a shadowy figure threading fine needles with brightly-coloured silks, lurked in the background.

He paused, 'Go on. Laugh if you must.'

Needing a distraction, Fay walked up the hill to the park and sat on a bench, watching the mothers and grandmothers who had brought their little ones to the play area. It was interesting to observe how the comings and goings of small children, demanding drinks and nose-wiping, removed barriers between strangers. She and Jack had lived in a terraced house, nearer the city centre, and she was working part-time when Caitlin and Dylan were this age. The nearest park was more than a mile away but, regardless of the weather, once a week, sometimes more frequently, she made the trek so that the children could let off steam, learn to take turns with their peers, and she could engage in some adult conversation.

Then, when Dylan was old enough to go to school and she was reclaiming her life, Kingsley came along. Having climbed a few ladders, he pushed her down a snake, forcing her to go back to the beginning. But the rules of the game had changed. It was as if she'd had too easy a time with Caitlin and Dylan, and Kingsley had been sent as a tougher test of her mothering skills.

Kingsley was a colicky, non-sleeper; he walked too soon and talked so late that the doctor sent him for hearing tests. He was a fussy eater and still in nappies when he was three. He screamed when he went to school then cried with boredom at the weekend. He was stubborn, wilful and questioned whatever she told him to do, as if he knew best. When he was older, he liked to start arguments, getting her so incensed that her responses became illogical and she became the petulant child. He relished every opportunity to make her look inadequate. *But only, and always me.* As far as she could see, everyone else thought he was 'that good-looking, intelligent and charming Kingsley Waterfield' and she was his controlling mother. His leaving was his supreme victory and she would give anything to have him back; to have another crack at it.

On the way home, she mulled over Geoffrey's lecture on marriage, not sure what to make of it. The last time she'd heard marriage commended was at Dylan's wedding, but surely nobody fell for the sentimental drivel that flowed so freely at weddings. Geoffrey, who was under no obligation to promote the institution which had failed him so badly, may have been pompous and sermonising but she liked what he'd said.

'Was it okay to take the car?' Neil was crouching outside the back door, cleaning his shoes. 'How's the hand?'

'Sore, but I'll survive. And how did you get on at Vi's?'

'No problems. We opened the windows – gave the house a good blow through. Checked the garden. We picked loads of tomatoes. We thought we'd make soup later.' His unremitting good humour was becoming tiresome. 'And,' he laid his brush and polish on the ground and stood up, 'we've got a plan.'

'We?'

'Vi and me.'

'*I*. Vi and *I*. Vi and I *have* a plan.' He looked confused and she shook her head. 'Okay. You've got a plan. Carry on.'

'Maybe I should wait until Jack—'

'What sort of a plan?'

'Well, when Harry goes home, which will probably be at the beginning of next week, I'm going to move in with them. We get on great. They'll need someone to lend a hand for a while. And they've got a spare room. I can get some casual work at one of the pubs up there, 'specially if I buy a little car. Nothing fancy. I'll be able to take Harry to his appointments. It'll be handy for gigs, too. I've got a bit put away. Vi says they wouldn't want rent. And we'd all be out of your hair. It would be neat for all of us.' The details popped out, one after the other, making it apparent that he and Vi had been working on their scheme for some time. He raised his eyebrows. 'So, what d'you think?'

'I think it's a wonderful plan,' she said truthfully. 'And Neil…any news from Kingsley?'

Laura must have returned home and checked her last caller but, when she rang, she seemed surprised that it was Fay who picked up the phone. 'Who else would have rung you from here?' Fay asked. Then she told Laura about her accident.

'But you two never row. What was it about? It must be pretty…serious.' She sounded hesitant, unlike her usual no-nonsense self.

'It is. Jack's been keeping quiet about emails from Kingsley. They were to Neil, but Jack knew about them. I can't believe he could be so cruel, knowing how much I worry about him. Then he had the bloody nerve to accuse me of driving Kingsley away. He made out it was entirely my fault. It was ghastly.'

'Was it *just* about Kingsley?'

'*Just* about Kingsley? Call me peculiar but I can't actually imagine anything more important than the loss of a son. And it could well be the end of our marriage, but that's a minor concern.'

There was an extended silence whilst Fay waited for wise Laura to tell her how to put everything right again.

'That's for you two to sort out. You'll have to decide what's important – how you want things to go from here.'

Fay was exasperated by this wishy-washy advice. 'And how d'you suggest we do that, if we aren't speaking to each other? For all I know Jack's run away, too.'

34

Routine and instinct carried Jack through the day. He anticipated a bad patch at lunchtime, when there would be no teeth to fill or dentures to fit or crowns to replace, so to keep busy and avoid Sheila's searching glances, he went out to get something to eat. Queen Street was thronged and, caught up in the cohorts of shoppers and office workers, he allowed himself to drift with them for a while, finally breaking away and heading down a side street.

Although he had little appetite, he bought coffee and a sandwich and, assaulted by clamour and heat in the crowded café, he opted for a seat outside, with the smokers. A sleepless night in Dylan's old room and yesterday's clothes – he couldn't face going in to their bedroom for clean things – combined to give him the sour, light-headed sensation of having been to an all-night party. Even in the fresh air, he was unable to stop recent events clattering around in his head, like lumps of aggregate in a cement mixer.

His phone rang and he was both disappointed and relieved that it wasn't Fay. 'Hello, Stan. Yes. I'll be there. No, I hadn't forgotten. See you tomorrow.' Morris practice the following evening might be a welcome diversion.

The man at the next table rolled a cigarette, scooping tobacco from the green pouch and distributing it, with stained forefinger, down the gutter of flimsy paper. Two under-clad young women gossiped, simultaneously inter-rogating mobile phones. Another, not much older, read *The Da Vinci Code* and ignored the baby in the pushchair next to her, bawling and wriggling, trying to escape like its mother. All around, the human race puffed and prattled, drinking 'skinnies' or 'smoothies' or 'grandes'. Evolution had been a terrible waste of time.

The 'REPENT' man was declaiming in his favourite spot, halfway between the Castle and McDonald's. Passers-by, rather than pausing to catch his zealous message, sped up, averting their communal gaze. Then, from nowhere, an unremarkable woman, not unlike his mother to look at, marched up to the man and took a position directly in front of him, no more than two metres away. At the prospect of free entertainment, an audience began to gather, collecting in a loose ring around the pair. The would-be prophet continued to proclaim his message of doom but, after a few minutes, he showed signs of being rattled by her silent presence, glancing at her from time to time and faltering until he stopped altogether, muttering. 'What d'you think you're staring at, missus?'

She folded her arms, one of those patchwork leather shopping bags dangling from her bent elbow, brown shoes with Velcro fastenings across the instep planted slightly apart for increased stability. 'A bloody charlatan, that's what I'm staring at.' Her uncultivated voice was frail but confident and Jack was surprised that she'd used such an elaborate word.

The crowd tittered, waiting for the next act, but they were disappointed. The man glared at her then unbuckled the harness that held his sign in place, lowered it to the ground and sidled off amidst faint jeers, like a magician who'd botched a simple trick. His adversary, finding herself the centre of attention, looked confused and she, too, melted into the crowd. How easy it was to puncture a dream.

Jack arrived home later than usual, then managed to find several gardening jobs that required his immediate attention.

'How's your hand?' he asked politely as he and Fay sat down to a cold supper. These were the first words he'd addressed to her since they left the hospital the previous evening.

'Painful. Inconvenient. Frustrating.' She didn't look up.

They continued in silence, not the sulking, childish silence that usually followed their tiffs, but a heavy-duty, 'man-overboard' silence. There was no doubt that they were drifting away from each other, caught by an undertow of mistrust, and there would come a critical instant when they were too far apart ever to link up again.

His mother came into the kitchen, carrying two dirty mugs. 'There you are at last, John. They're working you too hard at that place.' Being one's own boss was an alien concept to his parents. She jerked her head towards Fay. 'Did she tell you?'

'Tell me what, Mum?'

'I thought she'd have told you. Neil's coming to live with us when Dad gets out.' She made it sound as though Harry was doing a stretch in Wormwood Scrubs. 'No use arguing. It's all decided.'

Jack glanced at Fay and she looked up, giving an imperceptible nod, confirming that the unlikely statement was accurate and instructing him to greet the suggestion with enthusiasm. For a few seconds, they were collaborators.

'Sounds like a great idea, Mum.'

'Well, you two don't want us hanging around here, cramping your style, do you?'

Fay had left a sheet, pillow cases and duvet cover on the bed in Dylan's room, making it clear where she intended him to sleep, but he needed clean clothes and he tapped gingerly on the door. 'Fay?'

'Yes?'

'I'll just get my things for tomorrow, if that's okay with you. And my toilet bag.' He tiptoed in as though, if he made no noise, she might not notice him. She was sitting at her dressing table, still fully clothed and he realised how awkward it was going to be for her to change, shower or wash her hair. 'D'you need any help?' he offered.

'I can manage, thank you.' She fiddled with her bandage, making her difficulty more apparent and her obstinacy more infuriating.

When he had collected what he needed, he returned to Dylan's room – perhaps he should start thinking of it as *his* room – leaving the door ajar so that he could see when Neil had finished in the bathroom, not wanting to reveal that he'd been banished.

Dylan had chosen this cosy room on the day that they moved in to the house – he must have been four – and he'd occupied it, throughout school and university days, until his marriage. There had been a spell of less than a year, when he'd shared a city-centre flat with two other 'young professionals', but ruinous quarterly bills and his accountancy training drove him back to seek fiscal security at home.

Jack undressed, placed the bedding on a chair and, taking pleasure in this petty defiance, got into the unmade bed. Despite efforts to resist, he began mulling it over again. There was no disputing the fact that Fay had been within her rights to berate him for keeping Kingsley's correspondence from her – had he genuinely imagined that she wouldn't find out? – but the abuse that she'd hurled at him, physical and verbal, had shocked him. He was horrified, too, that he'd pushed her to the ground but, if nothing had intervened to halt their quarrel, where might it have ended? Nor did he regret letting loose his salvo of accusations, although he knew she would blast him out of the water if she ever had an inkling of the Laura thing, or his summer escapades.

How long could they maintain this standoff? Forever, theoretically. Fay was unbelievably stubborn. When Neil and his mother moved out, there would be no need to keep up any pretence. They could stake out individual territory within the house and never speak to each other for the rest of their lives. Until yesterday Jack might have considered this a blessing – a sort of stepping-stone in his plan to escape – but having heard Non's fond, but disparaging, comments regarding Iolo's irresponsibility, he knew that, if he ran to her, she would label him as yet another flaky member of his untrustworthy sex.

He heard Fay flush the lavatory and checked the time. Two o'clock. Then, at four-fifteen it went again and he thought he could hear the strains of 'Sailing By'.

A small, if nasty, cut on the palm of her left hand didn't seem a valid reason to take a second day off work, especially as Neil had volunteered to drive her to school but, following a night of no sleep and very little rest, Fay doubted whether she was up to a day in the classroom. She waited until Jack left for work, then hurried down to the kitchen, desperate for a shot of caffeine before making the final decision about whether to go in. She was more than a little flustered when Jack reappeared.

'Sorry.' He apologised, pointing to the calendar, 'Thursday. I forgot my kit.'

She turned away, peering out of the window, as if something fascinating was taking place on the lawn, knowing that he was watching her and waiting for her to say something.

He cracked first. 'How's the hand?'

'You keep asking me that.' She hadn't intended to sound so harsh. 'It's not too bad. But I can't face work. I had a shitty night.'

'The hand?'

Is that all you can think of to say? It was as if her left hand had become a cipher for everything that was wrong between them. 'That. And other things.' She allowed the narrowest chink to open up in her defences and he spotted it.

'Ummm. Look. Ummm. Can we talk, Fay?'

She pointed to the clock: 'You're going to be late. Yes. If you want to. This evening?'

He grimaced, drawing air through his clenched teeth. 'I really ought to visit Dad. Then I've got practice. But I can give it a miss—'

'No. After practice will be fine.' Having made a little headway, she didn't want to lose ground.

'See you about nine-thirty, then.' He hesitated and she thought he was going to kiss her but, instead, he raised his hand in a clumsy salute.

'Don't forget your kit,' she reminded him as he was leaving, for the second time, without it.

'I did first aid as part of my Lifeguard certificate. I knew it would come in handy.' Neil grinned. 'Handy. Get it?'

The flesh around the stitched area was bruised but the

346

cut itself looked clean and showed signs of healing, and Neil made a neat job of re-bandaging Fay's hand. After that he prepared bacon sandwiches for both of them.

'Are you sure you're happy about moving in with Harry and Vi? It won't be a barrel of laughs. And you've been to the house. It's pretty pokey.' She felt duty-bound to offer him the opportunity of changing his mind, whilst dearly hoping that he wouldn't.

'No. Really. I want to. And, if I shift a few things round, there'll be plenty of room in that back bedroom.'

It was the first time that Fay had been alone with Neil since his revelation. 'Any word from Kingsley?'

He gave a nervous smile. 'I didn't manage to check—'

'My fault. Sorry. I did rather jump down your throat the other evening, didn't I? It was a misunderstanding.' She sipped her coffee and counted to ten before suggesting, 'We could check now.'

'Cool.'

There were several unopened mails in Neil's 'in box' but nothing from Kingsley. 'He doesn't write often. And he doesn't say much when he does.' Could Jack have primed him in an attempt at damage limitation? 'Here. Have a look. I've kept the most recent ones.' He was right. They consisted of a couple of unfathomable phrases and no useful information. 'D'you want to let him know about your hand? We can do it from mine – save you logging on.'

It was tempting but it didn't seem proper without conferring with Jack – even if *he'd* shown no such scruples – and it might jeopardise future diplomacy. 'No. Not at the moment, thanks.'

The morning post flopped through the letterbox and Vi got to it first. 'Gas bill, by the look of it. Letter for Jack – looks like a circular. Something from the HSBC

Bank. And a postcard.' She turned it over. 'There's nice. It's from Kingsley. Addressed to N. Bentley. That must be you, Neil.'

Neil read the card to himself, his lips moving silently, like a small child with a new reading book. He turned it over to study the picture then flipped it back, reading the text again. 'Coincidence, or what?' he asked Fay, who was standing very still, as though he were a timid animal and any movement might scare him away. 'We were talking about King only a couple of minutes ago, and now this,' he explained to Vi.

'He sends *us* a card, now and again, too,' Vi said.

Is my son writing to every sodding person in the world except me? 'Where's it from?' Fay kept her voice light and casual.

'Kefalonia, it says on the picture, wherever that is.' Neil looked to her for help.

'Greece. It's a Greek island.' *A mere two thousand miles away. Four hours by EasyJet.* She'd curled her fists tight, the left one pulsing inside the unyielding bandage. 'Does he say what he's up to?'

He handed her the card. 'It's all Greek to me. Ha-ha.'

Kingsley's writing, small and leaning to the right, had if anything become more self-assured.

Neil, mate.
   Folk techno fusion, eh? <u>And</u> Titch Rowson.
   An irresistible combo.
      Cheers. K.
      Promise me though – no bells!

After lunch, Fay went back to bed and slept soundly, waking only when she heard them come in from the hospital. Neil helped her seal her hand inside a sandwich bag and, once he'd gone out to Jack's practice and Vi was asleep in front of the television, she took a long, hot shower, revelling in the healing powers of expensive toiletries and the dream that Kingsley might be on his way home.

35

'YOU FEELING OKAY, JACK? You cocked that up good and proper.' Stan never minced words.

'Sorry, Stan. Must be low blood-sugar. Didn't have time for tea.' Try as he might, Jack was failing to lose himself in the dance.

'Let's take a break, lads, then we'll go through the sets we'll be doing on the twenty-seventh. We've got two spots,' Stan took a piece of paper from his pocket and unfolded it '... the first session will be outside the pub and the second, on the school playground.' He looked at Jack. 'You're familiar with Llangwm, Jack. What's the pub called?'

Jack panicked, for a moment dreading that his secret was out, but then he remembered his encounter with Stan and Muriel on the day of the carnival. He pictured the jolly pub, decked with bunting, the charming painting of a rusty-red dog-fox hanging over the entrance. 'I *think* it's the "Fox".'

Neil was ensconced in a corner, deep in conversation with Trevor and Malcolm. He'd brought his guitar along and was running through some of the tunes, jotting down chords and titles in a spiral-bound notebook. Jack was irrationally disappointed that the lad wasn't showing more interest in the dancing side of the whole business but he appreciated that, for anyone interested in making music, the bouncy, cyclic tunes were compulsive.

On the way home, Neil was full of it. 'It's all kicking off. Titch is up for it and he knows a keyboard player. A girl from the College of Music. She's great on the technical side and she can sing a bit.' He prattled on, unintelligible with enthusiasm.

Jack recalled how, with Geraint, Griff and Jonesy – names that tripped off his tongue as readily as 'Mae Hen Wlad Fy Nhadau' – he'd spent long summer days – probably the last *perfect* days of his life – on the scrubland above the village. They'd collect scrap timber and cardboard boxes to construct rickety dens, headquarters for the 'Valley Victors' or 'Masked Avengers'. Concocting a name and formulating gang rules was always the best part. An image of the tough little highwayman who'd ambushed him a few weeks ago flashed through his mind. Perhaps things hadn't changed so much.

'Got a name for this band of yours, yet?'

'Not yet. We need to have some kind of folk reference but we've also got to make it clear we're totally twenty-first century. Kingsley's sure to come up with something. He's brilliant at that sort of thing.'

Jack concentrated on the road. 'Kingsley?'

'Oh, of course you haven't been home, have you? He sent me a postcard. From Greece. It didn't make much sense but it sort of mentions the band, so he may be—'

'Does Fay know? Did she say anything?' Their scheduled 'talk' suddenly promised a different agenda.

'Yeah. No.' Neil seemed jumpy about his role as informant. 'Yes, she knows. No, she didn't say anything.'

Vi was occupying the living room and Neil was doing something noisy in the kitchen.

'Where shall we go?' Fay asked.

'Definitely not the shed.' Jack was pushing his luck but Fay smiled.

'No. And we'd best not chance the garage, either. So – your room or mine?'

Your room or mine. It sounded so permanent. 'Why don't we drive somewhere,' he suggested. 'How about the Bay?'

She nodded. 'Good idea.'

He shouted towards the living room door, 'We're off out for an hour or two. Don't wait up.' He felt as if he were collecting Fay for a date and needing to keep her family sweet.

The restaurants and clubs, ringing the inky expanse of the bay, were bustling. Fairy-lights reflecting off the water, bobbing boats and urgent music escaping from the chi-chi bars, gave it an air of trying-too-hard, and he could see why he and Fay only came here when they had visitors to amuse. To be truthful, they rarely went out these days, unless it was a special occasion and then they played safe, returning, time and again, to familiar haunts. It was a shame, because there were so many things to try – and so many things that he never would. Scuba-diving. Learning Italian. Playing the piano. Come to think of it, their astonishing encounter in the bedroom had been something entirely new – but, considering subsequent events, it was most likely a one-off occurrence.

The evening was warm, without a breath of wind, and they bought coffee from a stall then wandered along the walkway until they reached the Norwegian Church, squat and plain and white, nothing to do with the illuminated fakery across the water. They sat side-by-side on a picnic bench, cardboard cups in front of them on the splintered table, facing the twinkling lights of Penarth Head, and now nothing was preventing them from talking.

353

'I'm not sure how we got in this muddle,' Jack began, Fay's silence encouraging him to continue. 'But if we don't sort it out soon, I'm afraid it might be too late.' The thought, once articulated, sounded melodramatic and by saying 'I'm afraid' he'd made it seem as if he wanted to patch things up. He still wasn't sure what he wanted – so much would depend on her reaction – and he touched her bandaged hand cautiously, directing the conversation to something concrete. 'I'm really sorry about your hand. I never intended to hurt you.'

'I know you didn't. And I never intended to use the c-word. It's an obscenity too far.' She might have been joking but he couldn't be sure.

If they were to achieve anything, they needed to get away from nit-picking about bandaged hands and foul language. He tried again. 'I should've told you as soon as I found out about those emails. I don't know why I didn't.'

She turned towards him. 'If you thought Kingsley left home because of me, I can see that you wanted to punish me. That's a reason, mind, not an excuse.' She was right, of course. 'And maybe I *was* too hard on him but I couldn't bear to watch him under-achieving. He's probably the brightest of the kids, but he was always so bloody lazy. And he let himself get distracted so easily. Whenever I read the riot act, he'd carry on regardless. I assumed it was water off a duck's back. I didn't realise he hated me for it. But isn't that what parents are supposed to do? Keep after their children. Make sure they succeed.'

Jack was surprised how calmly she was dealing with his criticism, especially as self-reproach wasn't her style. To offer reassurance and, to some extent, excuse his behaviour, he volunteered, 'King didn't say much in his emails.'

'I know. Neil showed me.' She tapped the back of his

hand urgently, 'And did you know Neil got a postcard from him today? From Kefalonia.'

'He told me. He seems to think King might be coming home to join this crazy band of his. We musn't get our hopes up, though, until we have something less airy-fairy to go on.' What a futile thing to say – as futile as telling someone to 'take care' or 'drive carefully'. He felt compelled to add, 'Perhaps I'd better warn you, love, the music they're planning to play is based on Morris tunes.'

She nodded, 'That's probably why he'd come. There's nothing he liked better than to get right back up my nose and he knows that's a sure way of succeeding.'

So far they'd only spoken about Kingsley, but Fay seemed to believe that he was their only problem. He'd hoped to discover if his wife was happy – or happy *enough*; whether the thirty years they'd spent together had been fulfilling and what she hoped to achieve in however long she had left. These were huge, huge, questions. Questions he could ask a stranger on a train but couldn't broach with her, because it would be like asking for her verdict after a thirty-year trial. Since his flirtation with Existentialism was over – he couldn't make the philosophy fit his circumstances nor put up with the itchy polo-neck – there were several dilemmas he'd have to face alone. Insubstantial though tonight's conversation had been, it was a start and, as they drove home, he felt relieved that they might, after five destructive years, be able to mention Kingsley without engaging in silent but undermining conflict.

The house was in darkness and they tip-toed up the stairs, giggly and intoxicated with the absurdity of sneaking into their own home. How odd that they were having most success, feeling most at ease, when they were unable to see each other clearly. The shed episode couldn't be classified as a success, of course, but what had taken place there might prove to be less of a disaster than it at first appeared.

He wasn't quite ready, yet, to surrender the *other* Jack Waterfield and he suggested, 'Look, love, why don't you have the bed to yourself for another night or two? You need to catch up on your sleep and you know how restless I am.'

She paused, 'That's very considerate.' He couldn't make out her features in the gloom – couldn't tell from her voice if the comment was ironic.

Fay must have come in to the room during the day because his bed had been made up properly and he wondered if it had been an excuse to snoop around. What if it had? There was nothing to find. He was about to put out the light when he spotted one of the family photograph albums, lying on the bedside table. It hadn't been there last night.

The plastic pockets, containing the white-bordered prints, had become brittle and lost a little of their transparency, giving the impression that the world they captured was enveloped in a light mist. He prised the photos out of the pockets and the mist cleared, revealing his family, beaming and standing to attention, bathed in endless summer sunshine at Saundersfoot or Bristol Zoo or in Fay's parents' garden. He turned the pictures over. Nineteen eighty-five. Caitlin, lanky and big-toothed, would have been ten or eleven; sturdy, olive-skinned Dylan, just seven; Kingsley, features yet to emerge from the layer of pudge, a beguiling toddler.

One particular picture held his attention. He and Fay, twenty years younger, leaned against promenade railings – *Weymouth or Aberystwyth?* – his left arm curled around her shoulders and her hand, reaching up, held his. The horizon dipped at a mad angle – Caitlin or Dylan must have taken the photo. Next to Fay's bare feet, a stripey beach-bag bulged with towels and picnic things. Taking the picture closer to the light, he studied their laughing faces, noting their natural intimacy and marvelling at their teeth, startling white against the seaside tan. At some point those carefree young parents, who squinted and waved and dug dams to hold back the tide, had grown complacent and allowed this stash of gold to trickle through their fingers.

Although it had gone midnight, he phoned Laura, trying to make up his mind if it would be wise to leave a message, should she choose not to answer. He was unnerved when, after a few rings, a man's voice replied, 'Yes?'

He remembered that her son still lived at home. This must be Cassidy Ford. 'Ummm. Is … is Alan there, please?' He had no idea where 'Alan' came from but he was proud of himself for such quick-thinking.

'No Alan here, I'm afraid. You must have the wrong number.'

'Yes. I must. Sorry to disturb you.'

It was some time before he fell asleep.

36

THE CONSULTANT CONFIRMED that Harry would be discharged on Monday and they spent the weekend sorting out a car for Neil, then ferrying his few possessions up the valley. Jack had, rather generously Fay thought, lent him the money for a four-year-old Fiesta, to be paid back 'as and when'.

'I'm going to get Neil one of those chauffeur's caps with a shiny peak. Then, watch out... Rest Bay. McArthur Glen. Lidl's. The world's our oyster,' Vi proclaimed, revealing a woman that Fay didn't recognise – skittish and ready for anything.

The ex-lodgers couldn't wait to establish their new household, behaving like children embarking on a new adventure – getting keys cut, making lists of favourite meals and planning jaunts. Neil and Vi had only lived with them for three weeks but they had been anxious, turbulent weeks. No one knew how the new regime would pan out and Harry's health was still precarious but, until the next crisis, she and Jack were on their own again.

On Sunday evening they were sitting in companionable silence, catching up on the papers, when the door bell rang. 'Sod's law,' Jack sighed.

It was Caitlin. 'I spoke to Neil this afternoon and he said that the move went smoothly. Gran was too busy baking a fruit cake to come to the phone. I'm afraid she's going to force-feed poor Grandad when he gets home tomorrow.'

While Caitlin was in the kitchen making coffee, Fay whispered to Jack, 'Should we tell her about Kingsley's postcard? I wouldn't like her to think we're keeping anything from her.'

'Let's tell her what it said and let her draw her own conclusions.'

'You're right. I keep forgetting the children are grown-ups.'

Fay told Caitlin about Neil's card, reporting Kingsley's exact words and no more. Caitlin obviously understood the implications but seemed unconvinced and negative. 'Don't set your heart on it, Mum. He might be winding you up. He was always good at that.'

'What about that Anya girl he used to talk about? And the child. D'you think that was that a wind up too?

Caitlin shrugged. 'Who knows? All I'm saying is that he's been pretty callous over the years.'

'Perhaps he's seen the light,' Jack suggested. 'Or not "seen the light", that's too instant. Maybe he's weighed things up and realised that there has to be some give and take – the grass isn't always greener…' He glanced at Fay. 'Sorry, love.'

Caitlin cleared her throat. 'I've never said this before because it seemed rather like speaking ill of the dead, but Kingsley's no saint. We've got into the habit of talking about him in whispers, as if he's a holy man. And he's perpetuating the myth, with his snide emails and obscure messages from Australia or Greece or wherever. You can't have forgotten how he used to play us off against each other? Stirring things up whenever he had the chance. It was unforgivably cruel not to come to Dylan's wedding. And I hate what he's done to you two. Okay, he's my brother but there comes a moment when he's got to do something to regain my love. Sorry, but that's how I feel.'

Fay was shocked by her daughter's outburst. She'd always imagined that Caitlin sympathised with her younger brother; that it was Caitlin's desire to conceal her disloyalty to *her* that prevented her from talking about him.

Watching Jack pour a small measure of brandy into each mug of coffee, she could see that he was equally shaken.

After three days of being an invalid, Fay was ready to get back to school. Her hand was healing well. The nurse at the surgery had confirmed that the stitches were the dissolving kind and replaced the unwieldy bandage with a neat dressing, making it possible for her to use both hands. On Monday morning she was in the staffroom a good fifteen minutes earlier than necessary.

'You're keen,' a colleague remarked. 'Trying to make a good impression?'

'Why would I want to do that?'

'The job. I assume you'll be going for it.' Seeing her bewilderment, he filled her in on the unexpected resignation of the deputy head. 'Applications have to be in by half-term. Seriously, Fay, you'd stand a pretty good chance and it would be a great way to round off your teaching career.'

'Why's he going?'

'Rumour has it that he's left his wife…for another man.'

That wasn't the only disclosure. Having decided to wait a while before dealing with Darren's disconcerting essay, more pressing matters had occupied her and she'd forgotten about it. She was checking the examination syllabus, when Linda Judd, the school secretary, approached her. 'Fay, I hear that you were asking about Darren Taylor?' Linda never missed a trick.

'That's right.' She was reluctant to give too much away, knowing that whatever she said would be all around the staffroom before the end of afternoon school. 'I was looking for a bit of background on the kids, before I do my half-term assessments. No one had much to tell me about Darren.' Was that convincing enough?

Linda folded her arms. 'The Taylors used to live down the road from us. Nice family. I remember Brian Taylor was a very neat bloke. Always tied the tops of his rubbish bags with garden twine.'

Fay waited patiently.

'Three children. A girl and two boys. Darren is – *was* – the middle one.' She lowered her voice, although there was no one within earshot. 'One day the girl, Anne-Marie her name was, got hit by a car. She was on the pavement with a crowd of her friends. The inquest said the driver had a heart attack or a stroke and lost control. The car mounted the kerb and ploughed into them. The other kids were okay but she was killed outright. I'm surprised you didn't read about it. It was all over the *Echo* for weeks.'

'How long ago was this?'

'Oh, five or six years. She was only twelve.' That was around the time that Kingsley left, the time Fay wouldn't have been interested in anyone else's tragedy.

'But she didn't attend *this* school?'

'No. The Taylors moved up this way a few months after the accident. Trying to make a fresh start, I expect.'

Regular progress reports from the '*ménage à trois*', as Neil insisted on calling them, sounded positive, and when they visited Harry on his first evening at home, initial impressions were that it might work. It wasn't exactly what she'd had in mind for Neil Bentley. She'd hoped to find him a trainee-ship in a reputable organisation with a decent career structure, a stepping off point for better things. But he seemed ideally suited to the role of carer and the arrangement *was* very convenient. Perhaps one day, when the situation changed, he could get some formal training. With people living so much longer, there had to be endless opportunities in the caring professions.

Despite the almost party atmosphere, it was clear that her father-in-law wasn't a well man. It took two pill-dispensers to accommodate his medication and he had a string of out-patient appointments for various consultant clinics. Displaced from the security of the hospital, he looked anxious and much smaller than she'd remembered, but, sitting in his favourite armchair, swathed in blankets, he put on a brave face. 'A few lamb stews and suet puddings and I'll be my old self again, won't I Mum?'

Before they left, Neil insisted on showing them around, as if they were prospective purchasers who had never set foot in the house before. 'There's a great view down the valley from my bedroom window. And stacks of storage space under the stairs.'

Fay had been feeling guilty that, having offered Neil a temporary home and assistance in finding a worthwhile job, they'd done nothing but taken advantage of his good nature and willingness to help. The speed at which he'd made Kingsley's room 'home', followed by his readiness, a mere three weeks later, to up sticks and start again was unnatural, but he seemed content with the way things were panning out. Then again, she wasn't convinced that he was capable of showing displeasure. Things would have been very different, of course, had Harry not been hospitalised but, now she knew the boy better, she wasn't sure where his future lay or whether she would ever have found him the right job. Amiability, Neil's defining quality, didn't qualify him for much.

In odd moments, Fay reflected on the sad story of Darren's sister. Fay wasn't trained in that sort of thing but she wondered if his poignant essay and the palpable agitation that followed could be connected with Anne-Marie Taylor's death. It had to be. A teenage girl is killed in appalling circumstances – her brother fantasises about dressing as a teenage girl and returning to the family home.

A few days later, Fay spotted Darren, loitering on his own outside the gymnasium. She hadn't seen him, or the rest of his English set, since they'd handed in their homework. 'Darren. I'm glad I caught you. Have you got a moment?'

He checked both ways, as if not wanting to be seen with her, then stared at the floor. 'Yes, Miss.'

Her lecture on making eye-contact, standing straight and taking hands out of pockets, could wait until another day and she said gently, 'I liked your story.'

He glanced up nervously then resumed his study of the vinyl tiles.

'It was well written. Excellent use of language. A few spelling mistakes but …' she was sounding too much like an English teacher and he looked longingly down the corridor. 'I know that it's a…very personal story. A poignant story.' If she were too subtle, too oblique, he wouldn't understand what she was getting at, but she continued warily, 'It's about your sister, isn't it? About Anne-Marie. I know you miss her dreadfully – and you always will. Your story is about bringing her back to life, bringing her back to the family, isn't it?' Her throat tightened as she watched the boy, face still averted, drag the back of his hand across his eyes. 'Don't say anything now but I wanted you to know two things. First, I promise not to read your story in class, although I'll be giving it my highest mark. Secondly, if you ever need to talk about Anne-Marie, what you feel about her death or anything at all, I'm always here. And Darren, it's perfectly natural to feel anger and guilt, as well as sadness, when someone dies.' *Or when someone chooses to leave.*

A string of clear snot dangled from his nose and she handed him some tissues from her bag. 'Thanks, Miss. C'n I go now, Miss?'

'Of course.' He slouched off down the corridor and when he reached the corner he turned to look back, but she was too far away to see the expression on his face.

She could see that Jack was trying hard. A rosemary plant and a monstrous vase, shaped like Nelson's Column, had appeared like ritual offerings on the kitchen window sill, and twice during the week he'd brought her flowers. They were both on their best behaviour, courteous and considerate towards each other. They ate together, discussed the latest on the local road-widening scheme, whether Fay's car needed a service, and exchanged news of work – Jack thought she should certainly try for the deputy headship. However, they were still occupying separate bedrooms and each evening, as bedtime drew nearer, a 'will-we-won't-we' tension built up, defused only when one or the other found a plausible reason for keeping it that way. Anything would do. An incipient cold. Restlessness. The heat. It was as if they were half way through a Sudoku puzzle, unable to proceed until they'd fathomed out the one elusive number that would unlock the grids.

It was still September but the shops were already full of coats, boots and chunky jumpers so, when Jack was at Morris practice, Fay decided to assess her clothes and see what she was short of for the coming winter. Oxfam bag at the ready, she took everything out of her wardrobe, heaping the clothes on the double bed, horrified to see how, once released from captivity, their volume doubled. Out, too, came shoes, hats and bags, until the bed and half the floor was covered with things she scarcely knew she had. Before the guilt became overpowering, she began the reverse process, determined to make her sacrifice the Third World's gain.

Some decisions were clear-cut. She couldn't part with the outfit that she'd worn to Dylan's wedding, although the turquoise *was* quite harsh and she doubted whether she'd wear it again. It had cost hundreds of pounds and charity shops never priced anything at more than twenty, so back on the rail it went, along with several evening dresses, a fake-fur jacket and a trouser-suit which she'd never worn because there was something odd about the lapels. She thought hard about the camel coat – the sleeves too long and the shoulder pads passé – but it would be a godsend if the coming winter turned out to be as cold as the papers were predicting.

Jeans. Smart black trousers. Tailored jackets. A genuine Burberry. Straight skirts and cotton shirts. All went back in.

She worked her way down the pile, coming eventually to silk and linen, symbols of her failure to become the Mrs Robinson of the Cardiff suburbs. How pathetic she'd been – planning intimate lunches; imagining meaningful glances and lingering looks; tearing across the country on the off chance of a kiss on the cheek. Was it merely a menopausal fantasy? Given the opportunity, she certainly would have taken Cassidy to bed, and even now, she wasn't wholly confident that she'd be able, or *want*, to resist. She shook her head, struggling to dislodge improper thoughts but, in doing so, released explicit memories of her wild night with Jack. Was there something wrong with her?

She opened her underwear drawer. There, at the back, beyond the wholesome cotton bras and briefs, behind the folded petticoats and thermal vests, lurked scraps of slippery satin. She snatched them up, holding them at arms length as if they were gobbets of decaying meat and, rushing downstairs, she shoved all ninety-eight pounds-worth into the rubbish bag, concealing it beneath chicken skin and tea bags. If she were out to seduce her husband, or anyone else, she'd do it without Moll Flanders.

By the time Jack came home, everything was back where it belonged and the half-filled charity bag contained two floral blouses, a pair of pale green shoes, a cotton jacket and – she remembered seeing a delightful charcoal-grey replacement in Robertson's – the camel coat.

Jack kissed her forehead. 'Sorry I'm late. Neil turned up so we had a bit of a chat.'

'Any problems?'

'No. He's full of it. There's something quite surreal, though, having him tell me about my own parents. What my father watches on television. What my mother's cooking tastes like.'

'Has he heard from…?'

Jack put his hand on hers. 'Caitlin's probably right. It could all be a wind-up.'

37

IF FAY WERE A FANCIFUL WOMAN, she might have studied the purplish-red scar on the palm of her hand, noting how close it ran to her life-line, seeing it as symbolic of something or another. She and Jack were still occupying separate bedrooms but, oddly enough, their physical separation was making it easier to re-connect, as if they were two sections of broken bone, knitting together nicely because the weight had been taken off. During the past week they had rediscovered the knack of being in each other's company – chatting about nothing in particular, reading or watching the television, making each other laugh. Jack had described a very funny incident, concerning an old lady and one of those ranting lunatics that preach doom and gloom. When Friday evening came, they celebrated the start of the weekend by preparing a meal together and washing it down with an expensive bottle of red wine which had been overlooked during the wedding festivities.

'Delicious.' Fay popped the last spoonful of crème brulée into her mouth. 'I'd forgotten how much I love Friday evenings. What shall we do this weekend?'

'Aahh,' Jack looked sheepish. 'The Wicker Men have got a booking tomorrow. I think I probably mentioned it but, what with all the toing and froing—'

'Where?'

'Llangwm, I think. Yes. Llangwm.'

If they were to set things straight, she would have to make some concessions and this was the moment to start. 'Shall I come along? See what it is you get up to every Thursday? Where is Llangwm, anyway?' Her suggestion appeared to have deprived him of the power of speech and, when he didn't reply, she prompted, 'Jack? Don't look so flabbergasted.'

'It's not far from Brecon. I believe.' He started clearing the table, clattering the plates and scraping leftovers into the waste bin.

'Leave that for a minute. What d'you think? Shall I come?'

'That's very thoughtful, but I don't really think it's your cup of tea.'

For years she had at best, ignored, at worst, ridiculed his hobby and could understand his caution. 'Well, someone thinks Morris dancing is worth watching or they wouldn't have booked you. Anyway, I fancy having a look round somewhere different.' She rubbed her palms together and smiled. 'That's settled, then.'

Jack went to the shed to clean his shoes and prepare his kit, whilst Fay, eager to tell someone about her conciliatory gesture, phoned Caitlin. 'Guess what? I'm going to watch your father dance tomorrow. At Llan-something-or-another.'

'That's nice.' Caitlin didn't sound impressed but was plainly keen to inform her mother that she'd booked two tickets for *The Magic Flute*, and that Cassidy was driving down the following afternoon. 'I thought we might go to Gower on Sunday, if the weather's reasonable. Cass is bringing his surfboard.'

It was a long time since her daughter had taken this much interest in a man. Cassidy and Caitlin. Cass and Cait.

It would be as well to get used to it. 'Might we be seeing you?' She felt the idiotic fizz of excitement in her stomach as she waited for a reply.

'I shouldn't think we'll have much time. Anyway, you two go and have some fun. Oh, nothing from Kingsley I presume?'

'No.' There had been nothing from Kingsley but, since it was no longer a forbidden topic, the disabling ache had eased slightly and she almost believed it when she replied, 'I'm sure he'll turn up, sooner or later.'

Safe in the shed, Jack bolted the door. He could drive a six-inch nail through his foot – that would solve the problem but it could also lead to terrible complications, like blood-poisoning or gangrene. How about a car-crash? He wasn't confident that he could stage a *harmless* crash and it wasn't fair to put Fay's life in danger merely because he'd got himself in this pickle. There were less flashy options, of course – a tummy bug or a bad back – but these were hackneyed excuses and teachers were dab hands at spotting sham illness.

And it was a shame, because things had been going well. The pact between his parents and Neil Bentley could work, enabling them to remain independent for a while longer and giving Neil somewhere to call home. If it came to a point where his father needed in-patient treatment or – he had to face the possibility – died, the lad might be prepared stay on as his mother's lodger and companion. *Whoa.* There was no point in thinking too far ahead. Neil might even make it as a funky folk-rocker and abandon them for the rock 'n roll life-style. But, as things stood, there was no one whom he trusted more than Neil to keep a watchful eye on his parents.

He'd spoken to Laura a couple of times – vague, Kafkaesque conversations which left him feeling that he'd come in three-quarters of the way through a film, where something pivotal might – or might not – have happened. In the end, all he could do was tell her that he was there, if she needed him – an offer which was twenty-eight years too late. It was all so precarious. *If only* Caitlin hadn't taken up with Cassidy Ford, *if only* they hadn't gone to visit Sadie in London, *if only* Caitlin hadn't been so on-the-ball, none of it would have come out. Had he not asked, Laura would never have disclosed that he was a contender in the 'who fathered Sadie' stakes, and now he would have to learn to live with that uncertainty.

He polished his shoes and, by the time they were gleaming, he'd made up his mind to speak to Non. Now that he'd come clean and told her about his family and his difficulties, it was possible that she would agree to help him out. All he could do was ask and then, if she weren't prepared to do it, he'd drink enough salt-water to guarantee authentic vomiting.

He rang Coed Melyn Cottage, crossing his fingers that she wasn't involved in a concert or a dance as part of the weekend festivities, but she answered, not seeming at all surprised to hear his voice. 'Hello, Jack. Ruth and I were just talking about you. I'm taking an early lunch break tomorrow 'specially to watch you dance. You are coming, aren't you?'

'Yes. Probably. Possibly. It's in your hands, actually.'

'How's that, then?'

'It's tricky. You see, completely out of the blue, my wife's decided to come with me. And…I don't know how to put this…'

'And I've never seen you before in my life?'

'Exactly. But it's more complicated than that…'

It only took her a few seconds to work it out. 'And my

parents haven't seen you before, either. Is that it?'

'I feel really bad—'

'Shh. It's okay. Remember what I said?'

'Of course I do.' *A place to catch your breath*. The exquisite phrase had been hard-wired into his brain from the moment she'd uttered it.

'But wait a sec', Jack. You met quite a few people on carnival day, didn't you? What are we going to do about them?'

'Don't worry. I think I've got it covered.'

In the utility room, Jack ironed the white pleated shirt, moleskin breeches and large white handkerchiefs. Next he pressed the red and yellow satin ribbons, attached to the bindings that encircled his wrists and elbows; he rolled the red braces and balled the white, woollen socks; he placed the black shoes, still smelling of polish, inside a carrier bag before putting everything into the holdall. Finally, in went the bells, shining and chinking, and he gave the bag a spirited shake – for luck.

Fay must have heard him coming upstairs and called out, 'What time are we off in the morning?'

He pushed the bedroom door open and stood, half in, half out of the room. She was in bed, reading, and, despite having had the opportunity to colonise the whole mattress, seemed to be keeping to her own side. 'Well, we don't want to get there too soon, so, let's say about ten? And if the weather's foul, or you think of something you'd rather do, or anything crops up, that's fine with me.' Simply by standing there at this time of night, he felt ill at ease, not sure if he was supposed to come or go, so he did neither. 'Good book?'

'Not very.'

'Anything I can get you?'

'I don't think so, thanks. D'*you* need anything?'

The dialogue was absurdly Noel Coward-ish, clipped and polite, and suddenly he wanted to hurl himself, whooping, across the room and bounce on the bed, simply because he'd never, ever done it before. 'Me? No. I'm fine.'

'Goodnight, then.'

'Goodnight.'

38

FAY SPENT A FRUSTRATING HALF-HOUR fiddling with her hair. The new style was proving to be high-maintenance and she was debating whether, with colder weather ahead, it was going to be worth the bother. Two minutes under a hat and she'd be back where she started. Anyway, who was she making all this effort for? Cassidy? Did he give two hoots what his mother's best friend's hair looked like? To emulate Isabel? The woman hadn't even managed to hang on to her husband so why adopt her as a role model? And besides, Fay doubted she'd be seeing much of Isabel. That left Jack, and he'd never commented on it, apart from suggesting it needed brushing.

When she went downstairs, there was no sign of him but, assuming that he would benefit from extra calories to get him through his strenuous day, she began preparing a cooked breakfast. While the bacon sizzled, she called upstairs, 'Jack? Breakfast in five minutes.'

She was lifting the eggs out of the frying-pan, when a stranger entered the kitchen.

'Morning, love.' He sounded like Jack and was wearing Jack's clothes. 'What d'you think?'

'What on earth have you done?' She could see what he'd done. He'd shaved off his beard. For the first time ever, she looked at his unadorned face; thinner than she expected and dotted with razor-nicks. He'd had a go at his hair, too, which he appeared to have given a rough trim, before brushing the ragged clumps forward, losing the neat side-parting. 'Gosh.'

'I thought it was time for a change.' He glanced at the stove. 'The sausages are burning, love.'

Whilst they ate, Fay studied her new-look husband. In accompanying him today, she was showing him that she was prepared to compromise over a thorny issue. She hoped that he would recognise this concession and, in return, examine his own conduct. He could sharpen up; be more assertive; take the lead now and again, instead of leaving everything to her. She hadn't, however, expected his first gesture to be so immediate and so tangible but she'd done more or less the same thing in setting about her own reconstruction, hadn't she?

'You haven't said what you think.' Jack looked up from his plate and smiled. His lips seemed fuller than when they'd been surrounded by bristles; his nose more prominent and his chin less so; his cheeks were an entirely different colour from his forehead – paler and pinker – not surprising as they hadn't seen the sun since he'd been a schoolboy. The overall effect wasn't so much a *younger* as a more refined, more subtle, man.

'You've got to give me time to get used to it. But why did you choose today? Wouldn't it have been better to let the barber do it?'

He ran the palms of his hands over his face and down his neck. 'Probably. But you know how it is.'

Did she?

When they reached Llangwm, she stayed in the car while Jack chatted with Stan Colley and the others. From the pointing and laughing, she guessed that they were teasing

376

Jack about his beardlessness but he didn't appear to be taking it too hard.

He came back to the car. 'We're going to get changed in the pub, then do a half-hour session. Kick off – actually 'Morris On' is the correct term – at noon. It's a pity none of the other wives—'

'Don't worry about me. You carry on. I shall enjoy having a little look round. There's bound to be a coffee shop somewhere.'

'There's the Corner Café and they do excellent bacon baps in the second-hand bookshop … or so they tell me.' He clapped his hands. 'Okay? See you later.' Grabbing his bag from the back seat of the car, he rushed off to join the rest of them as they ambled towards the main road. Anyone who didn't know might have taken them for train-spotters on their annual outing.

There wasn't much to Llangwm, making it all the more surprising that its Harvest Celebrations were so ambitious. According to the programme pinned up in the window of the odd little craft shop, the main attractions were 'The Annual Dahlia and Chrysanthemum Show', a 'Tramps' Supper', a brass-band concert with a bingo session in the interval and, of course, 'All the way from Cardiff – The Wicker Men'.

Fay's gaze wandered from the programme, across the chaotic window-display – ghastly chunky-knit jumpers, ridiculous felt hats, clumsy mittens and garish bags – things grandmothers bought as 'fun' presents for teenage granddaughters and which sat in the back of wardrobes for years, until the moths got to them. Despite this, something drew her inside. The woman in the corner, who to Fay's astonishment was half-way through *Ulysses*, smiled but said nothing, leaving her to browse the cluttered shelves, undisturbed.

A rotating stand stood in one corner of the shop, displaying assorted craft booklets and a few postcards. One card caught her eye. It showed a cross-stitched sampler – 'the original can be seen in Norwich City Museum' – with the simple declaration, worked in dark red letters;

BLESSED ARE
THE PEACEMAKERS
Annie Lewis: Aged 9 years: 1869

These wise words were surrounded by a border of virtuoso stitches, depicting leaves and flowers. She bought two copies of the card and, with plenty of time in hand before the Wicker Men were due to start, went in search of the bookshop.

Jack was right. The bookshop doubled as a café and half-a-dozen tables, jollied up with bright tablecloths and jars of pom-pom dahlias, occupied the area next to the poetry section. She slung her jacket on the back of a chair, then went to the counter and ordered a filter coffee from the middle-aged woman, who, wearing frilly blouse, a gathered skirt and hooped earrings, would have looked more at home in a Romany caravan.

Whilst her coffee cooled, she wrote one of the cards.

Llangwm - Saturday
Dear Geoffrey,
    I'm here watching Jack dance.
    So how many Brownie points do I get?
    Thanks for the advice. Fay

The aroma of coffee and grilling bacon stirred up memories of her sausage-sandwich breakfast. If the incident were written as a short story – 'Raj's Recommendation' perhaps or 'The Newsagent's Daughter' – she would tell the writer that, without a beginning, middle and end, and lacking a revelatory moment, it didn't comply with literary convention. But the encounter continued to pop into her head at the oddest times, as if some truth *had* been revealed but she had failed to spot it.

A crowd was gathering outside The Fox. From the banter it was clear that the majority of them were locals. 'I'll budge up.' The offer came from a stocky young woman with an open, but rather plain, face. Her dark hair, plaited and fastened with knitting wool, could have done with a decent cut and her clothes – a droopy skirt, creased tee-shirt and battered clogs – were rather unflattering. 'Plenty of room.'

'Thanks.' Fay perched beside her on the low stone wall.

'Here for the day, are you?' The girl's voice dipped and rose.

'Yes. I've never been to Llangwm before. It seems a very go-ahead place.'

'It's like anywhere, I suppose. We have a bit of fun, now and again, and the rest of the time we just get on with it.' She nudged Fay and pointed. 'Look, they're coming out.'

To the strains of accordion and fiddle, and much applause from the onlookers, the Wicker Men processed from the door of The Fox to take up position on the pub forecourt. Fay was surprised to feel her throat tighten, the way it had when she'd watched the children in their end-of-term concerts, and she craned her neck, looking for Jack. There he was, in the middle of the row facing her, almost unrecognisable in the outlandish outfit and without his beard.

The Wicker Men began to dance, handkerchiefs and

ribbons flying, whacking the tarmac with thick-soled shoes, stamping out the beat, kicking and twisting and leaping as they executed intricate progressions. All the while the *chink-chunk-chink-chunk* of the bells reinforced the rhythm. The spectators were soon hooked, clapping and stamping too, infected by the spirited performance and eager to join in. Fay didn't resist, clapping and tapping her feet.

'Look at those calf-muscles. They must be incredibly fit.' The young woman was standing on the wall to get a better view. 'It's ever so sexy, don't you think?'

Unable to suppress a surge of pride, Fay pointed at Jack, 'Actually, that's my husband.'

'Which one?'

'That one. In the middle. The one without the beard.' None of the dancers were bearded and, realising how silly it sounded, Fay laughed. 'Sorry. You must think I'm mad. It's just that Jack *did* have a beard until this morning.'

'Oh, look at the time.' Pointing at her watch, the young woman jumped down from the wall. 'I've got to get back to work. Enjoy the rest of your day, won't you.' And she was gone.

The Wicker Men danced on for a further ten minutes, their faces growing redder and sweatier, the music more riotous, until Stan shouted 'Morris Off, Wicker Men' and to wolf-whistles and loud applause, they danced back in to the pub.

Fay waited until the appreciative crowd had filtered away before she went to find Jack. 'You must be exhausted.'

He nodded, still breathing heavily. 'What did you think, then?'

'I'm very impressed. Everyone loved it and the girl next to me thought you were all extremely sexy.'

'Really? What did she say exactly?'

Stan interrupted. 'Hello, Fay. Nice surprise. I would have persuaded Muriel to come along if I'd known she'd have company. Next time, maybe. Good work.' He slapped Jack on the back. 'Fay, the landlord's put up a lunch for us but I'm sure he can rustle up an extra—'

'Thanks, but I wouldn't dream of crashing the party, Stan.' She turned to Jack. 'Why don't I meet you at the school, after you've finished the next session?'

'I could come and have lunch with you.'

'Absolutely not. I'm going to have another leisurely browse around the bookshop. Maybe pop into the flower show. I'll see you later.'

She wandered down one of the side streets, stopping to buy two jars of honey – the *ménage à trois* might like one – from a makeshift stall in the garden of one of the larger houses. Carrying on, she rejoined the main street, coming out opposite a double-fronted villa, its doorway festooned with hop vines and sheaves of corn, very much in keeping with the harvest theme. Fay read the sign above the entrance and smiled. It had crossed her mind that a 'spur-of-the-moment' night away from home would, without risking an embarrassing post-mortem, get her and Jack back together in the same bedroom. It would also ensure that she wasn't tempted to make a fool of herself when Cassidy Ford visited Caitlin. In her experience, spontaneity benefited greatly from forward-planning and, with this in mind, she'd packed an overnight bag and concealed it in the boot of the car, beneath the travel rug. She read the name again, 'The Welcome Stranger Guesthouse'. How ridiculous, but there was no harm in taking a quick look inside before making up her mind.

She knew the man in the foyer couldn't possibly be a farmer because farmers wore green nylon overalls, not calico smocks and battered felt hats; nor did they play the

381

mouth organ. He was concentrating hard, eyes shut tight, sucking and blowing his way through what she suspected was 'Oh, My Darling Clementine'. Several seconds passed before he registered her presence.

'Hello, there. Not as easy as you think,' he confided, waving the instrument in the air. 'I expect you want to book a room.'

Fay wasn't used to familiarity from people in the service industries and this, coupled with the man's odd garb, convinced her that the shabby guesthouse would not be suitable.

'Well, I'm afraid we're full up for the weekend.' He flicked through the large diary which lay on the reception desk, 'And all next week.' His apologetic smile was disturbingly charming and, despite having decided that nothing could persuade her to stay here, she felt a pang of regret. 'Anyway,' he continued, 'You probably wouldn't want to share a bathroom. Some people don't but we think that makes it more like home.'

'Actually, I need a room for tonight. Would you know of anywhere nearby? A hotel, maybe?'

He studied her, starting with her wedge-heeled shoes then up through her smart wrap-around skirt and boxy jacket to her well-organised hair, before passing her a glossy brochure. 'Henllys House. Just been done up. Excellent food, or so I'm told. Landscaped grounds. Quite posh. It'll suit you fine, I'm sure.' Although she detected no hint of disparagement in his voice, it was as if he'd weighed her up and reached the conclusion that she wasn't quite up to whatever went on at The Welcome Stranger Guesthouse.

She remembered seeing a small-ads board in the craft shop and made her way back. The board was chock-a-block with adverts for jumble sales, electricians, computer lessons and 'free' kittens; there was a six-berth caravan to rent in Tenby and a two-bedroomed flat for sale in Brecon, but no mention of a hotel – posh or otherwise.

'Hello, again,' the woman looked up from her book. 'Can I help at all?'

'Well … It's such a beautiful day and I'm having such a nice time here, it seems a shame to leave. I was checking your board – hoping I might spot somewhere out of the ordinary to stay.

'Have you tried The Welcome Stranger? Iolo and Zena are certainly out of the ordinary.'

'Full, I'm afraid.'

'There's Henllys House—'

'Mmmm. I saw the brochure. It looks nice but I was looking for something more…more…' She recalled her coy conversation with the assistant in La Passionata, but this open-faced, literate woman was a different species. 'I'm actually looking for something more romantic.' She cleared her throat. 'Don't laugh, will you? I want to surprise my husband. Show him that I still can.'

'That's a really lovely idea. And what a lucky man he is.' No smirk. No innuendo. The woman thought for a moment then clapped her hands. 'Hang on.' She rifled through the clutter near the till. 'A friend of a friend just brought…where did I put it…this in.' She held up a sheet of paper. 'She's had a last minute cancellation. It's not cheap but it's definitely unusual.'

The Wicker Men's second session was, if anything, more rumbustious than the first and a larger crowd had turned out to watch. Many sat on the grass, picnicking in cheery groups, whilst children and dogs careered around, safe in the confines of the school grounds. This time Fay felt less of an outsider. Clapping along to the now familiar tunes, watching her new-look husband leaping and jingling, she was sorry when the dancers skipped away into the school and the strains of the music faded.

'Thanks for hanging about, love.' After the merriment and the gaudy ribbons, she was almost disappointed when, ten minutes later, Jack, in navy shirt and khaki chinos, came to find her. 'Let's be on our way' He evidently assumed that she was eager to get back home and she was touched by his consideration.

Instinct had told Jack to bolt when he saw Non and Fay sitting together on the wall but he concentrated on his hanky-work and, the next time he had chance to look up, Non had disappeared. There was another iffy moment when Iolo's mate, a ham-fisted chap who'd hindered Jack considerably when he'd helped erect the jumper-rainbow, gave him a quizzical glance then, fortunately, was called away to move his car. Jack also spotted Iolo, in a smock and Zena, looking fetching in a gypsy get up. Both gave conspiratorial winks and raised their thumbs but, apart from that, he was confident that he'd gone unrecognised. He had taken a calculated risk but appeared to have got away with it and he felt heady with success.

Fay's last-minute decision to come with him had scotched his plan to spend the night in Llangwm – *Sorry love, we've been cut off by flash floods. I won't be able to get back tonight* – and join in whatever craziness Iolo had dreamed up for the Harvest Celebrations. He was disappointed, but it wasn't the end of the world. He'd negotiated a dodgy day, when his two lives had overlapped, and it had given him quite a buzz.

He'd seen how unfazed Non and her parents were by his visits even when, like today, they were in such peculiar circumstances. Could it be – and why had he never considered this before – that he was just one of a stream of 'regulars' who dropped in at The Welcome Stranger? The Evans's seemed happy enough to see him when he turned up, once in a while, and sporadic absences from home should be easy to wangle. It meant that he would be living in a constant state of anticipation – as if he had a never-ending supply of home international tickets stashed in a secret drawer. Bliss.

Jack dumped his bag in the back of the car and they drove out of the car park.

'Go left here,' Fay instructed, peering at a piece of paper. 'Then take the second on the right.'

'But that's not—'

'Do. As. You're. Told.' She tapped his knee in time with her words and looked smug.

'Okay. You're the boss.'

The road she indicated, and which he'd never noticed before, left the village and ran alongside a fast-flowing river through gloomy woods. Out of the blue, as if someone had pulled a plug out, his energy drained away and, realising how keyed-up he must have been all day, he was thankful to be putting some distance between himself and potential catastrophe.

He couldn't work out why Fay had wanted to come with him. For days now she'd been going out of her way to be agreeable and the atmosphere in the house was a lot more relaxed. But what if that were part of a plan? What if she had put two and two together about Sadie? Or discovered that there was a large dollop missing from their savings? What if she was, even now, luring him in to a trap? Hadn't he come home the other evening to find her watching 'Fatal Attraction'? He shivered. A lonely road; secluded woods; a raging river. He shook his head. His wife did not have one devious bone in her body. Were she ever to plot revenge, she'd place a large advert in the *Echo*, inviting everyone along to watch him suffer.

He drove on, gaining height and leaving the river behind.

'We're looking for a turning on the left.' She studied the piece of paper, then rotated it through one hundred and eighty degrees. 'No. On the right.'

He was too tired to speak; too tired to disagree.

'Here. Down this lane.'

Jack turned off the road as she instructed then stopped the car. 'Okay. What's this all about, Fay?' He massaged his forehead. 'To be honest, I'm pretty knackered.'

She swivelled round to face him. 'I've been thinking. We've had a…a difficult summer, what with one thing and another.'

He couldn't argue with that.

'And I was thinking…a night away from home…might be...I don't know.'

He said nothing, unwilling to sign up for anything until he'd heard the small print.

'On the spur-of-the-moment I tried that guesthouse. Did you notice it? The one with the twee name—'

'Any good?' Jack was wide awake now.

'*Strange*, to say the least. There was the weirdest man behind the desk. At first I assumed he was simple, but I think he was anything but. He was playing a mouth organ, would you believe?'

Playing a mouth organ. *Brilliant.* 'What was the tune?'

Fay smiled, as if he'd made an amusing observation. 'Anyway, the nice woman in the craft shop put me on to this,' She pointed down the lane. 'I thought, why not give ourselves a treat? Why not try something…different?' She seemed unsure and he sensed that she wasn't only talking about a night in a hotel.

As they drove on, the sheep, grazing in the fields beyond the hazelnut hedges, raised their heads in mild interest, their wool taking on an orangey-pink tinge in the late afternoon sun. There was still no evidence of human habitation and Jack prepared to make a ten-point turn once Fay owned up to her navigational error. The lane came to an abrupt end, widening out into an area large enough to park a couple of cars. A chunky wooden gate gave access to a footpath, leading around the belly of the hill, towards a copse. Carved in to the top rail of the gate, in bold letters, was 'Y Clochdy'.

'Well, this is it.' Fay opened the car door and stood looking over the gate. 'Listen.'

'I can't hear anything.'

'Exactly.'

Jack pointed to the gate. 'What d'you reckon that means?'

'Be patient,' Fay raised her finger. 'All will be revealed.'

It was a beautiful, peaceful place but, in the school changing-room, folding his crumpled gear into the bag, he'd been looking forward to an evening at home; pottering in the shed; reading the paper; watching rubbish on the television.

Fay lifted the back door of the car, flicking aside the tartan rug to reveal the holdall that they used for holidays. He felt a prickle of curiosity.

'Could you bring the bags, Jack?'

He followed his wife along the footpath. Down to his left, he could make out Llangwm, nestling in the valley; the place where he could catch his breath. Somewhere down there, Non would be cashing up at the nursery; Iolo and Zena togging up for the 'Tramps' Supper'; Llangwm preparing itself for yet another night of fun. He sighed.

Suddenly, up ahead, he could make out a building, half-hidden amongst the trees. A diminutive, stone-built tower with an open gallery at the top. Were they not sixty miles from the sea, he might have taken it for a lighthouse.

'What d'you think?' Fay beamed, as though she'd popped up here and built the thing herself whilst he'd been lunching in The Fox. She lifted the flower pot that stood near the entrance, removed a large, ornate key and unlocked the oak door, 'Come on.'

The room they entered – a sort of living-dining-kitchen – was equipped for two. Bold, modern décor; lots of wood and metal; no chintzy covers or fitted carpet to be seen. Scandinavian, was Jack's immediate thought, with hints of boat in the ingenious use of space.

Fay squeezed the arm of the black leather chair; ran her hand across the top of the birchwood table; lifted a stainless steel pan from the hob. 'It's spotless.' She opened the fridge. 'Wow. Look at this. Pâté. Olives. Smoked salmon. Strawberries. *And* champagne. If this is self-catering, I'm a convert.'

They climbed the spiral staircase to the first floor. The bedroom was not much bigger than their room at home, but the off-white walls and pale oak floorboards gave it a spacious and airy feel. In place of curtains, the recessed windows had wooden shutters, flick-flacked back, the deep sills padded to create window seats. There were fresh candles in unfussy iron candlesticks. Slap in the centre, and the unavoidable focal point of the room, stood the largest bed that Jack had ever seen. This, too, had white covers, making it appear wholesome yet tempting, like a bowl of porridge, sweetened with a swirl of syrup. Not feeling quite ready to confront bedroom issues, Jack pointed at the holdalls. 'We ought to unpack these.'

'Leave that for a minute. Look, there's another flight of

stairs. It must go up to the roof.'

Jack led the way this time. At the top of the stairs was a door. This opened on to a lookout platform which was exposed to the elements, with a solid wall to waist-level and a stone pier at each corner, supporting its pitched slate roof. He shook his head. 'What the hell is this place?'

'*Y clochdy* means the belfry. It's terribly romantic. Originally it was a folly, in the grounds of a *faux* Italian villa. The house must have been down there somewhere.' She pointed, vaguely, down the hillside. 'A rich Englishman built it for his Welsh mistress.'

'Colonialist pimp.'

'There was a bell…up there, I imagine.' She pointed up into the roof, at remnants of a cast iron housing. 'The legend is that she used to come up here and ring the bell to welcome her lover.'

'A bit of a giveaway, wasn't it? And, don't tell me, she threw herself over the edge, when the bastard did the dirty on her.'

'Of course. All the best stories are about sex and death.'

They spent a little while admiring the view then Fay went down to the kitchen to see exactly what the landlady had provided for supper and Jack took the opportunity to see how prepared Fay was for their 'spur-of-the-moment' night away. He eased open the zip of the holdall. Two toilet bags – she'd forgotten a razor but that was understandable; his dark jacket, white shirt, tie, underpants and socks; some sort of wispy dress and the gold sandals she'd worn to Dylan's wedding. A bit formal for a folly. She'd obviously planned it but maybe not down to the fine detail.

Digging deeper, he came to her underwear – white with an edging of soft lace. He was sure he hadn't seen it before but he wouldn't have, would he? He was still sleeping in

Dylan's room. Chic. French. Very sexy, anyway.

He sat on the bed, holding a pair of knickers in one hand, a bra in the other, running his thumbs back and forth across the silky fabric. Women might wear this delicate stuff but they were the tough ones. Look at them. Fay, Laura, Non, his mother – all 'sorters' and 'stickers' and 'fixers', in their own way. Their men – his father, Iolo, himself – would have gone under if they'd been left to their own devices. Wasn't what he'd considered Kingsley's courage, in reality, spinelessness? A daughter wouldn't have run away.

Fay appeared with the champagne and two glasses, blushing when she caught sight of her underwear, but saying nothing as he pushed it back in the bag. 'I thought we might have a drink.'

'Good idea.' He opened the bottle and filled the glasses, bubbles spiralling up through the pale liquid.

'Jack, I wanted to say…I wanted to tell you…I've really enjoyed my day. The dancing was great and I loved the music.'

'It can't have been—'

'Can I just finish?' There was no reprimand in her voice. 'I know I've been a bit…but I think I can see… I'd like to come with you again sometime.'

Listening to her stuttering words, he understood that she was struggling to convey something more important than a conversion to Morris dancing, 'Thanks, love.'

Fay drained her glass. 'Now I'm going to take a long, hot shower. Make the most of all those white towels and swish toiletries.'

Jack unpacked his dancing togs. It was silly really. They'd be going straight in the wash when he got home. But, whenever he spent a night away, it felt right to hang a shirt in a wardrobe, lay a book on a bedside table…or leave a clean, folded handkerchief in a chest of drawers. He was the male of the species, marking his territory.

He re-filled his glass and took it up to the roof. This was an extraordinary building, plonked up here on the hill, remote from the certainties of life. How many people before him had stood on that very spot, watching the racing clouds and reflecting on past stupidity; contemplating future recklessness. A folly – that summed it up, somehow. He walked around the enclosure, running his hand across the rough stones, looking for evidence of previous visitors, proof that he hadn't slipped into a dream-world. On his second circuit, he found the evidence he needed – a sweet wrapper, folded and folded again, then wedged in a gap between two stones. Phantoms didn't eat Quality Street.

The sun was dipping behind the hills and a gentle breeze riffled the leaves around his vantage point. It was as if he were in the basket of a hot-air balloon – without the danger or the hot air – hovering ten metres above the ground, unable to proceed unless he shed some ballast. He was feeling buoyant, though, and there were signs that the process had already begun.

Ever since his confrontation with Fay, and their subsequent discussion, Kingsley had cropped up, quite spontaneously, in conversations and reminiscences. It felt okay, too, as if mentioning him, now and again, was draining the pus out of the wound. It might be an idea to drop him an email; tell him about their row and its resolution – in a light-hearted kind of way, of course. News that his parents were getting on well with each other, and getting over his leaving, might be galling enough lure him home. He would discuss it with Fay – see what she thought.

He was at ease with himself about the Laura business, and it wasn't because he was callous or lacked the full complement of emotions. Sometimes he thought he was going to explode with bloody emotions. No. The 'thing' with Laura had never been anything to feel bad about. They'd talked it through at the time and again, on the phone the other day. She'd explained that, from the day she discovered that she was pregnant, she'd been determined to go it alone; that she'd loved David and had never contemplated letting another man into her life; that she expected, wanted, demanded, nothing from him or the other putative fathers. And – he'd worked this out for himself – it was feasible that bearing a child, regardless of whom the father was, had saved her from going round the bend with grief. She'd also apologised for visiting his parents. 'It was a mad moment, Jack. I promise it will never happen again.' He was duty bound to accept her decision and he knew she would keep her word.

Fay. Non. Laura. Dafydd Morgan wouldn't make such heavy weather of it all, would he? Jack could hear him now, chuckling, 'Go with the flow, Jackie Boy.'

'Nice shower?' Jack asked as Fay emerged from the bathroom. She wore a white bathrobe, which reached to her ankles, and had twisted a towel, turban style, around her hair. And, seeing her like that, it was as if he'd been suffering from an undiagnosed illness but, in that instant, had taken a turn for the better. 'You look fantastic, love.'

'I look a sight,' she insisted, but he could see that she was pleased. She sat on the bed, towelling her hair and studying his shaven face. 'I'm starting to get used to the new you but I'm sure the patients will have plenty to say. And Sheila, too.'

'It's nothing to do with them. We'll decide. You and me.'

Fay nodded. Pink-cheeked and freckle-faced, wet hair combed back from her face – the banner-waving girl he'd spotted across the student refectory stood in front of him. And here they were, cocooned in this fairytale tower – no income tax returns to complete; no books to mark or reports to write; no mother, hovering outside the bedroom door.

He showered as quickly as he could, scouring every nook and cranny. When he dried his face, the fluffy towel snagged on his chin where his beard was already beginning to erupt, but there was nothing he could do about that. He wrapped a towel around his waist, then drew his hand across the steamy mirror to reveal a man he barely recognised – a little on the gaunt side, not bad looking, but, to be truthful, nothing out of the ordinary.

It was getting dark. Fay had lit the candles and, its starkness mellowed by flickering candle glow, the bedroom looked snug; less chaste. She was searching through the chest of drawers. 'Did you notice a hairdryer? I didn't bring mine.' She paused at the drawer containing Jack's dancing gear and, taking out the bells, she shook them. 'I never realised what a stirring sound these make. Sort of joyous and nostalgic at the same time. Do they have a special name?'

'They used to be known as crotals, but I don't know if anyone still calls them that.'

'Crotals,' she said, as if memorising a useful phrase in a new language. 'Crotals. What an ugly word for such pretty things.' She shook them again, the silver metal glinting in the candlelight.

Dropping the towel from his waist, he kissed her gently on the lips, then harder, breaking off only to apologise, 'Sorry love, no razor.' Then he loosened the belt of her bathrobe, prepared to stop instantly if he sensed any resistance. But she returned his kisses, giving him the consent he sought.

He slipped the bathrobe off her shoulders, coaxing the

thick fabric down her arms, but she was still gripping the bells, a set in each hand, and it would go so far, and no further. 'You'll have to let go, love,' he whispered.

'Okay.' She handed him the bells and the bathrobe slipped to the floor.

He stood a hand's-span away from her, not moving, afraid he might get it wrong.

'Jack, will you do something for me?'

'Anything.' He meant it.

'Will you put them on?'

'What?'

'Will you put the bells on?'

'Really?'

She nodded and he raised his foot on to the chair, flicking the leather strap around his shin.

'No. Not on *you*.' She smiled shyly, offering him her leg.

Naked, he knelt in front of his wife, strapping the harnesses around her shapely calves, kissing her on either knee, anchoring himself in the moment.

Tentatively, she stamped her left foot, then her right. 'How am I doing?'

'It's a start, but you're going to need lots of practice.'

'Good.' She looped her arms around his neck and he scooped her up, carrying her across the room and dropping her, tinkling, on to the bed.

A lot later, after they'd showered again – together this time – and eaten a delicious supper, they returned to bed with a bottle of red wine. Fay fell asleep first, curled on her side like a cat amidst the crumpled sheets. Tired, but not quite ready to let the day go, Jack perched on the window-seat. He could see Fay clearly in the candle-glow, her breasts rising and falling steadily as she breathed.

She murmured something that he didn't catch, rolling on her back, reaching towards his side of the bed. What was she dreaming about? Him? The children? Anne Saunders parties? Or something he could never – should never even try to – imagine? *You can't be in my dream...I can't be in yours.* That's what the man ought to have sung.

He opened the shutters. A gentle breeze drifted up the hillside, carrying the scent of damp leaves; the candles dipped and danced; a harvest moon hung, low and golden in the sky, as if it had just bounced off the horizon. And the lights of Llangwm winked at him, encouraging and comforting, from down in the valley.

*

Morris Off ... is farewell, with no sorrow in it; good-bye, but with no dread of loneliness tomorrow; ... When the dance is over, and the bells are quiet, there is neither surfeit nor exhaustion. Morris Off is like to make one think of sound sleep and clear awakenings.

The Morris Book,
Cecil J. Sharp and Herbert C. Macilwaine,
Novello & Co. Ltd, 1907

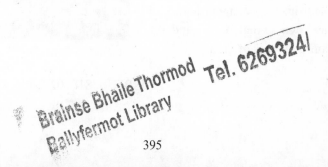

Other work by Jo Verity

Jo Verity was the **winner of the 2003 Richard and Judy "Write Here Right Now" short story competition**.

"Jo leapt out as the clear winner of our competition and we are over the moon that her writing talents have now been recognised." Richard and Judy

Everything in the Garden
by Jo Verity

When Anna Wren and her husband Tom buy a rambling farmhouse in Wales with three other couples the intention is to grow old with the support of tried and trusted friends. But life turns out not to be the bed of roses she had imagined... as she teeters on the brink of an affair the relationships that have shaped her life begin to crumble and Anna is forced to confront the changing nature of her own sexual desire and the consequences of giving in.

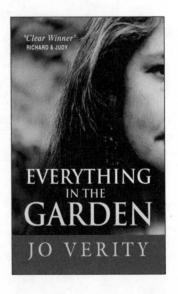

ISBN: 9781870206709 £6.99

My Cheating Heart
edited by Kitty Sewell

Jo Verity's story about a bitter end – *There Must Have Been Some Good Times* – features in this anthology of twenty-five original stories of intrigue, infidelity and betrayal.

9781870206730 £7.99

Safe World Gone
edited by Patricia Duncker and Janet Thomas

In these 28 stories, by turns funny, touching and scary, Welsh women authors explore the turning points that can change a woman's life forever. **Jo Verity**'s story on the nature of love and death is touching and human.

9781870206778 £7.99

Forthcoming titles from Honno

Big Cats and Kitten Heels
by Claire Peate

Fresh and funny: ideal beach reading.

Rachel – suffering from a Dull Life Crisis – embarks on an action-packed hen weekend. But there's a 'big cat' on the loose and only a handsome Welshman in wellies stands between Rachel and a vicious killer…

July 2007; 9781870206884 £6.99

More than Just a Hairdresser
by Nia Pritchard

A heartwarming belly-laugh of a book.

Mobile hairdresser Shirley and sidekick Oli use the tools of their trade to covertly trail a client's philandering hubbie...

August 2007; 9781870206853 £6.99

About Elin
by Jackie Davies

A haunting novel of love and loss.

Elin Pritchard, ex-firebrand, is back home for her brother's funeral. Returning brings all sorts of emotions to the fore, memories good and bad, her own and those of the community she left behind.

September 2007; 9781870206891 £6.99

Other titles from Honno

Hector's Talent for Miracles
by Kitty Sewell

Mair's search for her lost grandfather takes her from a dull veterinary surgery in Cardiff to the heat & passion of Spain.

9781870206815 £6.99

Facing into the West Wind
by Lara Clough

Jason may be lost and friendless, but he has a gift. He has a face people confess to. And those confessions are going to change everything...

A deeply felt and accomplished first novel" Sue Gee

9781870206792 £6.99

Girl on the Edge
by R.V.Knox

Just how did her mother die and what did Leila witness on the cliff top, if anything? A compelling psychological thriller set in the moors of North Wales.

9781870206754 £6.99

ABOUT HONNO

Honno Welsh Women's Press was set up in 1986 by a group of women who felt strongly that women in Wales needed wider opportunities to see their writing in print and to become involved in the publishing process. Our aim is to develop the writing talents of women in Wales, give them new and exciting opportunities to see their work published and often to give them their first 'break' as a writer.

Honno is registered as a community co-operative. Any profit that Honno makes goes towards the cost of future publications. Since it was established over 450 women from Wales and around the world have expressed their support for its work by buying shares at £5 each in the co-operative. We hope that many more women will be able to help us in this way. Shareholders' liability is limited to the amount invested, and each shareholder, regardless of the number of shares held, can have her say in the company and a vote at the Annual General Meeting.

To buy shares or to receive further information about forthcoming publications, please write to Honno at the address below, or visit our website: **www.honno.co.uk**.

Honno
'Ailsa Craig'
Heol y Cawl
Dinas Powys
Bro Morgannwg
CF64 4AH